PICTURE HIM NAKED

"I'm sure I don't have to introduce Averal Ballentine," Never began, telling the group he would be conducting this meeting.

As he took her place in front of the group she put the length of the entire room between them. She stood in the shadow near an exit door. He intimidated her. Yet she was responsible for all the lives in this room. She looked over the crowd. When her eyes came back to Averal's, he was staring directly at her. Her breath caught uncontrollably.

Naked. *That's it,* she told herself. It was hard to be intimidated by a man if you imagined him standing there naked.

Never's mind undid his tie. Slowly she pulled it free and dropped it to the floor. Then she went for the jacket. It joined the tie on the floor. The shirt came free one button at a time until his chest was exposed. With an imaginary fingernail she outlined the clearly defined squares of his muscular chest. His skin was warm and smooth. Reaching up she let her palms travel to his shoulders and pull the offending shirt down strong, corded arms.

When her hands went to the belt buckle, Never whipped around and lowered her head. She was breathing heavily. *This is not the way its done,* she scolded herself. *You're supposed to imagine him naked, not undress him, not touch him.* She couldn't imagine him dressed now that her mind had stripped him. She was glad she couldn't be seen clearly. Her body was hot and excited.

She had to get out of this room.

OPPOSITES ATTRACT

SHIRLEY HAILSTOCK

ARABESQUE
BET BOOKS

BET Publications, LLC
www.msbet.com
www.arabesquebooks.com

ARABESQUE BOOKS are published by

BET Publications, LLC
c/o BET BOOKS
1900 W Place NE
Washington, D.C. 20018-1211

BET Books™ is a trademark of Black Entertainment Television, Inc. ARABESQUE, the ARABESQUE logo and the BET BOOKS logo are trademarks and registered trademarks.

First Printing: March, 1999
10 9 8 7 6 5 4 3 2 1

Printed in the United States of America

DEDICATION

To Vivian Stephens
and
The Women Writers of Color

For believing in me and believing that
nothing is impossible.

ONE

The rhythm caught his attention; the steady tapping cadence of high heels clicking against hard wood flooring. No one else would have noticed—there were so many other sounds in the mall vying for dominance—but Averal Ballentine could pick out the tune those taps were making. He wished he had his saxophone. It might be fun to try to accompany the heels-to-wood-to-horn sound.

As it was, he sat cramped behind a table filled with books. Feeling confined even though the space was adequate for a man his size, he couldn't wait for this shift to be over. He wasn't used to being stationary or having a crowd around him. He wanted to move, stand, walk. He didn't like doing book-signings. Maybe that was why his mind had wandered, and he'd heard the tapping noise. If this hadn't been his hometown store he would have refused the offer to sign. He peered down the long line in front of him. All hope of getting away early was lost.

Looking up, he smiled at the woman in front of him and handed her the book he'd just scrawled in. "Happy reading," he said with a perfunctory smile. She returned the smile and moved aside for the next woman in line. He heard the sound again, heels against the flooring. His concentration heightened. The steps were unhurried, relaxed but determined, as if the wearer knew exactly where she was going. He glanced up.

The first things he saw were her feet. She wore red, shiny

shoes with heels like stilts. They supported shapely legs clad in black stockings with seams rising up the back. An assortment of running shoes had padded past him in the last two hours. Even women in business suits and silk dresses wore them. The floor of the Princeton bookstore was alive with the likes of Nike, Reebok, and Adidas. This woman, though, knew how to complete an ensemble—and what an ensemble it was. His eyes traced the seams of her sexy stockings from ankle to thigh, noticing as they disappeared like rose stems under a straight black dress. Around her neck hung a bright red scarf. A gold pin anchored the knot to her left shoulder, allowing the ends to cascade over her back and down her arm. The bright color contrasted with her dark skin tones and made him forget his purpose in being there.

A voice called him back to the desk in front of him, and he signed books almost automatically while his mind remained on the woman in the black dress straight down the aisle from where he sat. He hadn't seen her face yet, but the rest of her was packaged to his specifications. He'd say she was average height, by no means short, but neither would she stand eye-to-eye with him. Even from that distance he was sure her head would clear his shoulder if he stood, and he was six feet tall. From the back her dress angled in at the waist and rounded out over luscious hips. She stood straight, unlike many women whose postures gave away a major portion of their personality traits. This woman was sure of herself, confident in her ability to handle things, probably good at sizing up situations. Averal would bet she'd be asked directions by tourists, even in a foreign country. She had an I-know-what-I'm-doing kind of aura.

He cocked his head and signed another book. "Enjoy it," he said, and winked at a giggly college student who explained she was a business management major. His book was required reading, but she'd have bought it even if it weren't.

Averal wondered what attracted him to the woman. The personality assessment he'd just made wouldn't fit his usual type, but there was something about this one that got his juices flowing before he'd even seen her. She browsed through the nonfiction section. She didn't look as if she'd just come from an office. Neither did she look as if she were on her way to the nearest trendy party. She wasn't wearing or carrying a coat. It was thirty degrees outside, so she must work in the mall, although the small identification tag worn by store employees was missing from the unbroken expanse of dark material covering her from her throat to hemline.

The line for Averal's autographed book momentarily thinned, giving him time to watch her more thoroughly. She lifted a book from the shelf. It was *his*. He could see his face on the jacket cover as she opened it. He wondered where she worked, and why she was interested in a book on stress. She looked relaxed, more in control of herself than many of the women he'd seen today. Most of them were rushing back to work, to day care centers to retrieve children, or home to prepare meals. The woman at the back of the bookstore looked as if she never rushed anywhere.

She had clear skin the color of brown sugar. Her profile was tall and straight—almost queenly—and the way her dress fit was downright sinful. It molded over her breasts, angled in at the waist, and hugged her hips as it tapered down to legs that could rival the Garden State Parkway in length.

Averal shook his head. He hadn't assessed a woman this closely since . . . he couldn't remember when—it must have been as long ago as his college days—yet there was a magnetism that drew him toward this one.

She closed the book. He mentally telegraphed her a message: *Buy it.* At least he could autograph it and find out her name. She turned it over, looking at the photograph on the back.

His line was growing again. He stole glances at her between snatches of conversation as one person replaced another, each wanting a book. Everyone in line, it appeared, wanted a moment of his time. He tried to see her face, but her back was toward him. His eyes involuntarily dropped to her seamed hose.

Finally she moved toward the cashier. He followed her progress until a heavyset woman of about fifty blocked his view. She handed him his book and he warmly returned her smile, trying to keep an unnoticed account of Ms.-Black-Dress-Red Shoes. Lucky for him, there were three people at the checkout line in front of her.

"It's for my husband," the fifty-year-old said. "His name is George."

Averal wrote the standard inscription on the title page and signed it with his flowing yet unreadable signature. "Thank you, ma'am. I hope he enjoys it."

"Oh, he will," she said, beaming a tobacco-stained smile. "He enjoyed your last three books."

Averal smiled and she left. Another woman came to the table, which displayed several copies of his book, *Managing Business Related Stress: A Users Guide.* He took the book she offered and asked her name.

At the counter the woman was still there. Her long, black hair was mostly piled up on her head. Several curls spilled down her neck and over her shoulders. Its darkness disappeared down her back, lost in the midnight-colored fabric of her dress.

His customer left, and another appeared. This time it was a man. Even though his book was non-fiction and more men read non-fiction than women, women made more purchases.

He glanced at the counter. The cashier was waiting on the woman now.

Averal's mouth went dry. He had to force himself to remain seated. He wanted to go to her and introduce himself. He was *interested* in her—a stranger. He didn't know her name, but he wanted to. He was interested, and he hadn't been interested seriously in a woman in years. He knew why. It wasn't the women. He pushed them back. Women he dated knew he wasn't the marrying kind. Whenever someone got serious he immediately broke things off. He'd been serious once; even married once. The marriage didn't work, and he no longer wanted to be married or seriously involved. It led to complications he couldn't explain.

* * *

Nefertiti Kincaid clenched her jaws, then forced herself to visibly relax them. She was holding a book on stress, and she was as tense as they come. *Averal Ballentine.* She looked at the photo on the back of the book. Anger ran through her, swift as lightning. Every time she thought of him and the impact he would have over her life, her blood pressure went up. Beginning Monday, she didn't know how she would control it, or her tongue. Her grandmother, who'd coined her nickname, Never, had often told her, "You should think first, and speak second," but somehow she hadn't often remembered to do that until the words had already been uttered.

"Will that be all?" the store clerk asked, startling her out of her thoughts.

"Yes," Never said, stepping up to the counter.

The cash register made a high-pitched, clacky sound as it rapidly calculated the cost of her purchase. Never handed the clerk two twenty dollar bills. When the cashier counted her change she said, "If you'd like to have your book autographed, Averal Ballentine lives here in Princeton. We're lucky to have him here tonight for a book signing. He's sitting over there." She pointed somewhere over Never's left shoulder.

Never noticed the tone of the clerk's voice as she spoke of Averal Ballentine. She obviously thought there was sunlight just so it could shine on him. Never followed the line of the woman's finger.

It was on the tip of her tongue to say, "No, thank you. It's bad enough I have to buy the book. I certainly don't want to talk to the author," but she managed this one time to keep the words inside. She turned her head quickly to glance at the man at the table. He was looking in her direction. Light brown eyes captured hers, and something in her stomach changed. She couldn't put a name to it; lurched, rolled, dropped, she tested, but nothing in her experience fit what had just happened to her. She had to admit the photograph on the book jacket was far below the quality of the original. She pulled her eyes away.

Never accepted the bag and her change, then turned around. Averal Ballentine was signing someone's book. His head was down and she looked at the short, wavy hair that circled his head. On impulse she started for the table. She would have him sign her book. Never straightened her shoulders and lifted her chin slightly. In front of her was only one person. He moved before she got there. A wide smile was on Averal Ballentine's face when his eyes focused on her. She didn't return it, but her stomach flipped over and her feet faltered. She caught herself and checked the floor. She was sure she'd find a hole which had caught her heel, but there was none there. Nothing had caused her to trip except the look in the eyes of the man in front of her. And her hands were suddenly cold, yet her body was warm, more warm than the heat in the store called for. Her heart pounded in her chest, and she felt heat burning her ears. Again she felt herself clenching her jaw. She continued to walk forward.

He still smiled at her. She refused to respond. After all, what did she have to smile about? He had every reason. She doubted there was any stress in his life, yet in hers it was only beginning.

His eyes didn't move as she approached him. They were clear, amber-colored, and dancing as if he were happy about something. She could see only half of his body. She was glad she wore high heels. She needed the height to give her confidence to face the man. He had no idea of the impact he would have on her livelihood. He was having an impact on her person, too. She pushed it down, refusing to allow it to blossom into anything like attraction or arousal.

"Hello," he said in a clear baritone voice. It was dark and sexy, and exactly what his photo had told her it would be like. Hearing his one word made her feel as if she'd been touched; that somehow his hand had reached out and wrapped itself around her arm. She fought the urge to turn her head and check.

"The woman at the counter tells me you're Averal Ballentine."

"Guilty," he said playfully. Never still didn't smile. "Would you like me to sign your book?" He glanced at the plastic bag in her hand.

She really didn't want him to sign it. She only wanted to get a closer look at him. She wanted him to be old and staid and not abreast of current traditions and changes in business management, but she'd already seen his photo and knew he was only in his thirties. She wanted to know how much of an adversary he was going to be. Was he a reasonable man? Could she deal with him, discuss her future and those of the people she managed? She wouldn't be able to tell that from a look and a few sentences of conversation. She hoped the book would give her some insight into the man behind it.

She'd read Averal Ballentine before, but the analyzing she would do about this book this weekend hadn't been needed before the merger brought him into her life.

"Would you like me to sign your book?" he repeated since she'd taken so long to answer him. Never pulled the book from the bag and handed it to him.

He opened it to the title page and poised his pen over the blank space that looked as if it had been specifically left there for autographing.

"Would you like it inscribed to you?"

"No," Never said. "Just a plain signature will be fine."

While he wrote, Never gave him a good look. Objectively, she had to say he was good-looking. While she didn't think he would have turned her head if they'd passed each other on the street, he would most definitely have turned a few. Up close, his hair tended to wave. It looked soft and smooth, and she had the uncanny desire to reach out and touch it. His face was clean-shaven. When he looked up she saw his eyes, and knew they were his most devastating feature. They were a clear brown, almost transparent, and she felt as if he could look into her mind. Quickly she changed her thoughts, preventing him from reading what she was thinking.

She reached for the book. He closed it and handed it to her, but as she tried to pull it clear of his hand she felt a slight tug. She met his eyes again. He was holding onto the book, and unless she yanked it away she'd have to listen to what he had to say.

"Are you sure you don't want it personalized?" There was that smile again.

"Absolutely," Never returned a little too quickly. He opened his hand. She stuffed the book back into its bag and turned away without the customary 'thank you.'

It wasn't like her to be rude. It wasn't like her to be attracted to a man she'd only nearly met. It wasn't like her legs to wobble and her knees to threaten non-support. But all of that was happening.

She left the store without a backward glance and went directly to the bus terminal-style lockers outside Penney's Department Store, where she'd left her coat. Usually she kept her coat with her when she shopped, but after another day of discovering several more of her friends and co-workers had been fired she'd been too weary to cope with holiday shoppers plus a bulky coat. It was only October, yet Christmas decorations had sprung up seemingly overnight in the mall, and masses of Princeton's populace were rushing about as if it were Christmas Eve. She pulled her coat free of the locker and slipped her arms into the warm material. Turning up the collar, she headed for the parking lot. Minutes later she threw the plastic bag holding Averal Ballentine's book on the seat of her car, slipped behind the wheel, and headed home.

Inside her house, Never dropped her keys on the hall table. Her living room was done in a soft white; white walls, white drapes, white rug. The sterile expanse was broken by sofas done in hunter green and pillows picking up both colors. Wooden accent tables of dark cherry rounded out the room. She found that the color scheme had a strangely soothing effect on her senses. Stopping in the center, she took the book from the small plastic bag. Turning it to the picture side, she gazed at the color photo. The eyes grabbed her. Even in the store, when their eyes met, she had felt he was holding her.

Sitting down, she looked at him. Why had he made her legs weak? Why had his voice disturbed her? She could still hear the low tones as if they sang through her blood. She didn't react like this. It wasn't in her. Even in her teenage years, when most girls fell in and out of love every week, she'd wondered what it was about her that kept her from having those feelings. She had plenty of boyfriends and her share of dates, but there was no one with whom she wanted to swoon, giggle over, and talk to on the phone for hours and hours. She'd thought that it would come when she went to college, then when she graduated and started to work, but it hadn't. Yet today she'd forged new territory. She reacted with feelings she was unsure of. She'd wanted to stay and talk to him, but she was scared, too, and instinct told her to run.

Anger suddenly flared inside her. Why, she didn't know, and didn't ask. She didn't want to know. She wanted Averal Ballentine to go away and leave her alone, but she also knew that would not happen.

"What gives you the right to throw us out of work?" she asked angrily, then dropped the book on the polished wood coffee table and stood up.

In the kitchen Never made a cup of tea and took it back to the living-room. She slipped her feet under her as she sat down and used the remote control to turn on the television. She didn't hear much of what was being said. The photograph of Averal Ballentine stared at her from the book jacket. Her thoughts drifted to the merger, and to his role in it.

Looking back at the screen, she pulled her mind away from work. Her weekend began tonight, and she wouldn't give another thought to what was happening at Cedar-Worthington. Monday would come soon enough. Her tea cooled, and she went to pour another cup. As she returned, the first place her gaze fell was on the book. Never went directly to it and turned it over. She wanted no part of Averal Ballentine. Not even a two-dimensional replica.

The grandfather clock against the wall began its eight note Westminster chime, and then the deep, resonant gongs sounded out the hour. Never jumped when she looked at her watch. She had only minutes to get ready for the party, and Martin was notoriously punctual.

Martin Caldwell, owner of the Princeton Art Gallery, knew her well. He had a psychic sense that told him when she was in the middle of a crisis. His call to invite her to tonight's party had come while she was too busy coping with several delayed projects and the future of her department to argue with him. She'd have agreed to anything to get him off the phone. Again she was going to one of his theme parties. She hated theme parties, and tonight she didn't even know what cause they were supporting. She did, however, know Martin, and he always had a purpose to his parties. What was it this time, she asked herself as she started for her bedroom. Starving children in Ethiopia? A commune in the desert? Well, whatever it was it would keep her mind off the merger for a few hours.

Grabbing her shoes, she ran up the stairs and went into her large bedroom. Setting the shoes in the closet, she undressed and took a quick shower. She had barely finished brushing, twisting, and spraying her hair into the Nefertiti hairstyle when she heard the doorbell.

Martin, she thought, checking the radio alarm clock on the dressing table. She remembered his penchant for showing up early. Slipping her bathrobe on, she went to the door.

"I should have known I could expect you to show up early," Never chided as she pulled the door inward. Martin smiled and she returned it, letting him into the foyer and closing the door. He kissed her on the cheek. "I'm running just a bit late." She led him into the living-room.

"You, late!" His eyebrows went up in a gesture of surprise as he scanned the room with its many clocks. Never did have a fetish about time. There were at least two clocks in every room. "I thought those two words were mutually exclusive. What happened to cause such an uncharacteristic reaction?"

Never ignored the censure. Martin had often told her she didn't need a watch, yet he'd tried to give her a Piaget last Christmas to add to the collection of timepieces that were strategically placed about her house. She collected clocks. Miniature ones, anniversary clocks, oddly shaped clocks, even one that ran backward. Intellectually, Martin had informed her, she probably thought she had something to do, and that time was working against her. She ignored his drugstore psychology and equated it to his own need to find all the paintings of Raoul Garcia, a little known artist from the late eighteenth century.

"I dropped by the mall on my way home."

"Christmas shopping? I thought you'd be done by now."

Never frowned. "I picked up Averal Ballentine's new book. I thought I'd arm myself for Monday's meeting."

"Ah, the big day approaches." He bent down and took the book. "What is the book supposed to do—help you with the stress, or give you insight into his personality?"

"A little of both, I hope," she added. Then, noticing the time she said, "I'd better go and finish dressing. I'll be ready in just a moment."

"Need any help?" he asked.

"Thank you, no." She headed for the staircase.

"Well, you can't say I don't try." Martin spread his hands and turned innocent eyes toward her.

"No, I certainly can't say that." Never grinned at him. "Make yourself a drink while I finish." She started up the stairs.

Martin stopped her. "Not so fast. I went by Carver's this afternoon."

"Oh." Never stopped.

Martin pulled a ring box from his pocket. "I thought you'd like to have this."

"The rings!" Never raced down the stairs, holding the floor-length robe close to her body. The gallery director held a white velvet box in the palm of his hand. Martin knew everyone in Princeton, including a jewelry store owner. Never had asked him to have her grandmother's wedding rings reset for their anniversary. She took the box gently, then sat on the sofa. Martin sat next to her. He was a little closer than Never liked, but she didn't mention it.

Slowly, she lifted the top. What she saw took her breath away. Her free hand came up to her throat. On a bed of blue velvet rested a crown of laced gold which fell like overlapping leaves. Culminating at the top of the spray was a three-carat solitaire diamond anchored by four gold posts. As Never moved the box back and forth, light which hit the facets danced in sparkling wonder. Alongside the engagement ring was a wide, gold band which had been cleaned and polished.

"It's gorgeous," she whispered.

Martin leaned closer. His shoulder brushed hers. "I thought you'd like it." He took the box and pulled the engagement ring free. "Here, try it on."

Before Never could react Martin had taken her left hand and the ring on her third finger. "With this ring I thee wed," he quoted as he pushed the mounted engagement ring over her knuckle.

"Isn't this bad luck?" She extended her arm, admiring the matched pair. For once she was glad she had her grandmother's slender fingers, and that she'd taken the time to polish her long nails.

"No," Martin answered. "Just say the word, and I'll have an identical set made in time for a June wedding."

"Martin, you're not going to ask me to marry you again?"

"Are you going to say no?"

Never nodded.

"Then I'm not going to ask. But sooner or later you'll discover I'm what you want."

What do I want? Never thought, and without warning Averal Ballentine's picture darted into her mind. She quickly dashed it away, but not before she remembered the feelings that had washed over her when his gaze met hers. Averal Ballentine was good-looking, but she wanted more than good looks in a man.

"I'd better go finish dressing." She stood.

Martin stood, too. He caught her arm as she turned. "Think about it, Nefertiti." Martin voice was low and serious. "Marriage to me wouldn't be bad. You know I love you."

Never knew he was serious. He only called her Nefertiti when he was. "Martin, I love you, too, but not the way a woman loves the man she's planning to spend her life with."

"I'm willing to settle for less. I'm willing to settle for any terms you care to set."

"Don't, Martin," she chided. "Don't settle. You'll find it doesn't work."

Never knew this from experience. Once she'd tried to make the feelings happen. She'd reacted to a man's lovemaking, but it really wasn't there. When he asked her to marry him she'd accepted, knowing he wasn't the one but wanting to be like everyone else. She knew she was settling, and eventually so did he. She'd promised herself she wouldn't do that ever again. Never turned away from him. She faced the stone fireplace with its dead ashes from last night's fire.

"Somewhere there's a woman who'll stop your heart when you look at her," she said. "You'll have no breath when she's near you, and you won't know how you've managed to live so long without the part of you she fills. I don't do that for you, Martin. That's the kind of love you deserve." Never left him to go to the steps. She paused there and turned, realizing the words she'd spoken described her needs as much as Martin's. "Marriage between us is something I won't change my mind about."

"All right, I won't mention it again . . . tonight. Now you'd better hurry or we'll be late."

Never's shoulders dropped. She went up the stairs and back to her room. Martin had relented, she thought as she began to dress, but Never knew he would bring the subject up again. She liked Martin. He was one of the good guys; always fighting the

cause of the underdog. That was probably what she liked best
about him. He didn't come from any of the old money families,
but he'd made a success of his gallery and was respected by
everyone in the township. She wasn't in love with him, although
she should be. She liked everything he stood for, but there was
no spark between them—nothing that would last until they cele-
brated fifty years of marriage the way her grandparents would
in just a few weeks. She looked at the gleaming diamond on
her left hand. As many times as Martin had asked her to marry
him, she knew he wasn't any more in love with her than she
was with him.

She wanted a storybook romance. The kind Cinderella, Sleeping Beauty, and her grandparents shared. Martin was no Prince
Charming. He was just an inch under six feet, with dark eyes
and hair. His moustache was trim and neat, as was everything
about him, from his impeccable clothes and manicured nails to
the discreet amount of jewelry he limited himself to. She smiled,
pulling her dress up from the floor and reaching behind her to
slip the zipper up her back.

The man in the bookstore—Averal Ballentine—he looked
like Prince Charming. His light brown eyes reminded her of a
lion's she'd seen at the zoo one summer when she was ten—
sunlight flowed through them as if they were back-lighted. If
he were anyone but Averal Ballentine she'd want to pursue the
feelings that warmed her even now, since all she'd done was
think of him. But under the terms of the merger he was going
to have a significant impact on her life, and it wouldn't be in
the role of a loving prince.

Never took a final look in the mirror, pivoting and checking
the back of the dress over her shoulder. The black strapless
gown tautly pushed her breasts into half moons above the
straight line of the bodice. The dress dropped in a straight sheath
of satin that ended at her bejeweled slippers. A white sash was
tied at her waist, matching the floor-length coat lying across
the king-size bed behind her. A single, white diamond pendant
hung around her neck, and tear-drop earrings dangled from each

ear, matching the circle of stones that ringed her hair. The precious stones had arrived that afternoon from Martin's gallery. A comb that disappeared into the hair at the crown of her head made the circle of expensive jewels look as if they were suspended in each section of her hair. The adornment made her eyes sparkle.

"Well, Cinderella," she told the mirror. "You're ready for the ball."

Taking the coat, she left the bedroom. Martin was absorbed in Averal Ballentine's book when she slipped down the stairs.

"Martin," she called softly. He whistled when he saw her. Martin always whistled when he saw her. She knew why he continued to arrive early each time she agreed to go out with him. He liked having her on his arm. Sometimes she felt he thought of her as another of his artifacts, a living doll he could parade around and show off. Quickly she scolded herself. He did have a good heart, and he was very attentive. He was fascinated by her name, and loved her hair in the Nefertiti style. Never indulged him and often wore the jewelry he brought her, but refused to accept any of it as a gift.

"You're going to like reading this," he said, tapping his finger on the book.

She bit off the comment she wanted to make. There was no need to begin the evening angry. "I've read several of them, " she substituted.

"I'll have to get this one. It reads like a novel." Martin had regard for Ballentine in his voice, too. It wasn't as adoring as the store clerk's, but held just as much respect. She, too, had held respect for him until a few months ago, when the merger went from media speculation to reality. Then his theories on management became part of Cedar-Worthington, Inc. "I see it's autographed." Martin tapped the book cover. Never noticed the sticker. She didn't remember seeing him put it there.

"I hear he's a local author," Never supplied.

"Yes, we've met." He laid the book on the coffee table.

"You have?" she paused. Martin had been born and reared

in Princeton, New Jersey. Never knew his clientele gave him association with much of the township. She assumed Martin had met Averal Ballentine during the course of business.

"I know a woman who's very close to him," Martin said in a cat-that-ate-the-canary voice that had his eyebrows arching.

"I should have known," Never said, her tone slanderous.

Her eyes dropped to the book. Averal Ballentine stared at her from the jacket—sharp eyes, square chin with just the hint of a cleft matching a strong jaw, and skin that looked as brown and gold as autumn. He'd probably squired many women through the revolving doors of Caldwell's Art Gallery.

"It's nothing like that," Martin defended. "She's his mother."

"Are you sure?" Never's voice was dry.

"Nefertiti Kincaid, you have a dirty mind," Martin teased.

She laughed, a soft tinkling sound. "I think we'd better go." Martin helped her as she slipped her arms into her coat.

"You're going to wear it?" He indicated the ring. Never had forgotten she still had it on. Her right hand came up to remove the reset stone. "Don't," Martin's hand covered hers. "Wear it tonight. I'm sure your grandmother won't mind. And I can pretend."

Averal Ballentine hated these art world affairs; the kind where people milled about holding a wineglass in one hand and a plate of strange combinations of finger food in the other. He needed to grow a third hand to eat, as was evidenced by the empty wineglass and a saucer with six tooth picks that had stabbed bacon-wrapped shrimp. *Anne would be pleased,* he thought. The room was full of women in sequined finery and men in suits and tuxedos. He wore his own tuxedo, blending into the checkerboard of black and white clad men who dotted the space.

He wouldn't stay there too long. Anne knew he was only there for her. He wouldn't stay longer than the customary amount of time for politeness. Then he'd go home, or out. It had been a while since he'd seen Riddles. Maybe tonight he'd grab his sax and join the party at Riddles Place. He needed some relaxation, and that was exactly the place to get it.

He was actively thinking of the people at the popular bar when she came through the door. The woman from the book store, Miss-Black-Seamed-Stockings, the woman who hadn't really wanted him to sign her book. She came in smiling, on the arm of a man who looked familiar.

Averal reacted to her with good ole American male hormones. Who was she? She was so striking. Even with her hair done up like an African queen he'd recognized her immediately, as if he'd known her before, had always known her, yet they hadn't really met. She wore a black dress, not like the one she'd had on earlier. This one wasn't as formfitting, and the splash of color tonight was a huge white sash. The dress was strapless, leaving her deep brown shoulders bare and kissable. Her teasing, moon shape breasts peeking discreetly over the top warmed his blood and had him shifting position and checking the button on his jacket to make sure the physical evidence her entrance produced in him was hidden from prying eyes. Feeling awkward with the empty glass and plate in his hands, he set them down on a nearby table. His mother went toward the woman and spoke to the man. She hadn't been at any of Anne's other shows. He would have remembered her.

Averal had watched her walk away in the bookstore. He'd cursed himself, wondering what it was about her that attracted him. Obviously, she didn't return the sentiment. She hadn't smiled or frowned earlier, only held herself aloof. She smiled now, both at his mother and the man with her. The jewels in her hair caught the light and sparkled. He liked what he saw, and couldn't understand why she'd acted with veiled dislike in the store. They didn't know each other, and as far as he could remember he hadn't made any serious enemies in his life, so she couldn't be harboring secondary enmity. Yet in the bookstore the woman in black had had an air about her that would have glowed red hot under infrared inspection. In the gallery

light she radiated a different kind of heat. She was softer here,
sexier, if that were possible. She looked like the queen she imi-
tated, and he wanted to move into the aura that surrounded her.
He could feel the flow of her energy as if it were reaching across
the room and making contact with him.

Never saw him almost the moment they entered the gallery
hall. While she was still laughing at something Martin said, her
gaze found Averal Ballentine as if she'd been looking for him.
His eyes locked with hers. She was struck by the power of the
darkness in them. An hour earlier she'd been looking at his
photo. The force of the reality directed at her was physical,
powerful, demanding. A bubble seemed to descend over her,
blocking out everything except the two of them. Never pushed
at the solidity of the unexpected encasement, forcing her mouth
to smile and her mind to pay attention to what was being said.
She refused to be drawn to him, refused to allow the nick that
pierced her when he looked at her grow into anything. Her heart
lurched when the charisma that was nearly visible about him
touched her. She wouldn't allow it. They had a destiny. She
knew it, even if he didn't. Their lives would be meshed together,
but as adversaries, not . . . lovers. Lovers! the word caught her
off guard. She nearly gasped. Where had it come from? She
didn't care. Quickly she threw it out as if it were trash, and
forced her mind to the art show.

An author and consultant somehow seemed a little out of
place at an art show. Princeton was a small community, and
from the short bio inside his book jacket she knew he lived in
the township even before the store clerk had mentioned it. The
community did seem to support each other. Maybe he liked
BriAnne Ball. She did. She even owned a Ball painting. She'd
bought it years ago at an estate sale. Obviously no one had
known the real value of the painting, or its price would have
soared out of Never's financial reach. The painting was one of
the few possessions Never owned that had nothing to do with
computer generated images.

Martin's hand on her back felt like an anchor. She leaned

back into it, using it to keep her outside the bubble that made the room recede and bring Averal into focus. Approaching them was a woman with bright eyes, a wide smile, and her arms open. Never immediately recognized her as BriAnne Ball, the show's artist.

"Martin," BriAnne greeted. "I'm so glad you could come." Martin's arms clasped the small woman with salt-and-pepper hair.

"I wouldn't miss one of your shows, Bree," he said. "Mother sends her love."

"How is Louise?" she asked, leaning back to stare into Martin's eyes.

"She's fine. Loves living in Florida, but complains there's too many old people cluttering up the highways."

They laughed and Martin turned to Never. "This is Never Kincaid, a fan. Never, BriAnne Ball."

Never smiled her embarrassment.

"Thank you." The older woman's smile was bright and happy. "It's always nice to meet someone who appreciates my work. Now come and meet my guests." She took them both by the hand and led them farther into the huge gallery. "Never is a most unusual name."

Warm brown eyes smiled at her. Immediately she remembered Averal Ballentine's eyes. What was wrong with her? She was becoming obsessed with the man. Since the bookstore, every second thought seemed to be about him.

"My full name is Nefertiti Kincaid. Never is a nickname."

Martin's gallery wasn't new to her. She'd been here many times. Tonight, panels with large canvases had been strategically placed about the brightly lighted room. There were bars in several areas, where pockets of people gathered and talked. Throughout the room uniformed waiters and waitresses served hors d'ouvres. BriAnne stopped between two of the panels.

"That's even more unusual." She stepped back, looking at Never as if she were trying to decide how best to transform her features to canvas. "You do remind me of Nefertiti, especially with your hair up like that and all those stones circling your head."

"The stones come from Martin's gallery. They're usually displayed in the Gem Room." She nodded toward the other end of the gallery, where huge doors led to smaller galleries displaying sculpture, precious stones, and other kinds of artifacts. "He lends them to me now and then. The name is my grandmother's, not the Queen of Egypt."

"The queen would be proud," BriAnne said, resuming her steps.

Averal watched his mother. Her eyes sparkled with happiness as she greeted the couple. He had only first seen the woman this afternoon, yet his mother looked as if she knew her. The three of them were standing at a bar ordering drinks. He was drawn to her as if she were a magnetic pole. He started for them, but was hampered by several people who engaged him in short conversations, slowing his progress. The trio passed out of sight, behind one of the ceiling-to-floor panels, while he talked to someone who appeared to know him. Finally, excusing himself he continued.

Never followed him about the gallery with covert glances. He didn't look at her. Each time she stole a glance he was engaged in conversation. He seemed to give his total attention to whomever he spoke. And there was that smile, the one she'd seen in the bookstore, the one that had nearly made her trip over own feet. He looked good in a tux, too, she thought. His white dress shirt contrasted with his medium-brown skin. She liked the way he moved—sure, confident, as if he belonged there. He looked as if he knew where he was going, and could provide assistance in any situation. Well, there was one thing he didn't know, Never thought. He didn't know her.

But he would.

BriAnne introduced her to people in the art world. Being a friend of Martin's, Never knew many of them. She greeted those she knew, talking casually to them while BriAnne talked quietly to Martin about his mother. Never had a chance to observe

Averal. Turning her head, she found him in her direct line of sight. They stared at each other. She knew she should turn away, concentrate on what Martin and BriAnne were saying, but she couldn't. Invisible bonds held her as tightly as ropes.

She watched him move. His black tuxedo was cut to an exact fit. He had broad shoulders, the kind women loved to be held against. His movements were graceful. The vision of the lion flowed into her mind; graceful, sure, king of the jungle. Averal Ballentine wasn't an off-the-rack-type. Most men who wore custom-made clothes had custom-made minds. She wondered if he would prove to be one of them.

He stopped. BriAnne and Martin led her toward another canvas. She met several of BriAnne's friends. Martin left to refill his drink, and BriAnne was carried away by other arriving guests. Never found herself alone.

Averal Ballentine was several feet from her, and she could hear him speaking quietly. His back was to her, broad and straight. His head bent toward the woman, who smiled up at him. Never moved away. Somehow she had to wrench herself free of the magnetism which seemed to draw her to him. She moved about the canvases, captivated and absorbed by the talent of the artist yet aware of the handsome author's location no matter where she happened to be.

BriAnne Ball stood to make a small fortune tonight, Never thought; and to think she actually owned an original. She was glad she'd wandered into the small tent on the village green six years ago. It had been hot, and she'd been walking a long time. Inside the tent it was cool, and she could sit down. The auction began almost immediately. When the painting came up, a woman next to her bid a dollar. She said she wanted the frame. Never liked the painting. Her bid was ten-dollars. No one else bid, and the woman smiled her consent to Never. Today it was worth thousands, but she wouldn't part with it.

She circled the gallery, stopping briefly at each of the canvases. Sometimes she spoke to other people looking at the same painting, and sometimes everyone remained quiet and hushed, absorbed in their own appreciation of a very talented woman. Finally Never found herself in front of a painting in a large, gold frame. The card next to it read, *By The Sea*. When she ventured to look over her shoulder Averal was gone. For a instant an unexpected coldness ran through her. It had become a game, her walking about the gallery playing peekaboo about where he was located. She didn't like it that he'd eluded her.

As she searched the room, he came back into view. He was trying to get across the space of the gallery. She could see him, hampered by several women. She frowned. Each time he got close to her he was stopped by another of BriAnne's guests, and she strategically moved away. He remained polite, trying to keep track of her as she was doing with him.

Turning her attention to a painting to keep from looking at him, she became engrossed. The painting was the show highlight, and the only one not for sale.

"How do you like it?" he asked, coming up behind her. Never didn't show any outward reaction to that sexy voice. Inside, her stomach pitched as if she'd fallen from a high place, and her nipples pebbled under her dress. She'd forgotten his progress toward her when the showstopper commanded her complete attention.

"It reminds me of another one she did," she responded.

She didn't turn, not trusting herself. His voice was low, sexy. Never felt it surround her. She was looking at a beach scene. All the heat of sun-soaked sand gathered in her stomach as his voice caressed the words.

"You don't think it's rather lonely? With only the sea and sand, and a dog running toward the water. No people?"

She swung around to face him. She held a champagne flute in her left hand. Immediately, Averal noticed the engagement ring. He didn't remember seeing it earlier. He tried to remember if he'd looked at her hands.

"It's the kind of scene, Mr. Ballentine, I'd like to disappear into sometime."

He wondered if she were lonely. "You said it reminded you of another one?" He didn't ask her name. She'd seemed reluctant to give it to him in the bookstore.

"It's a small painting she did when she first started. It has a woman on the beach with a child. She's holding his hand and they're walking toward the water."

"The Edge," he whispered, almost to himself. "It's been missing for many years. Most of her paintings are now registered, and the owners known. We lost track of *The Edge*. Where did you see it?"

"At an estate sale. I thought it had a strange name. Before I go I'll have to ask her the significance of it."

"I can tell you what she'll say."

She lifted the fluted champagne glass to her lips. Averal watched her drink, his eyes following the ring on her left hand. When she lowered the glass he saw the imprint of her lipstick on the glass.

"What will she say?" she asked. Averal felt at a disadvantage. He wanted to know her name. Wanted to be able to identify her by more than the low voice that should have soothed him but was having the opposite effect.

"She'll say her paintings don't have people in them."

"I suppose that's true. I've seen many of her paintings, and *The Edge* is the only one with people in it. Even this one with the dog is not typical." She turned back to the canvas.

"You know her work well?" Averal asked.

"I first saw mention of her in a small newspaper in Paris." She moved away. He followed her, smiling and nodding at people as he passed. "I went to the gallery and saw several of her paintings. That's where I first saw *The Edge*. I wanted it then, but someone else had already purchased it."

"Are you an artist, too?"

She looked at him with large, clear eyes that gave nothing away. "No, my only drawings are on a computer screen." She paused. "And you, in addition to your writing, do you also paint?"

"No, I leave the painting to Anne."

"You know the art world well?"

"Only Anne's work. I come to her shows when they're in the area. Why haven't I ever seen you at one of them?"

"The shows aren't often in Princeton. I've only been to exhibitions in New York and Philadelphia, and they were not openings."

"Anne doesn't have them often. The exhibition travels without her."

"Have you known her long?"

"Quite a long time," he said with a sad smile. "As long as I can remember."

"Why did she call the painting *The Edge?*"

"She was divorced as a young mother. It was only a few years later that she painted that. She didn't tell me, but I believe it was the turning point in her life. If she hadn't painted, she might well have disappeared into the sea. *The Edge* is really the edge of despair."

Averal stopped when he saw the woman swallow hard. Her eyes glassed over, and she averted them to place the wineglass on the tray of a passing waiter. Why he'd told her the story he didn't know. Not even Riddles knew how he felt about *The Edge.* Anne didn't mention it, and he'd forgotten it until this woman said *By The Sea* reminded her of another one. Maybe that was why it was his favorite of the show. He knew the woman and child in the other painting.

"Why did she sell it? I can't imagine parting with such a beautiful painting."

"At the time she needed the money to feed her child, and selling the painting would change her status from amateur to professional artist."

Never looked across the room at BriAnne Ball. She was confident and smiling, totally in her element. She didn't look as if she'd ever had to contend with any crisis in her life. Yet, Never knew no one had a perfect life. Everyone had problems they needed to overcome. On Monday she would have to begin dealing with one of hers. After the story Averal Ballentine had told her, she wouldn't again look at *The Edge* in the same light.

"We almost met earlier today."

She turned back to look at him. "At the bookstore," she said. She nodded without a smile. "I hear it's required reading for anyone in stressful situations." The hint of a smile lifted her lips. It didn't fully form on her mouth, and he wanted it to. It was suddenly important to him. She'd smiled at his mother, at the man she'd arrived with, and at countless other people milling about the gallery, yet she hadn't smiled at him.

"I can't help but agree," he told her, a little embarrassed. "Although you don't look like anyone with stress in your life."

"Everyone has some stress, Mr. Ballentine."

"Averal, please," he interrupted.

"Averal," she repeated. He noticed she didn't give him her name.

"Is that the reason you bought it?" he continued.

"I could say I'm an avid student of the Ballentine School of Management. Let's see," she placed her finger against her chin. "This must be number six."

"You're laughing at me." It was a statement.

"And you're taking it so well." Never couldn't help but laugh. Tonight she had the upper hand. Monday they would meet on the battlefield. It was a shame, she thought. If Cedar-Worthington weren't between them could she fall for a man like him? Would he be the one person who could make her have more than brotherly feelings for a man?

"Have you really read them?" he asked.

She did have the number correct. He'd written six books on different aspects of management. He'd find his latest one on many shelves at Cedar-Worthington when he interviewed department heads regarding the merging of the two conglomerates.

"Some of them." The truth was she'd read five of the six. The last one she'd begun tonight.

"I assume that's how you know my name. I'm afraid I don't know yours."

Never was certain his expression would change when she told him who she was. After all, he did have an appointment with her Monday morning, and how many Nefertiti Kincaids could there be in the world?

"It's—"

"It'll be Mrs. Martin Caldwell, if I have anything to say about it," Martin interrupted as he joined them. His arm slipped about her waist and pulled her possessively into his side.

"Martin, how nice to see you again." Averal finally remembered where he'd seen the man before. He was the son of his mother's friend. They'd met once or twice at a few functions but they'd yet to become friends. Averal didn't think they would ever be friends now. "I didn't know you were to be married. Sorry, I monopolized your fiancée for so long." Then he turned to Never. "It was nice talking to you. If you'll excuse me, I have to say goodnight to the hostess." With that he left them. His parting words had been formal. Never felt as if he should have clicked his heels in a German salute.

"Martin, why did you do that?" Never rounded on him, angry at his declaration.

"I was only pretending." He lifted her left hand. "Just say the word. We could make it real."

"Martin, I'm not saying the word." She snatched her hand away. "Not now or ever. So stop it!"

"I'm sorry." He looked at her strangely. "What happened here? You've been acting strange all evening. You two didn't get into an argument over the merger, did you?"

"No, we didn't talk about it at all. In fact, I was just about to tell him my name when you usurped the privilege."

"If I'd known the joke would have you this angry, I wouldn't have said anything. Do you want me to find him and tell him the truth?"

"No." She felt deflated. It wouldn't do any good now. She watched him kiss BriAnne's cheek and disappear through the exit. She wondered why she was so angry with Martin. It wasn't the first time he'd implied to someone they were getting married. Usually she laughed and contradicted him. Why hadn't she done that tonight? Why didn't she act like the normal Never? Martin noticed there was something different about her. What was it?

Martin interrupted her introspection "So what did you and Averal find to talk about?"

"Mostly about the paintings." She turned, looking back at the end wall, giving the beach scene another look. "He seems to know a lot about BriAnne Ball."

"He should." Martin's eyebrows rose in a confused question. "Didn't he tell you?"

"Tell me what?"

"BriAnne Ball is a professional name. Her real name is Anne Ballentine. She's his mother."

TWO

"Good morning, Never." The chorus began as it did every morning when people arrived to begin the work day. Usually Never was at her desk by seven-thirty, even though she played a morning game of tennis with Mark Brown. This morning she had found it hard to concentrate, and Mark had beaten her easily. She could only attribute that to her encounter Friday night with Averal Ballentine. Her weekend of reading his book and constantly finding the image from his photo stalking her—as if he could rise up from the cover and speak to her—had contributed to her ill humor.

She'd also taken longer than usual to get dressed after the tennis game. By the time she arrived the office was fully populated, and morning conversation groups dotted the corporate headquarters of the Management Information Systems Department.

Going from the front door to her office, Never must have said 'Good morning' fifteen times. It wasn't a good morning. She dreaded today. Her first appointment was with Averal Ballentine. She had no wish to see him again or have him evaluate her department. And she had no wish to revisit the feelings he evoked in her.

What did he know about management information systems at her firm, she asked herself. He was an outsider. She resented him, resented anyone who wanted to come in and shut them down. Some of the people here had spent their working lives with this company. Soon they would be out on the street looking for work, like a newly graduated college student seeking his first job.

Reaching her office she placed her briefcase in its usual place on the credenza behind her desk. Her spirits rose slightly when she saw the new computer unpacked and waiting. Never's white wool coat slipped from her arms and she hung it behind the door, then began her morning routine of turning on all the equipment. She flipped the ON button of the beige box. Nothing happened. Checking the cables, she found that everything looked properly hooked up. Then she noticed the plug.

"You would think," she said to the air, "that even a fool would plug the machine in during an installation process." Dropping to the floor, she grabbed the plug. The phone rang. She looked up, lifting the almond-colored instrument, taking it with her as she stretched to reach the surge protector on the floor.

"Systems. Ms. Kincaid," she said into the mouthpiece.

"Aunt Gee."

"Stephen!" A smile split her face at the affectionate nickname only her two nephews used. Donald had inadvertently pinned her with the name when he was five. Never's sister, Samantha, had returned to Princeton with her husband, Ed, and their two children after several years in South America. Donald had looked at his Aunt Never and attempted to say, 'the aunt with glasses.' It came out 'Aunt Glasses.' The name stuck. She only needed glasses for reading, and by the time they started dating they had shortened her name to 'Aunt Gee.' "What are you doing calling this early in the morning?" Never asked.

"I just thought you'd like to speak to your favorite nephew before the worries of the day caught up with you."

"You're right. I could use a lift." She held the plug, no longer trying to push it into the socket but still crouched on the floor.

"Is anything wrong?"

"Not really. Mark killed me at tennis this morning, and I have a meeting I'm not looking forward to with a consultant."

"Why?"

Never nearly smiled. Why? Was Stephen's favorite question. Since Samantha and Ed had died in an accident, leaving her with custody of the two small boys ten years ago, he'd been curious about everything.

"Since the merger, nothing is the same. He's here to work on consolidating the two Corporate Systems Departments, but the real outcome will be the loss of jobs—mine included."

"I'm sorry. I wish there was something I could do."

"You're doing what you should be doing. You're in school, and I'm proud of you." In the last two years he'd made the Dean's List in each of the four semesters, and Donald had done the same.

"Did you read the book I recommended?" Stephen asked.

"I did." Averal Ballentine's book. Even by her family, Averal Ballentine seemed to be thrust on her. Stephen had told her about the new book. Since the merger, Ballentine books had become standard reading material for everyone—the theory being that they would learn something about his methods before they actually had to submit to his perusal. She admitted this one on stress was as good as the five that graced her bookshelf. The points were exacting, and should work if one put them into practice. She resolved to do just that during her interview with him this morning.

"Then you should be able to handle any situation."

"Thanks for the vote of confidence. The consultant I'm meeting *is* Averal Ballentine." His face loomed into her consciousness, and her heartbeat accelerated.

"You didn't tell me you knew him." Stephen sounded impressed.

"I don't know him," she quickly corrected. "I met him briefly Friday night at BriAnne Ball's opening. I discovered she's his mother." She had also discovered he was easy to talk to and laugh with. He had dominating eyes and a magnetism that attracted her. She liked him more than she wanted to tell anyone, including herself.

"He was here for a lecture series earlier this semester. A real nice guy. I met him one night at the student center."

There it was again, Never thought, that respect born of charisma. She had no idea how to handle this interview. She'd thought reading the book would give her some insight, but all it had done was confuse her. His methods were practical and systematic, and he'd dealt expertly with the subject of office politics—motivation in managerial decisions, logic and lack of logic, and how not to give in to the stress created. But it said nothing about meeting a man you were attracted to only to find out the two of you have vastly different views on the same subject.

"I understand things have to change, Stephen. I'm not arguing against change. I can see the impracticality of two legal departments, two tax divisions, even two MIS departments. Its just that everything changes on the Worthington side of the merger. On the Cedar Chemical side it's business as usual."

"It will get better," Stephen said in his eternal optimist voice.

"I know it will." *It has to,* she thought. The morale around the company had reached an all time low. "And you have brightened my day," she added on a cheery note.

Stephen changed the subject, to her other nephew. "How's Donald? Have you heard from him?"

"He made his customary call yesterday." She glanced at the smiling face of a tall, athletic-looking young man with brown skin and dark eyes who graced one of the gold frames on her bookshelf. He called her every Sunday. "He's fine. He told me he's going out for basketball."

"Basketball! When did he become sports minded?"

"I'm not sure, but he made the team." She paused, her voice rising. "However, I think there was a certain cheerleader who was the deciding factor." Stephen and Never both laughed. Donald was fun loving, and despite his muscular body was generally a spectator where sports were concerned. He had, however, been known to be quite creative when getting a date with a pretty girl. "He also told me about Brad Hilton recruiting everyone for a ski trip over the Thanksgiving holiday."

"You just can't trust him to keep a secret." She could almost see Stephen shaking his head. "You don't mind, do you? We're not committed yet. If you want us to come home, we'll cancel—"

Never cut in. "Don't be silly." She'd met Brad Hilton and his mother at the last Parents' Day gathering. He was an intelligent young man, battling adolescent acne, who was good at organizing. Apparently, so was his father, who hadn't been able to make the visitors' day. "Going on a ski trip with your friends is something you'll remember all your life. I'll be fine on Thanksgiving," she finished. The truth was she wished she could have done those kind of things when she was in school, but she'd had to work.

"Did Donald mention that the chapter is paying for this? The entire fraternity is going. We had a fund-raiser earlier this year, and it was very successful."

"Was that when Averal Ballentine came to speak?" Sarcasm laced her tone.

"You wouldn't believe the people who came to hear him. Tickets were selling faster than exam questions."

Never hadn't expected him to confirm her request. She didn't even know why she'd said it.

"You know, Aunt Gee, I've been thinking. Next semester I can get a job and go to night school. I talked to Mr. Jac—"

"You'll do nothing of the kind." She stopped playing with the cord in her hand, interrupting him. So there had been a purpose to this call. Other than to say hello, Stephen was worried about her and the problems the merger could cause. For the time being she still had her job, but for the future she had better find other means of support.

"Why not?" he asked. "You did it."

Never had done it, and felt she'd missed some of the best times of her life. She didn't want that to happen to Stephen and Donald, and she didn't want to tell them. Stephen would immediately remember her telling him how her days had been split between classes and working in the Sickle Cell Anemia Research Department at Howard University. During vacations she'd worked full-time, too, to get added money to pay tuition.

"It's still something I don't want you to have to do."

"But you're so concerned about money. The merger, the possibility of losing your job, a mortgage, car payment. You don't need the burden of two college students."

"I don't have the full burden." Never shifted her position to her knees and rested on her heels. "Both of you have good scholarships which offset a lot of expenses. So let's not talk about you going to work. There will be plenty of time for that later."

"But Mr. Jackson agreed to let me work in his office."

"Then you'll have a job when you graduate. How about we wait for that before we do anything drastic?"

"But—"

"No buts," she interrupted with finality, cutting off further argument from Stephen. "When they threaten to put my belongings on the street then we'll talk about you dropping out of school," she continued, the smile in her voice taking the sting out of her previous words. "Until then you'll remain a full time student. They'll be plenty of time for you to work after graduation."

"Graduation is two years away." He said it as if it were a lifetime.

"Who knows what can happen in two years?" she added, her voice sliding up scale. "We could be sitting on Easy Street by then."

"We would if you'd send some of those game programs out."

"I tried that, Stephen." She sighed, leaning forward again. Her legs were beginning to get tired. "It didn't work." She'd sent some of her programs for computer games to several manufacturers, but they'd been rejected. "You know I only started writing those for you and Donald. They're not marketable."

"Aunt Gee, that was years ago. They're a lot better now. The last one you sent me was a hit on three campuses."

"I'm glad to hear it," she smiled, pleased at his appraisal. He and Donald still loved playing with the videos she produced. She'd sent them programs, and both had told her their friends really enjoyed them.

"This isn't a fluke, Aunt Gee," Stephen went on. "There are some die-hard video game players in my dorm, and you have them standing in line for whatever you write. I hardly have time to get the package open before somebody is trying to borrow it. Give it a try. What have you got to lose?"

"You know this is only a hobby with me. I like working in the corporate world. I enjoy writing the programs, but they're for you and Donald. They really aren't marketable."

"Then make them marketable." He sounded exasperated.

"I'll think about it," she said. She remembered how devastated she'd been when she'd put so much hope into *World War III,* her best video game. It had been returned to her with a polite rejection letter. Her nephews were prejudiced. She was glad they felt she could sell them, but she knew better. And even if she did sell them, could they support her and her obligations?

"You know, if I took that job," Stephen began. "It would be one less burden you have to worry about."

"No it wouldn't," she contradicted. "All it would mean is I'd worry about you with a job and night school. Nothing has happened yet, Stephen. I can get another job if I lose this one. So let's put off dropping out of college until absolutely necessary." She spoke harshly, the words rising her up to her knees.

"All right," he agreed. "I'll pay you back, Aunt Gee. I promise."

"You don't have to pay me back. When I'm old and grey I'll live with you, and then I can be a burden." She ended with a slight giggle.

"That's a promise," he said.

* * *

"Her name's Nefertiti Kincaid," Barbara Dixon said as she hung Averal Ballentine's coat in the closet and led him toward Never's office. "Around here she's known as 'Never' because it's next to impossible to win an argument with her. So if you want a fight, you've come to the right place."

"I'm not here for a fight." Averal frowned. "I'm here to help with the transition, that's all."

"Well, when Never got in this morning she didn't look ready to negotiate."

Averal didn't like the sound of that. Nefertiti Kincaid disturbed him. His mother had supplied her name as Averal left the gallery. The moment he'd seen her he'd known there was something different about her. Then at the gallery they'd talked, laughed. He found her fascinating. Images of the woman in the sleek, black gown with her hair jeweled and looking like her namesake had been with him throughout the weekend. He'd slept and dreamed of rose stems that turned into black seams on long legs. Her image woke him more than once, and his body hated him for the cold showers he'd subjected it to at each instance.

It wasn't often a woman got under his skin, and even rarer for one to do it as fast as Never Kincaid had ingratiated herself into his psychic presence. An engaged woman was strictly off limits in his mind, but this one seemed to interfere with his normal thought processes. Even the time he'd spent at Riddles Place had been blurred by his mental portrait of her.

"This is Never's office." Barbara had led him around several aisles of modular constructed cubicles. He was a head taller than the high walls on his right and left. Inside them people were busy tapping out instructions on computers placed on sunken mahogany colored furniture. It was a study in efficiency, sprinkled with an occasional photograph of a loved one. Along the back wall were larger offices with dark wooden doors. The walls, however, were made of glass. Aesthetically it gave the full office light and made the space appear larger. He'd like to meet the person who designed the layout. A section of his next book was making the workplace more comfortable by providing a pleasant place to work that was adequately lighted and adhered to the basic needs of people.

Barbara stopped in front of an open door. Inside, Averal saw no one. Barbara went in. He followed her. The same deep red coloring of the modular offices was continued in the oversized desk, which held a computer on one depressed ridge, leaving plenty of work space on top of the desk. Averal looked around. Photographs lined the bookshelves, and prints hung from the walls. He liked them. There were company awards displayed on the glass ètagere in the corner and several framed certificates, one denoting ten years of service.

"You don't have to pay me back. When I'm old and grey I'll live with you, and then I can be a burden," Averal heard someone say. Then he saw the woman crouched on the floor. A hand came up, searching for the telephone.

"I'll take that," the secretary said, retrieving the headset and placing it in its cradle.

"Thanks, Barbara," the person under the desk answered.

"Never, your appointment is here."

"Would you go and get him, please?" She didn't raise her head.

Barbara opened her mouth to say he was already there, but was halted by the sound of her phone ringing. "Excuse me," she apologized to Averal, her body poised to run. "I'm expecting a very important call."

Barbara left Averal standing before Never's desk. He set his briefcase next to his foot and straightened, keeping his eyes on the woman huddling near the floor.

The back of Never Kincaid's head was barely visible over the top of the desk. She was on one knee, her face turned away from him, one leg extended behind her, prominently clad in a seamed, black stocking. Her hair was piled on top of her head, held in place by a tortoise shell comb, the Nefertiti hairstyle gone. He didn't need to see her face. He knew who she was by the sudden pummeling of his heart.

Never jammed the plug into the surge protector and raised her head. She stopped as her eyes became level with the desk. In front of her was a pair of legs covered in dark wool. From her vantage point she followed the line of the expensive English-cut suit up to the light brown eyes of Averal Ballentine. His eyes pierced through her. They reminded her of summer. The tremor which accompanied his stare shook her. She hoped it wasn't as visible as it felt. Her knees were suddenly weak, and there was no strength in her arms. She couldn't get up.

She'd known he was coming, known who he was since Friday night. So why was her body shocked and inert in his presence?

"Let me help you?" His voice had the velvet softness of a moonlit night. Never fought her reaction to it, but lost the battle. No wonder he'd been surrounded by women Friday night.

He stood above her, hands extended. Her gaze met them, open and inviting, as they reached for her. Lightly she lay both her palms in his. Sensation passed from his hands to hers, as she expected. She pushed it as far aside as it would go. His fingers were strong and slender. She liked the feel of his hands as he assisted her from her position.

Averal's gaze went straight to her feet. Business black, he thought, and smiled. He wondered where the red shoes were.

When his eyes returned to her face all the warmth of Friday night was gone. Today she was dressed in a black suit. The stiffly starched, white blouse, which rose to her throat and contrasted with her bronze skin tone, told him her mind was already made up.

"Good morning," she greeted nervously. He seemed to fill her office. Even the glass panel that faced Barbara's back and usually gave greater dimension to the space was humbled by his six-foot frame.

He smiled cynically. "The almost Mrs. Caldwell," he said.

"It's Kincaid. Never Kincaid. I apologize for Martin. He shouldn't have told you we were engaged. We're not." Averal was still holding her hands. He turned them over, hoping she didn't notice the tremble which went through him at the meaning of her words. The ring was gone.

"The ring belongs to my grandmother," she said, answering his silent inquiry. "It had been reset recently, and I tried it on and forgot to remove it before going to the gallery. I would have explained Friday night, but you left so abruptly." Never saw his jaw stiffen. "Martin had the rings reset for me. It's a present for my grandparents' fiftieth wedding anniversary."

"Fifty years. At today's rate of divorce, that's amazing."

"Yes, it is." Never pulled her hands free. "Won't you sit down?" She took her seat behind the desk. It was huge and uncluttered. Averal sat in front of her. She'd always thought the desk gave her the advantage—it made anyone sitting in front of it look smaller—but not with this man. He looked as if he owned the place. She felt like a subordinate, as if he were her boss.

Never began trying to get her footing back. "I've asked some of our staff to join us in a few minutes. First I'd like to ask exactly what your role here is going to be." She got straight to the point.

"I'm here to assist in as smooth a transition as possible of two businesses into one cohesive unit."

It was a canned response, but the way he said it Never thought he meant it. She shook her head slightly, clearing it of any sympathetic images that might crowd in to undermine her thoughts against this man. Averal Ballentine was not on her side, and she wouldn't fall into the trap of helping him eliminate her department.

"How do you propose to do that?" she asked, making an effort to keep her voice level. Never sat straight, her arms resting lightly on the padded leather arms of the chair. Her body language gave no clue as to her feelings. Averal had always been able to read his subjects well. Immediately he knew this woman would be different.

"Observe, ask questions, both here and on the Cedar Chemicals side of the business."

Never leaned forward, trying to forget how handsome the man across from her was. "Rumor has it, Mr. Ballentine, that you're here for our jobs."

Don't beat around the bush, Ms. Kincaid. Come straight to the point. Averal had heard she was direct. He could see she'd be a hard adversary. "That is not my intention. I am only here to study the situation."

"And what happens to this study? Is it to be bound and shelved, or are we talking about the lives of real people here?" She leaned forward in the chair, and he could hear the passion leaping into her voice. She was trying to control it. He knew that. He could also tell she was territorial about her department. That was common, and to be expected. Any manager who didn't look out for her people wasn't worth it, in his eyes. He wanted to smile, glad that she'd passed the unadministered test.

"Ms. Kincaid . . . Never . . . is it all right if we use first names?" Averal wanted to make the meeting as informal as possible. First names, he found, made proceedings appear friendlier, and Never wasn't the only hostile person he'd met. There was plenty of hostility in a new company; not just here, but in every division where he'd worked. Mergers did that. It was better in a hostile takeover, when people knew they were going to be terminated. In a merger, everyone tiptoed or walked fast, as if they were playing musical chairs and the music might stop when they weren't near a seat.

"First names will be fine." Never nodded. "My first name is actually Nefertiti." She knew the technique he was employing, and felt armed since she was aware of the ploy. She wouldn't give into him. In his book he had said *during stressful situations, try to reduce the tension between yourself and the other party or parties.* Never leaned forward and tried to smile. "Everyone calls me Never."

"Never, you must realize any merger requires some changes."

She was tired of hearing that. Every speech she heard these days began with that tiresome phrase. Never looked away for a moment. Her temper was rising. She laced her fingers together on the desk, much as she had done in Mrs. Gillespie's third grade. She hoped the action would help her maintain control.

"That's all that has happened here in the past four months, and all on the Worthington Pharmaceutical side. Nothing but people being fired. People who thought they had careers with this company suddenly find themselves unemployed. A lot of that has resulted from recommendations by Ballentine and Associates." She was angry but controlled.

Averal refused to be baited, but she was doing a good job on him. "No recommendation from me or my staff has resulted in anyone being unsatisfied with the settlement agreed upon."

"Are you saying they left voluntarily?"

"I'm saying they were made deals," he said succinctly.

"You're here now to make a deal with my department?" Her eyes widened.

"I'm here only as an observer."

"Well, I'll tell you what there is to observe. First, we don't have common hardware. Our software is different. Our methods of customer service are different." She ticked each point off on her well-manicured fingers. "Merging two ideologies as different as ours is impossible. We know what happens. The weaker one is eliminated. Since Worthington Pharmaceutical was bought, we're the weaker one."

"All decisions are not made based on who's the smaller company—"

"You're not going to tell me there's logic involved in this?" she interrupted with a mirthless laugh. He was probably used to people cooperating with him, Never thought. Most people just answered his questions; some of them with an undertone of hostility. Nefertiti Kincaid wasn't most people, and she wasn't about to lie down and die. She was up for a fight, and he was going to have to deal with her.

"Why don't you tell me what it is you think is happening here?" he asked.

Never recognized rule number three from his book on negotiations. *When confronted with hostility give them the reins and let them tell you what the problem is, or what they think the settlement should be.* In her case it was about the organization of the new MIS department.

"I think the consolidation of MIS will result in the elimination of the computer facility as we at Worthington Pharmaceutical have known it. Everything will be done the Cedar way. Regardless of logic and cost. It will be done the way Cedar Chemicals wants it, because they have the upper hand. We're the poor relation in this takeover, and the sooner we're eliminated the easier it will be for them to incorporate this unit into their mold."

"Does everything affect you this passionately?"

The question took Never by surprise. Her eyes opened wide, but she recovered quickly. Taking a deep breath, she continued. "I've known some of these people most of my life. Their whole lives are wrapped up in the security they thought they had with this company. Suddenly they've been thrust into a situation not of their making. You're damn right I'm passionate about this."

"Well, it's good to know where you stand."

"Where do you stand, Mr. Ballentine?" Never leaned back, intentionally keeping the smirk she wanted to give him off her face.

"I thought we were on a first name basis. Friday night you called me Averal."

Never didn't want to think about Friday night. She also didn't want to think about the way he was looking at her now. He wanted to melt her. She stiffened her resolve. Anger flashed through her. It was an unscrupulous act. This was business, and he had no right to try to corner her with those eyes.

"Averal," she said, low. "Where do you stand?"

"I've been hired by Cedar-Worthington. I'm impartial in this situation."

"I see. To you there aren't lives involved here. It's a cost savings to the corporation. You can measure your success based on the thousands of dollars you save the company. Don't worry about us. We'll survive. And if we don't, it's not your concern. You've done your job and been paid for it."

Averal was on his feet. Never pushed her chair back and stood, too. His voice was low, but unmistakably angry. "You know nothing about me. Nothing of how I work. You have no right to accuse me of stampeding over peoples' lives with no concern for their futures. I'm not some awful monster out for my own gain regardless of who falls into my path. I have a job to do, just like you. If we can't find a common ground to make this an easy transition, then I guess we'll just have to work around each other."

"I won't help you fire my department."

The battle lines were clearly defined as the man and woman glared at each other. Outside Barbara had her back to the wall. Her head was bowed and her concentration given to the person on the other end of the phone. Life continued without notice of the heated exchange inside the corner office.

"I don't think there's any point in discussing this any farther today." Averal's calm had returned.

Or any other time, Never thought, but held her tongue.

"Maybe we can talk about it later—on more neutral ground," he suggested.

"I will not help you fire my department," she said, repeating her earlier warning in succinct tones. Her pace was slow, giving each word emphasis, as if she were teaching a deaf child to speak.

"You won't be asked to do anything of the kind. All I ask is that you work with me and keep an open mind."

"And all I ask is that you remember this combination of businesses was supposed to be a merger, not a takeover, not a buy-out, as evidenced by the past effects on the Worthington Pharmaceutical portion of the business."

"Good day." Averal picked up his briefcase and left the office. She stared after him for several moments, then slumped into her chair, sighing heavily. Her hands went to her temples, and she massaged the thumping heartbeat she felt there. She hadn't been very professional. Reading Averal's book had done nothing to help her. Everything had gone wrong. What had happened to all the techniques she'd been taught during countless hours of managerial instruction? Where was her detachment, her ability to defuse situations? Why hadn't she remained calm and open-minded, as he'd suggested? How could she have been so unprofessional? How could she have accused a stranger of being the culprit in the recent firings? It wasn't his fault. She stood up and removed her suit jacket. She was hot, mostly from her argument with Averal, but not all of it was due to that. So many things had happened which had nothing to do with Ballentine and Associates.

He was going to beat her. She knew that. She'd seen the other departments where he'd been, knew it was impossible to maintain duplicate departments that had no need to exist. This was business. It wasn't personal. Yet she'd made it personal. The argument only involved Cedar-Worthington on the surface. Underneath was herself, the woman, and Averal Ballentine, the man. She'd used him, made him the scapegoat of her weekend frustrations. Her anger had built when she knew he was coming to her department next. He'd been to other departments in the company, and all of them had resulted in layoffs. Now it was their turn, and Never couldn't take it without a fight.

She looked through the window. Outside the sun was shining. Leafless trees stood in the crisp air, oblivious to her presence. She stared at them as if they knew the real reason for her hot-tempered actions against Averal Ballentine. She was uncomfortable with the way he made her feel. She had not had experience with the breathlessness, the heart-pounding, or her weak knees.

Why him? she asked herself. She met men all the time, yet none of them had affected her the way he did. All he had to do was look at her, and her skin threatened to liquefy. Checking her arms to make sure she hadn't melted, she pulled her anger back into focus. Anger was easier to deal with than attraction.

Averal threw his briefcase into the back of the Jeep Cherokee and slammed the door. His breath congealed in the air, telling him it was cold, but he was hot. He wanted to pull his coat off and have it join the briefcase in the backseat. Reason got the better of him, and he tore the driver's door open and slid behind the wheel. He was angrier than he'd been at anyone since his father had written him out of his life. Angry because she'd caught him off guard.

She'd deliberately withheld her name at the gallery Friday night. She knew if she told him who she was he'd immediately remember their appointment. Nefertiti wasn't a name like Linda or Susan.

"Well, 'Ms. Black-Dress-Seamed-Stockings', this is not the end of our association." Averal looked at the building through the windshield, speaking to the air. "No matter what you think of me, you and I will have more to settle than either of us thought, and none of it has anything to do with Cedar-Worthington."

THREE

Averal had long since divested himself of his suit jacket. His sleeves were rolled midway up his arms, and he'd been hunched over his desk for hours. Lacing his fingers behind his head, he stretched. Myra would be surprised when she came in the next morning to find a pile of folders on her desk completed and ready for filing. He'd also whacked out a ton of correspondence she'd been after him to clean up. The only motivation he'd needed was a sassy female with hair like midnight and eyes as soft as dark mink.

Never Kincaid pushed her way into his consciousness. She was back. Averal wasn't surprised. Since his seeing her last weekend, she hadn't been far from his consciousness. He'd delved into the work on his desk, trying to get her and the argument they'd had this morning out of his mind. It hadn't worked. He knew it wouldn't, but he'd tried, anyway.

Then he saw Caroline's message, the only incomplete item left—a pink While You Were Out slip in Myra's calligraphy-type handwriting. It told him his half sister wanted to return her call.

Averal glanced at the calendar. Caroline didn't bother him often, but he could expect a message from her three or four times a year. Usually he ignored them. Since his desk was clear of everything else and Caroline would get his mind off Never Kincaid, he pulled the phone forward and punched the digits with more force than necessary. He wondered what she had to say this time. Usually she gave him some excuse for her call, but didn't want anything more than to say hello. He should be able to withstand that. Why it still bothered him after all these years he couldn't rationalize. His brother had been gone for thirty years. His father deserted him, and he'd gone on. Why did it still get to him? Just a few penstrokes on a pink piece of paper, and back came the memories of years of feeling unwanted and unloved.

"Hello." The voice on the other end of the phone was sweet, and sounded older than her twenty-six years.

"Caroline, you called?" he said tersely.

"Oh, dear." Her voice dropped. "I'd hoped to find you in a good mood."

Averal clenched his teeth and kept quiet. With Never on his mind, he'd forgotten Caroline's uncanny ability to read his moods, even over vast distances and telephone lines.

"What's happened? You sound stern. Have a bad day?" She was teasing.

"What are you talking about?" He'd had an awful day—his encounter with Never, and the haunting he'd been subjected to for the past ten hours. Well, he wasn't about to confide in Caroline.

"I can hear it, Averal. Something is different about your voice."

"You haven't talked to me in months. How do you know what my voice should sound like?"

"I know," was all she said.

"I'm just tired, Caroline. Could you get to the point of this call?" She was irritating him, looking into his mind from two hundred miles away.

"I've heard tired before, and this is not it. This sounds more like a woman."

Damn, Averal thought. She had that you-can't-lie-to-me inflection in her voice.

"Am I right? Did you meet somebody new?"

Caroline sounded as if she were acquainted with all his female friends and knew there was someone different in his life.

"If you don't tell me why you called, I'm going to hang up." His voice was curt.

"I must be close, or you wouldn't be so disagreeable." He heard another giggle. "Maybe you should try reading your latest book. I've found it very good when I'm all stressed out."

"Caroline—" he warned.

"All right, all right. I recognize that tone, too. I called to invite you to Thanksgiving dinner."

"I can't. I'm busy."

"Busy doing what? Averal, everybody gets off for Thanksgiving—even men who hate their families, and own their own company."

"Caroline, I don't hate my family." That part was true. He didn't actually hate anyone. He just preferred to see them as little as possible. "I already have plans for Thanksgiving," he finished.

"Averal, you're lying." The last word dragged out like the end of a song. "It's only October, and I know you don't make plans that far in advance, unless . . ."

She let the words trail off. Averal knew she was doing it again. He closed his eyes, trying to close his mind to her, but he wanted to know what she was thinking. He couldn't read her as she could him.

"Unless what, Caroline?" he finally asked.

"Unless it's the woman."

"What woman?"

"The one who's got you so uptight."

"I'm not uptight," he shouted into the phone. "I'm sorry, Caroline," he apologized with a sigh. "It's just that I *am* tired." What a one-track mind she had? He wouldn't admit to it. Pressing his forehead against his hand, he held the phone hard to his ear.

"Not sleeping well?"

"No."

"How's your appetite?"

"Not good."

"What's her name, Averal?"

"Never."

"All right, I'll give up . . . for now. About Thanksgiving? Will you come?" All the playfulness had left her voice.

"Caroline—"

"Now, I won't take no for an answer," she interrupted before he could refuse again. "Besides, you haven't seen your nephew yet."

"Nephew?" Averal squeezed the instrument in his hand. His entire body went still and cold.

"Yes, dear brother. If you'd see your family more often than every three years, you'd know who was getting married, divorced, dying, or having babies."

It was true. He hadn't seen Caroline since her wedding three years ago. "Caroline, you have a baby?"

She giggled. "Twins actually. Laurence and Lindsay."

Averal paled. Babies. The thought made him sick.

"Are . . . they . . . all—" he stammered, barely able to get the words out.

"They're fine, Averal, and would love to see their uncle. So please come for Thanksgiving."

He couldn't. He didn't want to see Caroline or her children. It would be too much like seeing Gabe again. He knew he didn't want the added pressure of his father's relatives and Gabe's memory.

"No, Caroline. I do have plans, really."

"Just what are you doing that you can't take one Thursday out of the year and have dinner with your only sister and her family?"

He knew she could tell he was lying, but he repeated it anyway. "I've been invited somewhere else."

There was silence on the other end of the phone for a second.

"Well, if you change your mind," Caroline said. "Dinner is at three."

Averal wrote *Thanksgiving Dinner - 3:00* PM on the pink piece of paper, underlining it with two solid strokes of black ink.

"Thanks, Sis. Sorry I can't make it."

"He's dead, Averal." Caroline's voice was soft. "Please don't shut us out because of him. We all love you."

"I know." Averal didn't pretend he didn't understand what she meant.

"Will you at least think about Thanksgiving?"

"I'll think about it," he agreed sincerely.

"And Averal . . ." Caroline hesitated. "Bring her."

"Bye, Caroline."

He replaced the receiver and fell back in his chair. Caroline's calls rarely upset him. Tonight she'd told him she had children. Did they have the trait, or the disease? How long, he wondered. How long this time?

It had been the perfect evening to begin Christmas shopping. Never couldn't go home yet. She didn't want to be alone with her thoughts. Averal Ballentine had thrown her normally ordered life into chaos since she'd held his gaze for one brief moment in the bookstore. Her argument with him plagued her, but worse, her ability to concentrate had been shot. Several times she'd been tempted to call and apologize. Whenever she lifted the receiver her fingers only hovered above the keys, depressing none of them. Her hands remembered the electricity that flowed from him when he'd helped her to her feet. What would she say to him now? How could she explain that her attack had really been the result of the warm—Warm? That was a laugh. Warm was when you lifted clothes from the dryer and plunged your face into them. Warm was slipping your arms into a fur coat and sinking your body into its luxury. Warm was a glass of wine on a cold night that wrapped you in a cocoon of gauzy cotton. Averal Ballentine did not make her warm. He made her body burn.

She'd stayed late, working on *Falkan's Return,* her latest submission to the world of games. Disappearing into her fantasy programs had always been a panacea for whatever bothered her. Tonight nothing was keeping Averal Ballentine relegated to the back of her mind, where she wanted him. He was at the forefront of her thoughts, and refused to be moved.

She found it harder and harder to visualize him as her enemy. The mask she'd put on him slipped each time his image came into view. All she saw were the eyes of that lion she'd seen when she was ten. But it wasn't the lion whose face surfaced. It was Averal's.

Never found herself staring into the darkness outside her office window, her hands poised over the console. A light snow had begun to fall. She knew her concentration for the game was gone. During the day it had been easier to push him aside, with meetings and concentrating on the problems of the day, but it was dark now, and the office was quiet. There was nothing to keep her thoughts from running wildly toward him, a direction she had to keep herself from following.

Standing up, she switched off the equipment in her office and slipped on her coat. Reaching her car, she slid under the steering wheel and pointed the car toward home. Halfway there she suddenly turned toward the mall. She could get a jump on her Christmas shopping.

She meandered through the shops, purposely avoiding the bookstore. She knew it was irrational. Why should Averal be there? What difference could it make if he were? Still she avoided it, going to the lower level and passing under it. After an hour she'd only found two small gifts to use as stocking stuffers, and decided it was time to go.

Large flakes coated her hair by the time she reached her car, turning it the same grey color as her grandmother's. The season's first snowfall was predicted to drop five inches, but the ground was free of the powdery substance. She looked at the sky. Cold crystals kissed her face, with the promise of more tomorrow. As she reached for the door she saw John in the distance.

"John," she called, moving quickly toward him. "John!"

He looked in the direction of the voice, recognizing her, and waved. "Never!" John met her between the cars, clasping her in a bear hug and kissing her affectionately on the cheek. John Williams was in his fifties with sparkling blue eyes and a heart of pure gold. Until recently he had spent most of his working career at Worthington. His face was a ruddy red under a shock of blond hair that looked as if it were perpetually bleached by the sun. Never pressed her cheek against his cool one, noting the flakes of snow melting on his lashes.

"How are you?" she asked. She hadn't seen John for nearly four months, since he'd become a casualty of the merger.

"I'm fine," he said, releasing her but keeping hold of her gloved hands. "How are you?"

"I'm still at Cedar-Worthington."

"And your boys? How are they?"

"They're fine. They're both still away at college." Never pulled her hands free and turned her coat collar closer to her neck. "They're both fine. I talked to one today and the other yesterday."

"Have you got a few minutes? We could go somewhere and talk."

She nodded, shivering.

"Why don't you follow me? I know a place close by," John volunteered with a smile.

She agreed, and minutes later found herself with a glass of white wine as she sat across from John in a small bar in Princeton called Riddles Place. It had a restaurant, but they occupied a booth at the end of the crowded bar area. *It must be a popular after-work spot,* Never thought. She noticed turn-of-the-century photographs of Princeton's streets and houses. She hadn't been here before. There was a bandstand at the opposite end of the room. It was empty. Recorded music came from speakers concealed overhead.

John opened the subject. "So how are things going for you, Never?"

"Nothing has happened yet. I fear it will soon. We've been visited by Averal Ballentine himself." Never cringed, visibly shuddering as if she were cold or frightened.

John's head dropped. He took his glass and rolled it between his palms. A wet circle appeared on the polished brown surface.

"I'm sorry to hear that." He paused, bringing his crystal blue gaze back to her face. "You always seemed to enjoy your job so much." He paused again, then continued. "You can't tell what the future has in store, Never. It may be for the best."

Never was about to sip her wine. She set the glass down at John's comment. "What do you mean?"

"Everybody knows you love those games more than the routine of the department."

"That's not really true," she defended. "I like working."

"But the reward. That rush you get when the light bulb goes on. When you know the solution to whatever problem has prevented you from completing the program. It's not the same when you're working on departmental budgets or running off to a meeting to determine if it's feasible to upgrade the equipment to a new version this year."

Never knew exactly what John meant. She'd been in her position for over three years, and most of her day was a juggling act between one meeting or another. Fun was when she played with the games programs or when the workload was so heavy she had to go back into programming. She loved that, but she also loved the corporate routine. She might write the games, but they didn't replace the day-to-day rush of coming into a thriving business, knowing she was accomplishing something, making someone's life easier. And the pay wasn't nearly as good.

"John, I couldn't make a living with the games. Remember, I'm supporting two college students."

"I understand that. I just don't want you to lose sight of what's important in life. I worked at Worthington Pharmaceutical for twenty years before they fired me. In all that time, I never really liked what I did."

"I didn't know that." Her hand touched John's in an understanding gesture. "You were so good at it." Never remembered him teaching her, taking her under his wing and guiding her as if she were his daughter.

"And that's probably why I stayed. That, plus I lacked the courage to leave the security of my salary to pursue something else." He squeezed her fingers and released them. "Now I'm older, and because of the merger I've been forced to decide what I want to do with the rest of my life. I'm not bitter, Never. I look at it as an opportunity to do what I should have done years ago."

"What is that?" Never asked, sipping her wine.

"I've always liked working with my hands." He spread them open. "You know about my hobby shop in my garage. After I was fired I considered selling some of my crafts at shows and to the tourists along the shore."

Never knew of John's love for wood. He designed and made plaques, clocks, ships, anything he could, from all types of wood. Just as her moonlighting with games programs was no secret, everyone knew that John enjoyed fashioning wood into objects of art.

"Can you support yourself doing that?" she asked softly.

"For a while. There's only me now that Jinny's married and Ethel's gone."

Never couldn't imagine John as a beach bum. He was an office type, even if he didn't know it. Spending his days lazing about would kill him. He had changed after his wife, Ethel's, lengthy illness and her death. Then Jinny, his only daughter, had married and moved to Oregon. Now, at fifty-eight, he'd lost a job he'd held for thirty years.

"It wouldn't be too bad," John continued, a playful smile tugging the corners of his mouth. "My needs are small. If Jinny were still in college or I had medical bills to contend with I'd be more concerned, but I'm actually glad it happened."

As John's smile widened, Never's mouth twisted downward. He couldn't be serious about selling novelties along the shore, yet he looked so content.

"John, what about insurance?" Never lowered her voice a fraction. She wanted to be delicate. "Your needs may be small now. You're going to get older. You could have an accident, need medical care. I don't want to find you in some charity ward along the Jersey shore."

John laughed at the grim picture she painted. "I promise it won't come to that. I've had an offer from a furniture manufacturer in North Carolina. Apparently, Averal Ballentine sent them some of my designs for the wood items I make. They talked to me about working in their design department."

Never smiled, relief flooding through her. "That's wonderful, John. Why did you give me that story about selling trinkets along the shore?"

John laughed. "You're too serious, Never. You should stop letting this merger bother you and have some fun." He leaned back casually against the leather upholstery.

"It's hard to have fun when so many people are losing their jobs, knowing soon it'll be your turn." Never looked down, then back at John as she pushed her blues away. Tonight she'd be happy for him. "I'm glad for you. This will give you everything you want. I'm sure in a furniture company you can work with your hands and be able to see your designs come to life."

She knew how he must feel. It was how she felt when she transformed an idea onto paper and then made it work in her computer.

"You said Averal Ballentine sent them?" Never spoke as if the thought had only just registered.

"He's not a bad guy, Never. I don't know how long he talked to the others, but he spent a whole evening with me. I even took him back to my place and showed him my garage. When he asked to borrow the designs, I didn't know it would lead to a job."

"There were others?"

"Sam Harris, Greg Johnson, Bill Winston, and me. We met Ballentine right here." He used his index finger and tapped the table. "Let's see, it must have been two months ago. Talked for hours and hours."

"Have you seen Bill or Greg since then?"

John shook his head. Never made a mental note to call them when she got to the office in the morning. In the back of her mind a human being was emerging. She didn't know whether she wanted Averal Ballentine to be one just yet. She'd thought of him as a dragon out to cut headcount. Helping them to find other employment didn't fit into the character sketch she'd drawn.

"Remember, Never, it's not Ballentine who's doing this. It's the company. He's only doing a job he's been hired to do. Personally, I think he's trying the best he can. Mergers are hard on everybody, Never. There's no good way to combine two thriving businesses so everyone is happy."

Never took another sip of her wine. "I know what you're saying, John. But every day when I walk into that office all I see is uncertainty on the faces. They're all wondering when it will be their turn. We all know it's coming."

"I can't argue that. But make it easy, Never. Give Ballentine a chance. He'll do everything he can to make a fair deal."

It was clear John was on Averal's side. Why shouldn't he be? He had a new job, doing what he'd wanted to do all his life.

"I can't believe that. After all the people who have been let go. It's great he's gotten a job for you, but what about all the others? He can't possibly help them all."

"I understand that. The company is offering placement and education, if necessary. I'm just saying you should give Averal a chance. Talk to him." John paused, looking over Never's head. "Hey, there he is."

Never steeled herself. The instinct to turn and follow John's line of vision was strong. She fought it. Her back went ramrod straight. She wasn't prepared to talk to Averal Ballentine. To see him. She wanted to avoid him until she had time to prepare for an encounter. John wouldn't give her the opportunity. He lifted his hand and waved at Averal. "I'll call him over."

"No!" Never grabbed his arm, trying to pull it down, but it was too late. Averal Ballentine was already walking toward them.

FOUR

The instinct to run was the strongest it had ever been. She was trapped. No way out. She and John sat in the last booth. Across from them was the bar. Every stool was occupied. Behind it was a door marked Private which probably led to an office. She'd have to slide around the table to stand up and then pass Averal if she wanted to leave.

"He's coming over," John said, his smile widening in friendship.

Never could see Averal. He hadn't recognized her yet. He stopped briefly, speaking to the bartender. She noticed him pass a case to the man behind the bar before he continued toward their table. His easy familiarity with people he greeted was different from Friday night's artsy crowd. There he had been polite and friendly. Here he was easy and comfortable. As he worked his way toward them Never could tell he frequented this place.

She dropped her gaze. "John, I wish you hadn't done that. I'm not ready for a conversation with him, and this isn't the place to discuss my department."

John didn't have time to answer. Averal arrived and the two men stood, shaking hands.

"It's good to see you again," Averal greeted. "I hear things have worked out for you." Never's pulse skipped a beat at the sound of his voice. She gripped her glass in both hands. Suddenly her ears were hot, and she had no reason for her elevated temperature or the weakness that descended over her. John invited him to sit down.

"My house is up for sale, and I've been to North Carolina to find another one."

It was then he turned his attention to her. She noticed his eyebrows raise a fraction of an inch as he slipped into the booth next to her. She moved around the table to give him room. Still, his leg brushed against hers under the polished wood. She felt the heat of his closeness, and was surprised to discover she didn't mind it at all. Her heart suddenly pounded in her ears. She had to shift farther into the center to avoid continued contact with him. She wanted that contact. Slowly she let her breath out. This was getting way out of control, she told herself. He hadn't said a word to her, and already she was thinking of . . . she stopped herself. She wouldn't complete the thought. It was impossible, she told herself.

"Never tells me you two have met," John said. She concentrated on his words.

"Twice, actually," Averal said, his eyes holding hers in antagonistic scrutiny. She heard the censure in his voice.

"Good evening." She forced her voice to remain calm.

He nodded acknowledgment. "I hadn't expected to see you again so soon."

"Then we're both surprised."

John must have heard the tension between them. "I ran into Never tonight, and we dropped in here for a drink. I just finished telling her about my new job."

Averal took his gaze away. She closed her eyes a moment, trying to regain control of her pounding heart. She told herself to breathe in and out, that she was capable of being near him and not giving in to the strange feelings that assaulted her. Lifting her glass, she drained the last of her wine. Her throat felt parched, dry as hot sand. The liquid scalded against it on its way down. A waitress, who seemed to know Averal, appeared with a ready smile and a drink he had not ordered. Never watched as their hands took too long to pass the glass from one to the other. Averal returned the woman's smile with an air of familiarity. Suddenly, Never wanted to snatch the glass from their hands and dump the brown liquid over them.

"Thanks, Rhonda" he said, confirming her earlier thought that he was known here.

She turned her head to John, feeling more than seeing her empty goblet being taken away and a fresh one replacing it.

John gave her a be patient look. Then he and Averal Ballentine talked quietly for a few moments, leaving her to her own thoughts, which were chaotic at best. After a while Never's heartbeat slowed but didn't return to normal.

She was attracted to this man. Why?

She looked toward the bar. It was a long, high table with a brass railing and worn leather stools. Most of them were occupied by laughing couples. Briefcases lined the inner footrail. It was a comfortable place. She could see why people gathered here to unwind after a long day.

"I hate to have to leave you two," Never heard John say. "I'd like to spend more time with you." He looked at Never. "I have to go, and you two need to talk." He winked at her conspiratorially.

John and Averal stood. Again they shook hands. When he bent to kiss her on the cheek she whispered, "You planned this, John."

"Give him a chance," was his response. Then he was gone. Averal slipped back into the booth. She was alone with her enemy. Two enemies. One of them was herself.

She knew the moment would be awkward. It stretched on until she became aware of the noise surrounding her. Never groped for something to say.

"I'd like to apologize for John," she began. "He seems to have thrown us together. After this morning, if you'd rather not talk to me . . ." She made an effort to slide out of the booth.

"I don't mind." His hand grabbed hers. She stopped. He wasn't going to make this easy for her. Never felt hot and tongue-tied. She didn't know what to say.

"If you're meeting someone else—"

"I'm alone tonight." He lounged against the booth wall, lifting his highball glass and sipping the liquid that was the same amber color as his eyes. His body looked relaxed, and she knew his crooked smile was at her expense.

Never glanced at her drink. She held the glass by its stem. She swallowed. They couldn't sit there all night and not say a word. She might as well apologize.

"Mr. Ballentine," she began. "I know we didn't get off to a great start."

"I thought we did." He swirled the liquid in his glass, staring at it. Then he looked up at her. "Friday night."

Never felt heat pool into her face, then surge up her ears. She remembered the way she'd felt talking to him about the beach; the way she'd wished the merger wasn't between them.

"I meant this morning," Never said, letting the Friday night comment die the way her feelings would have to die. "I didn't plan to be so hostile. You were very professional, and I acted like . . . like—"

"Like a woman who might lose her job?" He leaned closer to her. She could smell his cologne, feel the heat of his body as it mingled with her own. "It was refreshing, albeit surprising." His voice was quiet, causing her head to come up and search his face. She thought she'd heard concern in his voice. After a moment he smiled. She returned it. Her blood rushed through her veins as she noticed the small lines that creased his eyes.

Suddenly Never knew why this man ran a successful business. In less than five minutes after John left them he'd managed to sap her of her anger, put her at ease, and allow her to save face about this morning's fiasco. "Is this more neutral ground?" she asked, encompassing the room with her arm.

"It's quite neutral." He followed the line of her hand before coming back to stare at her. He leaned forward, setting his glass on the table. "Let's not talk about Cedar Chemicals or Worthington Pharmaceutical, or Cedar-Worthington." Resting his chin on the heel of his hand, he asked, "Why don't you tell me about Nefertiti Kincaid?"

Never's guard went up. Her body washed over with heat. She was hot and cold at the same time, but she steeled herself not to shiver. She hadn't felt like this before. Why did this man do this to her emotions? Lifting her glass, Never felt the cool liquid wet her lips. She didn't know how to answer him. She didn't want to. There was nothing in any of his management books to give her a clue as to where he was leading.

"There isn't a whole lot to tell. I live in a normal house with my two nephews, and I work."

"That's all?"

"That's all."

"How old are your nephews?"

"Nineteen and twenty. They're away at school."

"Sister's children or brother's children?"

"My sister . . . Samantha. She and her husband died in a small plane crash just after I got out of college. The boys survived. They came to live with me then," she added quietly.

Averal had the feeling she'd shared a piece of herself with him that she didn't usually give to anyone. The knowledge made him heady. He wanted to reach for her hand, but thought better of it. He'd already told himself Never Kincaid was different and he would have to treat her differently. He knew touching her would make her clam up. He could tell she wanted to run. She'd wanted to run the moment she saw him. His problem was he didn't want her to go anywhere. He wanted to keep her around. Wanted to keep her close, and find out everything there was to know.

"I'm sorry," he said. "That must have been a very difficult time."

She nodded. "It was a long time ago."

"John tells me you write computer games." Averal changed the subject.

He and John had discussed her. When? Why? "I send them to my nephews."

"He says they're quite good." He took another drink from his glass, his eyes trained on her face.

"John is prejudiced. He thinks I'm his daughter."

"He told me that, too."

"When did you two talk about me?" Her stare was steady and unwavering.

"At his house. The night he showed me his garage. There's a photograph of you and his daughter on the desk in his shop."

"It was taken at Jinny's wedding," she told him. Never remembered the picture. She and Jinny were good friends although five years separated them in age. When she first came to work for John, he'd included her and her nephews in several family picnics. Over the years they'd bonded into a pseudo-family unit.

"Tell me about the games?"

"Why, are you planning to find me a job, too?" She was sorry the moment the words fell, but she couldn't take them back. "John told me you got him a job."

"I only sent his designs to someone I knew was looking for a good designer. John got his own job on the strength of his talent. I was only a go-between."

"And do you know someone who needs a good person to write games programs?"

He shook his head.

A man with straight black hair pulled into a ponytail appeared and smiled at her. He wore a suit with a turtleneck sweater. Everything was in navy blue except the gold ring he wore on the small finger of his left hand. His eyes could only be described as piercing. She felt he could look into her mind.

He didn't speak, but turned to Averal. His hands moved with lightning speed and Averal answered him, using movements equally fast and equally indistinct. Never had seen people signing before, but she hadn't been this close since her days at Howard—when the basketball team had played Gallaudet College and she'd helped host the party following the game as a cheerleader.

Never's problems dissolved in the knowledge of two people communicating without the spoken word. She could not follow what was being said, but both men exchanged smiles at intervals and then the man nodded a farewell to her and left. She felt at a disadvantage. Never had a quick ear for language, but signing was a code she couldn't pick up through sound.

"What did he say?" she asked.

"Are you sure you want to know?" There was a twinkle in his eye she hadn't seen before.

She nodded.

"He said you don't look like my usual dates." Averal's arm went along the back of the booth and he leaned conspiratorially toward her. "He said you're beautiful, and have intelligent eyes."

Never smiled, shooting a glance in the direction which he'd gone. She didn't see him, but picked up on the word *date*. This was not a date. She wasn't with Averal. He hadn't brought her. Why should she look like his usual dates? What did his usual dates look like?

"What did you say?" she asked.

He paused a moment, deciding before answering her question. Never noticed the shades that closed over his eyes before he answered her. "I agreed." She wondered what he had really said.

"In all that flashing of hands that's all you two said?"

Averal shook his head and a slight twist played at the corners of his mouth. "He asked if I'd made you sad, and told me I should apologize because eyes like yours should always laugh."

Never did laugh, joy reaching her core. Without a word between them, she liked Averal's friend.

"It's a sure thing he likes you," he went on as if he'd read her thoughts.

"How did you learn to sign?"

"Riddles taught me." He gestured in the direction which the man had left. "We met when I lived in Paris with my mother." The tone of his voice caught her ear. There was a definite emphasis on the last word. "In those days I needed someone to talk to. Riddles was my friend. I talked, he listened. Signing came easy. We needed a common ground to communicate, and since he couldn't learn to speak I learned to sign."

"Paris," she said. "I saw my first BriAnne Ball painting in Paris." Averal said nothing. Never stared at him, waiting for him to speak. "At the gallery, why didn't you tell me she was your mother?" The tenseness that entered his body at the mention of his mother could be seen.

"We haven't been on the best of terms for several years," he explained in precise terms.

"She's your mother."

He looked away. Never thought of her own mother, who died soon after Never was born. Her grandparents reared her. She couldn't have survived without family support. She felt sorry Averal didn't have the same relationship with his mother.

"My parents divorced when I was a child."

"Did you ever get over it?" The words were out before she could stop them.

His head snapped around and he stared at her. For the space of a nanosecond he thought Caroline had spoken to him.

"Why did you ask that?"

"Something you didn't say. You didn't tell me BriAnne was your mother, even when we talked about *The Edge,* and just now your tone was harsh."

"I don't want to talk about my mother."

"Yet her paintings touch you." She watched him. "I could hear it in your voice the other night when you spoke of the paintings."

"She has talent," he conceded.

"That's all you have to say about her? What did she do to you to make you hate her?"

"I don't hate her," he snapped. "I just don't want to talk about her."

Never didn't say a word. She leveled her gaze in his direction and waited. She could see that Averal could be a stubborn man if he wanted to be.

"All right. What do you want to know?" he finally asked.

Never remembered wondering if the custom-made suit came with a custom-made mind. She was sure it did where his mother was concerned.

"Your book jacket said you lived in Paris. Tell me about it?" She hoped this was a safer subject.

"We went there when I was ten."

"You and your mother?"

He gulped the remains of his drink. "She was divorced. Her whole life went into her painting. Nothing was more important." That included him. Averal remembered her going away to paint. Every day was spent in front of her canvas. She didn't talk to him. She didn't even listen when he talked to her.

"She produced some very famous paintings."

"At what expense?" He glared at her. "She pushed me aside. Both of them did."

"Both?"

"My father, too. He remarried and lives in Virginia." He stopped, looking into his empty glass. He hadn't intended to be so intense, but it still hurt him to think about his childhood. If only Gabe hadn't died, his life would have been so different. But Gabe *had* died, and his parents had divorced leaving him lost and disconnected.

"You told me she sold her paintings to feed her child."

"She did. I won't say she didn't provide for me, but it was years before she was established. Years she sat on a stone step, painting and painting. Everywhere we went—the beach, a restaurant, even hitchhiking—all she thought of was painting. I got so I hated it."

"Don't . . ." Never's hand went to his automatically. "She wasn't pushing you away. She kept you with her. She could have left you with your father, placed you in a boarding school and gone off alone."

"My father didn't want me. A boarding school would have been better."

"Would it?" She looked at him for a moment. "Tell me something good that happened while you were in France."

"I met Howard Ridley." He glanced at the man with the ponytail streaming down his back. He was behind the bar now. "Riddles," he explained.

Averal turned her hand over, keeping it in his. It was warm and strong, and Never didn't mind him holding it. "I was out riding my bike near the entrance to the Tuilleries gardens outside the Louvre when I heard the most beautiful music coming from a bearded black man with hair as long as Jesus's. He was playing a saxophone, and a small crowd surrounded him. I stopped to listen." Averal laughed then, remembering. "I stayed there as long as he did. Every day I came back. Finally he had to talk to me, but the only way he could speak was through the saxophone and with his hands."

"So you learned to sign?"

"Not at first. I asked him if he'd teach me to play like he did. I didn't see him for a week after that. Then one day he showed up at the house my mother occupied and pushed a saxophone in my hands. I had my first lesson that day."

Never's eyes misted. "That's a wonderful story." Unconsciously she squeezed his hand.

Averal nodded, looking toward his friend at the bar. Never followed his gaze. Howard Ridley was the best friend he'd ever had.

"How old were you?" she asked, her voice hushed.

"When we met I was thirteen. Riddles was almost thirty, but it was rare I ever thought of our ages. I thought of him as a father figure only when he insisted I go to school, but that's exactly what he was."

He turned back to her. Never smiled. She wondered what could have happened to make Averal feel his parents were lost to him. Yet, he'd found a different figure to make up for their absence. Riddles must have given him the love he needed, for Averal was a well-respected man in his field.

"Would boarding school *really* have been better?" She returned to his earlier comment.

Averal gave her a direct stare, then briefly looked at Riddles before bringing his gaze back to Never. "I guess not," he said softly.

"I'm sorry your parents weren't more supportive," Never said. She wanted to tell him his parents didn't know what a wonderful son they had. She pulled her hand back and put it in her lap. She liked having him hold it, but it was screwing up her thought processes, not to mention the other parts of her body. She couldn't keep her mind on what he was saying. Her thoughts kept wavering to dark nights and warm fires. That voice, combined with his holding her hand, was too heady a combination.

"Don't be." Averal's voice pulled her attention back to the bar. "It happened a long time ago, and the wounds are all healed now."

Never knew better. Wounds such as that might be covered, but they didn't heal without a lot of compassion.

"My parents died in an automobile accident when I was a child," Never said. The contrast between them was like fire and ice. "I don't remember them clearly. My grandparents reared my sister and me. They were supportive of our dreams." Never paused. "No matter how outlandish the dreams seemed at the time, they were there if we needed help or someone to talk to."

"You're lucky," Averal told her. He envied her the happy memories she must have.

She turned her head toward the end of the room. Riddles's ponytail hung in a black line down the center of his straight back. He moved easily, with the same kind of confidence Never noticed in Averal's manner.

"So were you," she said.

He followed her gaze, and had to acknowledge the truth. He hadn't thought about all Riddles had given him in the years since he was thirteen-years-old. Allowing him to follow him around like a shadow. Answering any question he asked. And being with him when he was confused and depressed.

He liked Never Kincaid. She made him see the better side of life. Riddles had been a driving force in his life. He knew that. When Riddles uprooted himself from Paris, which he called home, and settled in Princeton, Averal had been happier than he could admit. He knew Riddles looked upon him as a son, and he loved Riddles as no father could be loved.

Rhonda came back at that moment.

"Anything else, Averal?" she asked. Her eyes were wide open and her expression suggestive.

Averal looked at Never. Her glass was empty. He ordered them another round.

"Not for me," Never said. "I've already had two, and I have to work tomorrow." She checked her watch. "I'd better be going, anyway."

Averal didn't want her to go. "Why don't I order you a coffee, or dinner?" he asked.

Never nodded. "Coffee would be good."

The tall, thin waitress wrote on her pad, then sauntered away with a sway Never knew was for Averal's benefit.

Never smiled at the display.

"Why are you smiling?" he asked.

"Inside joke," she said, refusing to tell him. If he didn't know the woman who'd just left the table was vying for his attention, he must be blind. Never told herself to be careful of her own body language. While Rhonda had been obvious, she was sure her own feelings weren't being communicated. She couldn't let that happen. Despite them being friendly tonight, they still stood on opposite sides of Cedar-Worthington, and nothing would change that.

Riddles returned with a fresh glass for Averal and a cup for her. Never scanned the area for the young woman who'd taken their order. She found her at the bar. A pout covered her face as a woman with braids filled her order. She wondered why

Riddles had returned, and what relationship Averal had with the waitress.

Riddles set the tray down and flashed her a message in an unreadable language. She looked to Averal for translation.

Riddles began his hand dance again. It was gibberish to Never, and she looked again to Averal, who was shaking his head and continuing the dance of fingers, thumbs, and fists. When he finished, Riddles took the tray and, with a wink, left them.

"He said it's early yet. You should stay longer. You dress up his place."

"Why did you shake your head?"

"He asked if I were playing tonight."

"You play here?"

"Sometimes."

Never remembered the case he'd passed to the bartender before coming to the table. She had thought it was a briefcase. Now she realized it was an instrument case.

"Why aren't you playing tonight? You brought your sax."

"You're here. I'd much rather spend the time with you."

Sensation fissured through her. She'd had two glasses of wine and she did feel unusually warm, but she was far from drunk. So why did her stomach feel nervous and giddy when he told her he'd rather stay with her than indulge in something he'd planned to do?

She hadn't realized she had moved, or that Averal had. She found herself knee to knee with him. The emotions singing within her confused her, and she shifted away.

"I'd like to hear you play," she said, dropping her eyes a second before looking directly at him.

Her eyes held only sincerity when Averal looked at her. He would like to play for her.

"What would you like to hear?" he said by way of acquiescence.

Never cocked her head and thought a moment. "If I Were Your Woman" flashed through her mind. She was amazed the words didn't tumble from her mouth. "Jingle Bells," she finally answered.

A lazy smile crossed his face. He slipped around the booth and rose, his gaze concentrated on her face.

"Jingle Bells," he repeated.

She nodded and he walked toward Riddles, who stood behind the highly polished bar. As though planned, the saxophone case was passed to Averal, and he took his place with the small group on the tiny raised platform.

Never could look at him openly. He was a different man than the one she'd met earlier today. He was more like the man she'd met in the gallery last weekend, but he was even different from that one. Somehow she felt that in this place he was comfortable, in control, and knew that he was within his family unit. He turned to face her as he raised the sax to his lips. On a count of three the guitar, drums, sax, and piano began her request.

Suddenly she realized she wasn't just looking at Averal, that she was staring, but she couldn't stop herself. Her eyes were riveted to him. He was clearly the most handsome man she'd seen in some time. His dark brown hair with flecks of gold matched the sunlit quality of his lion-eyes. His golden brown skin tone reminded her of dark topaz. He had broad, athletic shoulders and legs that were hard and strong, even concealed under trousers.

Her song ended, and they began playing another. She knew it but couldn't name it, since her entire attention had been captured by a man she'd only met three days ago. A man she'd argued with. One whom she respected for the brilliant books she'd read before the merger was even a dream. She was definitely attracted to him. She couldn't deny that. Every time she found herself in his presence she had to fight feelings that surfaced like oil under furnace heat.

These sensations were new, different from anything she'd known in the past. Often she was unaware of how to handle them. So far he'd only held her hand, placed a hand on her back. What would it be like if he took her in his arms? Kissed her?

She shook herself. Thoughts like that made her hot. She could feel her body melting, her nipples tightening under her blouse, and the area between her legs becoming hot and wet.

Never didn't realize how long she'd been staring, or how many songs the band had played. When she came out of her dream it was to the low, sexy sound of "Hungry Eyes." Averal wasn't looking at her. His full attention was on the instrument in his hand and the music he was playing. Never knew the song, and wondered if he were trying to give her a message, or if he'd seen that message in her eyes. Her body pulsed with heat and embarrassment that the entire bar knew how hungry she was for the man on the platform.

At the end of that song they took a break, and Averal rejoined her.

"You play wonderfully," she said as he slid into the seat beside her. "I always wanted to play like that."

"You play the saxophone?" he asked with raised eyebrows.

Shaking her head, she said, "I tinkle with the piano. Nothing more than Christmas carols."

"You must play one for me soon." He took a drink from the glass the waitress had left. The ice had completely melted.

Never was already shaking her head before he finished the sentence. "I don't play for anyone. The only music I make is on my computer, and there I will play anything for you."

"I'll hold you to that," he said teasingly, catching her off guard.

She looked away nervously, wondering what he meant by that.

"Can computers really do that?"

"Do what?" She turned back to him. Her distraction after his previous comment had made her forget what they were talking about.

"Make music." He smiled lazily.

"Computers can do almost anything you program them to

do." The way he looked at her told her his words had a double meaning.

"They can play the saxophone?"

Never nodded. "And the guitar, piano, drum," she shrugged.

"Have you done that?" He sounded impressed.

"In a game program you use lots of music to complement the graphic display."

Averal rested his chin on his hand. "I'm very illiterate when it comes to computers. I can turn one on and work my way through the windows, but anything more than that I call my secretary."

Never had heard that many times before, but usually from men older than Averal appeared to be. "How do you produce all those books? Don't tell me you write with a pencil and yellow legal pads?"

"Is that out of the question?" He leaned forward, disarming her with his smile.

"It's archaic." She assumed the same position and leaned toward him.

"Somebody has to keep typing services in business."

"You have a typing service?" Her eyebrows went up, and her eyes widened incredulously.

"My secretary handles the heavy part. I can do simple revisions."

Never was shaking her head. Just when she'd thought all the people fearing the computer age were dead, she'd come across another dinosaur.

"I do have a computer on my desk. It's not state-of-the-art with enough memory to catalog the entire history of the world from the big bang to yesterday, but it's adequate for my needs."

Never had been duped. He was no illiterate, and he'd convinced her of an inadequacy which did not exist. "That was unfair," she told him, sitting back and resting her arms along the table.

"It was, but you took it so well." He looked at her, his eyes as innocent as a baby's.

Never couldn't keep her lips from turning up at the edges, or the grin that seemed to take over her face.

"Are you going to play again?" She looked toward the stage. The other men who had played with Averal were taking their instruments for another set.

He nodded as he glanced toward them. "Do you have another special request?" His smile was obvious. "We could do 'Rudolph, The Red Nosed Reindeer' or 'Silver Bells'." He stood, preparing to leave.

"How about 'Unforgettable'?"

Averal stared at her for a long moment as if he were deciding if he wanted to say something. Then, with a smile, he turned and headed for the bandstand.

The music warmed her. It was slow and velvety soft, and Never had the feeling it was being played only for her. It wrapped her in a cocoon of pleasure and made her relax. She could have sat and listened all night. Checking her watch, though, she knew it was time to leave.

She pushed her arms into her coat and slid out of the booth. Averal watched her with a questioning look in his eyes. She paused near the platform to wave. The question remained on his face, although the sounds he made with the instrument were clear and sweet.

When she reached the door Riddles was there. He spoke to her with his hands in a language totally foreign to her, yet the smile in his eyes was universal.

"I have to leave now," she explained, pulling her coat together and pushing the large buttons through their holes.

Riddles threw a glance toward the bandstand. Never followed it. She felt a pull to stay, stay and talk to Averal. She wanted to be in his company. She wanted to know more about him, much more. She wanted to know everything. Again she stared at him, lost in the music and the power of the man making it.

A flicker in the corner of her eye snapped her attention away, and she returned to Riddles. "I will come back," she said. He smiled at her and held the door as she went out.

Never was halfway across the parking lot when Averal caught up with her. The snow had stopped. A light coating could be seen on several cars, but most were clean. The air was colder, and Never shivered when a gust hit her.

He didn't ask her to stay longer or offer to go with her. "I'll walk you to your car," was all he said. Averal took her arm and guided her across the lot. Never didn't know what was happening to her. His hand on her back feathered warmth through the cold of the night and onto her back. Quickly it spread throughout her system.

They reached her car. She opened the door and dropped her purse on the seat. She turned to say goodnight, but her voice caught in her throat. All she could do was stare at him. It had been a wonderful evening.

He broke the spell she was under. "Goodnight, Never. I hope we can do this again, soon."

"I enjoyed myself," she told him.

"Tomorrow?" he asked. She wanted to say yes. It was on the tip of her tongue when he continued. "Why don't we meet tomorrow at ten, and pick up the appointment that didn't work out today?"

"I'm afraid my day is full tomorrow. And for most of the week," she told him. She deliberately attempted to put him off until next week.

The air of friendliness was gone. She was back to being the head of the MIS department, and he was the consultant coming to eliminate them. She felt as if her plane had abruptly crashed to the earth.

"All right, Friday." He rocked back on his heels.

She nodded. "Friday."

"Ten o'clock?"

"Ten o'clock isn't good for me. I have to take my grandmother for her fitting in the morning."

"Fitting?"

"She and my grandfather are renewing their wedding vows,

and we're having a big reception." She'd told him that when she explained about the ring.

"I see." He nodded.

"I'll be in later. How about one o'clock?"

"One o'clock it is."

He stared at her after he said it. She saw the hesitation, as if he'd planned something more. Never had that awkward feeling she'd had at the beginning of the night. Then he leaned forward. She couldn't move. She felt frozen, as if she'd suddenly been turned to a statue—a living, breathing entity that was rooted in place and couldn't move if her life depended on it. Her heart pounded harder, aching to escape her chest. Heat poured from her toes throughout her system when he pressed his lips against her cheek. Balling her hands into fists, she kept them at her sides. His lips were cool, her cheek cold, yet she felt flushed with a heat consuming and ready to flash out of control. He lifted his mouth. She let go of her breath.

"Goodnight," she said, and took her seat behind the steering wheel. Averal closed the door with a tight smile which Never returned. She turned the key, and the engine came to life. He stepped back as she drove away, waving. She checked her mirror at the end of the parking lot. He was standing where she'd left him. She paused for a long time, checking for traffic coming on the main road. Nothing passed her, and finally she turned onto the roadway and lost sight of him.

FIVE

"Oh, Grand!" Never cooed. She turned away from the mirror. "You look wonderful." Never's grandmother and namesake came out of the dressing room. Today was her final fitting for her gown. The ceremony was only a couple of weeks away, and Never knew she was looking forward to it.

"That dress was made for her," Jessie, the store owner, commented.

Never stared at the soft, beige lace. Her grandmother didn't fit the standard mold—overweight, large bosomed, grey-haired, with a bun and glasses. While she did wear glasses and had grey hair, Nefertiti Kincaid the elder stood five-foot-nine inches at a trim 127 pounds, with a figure that rivaled Aphrodite's. She had a long neck which complemented the gown's Victorian collar, small waist, and full skirt. She was slender, energetic, and wore her thick hair cut short and stylishly.

"Look at you," her grandmother said. Never turned and stood next to her grandmother. Her dress, covered with blue sequins, was soft and warm, making her feel good. "This is a lovely dress." Never pivoted to show the complete outfit. "It's too bad there isn't anyone to wear it for."

Martin would be out of town during the week the ceremony took place, and she didn't feel comfortable asking anyone else. She knew how Martin felt about her, even if she didn't return the same feelings. She didn't really need to have a man with her. She knew she'd be fine, and she'd be very busy making sure all the details of the evening came off without a hitch. Having a date she needed to attend to and entertain wasn't something she wanted to add to the evening's events.

"I can hardly wait for your wedding day," her grandmother said.

Never managed to hold herself still without an apparent cringe. She didn't think marriage was in her future. She had read about love, seen countless movies, been involved in several relationships, and witnessed her own grandparents' love. She had yet to come close, though, to feeling the kind of storybook love her parents had shared and her grandparents, after fifty years of marriage, still exhibited.

"You know I'm getting old. I may not live much longer."

Never knew where she was going with this. "As a psychologist, Grand," she told her, "you're terrible."

"I may be." She hugged Never. "But my words are true."

"Grand." Never pulled away and looked at her. "It may not happen. There aren't any men I know that I'm the least bit interested in, let alone want to spend my life with." She took her grandmother's hand. "I know you want me married, settled, but being married isn't for everyone."

"Are you saying you're one of those feminist career women who puts all her energy into boardroom discussions so there is nothing left for the bedroom?"

If any other grey-haired, eighty-five-year old had said that to her she'd be embarrassed, but Never had grown up with this woman and knew she would no more hold her tongue than eat dirt.

"I hope not, Grand. It's just that I'm twenty-nine, and no man has ever made me weak in the knees." Suddenly Averal Ballentine's face came into her mind. The shock jolted her.

"Come on," Never said to cover the astonishment that must have manifested itself on her face. "Let's change and get some coffee before I have to go to the office." There was Averal again. The reason she had to get to the office was that she had an appointment with him. She checked her watch. She couldn't believe she was going to be late. Ever since she'd met him her routine had been thrown out of sync. She was rarely late for appointments, yet she'd forgotten Martin was coming to pick her up until she had too little time to dress. Now she hadn't concentrated at her tennis game, and she wasn't going to be on time to meet him for their appointment. He was going to be angry—again.

"Don't worry, Never. You'll find him when you're least expecting to." Her grandmother smiled, patted her hands, and turned toward the dressing room. One of the clerks hovering nearby followed her grandmother to help her out of the dress. Never's friend and shop owner, Jessica Clark, followed her to unhook, unzip, and hang up her gown while Never dressed in her own clothes.

"I couldn't help but hear that," Jessie said, working the hooks at her back.

"Jessie, you know how parents are. They always want you married."

"I know, I know," she agreed. "My mother won't give up, either, but in your case your grandmother is in her eighties."

"And in perfect health."

"For a woman her age."

Never stepped out of the gown and turned to face her friend. "What do you suggest I do, marry the first man I meet?"

"Of course not."

"Then—" she prompted.

"You have been dating Martin Caldwell for . . . how long now?" Jessie had mastered the pregnant pause from years of religiously watching soap operas. She used that ability now on her friend.

"I'm not dating Martin. We're just friends."

"Not if you ask Martin," she said under her breath. "I heard he claimed to be engaged to you already."

Never stopped in the act of pulling her own dress over her head. "And just who imparted that bit of gossip?"

"It doesn't matter, does it?"

"No," Never agreed. *Jessica's Bridal and Boutique* was like a beauty salon. Everyone frequented it often, and left all the local gossip with her or her salesclerks. "However, if anyone else comes in with that story, I trust you'll be sure to set them straight."

She paused for effect, then said, "I'll do my best." Together they laughed. When Jessie sobered she stared at her friend, looking her up and down as if she were a new client and Jessie needed to size her in her mind.

"What?" Never asked checking her reflection in the mirror.

"I have an idea. Wait here."

Jessie left her. Never had pulled her dress on and was struggling with the zipper when Jessie returned. The unmistakable sound of plastic covering accompanied her.

"Don't dress," Jessie said, hanging the bag up. "I want you to try this on." She pulled the zipper Never had gotten halfway up her back all the way to its base.

"What are you doing? I already have a dress for the wedding."

"This one's different." Jessie turned and opened the clear dress bag. Never gasped.

"That's a wedding gown!"

Jessie pulled it fully out and held it up. It was beautiful; all white with a fitted bodice overlaid with lace as delicate as webbing. Pearls had been hand woven into the lace. A chiffon skirt that swayed like a cloud even as she held it reminded Never of a soft prayer. It was clearly the most beautiful gown she'd ever seen.

"I want you to try this on."

"Why?" Never stared at the dress. "I can't wear that to the wedding," she whispered for no apparent reason.

"You won't be. You'll just wear it for her." Jessie raised her arm toward the wall. Her grandmother wasn't in the next dressing room. "The woman down the hall wants to see you wearing a wedding gown and walking down a church aisle. I can't provide the church or the aisle, and at your rate you may not get the white lace and promises." The last she delivered out of the side of her mouth. "We can do the next best thing. Now put it on."

Never hesitated. She touched the pearls. She wanted to try the dress on, and Jessie had pushed the right buttons.

"Isn't it bad luck or something?" She frowned.

"Where did you hear such a thing? Now take that off."

Never pulled her dress off for the second time and pushed her arms into the gown Jessie held. It floated over her. She heard the whisper of fabric as it dropped to the floor. It was beautiful on the hanger, and as she turned to the three walls of mirror she couldn't believe her eyes. All brides *were* beautiful, she thought.

Her eyes filled with tears. "Jessie . . ."

"Hold the tears," Jessie said, emotion in her own voice. "We're not done yet."

Jessie lifted the veil over her head and set it in her hair. "I wish you'd worn your hair down," she complained, pinning the veil and then adjusting Never's hair around it.

"Can I cry now?" Never asked.

"No! If you start I'll cry too, and what will Mrs. Kincaid think?"

Never swallowed hard and clenched her teeth.

"Smile," Jessie ordered. A second later she opened the door. Never didn't move. She could see her grandmother sitting on the sofa thumbing through a bridal magazine as she waited.

Never moved slowly out of the dressing room. Her grandmother looked up. For a moment she appeared not to recognize her. Then her mouth dropped open as recognition froze her to her seat. Never waited, standing in the middle of the room, alone in the store except for her grandmother and Jessie. The tears she'd wanted to shed crowded in her grandmother's eyes and fell unchecked down her cheeks.

"Nev—er." Her voice cracked, making the word two separate syllables. Her hand went to her breast. "You should have warned me." She tried to get up. Jessie went and helped her to her feet.

Nefertiti Kincaid circled her granddaughter slowly. When she'd made a complete revolution she stared, speechless. Then she opened her arms and Never went into them. Tears ran from each woman's eyes. Never heard Jessie sniff, and knew she was crying, too.

"You're going to make a beautiful bride." Her grandmother's voice was hoarse with emotion. She wiped at the tears with her fingertips. Jessie handed the elder Never a tissue. She'd told Never more times than not that the mother or grandmother of the bride cried when they saw the bride in full dress. She wiped the tears away and, balling the tissue in her hand, continued to study Never. Then suddenly she hugged her again. Never felt as if she'd given her a precious gift. It's too bad she wasn't *really* a bride.

She didn't know how long they stood like that, but they separated when the doorbell tinkled, announcing the arrival of another patron. Never straightened and turned toward the door.

Averal Ballentine stopped just inside the full-length glass door.

Never's knees threatened to buckle.

Living in Paris, Averal had seen some of the most beautiful women in the world. Models and would-be models flocked to the city year after year in hopes of becoming the next cover girl. It was nothing for him to see everything from women clad in bathing suits to ball gowns on any given corner. But the sight of dewy-eyed Nefertiti Kincaid in a white bridal gown literally left him without the ability to speak. He was lucky he could keep standing.

He'd come here because they had an appointment. It was technically scheduled for her office on Friday, but remembering their last encounter in her office he thought he'd take her to a working lunch, instead. It was an excuse, and he knew it. He just wanted to see her again. He'd kissed her earlier on the cheek. Nothing to speak about, but it had disturbed him enough to keep him awake most of the night thinking about her.

He'd called her office to talk to her, just to hear her voice, but Barbara told him she wasn't in yet and he remembered the appointment she'd mentioned. Getting the name of the shop was easy, and he'd come over hoping to see her again. He hadn't expected to find her dressed in a white gown, looking as if she were about to float down the center aisle.

Anger balled in his stomach. She'd told him she wasn't engaged. Maybe it had been true last week. Was it still true today? Had she changed her mind? Why was she dressed like this? Why was he so angry? He shook himself, trying to get rid of the bond that seemed to hold him in place. He took a deep breath. This job wasn't going to be easy, and now that he'd seen her dressed like that it was going to be hell. How could he resist her, when every time he thought of her from now on he'd have this picture in his mind?

And he liked the picture.

The thought surprised and scared him. He'd been married once, and he'd promised himself it was the last time. Marriage wasn't for him. Marriage or children.

"If I start the introductions, will I get to meet this young man?"

For the first time since he'd entered the shop he moved his attention from Never. In front of him stood a tall woman who reminded him of Never. She had white hair and eyes that were greying around the edges but still showed the sparkle of what they used to be. She was taller than her granddaughter, and Never's smile was a duplicate of hers.

"I'm Never's grandmother," she told him. She swung her gaze between them. Nefertiti Kincaid. "From that look I guess you already know my granddaughter." There was a volume of knowledge in the short sentence.

"Averal Ballentine." He took the hand she offered and shook it.

"Never hasn't mentioned you."

She wouldn't, he thought. She'd probably try to put him as far to the back of her mind as possible. Why he couldn't relegate her to the same location he didn't know.

"We only met recently." He glanced over at her. She remained in the same place. When she'd turned, the train of the gown positioned itself at her feet as if in a portrait. She stood straight and still as in a live portrait except for the rise and fall of her breasts and the wildly beating pulse at the base of her throat. She looked beautiful, delicious enough to eat. "We have an appointment." Averal's explanation of his presence seemed weak now.

Never spoke for the first time. "Our appointment is for later."

"Maybe we could get some lunch first."

She turned toward the dressing room. "I can't go to lunch. I have to take my grandmother home. She doesn't drive."

"Don't worry about me. Jessie will drive me back."

"No problem," agreed the obvious Jessie, standing off toward the rear of the store.

Averal almost smiled when he saw the discomfort on Never's face. She looked at him as if he'd planned this. He hadn't, but things seemed to be working in his favor. She lifted the skirt of the gown and went into the dressing room. Jessie followed her, leaving him alone with her grandmother.

"I didn't know Never was getting married," he began as they walked to the middle of the store. She took a seat on the sofa, and he sat next to her.

"She isn't."

He looked at the closed dressing room door. A sigh escaped him, and his heartbeat slowed a little.

"My husband and I are having a ceremony to renew our vows." Leaning toward him in a conspiratorial manner, she whispered, "It's really for the kids we're doing it."

"Never told me you've been married fifty years."

She nodded. He noticed the twinkle in her eyes. Never had told him her grandparents had reared her and her sister. He could feel the love they shared. He wondered what that felt like—for a person to truly love their child.

"I've always liked a party, and I'm looking forward to the reception." She sat down. Averal sat next to her.

"I'm sure it will be a lot of fun."

He smiled at her. Averal liked Mrs. Kincaid. He could see a lot of Never in her. He imagined Never at the reception in the lace-covered gown she must be changing out of. His mouth went dry again. He wanted to be there with her, dancing with her, holding her in his arms and squiring her around the floor. He wanted her smiling up at him the way she had Martin Caldwell.

Mrs. Kincaid asked him a question, breaking his concentration on the mental picture he'd stored of Never. She wanted to know what he did, and how he and Never had met. She wondered if he had any relatives in Arizona named Ballentine. She'd met a couple named Ballentine on a cruise several years ago, and they still kept in touch. Averal didn't know them. She was a lively woman full of wit and love, and he enjoyed talking to her. Growing up with her had to be fun, and he envied Never her memories.

Never came out of the dressing room. She wore a black suit and a white blouse. Red was the splash of color for the day. It came in the form of a wide belt at her waist. His gaze dropped to her feet. Her shoes picked up the color of the belt. He smiled, noting the differences between that pair of red shoes and the others she'd worn. He'd become used to looking for the signature stockings, and when she turned to pick up her purse, also red, he wasn't disappointed. The nylons had seams angling up her legs and tiny red bows at the bottom. He swore to himself. Those stockings would be the death of him. His body grew taut and warm at the small act of watching her pick up a purse. He shifted on the sofa and stood up.

Jessie returned and hung up a dress. "I can take you now, Mrs. Kincaid, if you're ready." Averal took Mrs. Kincaid's arms and helped her up.

"I've enjoyed talking to you."

"And I you," he told her. Jessie held a coat and she turned and slipped her arms inside it. Jessie disappeared for a moment to get her coat. Averal could hear her speaking low to someone in the back room. Never got her coat and pushed her arms through the sleeves. He would have helped her, but thought she didn't want his help.

"I'm ready when you are," Jessie said, dressed now in her own coat.

"I'll see you at home later," Never said and kissed her grandmother on the cheek. The two women started for the door. Then Mrs. Kincaid turned back.

"Averal," she called. "I have an idea. Why don't you come to the wedding and reception? You can bring Never."

"Grand!" Never interrupted. Her eyes seemed as large as dinner plates. "I already have a date."

"No, you don't. You just told me Martin is going to be out of town."

Averal looked down so she couldn't see the grin that threatened to spread over his face. He listened while she sputtered and tried to backpedal.

"I didn't say he would be out of town for sure. He could get back in time."

"If Averal brings you, you don't have to worry about Martin, and he doesn't have to change his plans." The old woman smiled. Averal wanted to hug her.

"Are you busy, young man?"

"No," he answered before Never could say anything. He didn't know what day the ceremony would be on, but whatever day it was, he would be free to escort the woman in black.

Never sat silently as Averal drove the fast car. She was too angry to speak. She wanted to blow up and direct it all at him. Somehow she thought better of doing that. She didn't want to go anywhere with him, especially not to her grandparents' mar-

riage ceremony. She wanted to rescind everything her grandmother had said. She'd tried to hear what they were talking
about while she was dressing, but Jessie kept chatting away as
if she were in cahoots with Averal to block her efforts. Her voice
prevented Never from eaves dropping on the conversation going
on in the main part of the store.

"You're angry." He stated it as fact. Never couldn't argue
with him. "You don't want me to take you to your grandparents'
affair." Still she said nothing. "You don't have to worry. I wasn't
planning to take you, anyway."

"What?"

"I knew you didn't want to go with me. I was only placating
your grandmother."

"She won't appreciate that."

"But you will."

Never didn't. What was wrong with her that he didn't want
to take her? And why did she care? A moment ago she'd been
angry that he'd wormed his way into her life, and now she was
angry that he didn't want any part of it. Something was definitely wrong with her, and it centered around this man.

It was too close in the car. She wanted to get out of it. She
needed air, and there was suddenly none inside the car.

"She's an old lady. If you didn't want to go you should have
told her the truth. She'll expect you to be there."

"What about you?"

"It makes no difference to me." She looked away from him.

"Liar." The whispered word was so soft she almost thought
she hadn't heard it.

"What did you say?"

"I said I'm taking you to your grandparents' wedding."

Each story was the same. Never dropped the phone back in
its cradle. She'd talked to Bill Winston, Sam Harris, and Greg
Johnson. Each had spent time with Averal, and each had found
new jobs. "Not just any job," Sam had said. "It's my dream

job. I couldn't have asked for better luck." She frowned. Could she be wrong about him? Never stuck a pencil through the tight mass of hair she'd arranged on her head. Right now she wanted to pull it down. She'd only talked to the four men, and from their accounts of his actions Averal Ballentine was the Wizard of Oz, bestowing wishes on all who came before him.

Never didn't believe that. The Wizard of Oz was a myth. On impulse she picked up the phone and dialed again. And again the story matched. Three additional calls couldn't shake the story. She'd found Averal had a hand in finding employment for all but one of the former employees, and she'd decided to work from her home. What was he running, a placement center, or a management consulting firm?

When she put the phone down she knew she'd been wrong about him. Averal Ballentine wasn't her enemy. He'd proved that the night she met him at Riddle's Place. Yet she'd tried to deny it. Whatever else he was, he was trying to help those people who were losing their jobs. She had to apologize to him, and that wasn't something she looked forward to doing.

She was expecting him in an hour, and she wasn't a person to put things off. She'd apologize as soon as he arrived. It had been four days since she'd seen him. And it was a disturbing four days. After his kiss in the parking lot, Never had gone away confused and at a loss for what to do. Her attraction was strong, and each time she thought of him it got stronger, but she looked on him as the man who would eliminate her job. A totally unfair view, yet she maintained it. Her thoughts had strayed to him many times during the past week, and many times she'd replayed the scene in the parking lot.

It would come to her unbidden. She could feel his cool lips on her skin, and the heat would wash over her. Every part of his face would be visible. She'd become aware of his face, the lack of a mustache, the smoothness of his shaved skin. Her mind would let her touch his face, turn her own and place his mouth on hers. This morning she'd come in humming "Unforgettable." That was how she was beginning to think of Averal

Ballentine. There was a chemistry between them with all the right ingredients. It could be explosive if left unchecked. She knew it would. They were both working on short fuses, and each tended to be a catalyst for the other. She shook herself, bringing her concentration back to her surroundings.

So how was she going to handle him? She looked at the domed anniversary clock she'd received at her five year luncheon. Less than forty-five minutes separated her from Averal's arrival. She'd been forced by her own sense of fairness to schedule a meeting. If her department were going to be cut, he was not the person holding the axe. If her people could find as much happiness as the people she'd spoken to this morning, maybe the future didn't look so dismal.

So she promised herself that she would give him access to everything when he arrived—everything except her heart. Sadness filled her, and she felt like crying. Moments later Barbara gave her the perfect excuse.

"Never, I'm getting married." Barbara rushed in, glowing, her hand extended to show her three carat diamond. Her words had barely registered when Never burst into tears. Never was on her feet hugging her secretary, congratulating her, and boiling over with questions. Had they set the date? Where would they get married? Had she told the others in the office? Soon both women were crying. Their reasons were different, but only Never knew that.

"Now I won't have to worry about that meeting," Barbara said when she was coherent again and Never had issued tissues for both of them. "Or be concerned about finding another job." The man Barbara was engaged to came from the 'old money' of Princeton. He also ran a lucrative law practice. If Barbara worked after the wedding it would be by choice.

They sat talking for a few minutes, then Never went to fix her makeup. She could see people drifting toward the conference room. When she returned, Averal Ballentine was sitting in her office. She stopped, gripping the doorjamb as the familiar weak-kneed reaction set in. He stood and faced her. He'd taken her by surprise. Her face paled, then blood rushed through her, making her ears hot. She had a sudden urge to run to him, but tightened her grip on the door instead.

She hadn't seen him since that day in the bridal shop when he'd come in and taken her to lunch; when she'd agreed to let him take her to the ceremony and reception. He looked a little different. His clothes were of the same impeccable cut, his hair had been recently trimmed, and his face was cleanshaven. It was the eyes, she thought. There was something in them that hadn't been there before. She couldn't tell what it was, and it was gone before she could identify it.

Her heart lurched in her chest. She wanted to say something to him about her attitude, about what she'd recently learned about him. Then he looked at her with something akin to raw passion in his eyes, and words stuck in her throat.

God! she was beautiful, Averal thought as he left the chair. He'd been on edge all day, anticipating this meeting. He'd wanted to see her again. Needed to see her. Purposely, he'd stayed away, giving her time. Giving himself time. He needed to analyze his feelings. Find out what it was that made him want to grab her and hold her against him, experience the delights of her dark body molded to the length of his. But time had only heightened his desire for her. He could still feel her cheek against his lips, and remember the small shiver that ran through him when he touched her. But he could see the wall she'd erected between them. She didn't trust him yet. And he wanted her trust.

She wanted it, too. No matter what she said or how she'd deny it if he confronted her, they'd sampled the magic between them when he'd kissed her. He wanted to kiss her again. Right now. And he wanted more than kisses. But he could see the doubt in her, then the quick straightening of her shoulders, bringing into focus the haughty confidence that seemed to reflect from her black and white outfit. Irrationally, he suddenly hated those two colors. Even if the contrasts made her skin glow, he wanted her to understand that everything wasn't that clear-cut. If it weren't for the moment in the bookstore, he wouldn't even know about the red shoes. He wanted to see her in colors, bright reds or yellows. For a moment he imagined what she'd look like in a hot pink swimsuit as she ran toward blue water on a white sand beach.

Never wanted to apologize, but something about the way he was looking at her made her throat dry, and she couldn't speak. Somehow she knew he was thinking about her, about the kiss in the parking lot or that day he showed up to take her to lunch. It wasn't like a real kiss, Never told herself. It didn't even count as a kiss. She'd been kissed before, really kissed, but no one had made her toes tingle with so brief a touch. And even now, with the space of the room between them, Never's feet began to feel numb.

She shifted a second and tried to smile. "Every . . . everyone is gathering in the conference room," she stammered. Never moved into her office and stored her purse in one of the drawers. She turned back toward the exit.

"Just a moment." Averal took her arm as she reach the door. The sea of empty cubicles stretched the length of the room in front of her.

Never felt waves of electricity shock her and she wanted to give in to the current and melt against it, but she didn't. She looked down to stare at the hand holding her arm. Averal released it. With steady control she allowed her breath to continue. The urge to gasp was so great it caused pain in her chest.

"We seemed to have gotten off to a bad start, and from there have gone downhill. I'd like to change that."

Never didn't move. She kept her gaze trained on the row of empty offices, forcing her mind to concentrate on what he was saying and not on that part of her body which seemed singed by the touch of his hand.

"It's going to be a busy day," Averal was saying. "But later on, at dinner perhaps, we can get together and talk?"

"I do want to talk to you. There's something I have to—"

"Never," Barbara interrupted. "Everyone is waiting."

"We'll be right there," she said. Barbara nodded and headed toward the training room at the back of the building. Never returned her attention to Averal. "There's something I need to talk to you about, but there are a lot of anxious people in the conference room." Never started for the meeting, leaving Averal standing in her doorway. She knew she should wait for him. She couldn't. The electricity around them was too active. He stood too close to her, and her thoughts were running wild.

The noise coming from the training room greeted her long before she reached the door. Everyone had been anticipating something. She hoped some of their fears would be laid to rest; maybe some of the rumors that had spread and accelerated like a forest fire would be stemmed. Averal caught up with her several steps from the entrance to the room.

"Are you ready, Mr. Ballentine?" she asked.

"Averal," he corrected.

Never didn't acknowledge that. She turned and walked into the room. The noise ceased as quickly as if a choir director had tapped his baton.

Averal followed her. They stood in front of the group. Never smiled, trying to put the room at ease. Barbara returned it from her seat in the back.

The room normally had tables with computers set up on them. Never had had it transformed into a large conference room, with chairs set up theater style so that everyone could have a seat. In the front of the room was a raised platform with a lectern and all manner of electrical devices, allowing the room to double as a conference room. The lights were brightly lighted on the stage and over the chairs. Only the back wall was dim.

Never looked over the faces of the people she'd worked with for years. She could see the sadness in their eyes, feel the anticipation of the sword they felt hung over their livelihoods. The hush over the room, allowing only for the sound of breathing, told her there was fear accompanying everyone present.

"I'm sure I don't have to introduce Averal Ballentine,"

Never began, telling the group he would be conducting this meeting. He would explain his company's role, what he expected of the department, and specifically what each person would be required to do. She advised them to fully cooperate with him, help him, answer any questions he had, and provide any information they were asked to the best of their knowledge.

When she finished she turned to Averal. He smiled at her and nodded, but she could see the question in his eyes. After their initial meeting he hadn't expected her to cooperate. Prior to this morning and her phone calls she might not have. She knew the merger was a done deal. They couldn't go back and reverse it or its terms. The only thing they could do was make the best of the situation, and the man she'd introduced wasn't there for their heads—even if she'd accused him of that.

As he took her place in front of the group she put the length of the entire room between them. She didn't sit down, but leaned against the bank of waist-high file cabinets that guarded the back wall. She was glad the lights were only on in spots. She stood in the shadow near an exit door.

The training room was large, long, and narrow. The group was large, too. They didn't fit into a regular conference area. Never looked over them from the back. How many families were represented here? How many people had spent their careers giving to Worthington? How much family lived in this room? Never knew her own loyalty to the people here. She knew how it felt to be torn apart from people she'd met morning after morning for years. None of them had ever said they were family, yet that's what they were. A unit working for the good of each other. They weren't perfect. What family was?

"Nothing will ever be the same," Averal began. "You can't go back. Worthington Pharmaceutical is dead, and Cedar Chemicals, Inc., is dead. You happen to be the relatives. And relatives grieve. Then they heal. We're here to help you heal."

Could he do that? Never wondered. She was intimidated by him. At her office door, all he had to do was touch her arm and breath left her body. Yet she was responsible for all the lives in this room, all the families, which couldn't be seen, depending on these people.

She looked over the crowd. When her eyes came back to Averal's, he was staring directly at her. Her breath caught uncontrollably. She couldn't stop the strangled escape of air if she'd tried, and she had no time to try.

Naked. *That's it,* she told herself. It was hard to be intimidated by a man if you imagined him standing there naked. She'd heard that before. Never returned his gaze, managing with great effort to keep hers steady.

"Losing friends hurts . . ." he went on, not knowing what she was thinking, ". . . and you have a lot of pain right now. Yet between the two companies a baby has been born. A child for you to nurture and feed."

Never's mind undid his tie. Slowly she pulled it free and dropped it to the floor. Then she went for the jacket. It joined the tie on the floor. The shirt came free one button at a time until his chest was exposed. With an imaginary fingernail she outlined the clearly defined squares of his muscular chest and allowed her hands to splay across his flat nipples. His skin was warm and smooth, and she loved the touch of it. Reaching up, she let her palms travel to his shoulders and pull the offending shirt down his strong, corded arms.

When her hands went to the belt buckle at his waist, Never whipped around and lowered her head. She was breathing heavily. *This is not the way it's done,* she scolded herself. *You're supposed to imagine him naked, not undress him, not touch him.*

Why did she do that? Why had she fantasized about him? She sucked air into her lungs. They refused to fill. Sound roared in her ears like a seashell held close, and she could hear nothing else. She didn't care. She hoped no one was looking at her, but even if every person in the room were staring at her there was nothing she could do about it. The image she'd created was all too real.

She couldn't turn around and look at him. It was too soon.
She couldn't imagine him dressed now that her mind had
stripped him. She was glad Barbara hadn't turned the lights on
in this part of the room. She was glad she couldn't be seen
clearly. Her body was hot and excited.

She had to get out of this room.

What was she doing? Averal wondered. He was prepared for
this meeting. His speech was designed to soothe the audience,
to put them at ease so that when he and his group came there
would be no fear, no need for them to be uncooperative. He'd
assumed Never would be the hardest person to get around, and
she'd surprised him by asking everyone in the room to be as
helpful as possible.

Then what was wrong with her? He could barely see her in
the subdued lighting at the rear of the room, yet he knew her
face had changed, and so had her body. It had become softer,
and sagged against the cabinets. Why had she gone to the back
of the room? Normally, a host would take a seat on the front
row, or at best stand against the front wall, but not Nefertiti
Kincaid. She took up command in the rear. Out of sight of the
room and out of his sight. He could almost charge her with
turning the lights off just to drive him mad.

In their short acquaintance he'd discovered Never wasn't
made from the mold of a normal person. She didn't fit the
standard pattern. Didn't conform to standard ideas. He could
see it in the seamed stockings with her business suits. She was
unique in everything. He liked that about her. He liked everything he'd discovered about her. He could even forgive her bad
temper. Most of it was out of loyalty, and loyalty was an admi-
rable quality.

She had surprised him with that, too. He hadn't met anyone
in a long time with as fierce a loyalty to their employer as was
housed in her thin body. What she'd briefly told him about her
sister and her family had probably helped mold her into the

kind of person she was. He envied her. If his parents hadn't divorced . . . but they *had,* and there was no need thinking about what might have been.

She left the room. Where was she going? Averal was jarred. He suddenly lost his train of thought and found a room full of people staring at him. He was completely blank. What had he been saying?

Suddenly he remembered. "Don't think the people who left voluntarily . . . or through staff reductions don't have names and faces, or that we're unaware of their pain and their day-to-day problems. We're helping them adjust, finding new jobs, and new careers. They will survive. A lot of them are handling their situations better than some of those left behind."

Averal continued to talk, telling the audience his staff would be conducting interviews and preparing a skills inventory. He then took questions.

Where was she? She hadn't come back.

The water was cold as Never wet a paper towel and placed it at the back of her neck. The dampness helped bring her body temperature back into place. Imagining a person naked and undressing him one garment at a time was a stupid thing to do.

She'd looked at him as a lover. Undressed him as if it were a prelude to making love. If he'd been old and fat she wouldn't have thought of it, but he was young and strong, and she could only imagine what his body looked like beneath that custom-made suit. Why did she even think of love in the same breath with Averal Ballentine? And why was it that when she thought of Averal it felt as if all the air disappeared? She'd find herself gasping to fill her lungs.

Then there was her body; how it reacted to him. In the bar she'd been mesmerized by him. And in the parking lot, it was so natural for him to kiss her. If he hadn't kissed her she would have leaned forward and kissed him. She'd better not think about

that kiss now, she thought. If she did she'd need more cold
water. As it was, this was the third time she'd wet her towel and
laid it against her nape.

She was going to have to go back soon. She didn't know how
long she'd been missing, and she didn't want anyone coming
in and finding her there. She straightened, moving the towel,
then found she'd soaked the starched collar of her blouse.

Never looked at herself and how her blouse lay limply against
her skin. It felt cold and uncomfortable. Wispy tendrils of hair
escaped her French twist and fell with the same unmanaged
texture as her blouse. She knew she was going to have to release
her hair. She reached for the pins and began pulling them free.
Long hair spilled past her collar, obscuring it from view. With
open fingers she combed through her hair. Then shaking her
head, she pushed it into a makeshift style. Thank heaven she
had manageable hair. Nothing else in her life of late had been
manageable. The ends curled under. She brushed them with her
hands, smoothing the surface and turning the bottom over her
hand.

After a final look in the mirror she reentered the crowded
room. No one noticed her slip back in. That is, no one facing
her, except the man standing in front of the room.

His eyes bored straight into her mind.

She had taken her hair down. Averal strained to see what else
had changed. She'd stolen back into the room, her jacket draped
over her arm and her hair cascading over her shoulders. Hair
which had topped her head in a tight knot was now loose and
unconfined. Why would she change it? Women didn't do that
unless something irreparable happened to their style, or they
were trying to hide something. Never's hair had been swept up
and coiled into some sort of a twist. Nothing had been left
falling about her face to give it a soft look. He didn't think she
wanted to look soft, at least not for him. She wore austere colored clothes and kept her hair neat. She didn't know her stock-

ings gave her away. The seams were her outward notice that beneath the black and white layers was a warm, passionate woman—how passionate, he had yet to find out.

Averal doubted her hair had been irreparable. The only other option was that she wanted to hide something. He wanted to know what it was.

The assembly's questions were apt and interesting. He answered them as best he could. When he'd answered everyone he turned the floor back to Never. She didn't join him in the front of the room, but walked forward into the light at the back and asked if there were any further questions. No one said anything, and she dismissed the group.

Averal watched as the crowd filed out in hushed silence. A few people talked to each other in whispers, but most exited silently. When the last one had gone through the door he made his way toward the back, and Never.

"How do you think it went?" he asked. "The part you heard, that is."

Never's eyes flashed at the insult. "As well as could be expected." Her answer was canned and it had a false ring. She knew he heard it.

"The attitude will change in time."

"Yes, I'm sure it will." She turned to the cabinet, picking up her leather folder.

"What were you doing?" His voice was soft, almost a whisper. He watched her closely. Something akin to panic swept over her, but when she turned back she seemed calm. "Why did you leave the room and return with your hair down?"

Instinctively, Never's hand went to the ends of her hair.

"It looks beautiful," Averal continued. "You should wear it that way all the time."

"I couldn't," she began. "It would fall in my face." She went to push it back over her shoulder, then remembered her collar. Never pulled the leather folder close to her breast and took a step forward.

Averal looked at his watch. "We haven't settled this evening.

I still want to talk to you, and you said you wanted to talk to me. Why don't we meet at Riddles' Place? The food's good, and Riddles would love to see you again."

"I can't. I'm busy this evening."

He knew she was lying. He wasn't put off.

"I'm late for an appointment now." He checked his watch again. "Why don't I call you later? We'll talk about it."

Never hesitated. Averal took it as consent.

"And your hair." He took a strand between his two fingers. "Wear it this way the next time I see you."

He took a step closer to her. He could feel her heat, smell the light perfume she wore. He liked the way women smelled, but he hadn't, before meeting her, been aroused by scent of a woman. She did that to him.

She licked her lips as if her mouth had gone dry. His was dry. She raised her hand to pull her hair from his fingers, but it closed over his hand and Averal slipped his fingers into the mass of tumbling curls. It was soft, like cotton. He hadn't ex-pected it to be. He liked the feel of it; the way it coiled around his hand, heavy and dark. He heard a slight sound from her—unidentifiable, but warm and touching. Then his hand contacted her collar. The coldness told him it was wet. He said nothing, just stared into her eyes. She'd put water on her neck, and it had wet her collar. He didn't stop to ask himself why. He made up his own reasons for her needing to cool herself off. In the half-light of the room he stared at her. Her eyes were half-closed and her lips trembled slightly. He nearly smiled at the involun-tary action. He liked knowing his presence affected her.

He lowered his head. Only a breath separated them. Never dropped her chin. Averal's hand pressed the wet collar against her nape, applying enough pressure to bring her chin up. He touched her mouth with a seductive kiss. It was brief, too brief. He lowered his mouth again. She moved her head from side to side, trying to avoid his kiss. Her body moved erotically against his. He grew hard, and he knew she felt it. He aroused her, too. Her nipples pebbled against the stiff blouse, and he could feel them, puckered and aroused. The more she moved, the weaker her defenses became. She stopped, only to discover it was a mistake. His mouth closed over hers.

This was a situation she couldn't win.

He captured her mouth, teasing her, playing an effective game of cat-and-mouse, knowing she had no chance against him. When he raised his mouth her eyes stayed closed.

Her arms still clutched the folder between them. He pressed her closer, taking her mouth, encircling her with his arms and deepening the kiss. God, she felt good in his arms! He could feel every bit of her, from her seamed stocking-clad legs to her thighs pressing against his. Her hips pushed into him and he shifted her, letting her feel the hardness of his erection at the juncture of her legs. Her breasts, small and firm, tilted upward. They could have been naked. Pulling her further into him, he wished they were. He wanted her in his bed, wanted to see her eyes as he made love to her, wanted to watch her waking in the early morning with the bed covers rumpled and love-worn. He wanted to see her whole, and without a stitch on. They could have been the only two people in the world. He could hear nothing, see nothing, but her.

Sensation passed through him. He felt himself groan as he lifted his mouth, only to reposition it over hers. This time he held back, fighting the urge to crush his mouth to hers, plunder her with his kisses. Instead he held her tenderly, as if she were breakable and he needed to be careful. His mouth brushed over hers, traveling her face, kissing her eyes, her cheeks, her nose, before settling over her mouth a final time.

Her hands moved. He pulled back, not breaking contact, only giving her enough room to free herself. Fingers closed around his upper arms. At first they hung there, limply, only tight enough to keep her balanced. Then they closed, squeezed, clung in submission. Her mouth changed, too. Everything about her changed. Her body arched toward his, and her fingers dug into the fabric of his jacket. Her tongue slipped into his mouth, tasting him, tangling with his.

Letting go of his arms, her hands moved upward, connecting behind his head aligning her body fully with his as she went up on her toes. She was thinner than he'd thought. His arms completely circled her waist. She was soft and warm in all the right places. His hands roamed freely over her back and the sensitive area of her hips and thighs.

Averal felt elation pierce him. He'd broken through that barrier she kept around herself, the one behind which she saw the world only in black and white. The woman in his arms had just discovered reds and golds, yellows and blues. She was part of the kiss, part of him. She pulled him closer. He felt the softness of her, felt the passion inside her that he knew wanted to burst out. He wanted it to burst, too. He no longer tried to keep the kiss light. Her mouth plundered his, and he couldn't control what was happening between them. He crushed her to him, grinding his erection into her until he thought he'd shout.

Then the leather folder that had been between them slipped to the floor. The sound slapped against the tile and penetrated his consciousness. He lifted his mouth, instinctively looking down. Never slumped against him, burying her face in his shoulder. He let her stay there, wanting to hold her for just a moment longer. Then he pushed her back and looked into her eyes.

"I'll call you later."

Never leaned on the file cabinets at her back the moment he went through the training room door. Damn! she cursed. Her body shook with reaction. She shivered in the coldness that took the place of the heat that so recently had surrounded them. Gulping breath into her lungs, she tried to control herself. Her heart beat like thunder, thudding and crashing against her chest. What had gotten into her? How could she let this happen? And in the office. With an open door. Anyone could have walked in and found them.

She felt the heat of embarrassment flush her face, replacing the chill. Her ears had to be red hot, and she could feel the blood rushing in her head. Turning back she leaned against the wall, then slipped down to the floor, discovering that her knees wouldn't support her. Her head fell forward onto her knees, and her arms banded her legs in a tight ball. She rocked.

Never didn't know how long she sat there. The lights were dark and the room was cool. Her heartbeat returned to normal. She wanted to cry, but her eyes were dry.

She wasn't just attracted to Averal Ballentine.

She was falling for him. And he was the only man on earth she couldn't love.

SIX

Averal's ears throbbed with the music coming from the bandstand. Normally he would be up there with them. Tonight he was in no mood. He sipped his club soda at the bar and thought of Never. He'd done nothing but think of her since leaving her this morning. Going to his next appointment was out of the question. He'd called and canceled, spent the afternoon driving. He'd taken the Cherokee and headed east. He'd driven as far as he could, only stopping when the sand of the beach dropped off into the Atlantic Ocean.

The shore had been deserted. He'd walked in the cold wind, listening to the caws of the gulls overhead, watching them swoop and glide searching for food, hoping the crashing waves of the water could tell him why he'd ignored every rule of management he'd ever learned and kissed Nefertiti Kincaid. First the wedding gown, and then the kiss. How was he supposed to work with her now?

"Rhonda, let me have a tray."

Rhonda was covering the bar tonight. She stared at him for a moment, knowing what the tray meant. Whenever he or Riddles took a tray it meant long conversation into the small hours of the night. She reached under the bar and came up with a small silver tray.

"What would you like on it?"

Averal set his glass down. He should take a bottle. Staring

up at her, he laughed—the first real humor he'd had since he left Never at her office.

Rhonda poured two glasses of club soda and set them on the tray. "You can really tie one on with this." Rhonda pushed the tray forward.

"Just keep them coming." He took the tray and headed toward the door marked Private. Behind it was a set of stairs leading to Riddles's upstairs office. The two of them had spent as much time there as they had in the cafés of Paris. In Paris it had been over ice cream, and he'd been fifteen when he poured out his heart to his surrogate father. Since then it had been Riddles he came to when things were important.

Averal took the first step and thought of this morning. What had happened to him? He wouldn't beat himself up for thinking of kissing Never. She was a beautiful woman, and he was as male as they come. He didn't mind the kiss. It was the whole incident that had him losing his mind—him trying to mold her to his body, him grinding her hips into his, trying to force her to swallow his tongue, living for the moment when she surrendered.

And she had. He'd felt powerful, knowing he'd pushed her past the world of black and white, knowing that she would have done anything he asked at that moment and not cared.

The fact was, she scared him. Scared him into running. That's what he'd done. He'd left her with a cryptic remark and gotten out of there. But he couldn't run from himself. So here he was in Riddles's bar, holding a tray of club sodas and wondering where she was and what she was doing. He wanted to call her, go to her, remove the fantasies he had in his head and turn them into reality.

Averal knocked once and opened the door. Riddles had his back to him. He didn't turn when Averal came in. The office was dark except for the light coming through the mini-blinded windows. Those windows looked down on the bar area. Averal knew at a glance that Riddles had been watching him.

Riddles had on a black dress suit with a white shirt. For a

moment Never and her penchant for the black and white color scheme flashed through his mind. His hair, as usual, hung down his back in a long ponytail.

Averal crossed to the desk and set the tray down. He switched on the desk lamp, giving the room some light but leaving them enough in the dark so that they couldn't read each others' expressions. He took his glass and drank most of the carbonated liquid.

Riddles turned and signed to him. "Woman trouble?" He didn't need to ask how it was that Riddles could always read him. Since he was thirteen-years-old, Riddles had known what was going through his head, even when he didn't understand it himself.

He'd explained everything to Averal, even told him why his body reacted violently when he turned fifteen, and why the sight of Alice Castleberry left him in a permanent state of erection at sixteen. Could he tell him why he couldn't get Never out of his mind? And the other parts of his body?

"What man doesn't have woman troubles?" he said, facing Riddles. He smiled, trying for lightness. Riddles knew him better than anyone else. He often knew when Averal was having troubles, and what the trouble entailed.

"Is it the new one?" Riddles signed.

"She's not a new one," he signed back, a little too roughly. Averal took Riddles's signs to mean he came in regularly with different women. This was clearly not the truth. He rarely brought a woman here. He hadn't brought Never. She'd found it on her own.

Riddles approached him, taking one of the glasses from the tray and drinking deeply. "What happened?" he signed when he'd replaced the glass and could use both hands.

I kissed her. The thought came unbidden. "Nothing," Averal lied, using both his voice and his hands to communicate. Something had happened. He didn't know if it was wonderful or terrible. People dreamt of the kind of feelings he was having.

Not him. He didn't want to feel like this. He didn't want her to make him feel like this.

"Then why were you sitting alone down there?" Riddles indicated the downstairs bar.

Averal didn't answer that. He lifted his glass and tossed the last of the club soda to the back of his throat as if it were scotch. At the moment he wished it was scotch.

"Is it Gabe?" Riddles persisted. Riddles was the only person, other than his parents, who knew the entire story of Gabe.

"No," Averal answered decisively. Then, feeling bad for speaking in anger to his friend, Averal dropped down onto one of the comfortable leather chairs in Riddles's office.

Riddles took the other chair. "I believe it is." He paused looking directly into Averal's eyes. They had always been up front with each other. Averal felt a pang of guilt for not being completely truthful, but he couldn't be completely truthful with himself, either.

"I have seen it often, Averal." Riddles's hands were a flash of light. Averal knew he was angry with him. "I know what you're doing. You're using Gabe as a reason to close your feelings off. You can't do that."

"I'm not doing anything of the kind." If he could, he wouldn't be feeling like this now. He wouldn't have felt the way he did this morning when he'd ignored his brain and let his—his heart—guide him. Was it heart or hormones?

"What happened today?"

Averal leaned forward. He set the empty glass down and told him. The story didn't take long to tell. He'd meant to kiss her. He'd thought about it since seeing her for the very first time, her heels tapping out a cadence on the tile flooring. When he leaned toward her this morning he'd had no idea it would get as out of control as it had.

Riddles didn't speak. He smiled slightly as he stared at Averal. The silence between them grew until Averal was uncomfortable with it.

"What?" he asked.

Riddles still said nothing.

"What?" he asked again, sitting back and staring straight at Riddles.

"She made you feel something?"

He had a knack for understatement.

The phone hadn't rung all day. He'd said he would call, but hadn't. He hadn't called the next day either, or the one after that. All day today she'd jumped each time the phone rang, thinking for sure it was Averal. It had been everyone *but* Averal. Yet he was coming. Barbara had received a message from Averal's secretary that he would begin his interviews tomorrow.

Never busied herself making hot cocoa, sweeping and vacuuming clean floors, turning on her computer only to sit and stare at the blank screen. She made a fire and watched it, purposely making herself think of something other than Averal Ballentine. Tonight she needed something to keep her hands busy and her mind off him. More importantly, she needed something to keep her mind off that kiss in the office Friday—and her own reaction to it.

She'd been helpless. It was a new feeling. Never didn't understand it. She'd always been in control. When her sister died and left her with two young boys, she'd shouldered the responsibility; grieving herself, yet helping them over the period of transition. She'd worked her way into the corner office, and looked forward to going in each day. Then Averal Ballentine had come along and destroyed her ordered little world with one kiss.

And she'd helped him.

She'd been part of it. She'd wedged herself to him like a second skin. If it hadn't been for the leather folder falling, she'd probably have torn his clothes off and made love to him on the floor of the training room. She'd wanted to. Then he'd left her standing there alone, incapable of supporting herself, her body on fire. She couldn't rid herself of that fire. She was hot even now. Why had she started a fire?

She glanced at the phone, frowning. He hadn't called, not while she was in the office, and not since she'd been home. Did he know her home number? She'd never given him her number. It was listed, though, and he could have called the office. She'd checked her voice mail three times since she'd been home. Why was she so disappointed? She should be glad he wasn't there. Maybe he was having second thoughts about her. They had both been unprofessional, as unprofessional as that first day in her office. His returning would mean the beginning of the end around the office. Yet each time someone passed her window this afternoon she'd looked out, hoping it was Averal, then become disappointed when it wasn't.

Now she sat in her living room, a warm fire crackling in the fireplace and a cup of hot chocolate cooling on the small table next to her. Her day had been a fight for concentration, and she'd lost. She had told Averal she wanted to talk to him. She wanted him to know she had seriously misjudged him for the things she'd said the first day he'd come to her office. She hadn't had time to apologize.

Getting up from the sofa, she decided to do it now. It had gone on long enough, and she couldn't put it off any longer. Tomorrow when he came to the office, if he came, it would be too late. She had to tell him. She looked at her watch. It wasn't too late. Maybe he was still in his office.

The cold air hit her as she left the house. Her car sat like a solitary sentinel in the middle of the driveway. She hadn't even put it in the garage when she arrived home. If she let herself think about that, she might change her mind. She always put the car away. Why had she left it sitting there tonight? Had she planned to go out?

Never got inside and started the engine. She switched the radio on while she waited a few minutes for the car to heat. Then, putting it into gear, she angled it toward the end of the street. There she stopped. Second thoughts stopped her. Should she go to his office? Riddles Place slipped easily into her mind. Would Averal be there?

She was hungry, and Averal had said the food was good. Maybe she should try it. She shook her head. Not tonight. Tonight was too close to Friday night. "Unforgettable" suddenly began to play on the radio. Nat King Cole's voice filled the interior, joined by that of his daughter Natalie. Never thought of the saxophone, and the attraction she'd felt for Averal when he'd played the same song.

When the song ended she was still sitting at the end of the small side street where she lived. There was no traffic coming from either direction. The car heater was working full blast, but the warmth she felt came from a source other than the car.

Finally she released the brake and pulled onto the street. It was time to eat crow. Averal hadn't called her. It was her move now. She had to make her apology, and she wouldn't go to bed tonight without doing it.

She didn't know where he lived, and she rejected going to Riddles Place. She made three stops at carryout restaurants before driving to Averal's office. The parking lot resembled her own office lot when she'd left it earlier tonight, deserted and empty except for a few lonely cars. One of them was Averal's jeep. Parking her BMW next to it, she got out.

Not giving her analytical brain time to think, she immediately walked into the building. The night guard must have been away, for the place set up for him was empty. She found Ballentine and Associates on the directory board. They were on the fifth floor. She stepped into the elevator and pushed five.

When the doors opened, an attack of nerves grabbed her. She stepped onto the carpeted hallway cautiously. Looking both ways, she had an urge to turn around and get back on the elevator. The doors closed behind her.

Taking a deep breath, Never found the door marked Ballentine and Associates and went through it. The place was deserted. She wondered if the cleaning staff had completed their rounds or if they would return to lock the doors later.

Never stopped in the doorway to Averal's office. He had his head bowed, engrossed in the papers he was working on. Everyone was gone, and most of the lights had been turned off. The beacon coming from his office had given her direction.

"Hello," she said quietly as she leaned against the doorjamb.

Averal raised his eyes at the voice, then blinked as if an apparition had appeared. It was Never! His stomach immediately knotted up. He stood, coming around the desk with a smile. He wasn't sure if this were a dream. If it was, he was grateful. He'd thought of nothing but her for days, and he didn't trust himself. In the past few weeks, since he'd met Never Kincaid, she'd interrupted many of his nights.

He wanted her, and finding her standing in his door did funny things to his heart. He wanted to rush to her and take her in his arms. Then he remembered what had happened the last time he did that—the small, almost harmless, firecracker that he had inside him had flared and burst in a TNT-size flash of desire.

"What are you doing here?" he asked, sounding surprised.

"Would you like me to leave?" She started to turn back to the door.

"No, you've come this far. You might as well come on in."

Never stepped farther into the room. "I went to three restaurants, but none of them had crow on the menu." She held up bags with the logo of three well-known Princeton eateries.

"Crow?"

"Don't you think I should be force-fed with a steady diet of it for a least the next six months?" She took another step toward him. "I've come to apologize."

"What are you apologizing for?"

"For not believing in The Wizard of Oz."

"Are you all right?" She looked the same. Her hair was loose. He remembered telling her he wanted to see it down. Right now he wanted to smell it, push his fingers through it. Her clothes were in the same color scheme, but she wore jeans and a sweater—white on top, black jeans. Her jacket was also black.

Somehow she was more relaxed. He felt like a toy wound too tight.

"I'm fine. I talked to several people last week—Greg Johnson, Sam Harris, Bill Williams. And the stories they tell . . ." She left the sentence hanging as she walked about the room looking at his desk, taking note of the small, foot-printed computer and the pink paper impaled on a desk set. She stopped near a wall of awards and certificates. "Well, if you're not The Wizard you must be a blood relation." She turned back to him.

"It was just coincidence. I happened to know people who were looking for the kind of experience they all had."

"And the rest?"

"What rest?" His eyes narrowed.

"You don't think I ended my investigation with just three people, do you?" She turned her back and dropped the bags on the small conference table in the corner.

Of course not, not Never Kincaid. "Just how many people have you talked to?" Averal sat on the edge of his desk.

"Illegal question." She smiled, shaking her head. "I asked my question first."

"There's no mystery. The answer is the same."

"You must know an awful lot of people. People who are looking for someone with just *the right kind of experience.*" She fed him his own words.

Averal pushed himself back, sitting on the desk and spread his hands. "It's not a crime."

"And what about the benefits packages? I suppose you just happen to have an in with the powers at Cedar Chemicals, and you convinced them to double the usual severance amounts?"

"Who told you about that?" He sounded as if she'd just breached security.

"It doesn't matter how I found out. Your cover is blown, Mr. Averal Ballentine. You're a human being, and I'm an evil monster." She frowned at him, closing one eye and screwing her nose into such a lovable nub he wanted to kiss it.

"I wouldn't say you were an evil monster," he replied. "Evil monsters haven't been known to apologize." And evil monsters couldn't possibly look like Never with her hair flowing about her shoulders.

He watched her, wondering what she was really doing here. Had she come just to see him? The rush that squeezed his heart at the thought threatened to force him off the desk.

"Thank you." She was sincere. "I hope you didn't judge me as quickly as I judged you. I'm sorry. Please accept my apology."

"Apology accepted."

"I suppose I should leave now." Never took a step toward the door.

"Why did you come here? You could have apologized over the phone." He stood, but didn't move from his position in front of the desk.

"My grandmother says you should always apologize in person. She says you don't insult a person over the phone, so you have to give them the opportunity to refuse to your face."

He weighed this for a moment, but couldn't resist teasing. "Apologies don't take much time. You could have done it while I was at your office Friday morning."

He checked her carefully to see if she reacted to Friday. He couldn't get it out of his mind. She acted as if it hadn't happened. It was a kiss. Nothing more. Had he read more into what happened than she did? Had he kicked himself for the last few days, while she thought it was only a matter of course? Anger crowded in on him.

"You did invite me to dinner." She picked up one of the bags.

"I suppose you've got me there." He came toward her, taking the bag from her. "What is all this?" He pulled the bags open.

"There are Buffalo Wings from Chuck's, and coq au vin from Lahiere's and arroz con pollo from The Alchemist and Barrister."

"It's a good thing I like chicken dishes. But I can't eat all this food myself." He smiled mischievously. "I guess as your punishment for vastly misjudging me, you'll just have to stay and eat with me."

Never smiled and held Averal's gaze for a moment. Then they delved into the bags and spread the food over the table.

"This should hold me until well after Thanksgiving," Averal said sometime later as he pushed himself away from the table and stood up. Empty bags, paper plates, and plastic utensils littered the table. Although the wineglasses were heavy crystal, everything else was disposable. Never hadn't brought the wine or the goblets. Averal had produced them from a bar in the corner of his office. "There are times when I entertain clients in this office," he had explained. His secretary made sure his bar was always stocked.

While he filled their glasses again, Never cleared away the debris.

"Why don't we sit over here?" Averal directed her to the sofa on the opposite side of the room. In front of it was a large, glass coffee table with consulting magazines on it. Never had taken her jacket off earlier and hung it on the back of a chair. She left it there and joined Averal on the sofa.

She took the glass he offered and sipped the sweet liquid.

"I'm glad you came by," he said.

"I kept you from finishing your work." Never glanced at his desk. "From the looks of it you'll be here until midnight."

"Myra, my secretary, says it always looks like that."

"Is that what you were doing tonight, cleaning your desk?"

"I'm always cleaning my desk. There's nothing there that can't wait for tomorrow."

Never felt nervous. Averal was more than polite, yet she felt a restraint underneath his surface. She wondered if he'd kiss her again. Then a surge of heat poured into her face at the thought that that was the reason she'd come here. She'd wanted to see him again, but she wanted more, more than food and conversation, more than a kiss.

The need to escape, to survive, roared into her brain, and she stood up.

"Speaking of tomorrow, I should be getting home." Never put her glass down on the coffee table.

Averal followed her. He didn't want her to go, but knew if he opposed her she'd fight him. He went to the conference area and got her jacket. Standing behind her, he held it while she slipped her arms into the sleeves. He resisted taking her shoulders and turning her around.

She waited silently while he got his coat and turned the lights out. He locked the doors, and they headed for the elevator at the end of the hall. They seemed strangely quiet after having talked so animatedly the past couple of hours. He knew he was reluctant to end the evening, but he wondered what her thoughts were.

The doors opened on a cushion of air, and they stepped inside. The ride to the lobby was short, too short. He wanted to ask her to go back inside. They could talk the night away, or go to Riddles Place, but he said nothing. They exited the building and headed for the only two vehicles still in the parking lot.

His office was in the middle of the business district of Princeton proper. Never could hear the traffic whizzing down the street. In the distance was Princeton University with its cathedral gates and centuries old buildings.

At her car he said, "Seems I'm making a habit of saying good night to you in parking lots."

Never nodded.

"Tomorrow since I'll be in your office maybe we can find a different forum to say goodnight." He wanted her to know he'd be there for the whole day.

"Goodnight," she said with a smile.

"Your secretary called and left me a message."

Averal nodded. They didn't move for a moment. Then he lifted his hand and pulled a strand of hair back from her face.

"Goodnight," he said and began walking away. Never stayed where she was, feeling disappointed.

Averal was only two steps away when he stopped. She held her breath. He turned back to face her. She stared at him, her eyes misting. The wind between them was no match for the concentrated heat that flared up and linked them like fingers. Averal retraced the two steps. Her breath caught in her throat, and her heart took off as if it wanted to get out of her chest.

This time when he leaned forward she went up on her toes to meet him. Lightly he brushed her lips with his. His hands came up to cup her face. He looked directly in her eyes. For the space of a heartbeat they stared at each other. Then his mouth covered hers, and Never was lost. She felt herself floating. Her brain was dizzy with sensation, and she liked the way she felt—weightless, airborne, free of any bonds.

The explosion came, rocking her. She melted into him. Her hands found the inside of his open coat, and she circled his body with her arms. His tongue drove deeply into her mouth, and a strange guttural sound that could only be erupting pleasure escaped her. Cauldrons bubbled about them in the heat they created. Averal's hands found their way into her hair. He twisted the silken threads as if they were the gentlest of fibers. His mouth devoured hers, but his hands were gentle and caring. She was a fine piece of porcelain, fragile to the touch but strong and resilient. Through her jacket she could feel the hardness of his body. Her hands slid up his back, separated from his skin by only a shirt. Muscles jerked and rippled in the wake of her touch. She reveled in the excitement the knowledge gave her, and fit her body closer to the groove of his. She heard the sigh of pleasure that matched her own.

When his mouth slid from hers they clung to each other like two limp weeds. Averal's head was buried in her hair, and Never was dizzy. The world sped around her and blurred the lights in the parking lot to soft rings. It took several minutes for her vision to clear and her strength to return enough for her to push herself away from Averal.

Her voice didn't immediately return. She didn't know what to say, anyway. No man had ever kissed her like that, and no man had made her feel the way Averal made her feel, made her heart beat so fast and had her breath coming in short gasps without even touching her.

"It's cold," he told her. "You'd better get in the car."

She didn't know if she could move. She didn't know if she were a whole person or merely atoms scattered about the Princeton parking lot. She didn't feel disconnected. On the contrary, she felt anchored to Averal, unable to exist without him.

"Never?"

The sound of her name snapped the world back into place. She heard the traffic, slick wheels on asphalt, the sound of her own heart thundering, and Averal's ragged breathing. She moved more like an automaton than a human being, seating herself in the car and turning the engine on, adjusting her seatbelt.

Averal watched until she started the engine before climbing into the jeep and turning his own key in the ignition. He needed a drink. He wanted Never Kincaid, more now than ever. And tonight when she showed up he'd been thinking about her, thinking what it would be like to really hold her again. But nothing had prepared him for the gut-wrenchingly weak feeling he experienced when he wedged her body into his. And the shudder that passed through him when her hands played across his back as if he were her personal instrument.

The thought paralyzed him. He was attracted to Never, yes, but could he be falling in love with her? He'd been in love before. Once. It was a consuming emotion that robbed him of his own will. It ended in disaster. He'd vowed he wouldn't fall again. Would it be different with Never? Could he trust her? Was she playing a game with him? She said she'd come in peace. He wanted to believe her, especially after he'd held her in his arms. He liked the feel of her, the taste of her, and the smell of her perfume. He liked her voice—when she purred like a kitten, and even when she was angry. He smiled at the thought. But was he in love with her? And if he were, what did it mean? Love brought demands he wasn't ready to confront, probably would never be ready to confront.

But with his arms around her nothing was clear. He'd sud-

Shirley Hailstock

denly felt as if he were hollow, and she'd filled the vessel within him. He wanted to go on holding her, protecting her from hurt, keep her with him, but he knew he couldn't protect her from his own ability to hurt. He remembered her nylons, the thought of the passion underlying the severity of her black and white wardrobe. Now his thoughts centered around family. She had two nephews she was proud of. She came from a happy family background. Wouldn't she want to duplicate that in her own life? Wouldn't she want marriage and a family?

He hit the steering wheel with the palm of his hand. Of course she would. He didn't. He couldn't. It would end in disaster for both of them. The same way it had ended for his parents. He wanted her more than he'd ever wanted a woman, but he knew they would have no future together. Not one that would result in a family. He'd let her go.

Never's BMW pulled out of its space. Averal noticed the movement, and realized he'd been sitting in the dark long enough for heat to come from the jeep's interior system. He reached for the lights button and pulled it. The license tag of Never's car illuminated like a large danger sign. At the exit he pulled up behind her and read the tag again. He laughed, throwing his head back and letting the sound fill the cabin. PLAY GMS it read.

"Is it a game, Never?" he asked as she turned left toward Palmer Square. "Is it all a game?"

SEVEN

"Game, set, and match," Mark shouted across the net. He ran on his long, athletic legs toward Never's side of the net.

She walked to the end and began putting away her racquet.

"What's with you today, Never? I've seen you play some bad tennis, but today you've given a new meaning to the word lose."

"I suppose my concentration is somewhere else." She knew that was an understatement. Her concentration was on Averal. She didn't think she'd ever be able to pass a parking lot without thinking of him, and thinking of him was all she'd done for the past week.

"I understand, Never. The merger is affecting us all." Mark zipped his racquet case and she heard the soft whoosh as he snapped the plastic top onto the can of yellow tennis balls. "I'm sure my department will be cleaned out. I'm just staying around for the severance package."

If it were only the merger, Never thought later as the water from the shower cascaded over her. Her problem had ceased being the loss of her job. It would end, she was sure of that. But she wasn't like Mark. She couldn't sit around waiting.

Her problem was a man. The feelings she had for Averal Ballentine. She was different with him. She laughed a lot and felt relaxed, and wanted to talk all night and listen to him. She wanted to hear him play his saxophone and tell her all the stories of his youth.

Never turned the dial to OFF. Pulling the plastic curtain aside, she reached for her towel. She needed to get away and think about what was happening to her. Maybe this weekend, after her interview, she would go up to the Poconos and think about what she was going to do.

She dressed quickly and repaired her hair and makeup. Thirty minutes later she was headed to the office.

"Good morning, Barbara," Never greeted her secretary. Barbara seemed to glow these days. She'd gone into wedding arrangements with the zeal of a mother-of-the-bride.

"Hi, Never. Here are your messages." Barbara handed her three pink pieces of paper.

"Where is everybody? It seems awfully quiet in here."

"There're all gawking at *him*." She nodded toward the end of the room.

Never's gaze followed the line of cubicles. The room looked the same as it had for a week—ever since Averal Ballentine had been conducting interviews. Secretaries who were usually busy at their keyboards at this time of the morning, and even some of the female managers, found reasons to pass Bill Winston's old office in hopes of getting Averal's attention.

Never found reasons to avoid going in that direction. Her traffic pattern had been altered by his presence. She'd come in a week ago, the night after her visit to his office, to find him installed in an office in her direct line of vision. Despite his ability to recommend the dissolution of her department, the female employees found him fascinating to look at. They gawked openly, each trying to get his attention.

She couldn't blame them. She wanted to do the same thing. In fact, she'd done more. Much more. Then she'd put a stop to it. They couldn't maintain a sexual relationship and still have Cedar-Worthington between them. Never understood where her loyalties lay, even if the women in her department didn't. She'd refused to see Averal again. Things were moving too fast for her. She needed time to think about her options. *None,* she told herself, where Averal Ballentine was concerned. He might not be the devil she'd originally thought, but he still held power over her and the people who worked for her. It was a relationship that had no place to go.

Averal hadn't fought her about it, either. He'd hadn't come to her office or even bumped into her in the small kitchen that serviced the floor with coffee, tea, and hot chocolate. She was grateful for that.

Glancing once more toward the end of the office, she shifted her briefcase and went in, snapped the computer on, and hung up her coat. Picking up her coffee cup, she headed for the end of the room. The group dispersed when they saw her, each person saying good morning in turn.

"Excuse me for interrupting." Averal stood when she came in.

"It's all right. We were just finishing." He nodded to Wendy Jordan, who left them alone. "It's nice to see you. I was getting the impression you didn't really work here."

She knew he was trying for lightness, but she couldn't be light around him.

"I've been in a lot of meetings, but if there was anything you needed you could have asked Barbara."

"Barbara has been most helpful. It's you I wanted to see."

Never's heart pumped up, the familiar need for breath attacking her. "I didn't get a message that you wanted to see me." She deliberately misunderstood. She'd wanted to see him, too, but she couldn't be sure of keeping her attraction for him a secret if she had to pass him every time she went for coffee or to another office.

"I didn't leave one. I just thought that if we were in the same office I might get to see you passing by once in awhile."

Never managed a smile. "I have been very busy with King Boris."

"Who?"

"I'm sorry. That just kind of slipped out." King Boris was Barbara's tag for Boris King, the squat, fat Vice-President of Information Services who had replaced John Williams. "We've had several meetings off site this past week."

"Why don't you sit down for a moment?" he invited.

"Aren't you expecting someone?"

"They'll wait."

Never took the seat opposite him. "How are the interviews going?"

"I'm not sure. Few people give me any feedback. They all ask the same question."

"Which is?"

"At the end of these interviews, how long will it be before the department is shut down?"

"That's a valid question. What answer do you give them?"

"I tell them I don't know. And that's the truth. I don't know what will be done when this is finished."

"How much longer will it be before you've completed all the interviews?" Never hoped she didn't sound too anxious. Now that he was here, she realized she did like seeing him once in a while, even if she did maintain her distance. After he finished she'd miss him.

"I should be finished by the end of the week."

Friday was only two days away. She should be calculating how long it would be before her department was phased out. Instead she was thinking she only had two more days to see Averal. After Friday he would have meetings with King Boris, meetings that she would not be privileged to attend.

Averal noticed her attention suddenly go to the window. She stood and walked to look down on the parking lot. He wanted to go to her, to stand with his arms around her waist and let her rest her head on his shoulder. He wanted to let her know everything was going to be all right. The glass wall facing him was one reason he remained seated. The other was the woman herself. He didn't trust himself for a moment to keep his hands to himself if he got within a foot of her.

"Never."

His voice was as soft as moonlight. *Two days,* she thought. *He'll be gone in two days.* And she wouldn't even be in the office to see him leave. Today was it. She turned back. Her coffee cup was still in her hand.

"Riddles asked about you."

"How is he?" The change of subject helped her, but also put her on edge.

"He wondered if you were coming back. Why don't you have dinner with me tonight?"

"You'll play your sax for me?" she asked.

"I'd be honored." He bowed his head.

"It sounds good." She wanted to go. "But I can't go tonight. I have plans." This time it wasn't a total lie. Never didn't have plans for tonight, but by the time she got back from New York she would be too tired to go to Riddles. New York tired her out.

"What about tomorrow night?" He expected her to refuse. The black and white outfit radiated no!

Never shook her head. She did want to see him again, but felt it was somehow disloyal to herself and the company she worked for to side with the hand that was about to axe them. The way he looked at her was almost her undoing, as if it were most important that she spend time with him. She wanted to.

"I'd better go now. I see Aletta coming, and I haven't had my coffee yet." She turned at the door to give him a parting smile. "Good-bye."

Seven hours later Never had finally finished her job interview in New York. Feeling that if she smiled one more time she'd have to carry her face home in a jar, she was completely robbed of any energy. Before her was a trip to Penn Station and an hour train ride during the busiest part of the day—rush hour.

Never left the Warner Communication Building at Rockefeller Center. Hundreds of weary workers jostled her as she walked toward the train station at Thirty-Fourth Street.

"Nefertiti," she heard someone call. She turned, glancing over her shoulder as the crowd carried her forward. She heard her name again. "Never." Flattening herself against the wall of a building, she turned around and found BriAnne Ball gesturing for her to join her.

Fighting her way against the crowd was like swimming upstream as she reached Averal's mother.

"What are you doing in New York?" BriAnne asked, helping her inside a small gallery.

"I had an interview, and I'm on my way home," she told the small woman dressed in purple from her blouse to her shoes.

"When I saw you go by the window I wasn't sure it was you. Can I get you a cup of tea or a drink?"

"Tea would be fine."

She followed BriAnne to the back of the empty gallery. "My friend Evan Dirkson owns this gallery. He goes to visit his mother once a month, and I come up to help him out. We both started out together in Paris. I went on with painting, and he opened a gallery."

Never took a bone china tea cup from BriAnne and sat in a Queen Anne chair in front of an uncluttered desk. Momentarily she was reminded of Averal's messy desk in his office. "I can see you've both been very successful." The gallery was airy with large front windows.

BriAnne smiled, taking the chair behind the desk. Never was struck by the resemblance Averal had to his mother. Why hadn't she seen it before? They both had the same piercing eyes and the smile which she'd recognized, but he also had her coloring. Never shook herself, forcing her mind away from BriAnne's son before she completed a full inventory of his attributes.

"You know, I'm very glad I saw you. I've been thinking of calling you since the night at my opening. I have an idea, but I didn't know how you'd feel about it."

"What idea?" Never sipped her tea as if it were a lifesaving elixir.

She hesitated for only a second. "To be rather blunt, I'd like to paint your portrait."

"What!" Never had expected anything but that. Her cup clattered in the saucer. "You don't paint people. All your paintings are landscapes. Only *The Edge* and *By The Sea* have any characters at all."

"You know *The Edge?*"

Never looked into her cup as if leaves would form on the top of the liquid and tell her what to say. She decided on the truth.

"I own *The Edge.*"

BriAnne's hand froze halfway to her mouth. She was stunned, but only for a second. Setting her cup down, she asked, "How did you come by it?"

"I bought it at a charity auction. At the time, I only knew that I liked it. I didn't know it was yours until years later, when I recognized the style at an exhibition in Paris. I talked to the gallery owner, and he told me the name of the painting."

"I wondered what happened to it." She spoke quietly, as if she were talking more to herself than to Never.

"Averal said the same thing."

"Averal knows you have this painting?"

Never shook her head. "We talked about it the night of the opening, but I didn't tell him I own it."

"It was hard parting with that painting. It was like a child had died. *The Edge* was my first sale. For a long time I didn't want to know where it was. Then I just couldn't face the pain again. It represented my broken marriage and the loss of my youngest son."

"I'm sorry," Never whispered. "I didn't realize you had another child."

"I had three miscarriages before Averal was born." She leaned forward, sipping from her cup. "He was such a wonderful baby." For a moment she was lost in memory. "Then I had Gabe." A cloud settled over her features.

"I didn't mean to bring up bad memories."

Never remembered Averal's tone when he mentioned his mother's name. Yet BriAnne spoke of him with only love in her voice. *What happened between them?* she wondered.

"I'm all right, Never." She stared directly at her. "Time has a way of dulling pain. The painting was a physical replica. It

didn't cause the pain. I think part of painting it helped we resolve the pain I felt."

"I'm glad," Never said. "I love it."

"I haven't painted any people since *The Edge.*" BriAnne put
her cup down. "For a long time I've been toying with the idea
of doing something different. The idea of a portrait hit me when
I first saw you." For a second the artist lowered her gaze, then
raised her eyes. They were brown and warm, as Averal's had
been just before he kissed her. Never shook her head, clearing
the memory. "I want you to pose for me."

"I haven't done any modeling."

"Martin tells me you model his gems all the time."

Never smiled. "That's what Martin calls it when he wants
me to go to something with him. He says he needs someone to
wear his jewelry. But to pose for an artist?"

"I've haven't used a model before. For landscapes you only
need light."

"I thought you didn't like people in your paintings."

"You're right. It's been over twenty years since I painted *The
Edge.*" Several expressions crossed her face. Pain was the only
one Never could put a name to. Quickly it was lost, and the
vibrant personality returned. She wondered what BriAnne had
thought. Somehow she knew it had to do with the time she'd
spent in Paris with Averal. She wondered if BriAnne regretted
that time, if she were thinking what she'd do if she could go
back and relive that period with a fresh canvas in front of her.

"It wasn't one of my best. In fact," she said, giving a mirthless
laugh. "It's one of the worst ones I've ever sold."

Never disagreed with that, but didn't contradict the woman.

"For the past few years I've been thinking of changing direction." BriAnne continued.

"I suppose everyone needs a new adventure sometime,"
Never said, thinking of the interview she'd just had. If she got
a job in New York it would certainly change her life.

"You understand," the other woman replied, a broad smile
splitting her face.

Never nodded.

"When I saw you the night of the opening, I knew I wanted to paint a portrait."

"When you looked at me, I had the feeling you were seeing me on canvas."

"You're right. I wondered if you would consider posing with the Nefertiti hairstyle and wearing the jewels you had at the gallery. I went to see Martin to ask him to call you for me."

"What would I have to do?" Never took a sip of her tea, considering the proposal. She liked BriAnne Ball, and to be featured in one of her paintings was like being made queen for a day.

"Mostly stand or sit, I don't know which yet." She didn't appear confused, more as if she was just thinking out loud. "I'd begin with some photographs, then sketches. When everything falls into place . . ." BriAnne was using her hands, trying to grab thought and mold it into a cohesive idea. "Then we can begin the final portrait."

"When would you begin?"

BriAnne smiled. "You'll do it?" she asked, moving her cup and saucer out of spilling distance.

"I have a busy schedule."

"I'm willing to work within it." BriAnne was eager. "I know you have a full-time job. I thought we could try Saturday and Sunday mornings. The light is best at that time. Other times, I can work from the sketches or the photos."

Never felt as if she were granting favors to a child. "Saturday and Sunday mornings will be fine," she said.

BriAnne held her cup out to Never as if it were a champagne glass.

"To success," BriAnne toasted.

Never saluted BriAnne with her own tea cup and took a drink. Looking into the hot, dark liquid, she thought of Averal. The small woman in purple reminded her of him. If BriAnne Ball were about to step into the pages of *Elle,* she was certainly dressed for it. The simple purple suit was a complement to her tiny frame. Never knew she had to tell this woman about the relationship she had with her son.

"BriAnne, the idea of sitting for you is intriguing, but I should tell you that I've had to work with your son for the past few weeks."

BriAnne came forward in her chair. "You don't work for those two chemical companies that merged?"

Never nodded. "At first we had a terrible encounter. Our argument was quite heated."

"And now?" BriAnne asked.

Never had the feeling BriAnne could read her quite clearly. "We're on better terms now." Never's ears were burning. "He's nearly finished with my department. I don't expect to see much of him after tomorrow." There was fear in her voice, but she hoped the perceptive woman across the desk didn't hear it.

"I saw the two of you talking the night of the opening. I didn't realize you and Averal knew each other."

"We met that night."

BriAnne stood and came to take Never's cup. She prepared two more cups of tea and brought them back to Never's side of the desk. BriAnne took the other seat in front of the desk and sipped the hot liquid.

"Never," she began cautiously. "What do you feel for Averal now?"

I'm falling in love with him. The words jumped into her mind. Never nearly spilled the hot liquid. "I'm falling for him," she whispered to herself, forgetting BriAnne was there to hear.

BriAnne was quiet, and Never felt as if the words were printed on her jacket. She couldn't be in love with Averal. He was going to be out of her life in a few days. How could she have fallen in love after two kisses? Granted, they were devastating kisses, but they couldn't possibly have made her fall in love with him.

Her body was suddenly hot. She remembered herself in his arms, and how nothing had been important when she was there. Emotion rocked her.

"Never, are you all right?" She heard BriAnne through a fog. "You look a little pale."

"I'm . . . all right." She hesitated, then raised her tea cup to her lips. When had she fallen in love? And why hadn't she known? She'd imagined when it happened she'd hear violins or feel an earthquake—something to tell her. It had come like a word that triggers a dream. But dreams were harmless. She couldn't say that for Averal.

BriAnne smiled. "I liked you from the first, Never. I don't know if Averal's told you about our relationship."

"He's alluded to it," she answered honestly.

"We have problems I want to work out. He still needs time."

"I understand," Never said.

"I don't think you do. What I'm saying is I want you to be my friend, no matter what you feel for my son."

Never was relieved. She liked BriAnne, and didn't want to cause any further ripple between her and Averal.

BriAnne smiled. "How's next Saturday morning? We could meet at Princeton University, and I'll take some pictures."

"Next Saturday will be fine." This coming Saturday was her grandparents' weekend, and she would be busy with college students and hotel arrangements.

She wondered what Averal would be doing. Even though her Grand had invited him, she knew he wasn't coming. A pang of regret pierced her heart.

Never leaned her chin on her hand. Her reflection waved back and forth in the darkness of the train window, but she didn't see it. She was too absorbed in the knowledge of being in love. The wheels revolved in a rapid chant. *I'm in love. I'm in love. I'm in love.* It seemed the wheels of the train had to keep telling her over and over.

The train ride seemed endless. When it finally got to the Princeton station she had a headache. And no car. She'd left hers at home and walked to the station. It wasn't very far away, but now she didn't feel like walking home. Looking around, she found the taxi area empty. People had quickly scrambled for the three or four that serviced the small station.

Resigned to her fate, she started up the hill toward Nassau Street. Only a few more blocks and she'd be home. But as she reached the crest, the urge to see Averal outweighed the pain of her headache. She stood on the windy corner debating whether she should turn right or left. Left would take her home and right would lead her to Riddles Place. Averal might be there. He had invited her.

She turned left.

Never was dressed. She'd left her car in the driveway after a full day of running errands. She'd been to the post office, the grocery store to stock up on food for her visiting nephews who would arrive this afternoon, then gone to Jessie's and picked up her dress, and had lunch in the diner across from Jessie's shop. Never had tried everything to keep her mind off of Averal. None of it had worked. She felt plagued by him. Her mind was always a step away from thinking about him, or he was at the top of her thoughts.

Tonight she would see her grandparents. As an added surprise for them she'd arranged for a limousine to pick them up to bring them to the party, and tonight they would stay in the Hyatt Regency Hotel.

Her nephews were too wrapped up in themselves and their games of one-upmanship to be concerned about her. She didn't blame them. They were college students.

The doorbell rang. Never looked at her watch. Who could that be? Martin had called earlier to apologize again for being out of town, so it couldn't be he, unless . . . Maybe Martin had returned, and he— She rejected the idea. Martin never surprised her. He was always exactly where he said he'd be. Tonight he was out of town, and nothing would have him returning. She started for the door. Maybe it was only a Girl Scout selling cookies. This was the time of year for them.

Never looked through the side windows. The man she saw standing there had her jumping back. What was Averal doing here? The doorbell rang again. She had to answer it. Her car was in the driveway. He knew she was home.

Straightening her shoulders, she reached for the knob and opened the door.

Averal turned under the porch light. God! he looked good. She held her breath a moment.

"What are you doing here?"

"I believe we have a date."

He passed her and walked into the foyer. Never closed the door.

"Your grandmother invited me to bring you. Remember?" He smiled what she'd begun to think of as the bookstore smile. It was there she'd first seen it. Never could refuse if she wanted to. Her problem was she didn't. It was only for tonight. She should be able to do what she wanted for one night. And what would she tell her grandmother if she didn't show up with him?

"I remember," Never said. They stood staring at each other, neither of them moving.

"Shouldn't you get a coat?"

Averal had thought he was prepared for the sight of her. He'd expected something in black and white. But tonight the signature colors had been retired. Never wore blue. Electric blue. The dress was like the formfitting one from the bookstore, except that it was covered with sequins. It covered her from neck to mid-thigh. Her legs looked long and sensuous, extending to blue shoes with heels that brought her eye to eye with him.

She turned to go for her coat. Her nylons had no seams. These had red rhinestones, forming a heart on each ankle.

"Shall we go?"

Averal took her arm and led her through the door. It allowed him to touch her. He helped her into his car and got inside, himself. As he turned on the lights her license tag reflected in front of them. He reversed down the driveway and headed for the hotel.

The Hyatt Regency Ballroom had been transformed into a garden. A white trellis with roses had been set up at the end of the room. Covered chairs awaited the guests on two sides of a center aisle, like in a small chapel. A white carpet ran up the center aisle. Flowers added scent to the room. Never inspected the setup and nodded to the banquet manager that she approved of everything.

"The reception area is this way." The woman led them through a door and into an adjoining area where a bandstand headed the room. A dance floor had been laid, and tables with blue and white table cloths and napkins made it festive. There were people about still setting up the center pieces, balloons with the couples' names and the date on them. Some of the band members had arrived, and were taking their instruments out of the cases.

"It looks wonderful," she said. The banquet manager smiled and left them. "They're going to love this." Never smiled as she looked at him.

They returned to the chapel room. It was a perfect setting for her. Everything about it sparkled like the dress she wore. They took seats on the first row. Averal looked over the setting. He could see Never as the bride tonight, floating down the aisle in that white dress she'd worn in the bridal shop, a bright smile on her lips. She seemed to shine in this venue. He just couldn't see himself as the groom.

"What are you thinking?" she asked. "You haven't said a word since we left my house."

"I'm thinking how lovely you look in blue."

"Flattery, Mr. Ballentine?"

His eyes took her in from head to toe. She'd pushed her hair back from her face and secured it with a comb. The rest of it flowed down her back in a cascade of curls. He wanted to slip his hand into the mass.

"Not flattery. Fact."

Her eyelids fluttered down as if he'd embarrassed her. Averal slipped his arm along the back of her chair and leaned forward. He kissed her lightly on the forehead. "It's going to be a perfect night."

His voice was no louder than a whisper. Never wondered what he meant, for at that moment she sensed a change in him. She took his hand, wanting to explore what had happened, ask him what had changed, but the door opened and the first guests arrived. Her nephews and their dates came in.

Never stood still, holding Averal's hand. The boys looked wonderful, but they weren't boys any longer. Her sister's death had sent them to her, and now they were young men. She'd lose them soon, probably to the girls they had on their arms. A lump formed in Never's throat as they approached her.

"Hi, Aunt Gee," said Stephen, the older one. She had to look up at them both now. They'd taken their height from their father. Each of them was already over six feet.

"Hello," she said. "You all look so nice." She took the group in.

"We just left Grand. She looks like a dream."

"And Pops is a nervous wreck."

They laughed. "Guys." Never glanced at Averal. "This is Averal Ballentine."

"I met you before," Stephen jumped in. He stepped forward and shook Averal's hand. "You spoke at my school."

"I remember," Averal replied. "We spent an afternoon in your student center, but I didn't know you were related to Never." He glanced at Never as if she'd betrayed him.

"That's because we don't have the same last name. This is Holly Barrett. She goes to the University of Connecticut."

"Holly." He shook her hand. "And I take it this is Donald, the other nephew?"

Donald only smiled and nodded.

"And this is Donald's girlfriend, Katherine Morrison." Kathy was the cheerleader Donald had gone out for the basketball team to capture. It seemed things were progressing nicely.

Stephen immediately engaged Averal in conversation, all the while holding onto Holly's hand. Donald and Kathy skirted the room, checking out everything. Never found herself alone. She looked at them, her family. It had been difficult when they left her to go away to college. She'd gotten used to being alone in the house without all the noise and phones ringing. Looking at them now she knew that when they graduated it was only a matter of time before they married and went off to lives of their own, with no intention of returning to the home they'd known for the past ten years.

Then she looked at Averal. Her heart beat a step faster. She knew Stephen liked him, from the day he'd phoned and told her to buy his book. Even though Never had tried not to get close to him, it hadn't worked. She felt closer to him now than she'd ever been to a man. But there was something about him that pushed her back, even when he had her in his arms. It was hard for her to see when she clung to him like a second skin, but when she wasn't in his arms she could tell.

Why had he shown up tonight? She hadn't expected him to come, and he knew that. He didn't really know her grandmother, and after only one meeting her grandmother couldn't be that disappointed if she didn't see him again.

They'd agreed to put a stop to their association. It wasn't the professional thing to do, since they sat on opposite sides of the merger. But her heart had thudded when she saw him, and she hadn't put up much of a fight with her conscience when he said he was there to fulfill an obligation. She wanted to be with him.

Averal reached for her and she went to him, taking his hand. His fingers curled around her hand, and she smiled at the way he could make her feel with only a slight touch. Never had often told herself she had everything she wanted. She had a good job, her sister's children, and her grandparents as staples in her life. She didn't need anything more. But she knew now how wrong she'd been. She did need someone to be in love with, and someone to love her. She remembered all her friends crying over lost loves, then finding new ones. She thought they were crazy to have such emotions. Now she knew what they meant, knew how love could make you want to fly and then as quickly drop you to the ground. She squeezed Averal's hand, and he glanced at her before returning himself to the conversation he was having with her nephew and his girlfriend.

She stayed close to him until the guests began to arrive. Then, reluctantly, she left him to greet friends. The room quickly filled, and Never went to the small room on the side reserved for her grandparents.

"Are you ready?" she asked when she saw them. "The room is nearly full."

"Well, tell them all to go home," her grandfather said. "I don't know why I ever agreed to this circus."

"It won't be a circus," she assured them. "Grand, you look wonderful. And Pop, no one ever looked as good in a tux."

"When did you teach this child to lie?" He looked at his wife, then went to hug his granddaughter.

"I wouldn't lie."

"No?" His brows raised. "I hear you're here with a young man."

Never glanced at her grandmother, who turned to face the huge wall mirror.

"Grand told you she set me up."

"She told me he couldn't keep his eyes off you."

Never remembered herself in the wedding dress. The way Averal had looked at her. She'd felt beautiful under his gaze.

"Tell me," her Pop asked. "Is he the one?"

"Pop," she pushed back. "He's just someone I work with."

"Well, if he doesn't change his mind after seeing you in that dress, the man has no blood in his veins."

Never smiled at her mischievous grandfather.

A knock on the door had them all turning. "Ten minutes." The wedding consultant came in. "Oh, Ms. Kincaid. You should take your seat."

Never kissed her grandparents and headed for the door.

"Remember what I said," her grandfather reminded her.

"He's got blood in his veins, Pop."

Never returned to the room set like a chapel and stood in the back hall. The music had barely begun, and already she was fighting tears. What would she do when the actual wedding march began? The wedding consultant joined her, nodding her head, signaling it was time for Never to be seated. She smiled, walking down the aisle. All eyes turned to her. She focused on Averal. She was unable to see his expression. She wondered what he was thinking. Her grandfather's words rang in her ears. At the front of the church she took a seat next to Averal and waited for her grandmother and grandfather to slowly march in. Why were her knees knocking with nervous tension? They'd practiced the ceremony, rehearsed the promenade, but she was as scared as a five-year-old facing a room of adults.

Averal took her hand. She turned to him. His eyes were soft and staring into hers.

God, yes, she thought. *He's got blood in his veins.*

The only wedding Averal had ever attended was his half-sister Caroline's. He'd sat in the back of the church, maintaining obscurity and a detachment from the proceedings. Almost immediately after the ceremony he'd returned to New Jersey. Weddings were family events, and Riddles was his only real family. Interacting with his father's second family made him feel as awkward as a fifth wheel. He'd come because Caroline had insisted he be there. She couldn't keep him there, however, and he'd left on the same wind that carried her down the aisle toward a life of Mr. and Mrs.

He held Never's hand, and for the first time in his life he thought there might be a chance for him.

EIGHT

Never hummed the last song as she lounged against the upholstery in Averal's car. He pulled into her driveway and cut the engine. Neither of them moved.

"Looks as if you have a full house."

In the driveway was her car and two others. One had Connecticut plates, and belonged to Katherine Morrison. The other was the old clunker Stephen had bought in high school and restored. It usually resided in the garage. Its presence in the driveway and the blaze of lights coming from the windows told her the boys were home.

"College students," she answered. "They'll probably be up all night."

"You like having them here?"

"I love them," she said. "I know they won't be mine for much longer. They grow up very fast."

Averal thought of his own home life. His mother hadn't seemed to notice if he were there or not. His father hadn't seen him in decades. He wondered how it felt to have someone like to have you around.

"They're really lucky to have you."

"I'm the lucky one. When they came to me we were all scared of the future. The only things we had between us were blood relationship and love. We loved each other, and that got us over most of the grief. It also helped solve a lot of the problems."

Never sat up straight and looked at Averal. He faced the front of the car, his hands on the steering wheel. She took one of his hands and brought it to her lips. He turned to her, then, and moved his hand into her hair. For a long moment he stared at her as if he were trying to memorize her features in the space of the light coming in the windows.

Then he leaned forward and kissed her lightly. His mouth only touched hers. Never's eyes closed and her hand reached for him. She touched his chest then he pulled back.

"Would you like to come in?" she whispered.

"No." He shook his head. Disappointment must have been evident on her face. "You can't know how much I want you. I'd like to take you home. My home. We'd skip the coffee, skip the small talk, go straight to bed."

Never couldn't speak at the images that crashed in her mind with his words. She was through kidding herself that she didn't want exactly the same thing as Averal had described. She did want him. She'd wanted him from the first, and now she had no doubt of the love she felt for him. But in this, was love enough? It had worked for her when her sister died and the boys came, but they had been children. There was nothing child-ish about the way she felt for Averal. She loved him the way a woman loves a man.

She brought her hand up to his neck and pulled his mouth to hers. This time she kissed him for all she was worth. The gearshift column kept her from moving closer to him. She could only let her mouth say what her body wanted to convey.

"I know the timing is wrong." Averal lifted his mouth. He kissed her eyes. "You have to go in."

"I don't want to," she said in a hoarse whisper. "I want to go with you."

His laugh was guttural. "How long have I waited to hear you say that. Now I have to be the sensible one." He kissed her again lightly and opened the car door. Never slumped back against the upholstery. Averal came around and opened the door for her. She took his offered hand and stood up, wrapping her arms around his neck and taking his mouth. She rubbed her body against his, feeling his arousal and knowing how much her own body craved release.

She kissed him until she was weak.

"Averal?"

"Shhh . . ." he said. He turned her around and led her to the door. "Good night, sweetheart."

He kissed her one more time and then pushed her through the door. Back in his car he sat for a moment. He liked her boys, but why did they have to be here tonight?

Then he started the engine and drove home, knowing he wouldn't be able to sleep.

She missed him. Averal's next assignment required him to spend time at the Cedar Chemicals site in upstate New York. Averal called her most nights. She pushed any thought of the situation at the office away to be with him, but her return to work and the sadness that had become as visible as storm clouds was there to greet her. Day after day Never would come into her office, automatically checking the office at the end of the hall. Averal wasn't there and would not return, yet she couldn't stop herself from looking. He'd finished his stay in her department. All that was needed now was his report. The atmosphere changed decidedly after his departure. Morale had been low before, but now its depth was below sea level.

Several people had given notice this week that they'd found other employment and would be gone in a matter of weeks. Others waited for the axe to fall.

Never felt torn. She was in love with the man who would put them all out of work. She hadn't seen Averal since the night of the party, the night she'd made a fool of herself and told him how much she wanted him, told him she wanted to go to his house and make love to him.

Where had her sensibilities been? It was the wedding, she rationalized—her grandparents getting married and the reception. Them dancing all night and kissing in her driveway. What had she said? What would she have done if her nephews hadn't been in the house?

She'd gone in. They'd made popcorn, and everyone had changed into jeans and sweatshirts. Videos were playing and everyone was talking. Never had stepped inside and smiled at them, then gone to bed. Most of the night she'd lain awake, wanting Averal to be there with her. The noise of conversation coming from below hadn't bothered her since she couldn't sleep, anyway.

Now her nephews were back at school, and she had returned to the routine of work. Her concentration had been off for the entire week. She'd taken today off to go to New York for a second interview. This time she didn't see BriAnne Ball at the small shop, but got on the train and returned to Princeton.

At Nassau Street she thought of this point a week ago, and how much her life had changed since that time. Today she didn't argue with herself about turning right or left. She turned right, passing Palmer Square and making a left on Witherspoon Street. Within minutes the restaurant came into view. Never wasn't in the habit of going into bars alone, but tonight she didn't care. She wanted to see Averal, and this was one place she knew he might be. She pulled the door open and stepped inside. The place was crowded, and the band was in place and playing.

She found Averal without any effort. His saxophone was raised to his mouth, and he was blowing out the tune. For a moment she stood in the shadows staring at him. Heat elevated her temperature, and she wanted him to hold her, kiss her, make love to her. She was in love with him. She loved everything about him, the way he looked at her, the funny cleft in his chin, the way she felt when he held her, the explosion that took place in her heart when he kissed her.

Averal didn't see her, but Riddles did. He came to her, greeting her with genuine pleasure and a smile that made his ebony eyes twinkle like dark stars. He took her arm. At the end of the bar was an empty stool. He helped her onto it, and signaled to the bartender.

A white wine appeared in front of her. Riddles smiled and worked his magical fingers. She smiled, but didn't understand anything.

"He said he's glad to see you again."

Never looked across the bar. The voice had come from a woman with dark red hair that had been braided into what seemed to be hundreds of small braids. The ends curled under. She was Never's height with clear, brown skin the color of cherry wood and the most unusually bright eyes Never had ever seen.

"I'm Vivette Brooks. I help Riddles occasionally."

Never offered her hand. "Never Kincaid."

"Averal has said nice things about you." She tossed her head toward the bandstand.

She wondered what he'd said. Never took a sip of the wine. "Averal said you asked for me." She spoke to Riddles. She watched his hands, but what he said was gibberish to her.

"He missed you, and Averal missed you," she interpreted. "He heard you were too busy to come in."

Never cast a glance at the bandstand. Averal had missed her. Her spirits soared, her decision to come to the bar sanctioned. "Most of my meetings these days last into the night. When they're over, I go home or do a little Christmas shopping."

Never looked to Vivette when Riddles finished speaking. "He says Thanksgiving is still two weeks away. You should wait and be frantic with the other shoppers on Christmas Eve."

Never laughed. "I suppose he does that."

Vivette nodded. "She's got your number, Riddles."

"I couldn't do that. I need plenty of time to shop and decide. On Christmas Eve I just like to stay home and build a big fire."

"I understand," Vivette said. "I want to be finished by then, too, but I'm usually still running around trying to decide what to buy."

"Excuse me, do you think a guy could get a drink here?" Averal stood behind them, a big smile on his face. Never's heart started to pound. "Hi," he said, looking directly at her.

"Hi," she whispered. For a moment they were alone. Never saw no one but him.

Vivette left and came back with Averal's drink. When she placed it on the bar she and Riddles left them.

"I've heard how things are in the office."

"We've had better days. We're all expecting your report soon." He took the stool next to her, but said nothing about the report. "Don't worry, I'm not going to ask you what's in it." She covered her embarrassment by lifting her wine to her mouth. "I won't mention it again."

Never ears were burning hot. She went back to her conversation with Vivette. "Vivette tells me you say nice things about me." She was pleased he'd thought of her when she wasn't around. She'd done nothing but think about him. Had he done the same?

The booth they'd sat in before emptied out. Averal asked if she wanted to sit there. He slid into the booth behind her. Her legs brushed his. An electric shock jolted her. "Did I hear you say you'd been Christmas shopping?" he asked.

She shook her head. "We were talking about it."

"It's not even Thanksgiving yet."

"Thanksgiving rushes up so quickly, and with preparing dinner and getting around college students in the house I don't have time to do anything until December. But this year I should be able to make great strides long before the holiday."

"Why is that?"

"No college students. They're going skiing, and won't be home for the holiday. So I don't have to plan a meal or wash mounds of dirty socks." Never's voice was jovial, but she really liked the hassle of having her nephews and their friends home for the holiday. She liked the big meals and football games all day, and not being able to have a free moment until they left Sunday night.

"Does that mean you're free to have dinner with me?"

"I wasn't fishing for an invitation and you're not free for dinner," she told him, coming out of her dream.

His eyebrows went up. "I'm not?"

"No." She shook her head.

"Where am I going?"

"To your sister's."

"Now how did you know that?" He cocked his head as if she could read his mind.

"The night we ate at your office. I saw a note sticking out of a pen on your desk." She closed her eyes. "It said, Thanksgiving Dinner, three P.M." She opened them. "And I believe your sister's name is . . ." Her eyes closed again, as if she could read the neural impulses on her brain. "Caroline."

"Caroline is my half sister. I'd forgotten it was there."

"You forgot where you're having Thanksgiving dinner?" Never sounded as if forgetting was unforgivable.

"No, I forgot the note was there." He hadn't given Caroline's call a thought. And it wasn't his intention to have dinner with her until he discovered Never would be free. "I'll call Caroline. She loves having a lot of people over for the holiday. I'm sure she'll have no problem with you joining us."

"You're not inviting me because you think I'll be home alone?" Never had at least a score of cousins she could spend the holiday with.

"I'm inviting you because I can't think of anyone I'd rather spend Thanksgiving with."

She couldn't think of anyone she'd rather spend the day with, either. "What about BriAnne?"

"Anne spends Thanksgiving in New York. She has friends there." There was that note of sarcasm again.

Never didn't think she'd be able to speak over the beating of her heart. "Are you sure your sister won't mind?"

"I think she'll be thrilled, but there is one thing I should tell you."

Never waited.

"She lives in Northern Virginia, just outside of Washington, D.C."

Never hesitated for a long second. She wondered if Averal

thought she would refuse because he was actually asking her to go away for the weekend. She'd told him she wanted to go home with him. Why would a weekend make a difference? "I guess I should pack a bag," she said, beaming.

He nodded. "Would you wear your hair down?"

"Men certainly like women's hair."

"Can't you tell I'm having a hard time keeping my hands out of yours?" He leaned toward her, his hands going for the tight knot at the back of her head.

"What happens when it's loose? Will it be more of an effort?" She stilled his exploring fingers.

"It's always an effort to keep my hands off you."

Never was suddenly hot, and her throat was dry. She looked away and happened to see the guitar player trying to get Averal's attention. "I think it's time for you to play again."

He looked around and signaled, one hand still in her hair. "Promise me you won't leave before I get back?"

"I promise." She paused. "I came here straight from the train. I thought you'd give me a ride home."

"No problem." He stood up, and before leaving he asked, "Any special requests?"

All the love songs came to mind. Never looked deep into his eyes. She knew several messages were in hers, but she couldn't read anything in his. She shook her head, knowing anything she said would have a double meaning.

NINE

The Township of Princeton, renamed for the Prince of Orange-Nassau in 1724, was established in 1681 when Captain Henry Greenland built his plantation. The Quakers first settled the land in 1696, when it was known as Stony Brook. George Washington quartered his troops there shortly before the turning point of the Revolutionary War, when he crossed the Delaware River, only fifteen miles away. It even served temporarily as the headquarters of the Continental Congress, in the summer and fall of 1783.

The houses in the seventeen mile tract were of mansion proportion, and predate the 1777 Battle of Princeton, when Washington defeated the British.

Never lived in a blue Victorian house at the end of Library Place. Averal drove there when they left the bar. Her car sat in the driveway.

"Why do you have PLAY GAMES on your license tag?"

Never's smile was mischievous. "I'll show you."

She opened the car door and jumped down from the high seat. Inside her foyer she switched on the light and took her coat off. Averal followed her and handed her his coat to hang in the closet.

"Come on," she said, moving through the living-room and kitchen, turning on lights as she went. The house had a center hall with a living room on one side and dining room on the other. At the end of the kitchen she opened a door. Down a

flight of stairs, Averal found himself in a room with a large
screen television and several sofas. There was a stereo rack
against one wall with a bookcase of CD's next to it. At the other
end of the room was a bar. This was obviously where she relaxed. What struck him was the color scheme. As he'd passed
the two rooms on the upper floor, he expected to find Never
Kincaid had fixed her life with shades of black and white. What
he saw was a living room of green and white, and a kitchen
done in a subtle yellow. The basement furniture was a beige
and rose floral.

Never was opening yet another door. This one led to a game
room. In its center was a huge pool table. Over it hung a Tiffany
lamp almost as large as the green felt table. But what dominated
the room were the video machines that lined the walls. She had
her own arcade.

"How did you get all these?"

"My grandfather owned an amusement gallery at Asbury
Park. When he retired he gave me the machines for my nephews."

She went over to a pinball machine that must have been an
antique. "I must admit," she continued. "I was as fascinated as
the boys were. Before he retired we used to go to the beach
every chance we got because he'd let us play for free."

"That must have been where you first started to like the
games."

Never turned to the machine she stood in front of. "On this
machine I've logged hundreds of hours." She pulled the button,
and one silver ball started up the track. Pushing the side buttons
to make it hit the markers, she racked up thousands of points
before the final ball slipped through the wings and disappeared
down the hole.

"Would you like to try?" Her face glowed when she looked
at him. Averal could tell she was at her best in this place.

Averal stepped up to the machine. "I used to be very good
at these when I was in college." He pulled the lever and a ball
went up the track. Never watched his concentration. He was

good. She liked the way he went to the task, giving it his full attention and trying to better her score. She watched him rather than his game. She loved just having him there. The week they'd been apart felt like a year.

His second ball started. The points he attained were good and earned him a free game, but they were nowhere near the record she held. Stephen and Donald were gaining on her, but she outdistanced Averal with ease.

"My nephews like the video games better than pinball." She moved to a car-like machine with a hooded seat. Never got in and took the steering wheel. She switched the button, and a raceway appeared on the tiny screen. As the engines revved she applied pressure to the accelerator and started the course.

"You're very good," Averal praised, squatting down to get a better view.

"It's all a matter of practice." Averal could see that. Her eyes didn't leave the screen. She mastered the obstacles as if the wheel in her hand was an extension of her arm. "Your turn," she told him.

Averal didn't give her time to get out, but climbed into the small seat beside her. Never was pinned against the wall, her head brushing the ceiling. Emotion paralyzed her. She couldn't turn in either direction. And her hands had nowhere to go that didn't touch the man beside her. Averal slipped his arm around her waist and shifted her in front of him, between his legs. His arms cradled her as he took the wheel. She felt his legs spanning the length of hers as he reached for the pedal control.

Never sat rigidly still. Averal's breath stirred her as it fanned the sensitive skin at the back of her neck. Her lungs deflated and refused to fill. Weights seemed to hold her arms down.

When the cars appeared on the screen she was too distracted by sensation to see them. Averal's hands on the steering wheel made his arms brush against her breasts, which hardened to the touch. The air was too low in the tiny cavity. She gasped to fill her lungs. Averal stopped trying to steer the simulated cars on the viewer. Instead, his hands closed around her upper arms, and his mouth brushed the erotic spot near her ear.

Never shuddered at his touch. Her head fell back against his shoulder as a soft purr escaped her throat.

When he swung her around to face him she was as pliant as putty. Her knees were on the floor now and her eyes level with his throat. She watched his Adam's apple bob up and down, and she knew his reaction was equal to her own.

His hand came under her chin and she lifted her eyes to meet his. In the semidarkness of the video machine she heard the game cars crashing into signposts and veering off into the embankment, but she could say nothing. Averal's mouth was moving toward hers in a manner that said speech was unnecessary. His mouth was soft on hers, persuasive, teasing. He tempered their touch slightly, allowing his lips to feather hers, as if to fully kiss her he'd pull down barriers that couldn't be erected again. But when her arms slid up his and circled his neck, he crushed her against him. His tongue plunged into her mouth, and he dragged her to him in a kiss so hot it could melt diamonds.

Never was newly in love, and the floodgates of emotion were crashed by the force of outpouring passion. The seat was a barrier to her fully reaching him, but she could feel the heat they created. It was intense, as much out of control as the unseen graphical images exploding behind her. The miniature enclosure seemed to shrink around them. Burning in the flames of passion, their bodies erupted in a thousand explosive lights. Her hands stroked his hair as her long nails caressed the tips of his ears. She was rewarded with the sound of raging passion. His mouth fused with hers, each joining the other in a tango of tongues, lips, and teeth.

His hands traveled up her body until they came to rest on her already taut breasts. She was dying of the heat, wanting desperately for him to loosen her blouse or remove her jacket, but his hands had designs of their own. With open palms he rubbed the sensitized skin of her nipples until they threatened to break the bounds of her lacy B-cups. Never thought she would scream.

Averal left her mouth to cover her face and neck with wet, sweet kisses. Her blouse with its tight bow tie prevented him from reaching her hot skin. His hands came up as his mouth reclaimed hers. Pins fell to the floor with a quiet tap, and her hair tumbled in long curls over her shoulders and down her back. The tie was the next to be released, and then her blouse was open and his hands were inside. She arched toward his touch, wanting the feel of him, wanting him to go further and further until every part of her body had been touched. His hands were wonderful, like a musician's, skillfully playing her, giving her pleasure. They moved with the slowness of time passing. Never's body was like soft wax in the hands of a master craftsman. She moaned under his tutelage, straining to defy the physical obstruction preventing her from merging her body completely with his.

Driving his hands deep into her hair, he lifted her face again and covered her mouth. A low sigh escaped her. She felt the snap in Averal. Caution and control were lost in the brilliant light that burst around them. Averal's mouth ravished hers with a hunger so deep it reached her soul. Wildly they rocked the video car, its confines too close, the heat too intense. Never was dissolving in her suit. She had to get out of it if she had to tear it apart. Averal helped her, pushing her back against the steering wheel and freeing her arms of the offending fabric.

When his hands took the place of the silk they were like fire searing her skin. He released the catch on her bra, and his head dipped to take one of her nipples into his mouth. A tiny scream shattered the quiet as sensation rocked through her like bolts of lightning.

"Never, we've got to get out of here." Averal's breath was hot and ragged as he raised his head to move from one breast and pay homage to the other. She pressed herself to him, her fingers raking through his hair and her tongue making tiny circles in his ears. He groaned with pleasure and squeezed her closer to him.

Averal scooped her up and pushed her backward through the tiny car door. He followed her. Never sat on the floor. Taking her hands, he pulled her up the length of him and looked deeply into her eyes. They were dark with desire and a primal hunger.

He didn't speak, but took possession of either side of her face, taking in her hair with his caress. Dark eyes filled with emotion stared at her. She could feel every inch of his hard body pressed into hers. Her hands found the buttons on his shirt and one by one she freed them from the security of the buttonholes. His jacket and shirt crumpled in a heap at his feet.

Without a word Averal lifted her into his arms and, passing the pool table and video machines, made his way to the stairs. Never didn't say a word or give directions. She was captivated by him. With a sixth sense he found her bedroom and went in. With the slowness of sustained pleasure, he let her slide down his frame. His body was hard compared to the softness of hers. Her breasts pressed into him as his head moved down again. Their mouths met and worked a frenzied dance.

Never didn't remember what happened to the rest of their clothes. They seemed to burn away like distant memories. Moonlight draped them in naked wonder as each took in the beauty of the other. She reached for him. Her hands met his chest, moist and warm, his heart pounding against her hand. Her hands slid over his male nipples, making them erect pebbles to her fingertips. She continued to sculpt his body, outlining the contours of his strong chest and shoulders until she reached his neck. Then, pulling his head to hers, she closed the step between them and allowed the heat of his hardness to press into her flesh. Their mouths melded like liquid metal.

Averal's hands spanned her waist. He pushed her back to the bed. Softly it gave under their combined weight. He spread her hair over the satin comforter, his eyes watching the silken threads as if he had never seen anything as beautiful as the dark strands he fashioned about her head. Then, in a flash of movement his body covered hers. Never couldn't stop the purring sounds of pleasure that thrust forward at the feel of him against her.

When she expected Averal to enter her body he lowered his head and kissed her with a reverence that brought tears to her eyes. Releasing her mouth, he covered her body with slow, drugging kisses that had her moaning and purring like a loving kitten. The trip was a road map of her erogenous zones. At her feet, he took one in both hands, lightly massaging it as if it were the focal point of all passion in her lithe body.

She didn't know how she survived the frantic emotions that gripped her body with a longing that must be assuaged. He replaced his hands with his mouth. Never jerked with sensations as his lips moved against her feet. He retraced his steps back to her mouth, covering her inch by hedonistic inch with his warm body.

"Averal." Never's voice was unrecognizable, filled with passion.

"Now," he said. She heard the opening of cellophane and felt his hands between them as he slipped protection on himself. Even that movement was erotic as his knuckles brushed against points straining for fulfillment.

Averal filled her easily, yet she shivered with the newness of him. The primeval rhythm between them began slowly, but quickly flared out of control. Never hadn't thought she could let herself go as she was doing now, but she couldn't stop the feelings that raged within her and pushed her to complement the movements of Averal's athletic frame.

His hands reached under her, lifting her buttocks and plunging deep into her. Never cried out with each stroke, lost in the pleasure they created in each other, and wanting it to go on and on and on. Waves of heat crested over her, burning her in its desire to please, to be pleased, making her fight to prolong the ecstasy. They balanced there—at the top of the peak. Never felt her stomach harden. The uncontrollable urge to scream began deep within her, and no amount of fighting would keep it from breaking forth.

At the pinnacle of fevered rapture she cried Averal's name. He climaxed at the same time, calling hers over and over.

She finally knew what it meant to make love. It was all-consuming. She fell limply back to earth, wet with the sweet sweat of their combined bodies. She wanted nothing more than to die there now.

Weak arms slid over Averal's back and brought his head up for her to kiss. His eyes were slits of satisfied desire, and Never held him tighter. His arms gathered her and he kissed her eyes, nose, and mouth. Then he slid to her side, pulling her with him, fitting her back into him and drifting off to sleep.

A smile curved Never's lips, and she closed her eyes.

"Averal." He stirred, pulling the pillow further under his head. Memory of the night before flooded his mind, and his body instantly began to harden. He reached for Never, but his arms closed around her pillow. "Averal," he heard her say. Opening his eyes he found he was alone in the king-size bed. The sheets were rumpled, and torn from their usual tucked-in state as if there had been a fight. Dragging the pillow closer, he breathed in her essence—Passion perfume mixed with a clean smell that was all Never.

"I didn't want to wake you." He squinted, looking for her, but the room was empty. "You looked so like a little boy sleeping. I couldn't."

Averal turned over, hoping to find her behind him, standing in the light of the sun with her hair down and her body clothed in a sheer nightgown. A gown that would soon be on the floor.

But she wasn't there.

"I have an early appointment, but there's a pot of coffee in the kitchen." He traced the sound to an audio cassette in the clock radio.

"Damn," he cursed, falling back on the bed in frustration.

"I won't be in the office today, but I am looking forward to dinner tonight. I'll see you at seven."

There was a pause, and Averal turned over to shut the machine off. He had to find the button for the alarm. Just before he pushed it she spoke again.

"Averal." She paused. "I had a wonderful time last night."

All the muscles in his body collapsed and he fell back onto the bed again. A Chopin nocturne began to play, and Averal lay there listening to it. When it ended he switched off the machine. Last night had been more than wonderful. It had been like balancing on a live wire in a thunderstorm. Frantic particles of electricity had flown about him, making him dance in the exotic light of passion. It was dangerous and exciting.

Never had found the well within him and filled it, temporarily. He wanted her more now than he had last night. He wanted her forever.

Where the hell was she? He kicked the sheet aside and sat up, dragging the pillow with him. Why did she leave him to wake up alone? Didn't she know he wanted to wake slowly with her in his arms, so he could make love to her all over again? Muscles knotted in his stomach, the beginning of an erection. How was he going to survive? Just thinking about her could make his body hard.

She wouldn't be in today, the tape had said. He wanted to see her, hold her, make violent love, go back to that place of supreme pleasure where she'd taken him last night. What damn appointment could be more important than that?

Frustrated fists beat at the pillow. Then, getting up, he left the bed and took a cold shower. He wrapped one of the huge pink towels around his middle and thought of the coffee in the kitchen. Leaving the bathroom, he stopped cold as he saw a painting. Hanging on the wall next to the door was *The Edge*. She owned it. Why hadn't she told him?

He stepped closer to it, as if drawn. He touched the paint. Gabe and Anne headed for the water. He knew it was his brother. Averal had always been tall. Even at twelve he was taller than his mother. And Gabe was shorter. The child in the painting was shorter than the woman. Averal wasn't even part of the scenery. Not even in those days had she thought of him as her son.

Yet somehow he no longer hated that painting. At twelve, when she'd sold it, he was glad to see it go, hoping she would finally begin to remember he was alive.

"But you didn't," he told the woman on the beach.

Turning abruptly, he headed for the kitchen, pushing Gabe and Anne to the back of his mind.

Everything was orderly. There were no appliances on the counters except the coffeemaker, which appeared to have been placed there this morning. Averal found a cup behind the first cabinet he opened. The coffee was good. He drank it looking out over the wooded backyard, wondering where Never was and if she was thinking of him. Pouring himself a second cup, he took it back to the bedroom.

Never was neat. The only thing that looked out of place was the unmade bed. Even his clothes, which had been discarded in the game room, were neatly folded on a chair in the corner. Suddenly he remembered that her office looked the same—everything in its place.

Setting his cup on the dresser, he threw her closet doors open. First one and then the other mirrored door gave way in his hands. It was as he expected. Slacks all in one place, skirts and suits together, blouses hung with care. Even her shoes stood at attention. And no color stood out, different from the next. The red shoes were missing. Where were they, he wondered.

"Never, you need a little chaos in your life." He spoke to her clothes. Then, picking up the phone, he dialed a familiar Princeton number. "Chaos, and color."

"Game, set, and match," Never called to Mark. A wide smile made her face glow.

"What's happened to you?" Mark asked. "You're certainly not the same woman I've been playing with for the past month."

She wasn't. This Never was in love. This Never had spent the night making love to Averal Ballentine. This Never didn't have her feet on the ground. She was up in the clouds somewhere—the place where lovers live, and where nothing is ever wrong.

"I took your advice, Mark, and stopped letting the merger dominate my life," she finally answered.

"Well, maybe next time I'll keep my mouth shut." They both laughed and headed for the showers.

Never had a lot to do today. She was glad she'd taken the day off. Initially, she'd planned to go up to the Poconos, but after meeting BriAnne in New York she would have had to postpone that until after they had their Saturday morning photo session. But now, after last night, she wasn't going at all. She was going to spend every moment with Averal.

Waking up against him had been heaven. His legs were tangled with hers, and his body covered her with a heavy warmth. His breath caused a gentle stir in her hair. Each time she shifted he'd gathered her closer. Even in sleep he'd wanted her close to him.

She had her arms draped over him and her head pillowed against his chest. His strong heart beat in her ear, and she'd remembered the ageless rhythms of the night before. Wild fire raced to her loins, and she wanted him again.

It had been inhuman to leave him, but she had to meet Mark for tennis. There was no way of reaching him on such short notice, and they were committed to a game each morning. Through Mark's divorce and his daughter's surgery he had come to every game. How could she not show up because she'd fallen in love? Averal would understand.

Never took longer showering and dressing this morning. Since she didn't have to go to work, there was no hurry. She had to go to the post office and have her hair done, and she thought she might buy a new dress for tonight. A red one.

When she emerged from the Princeton Racquet Club she had just enough time to make her appointment at the beauty shop. She'd told Michael tonight was very special, and she needed a style that would allow her hair to be free. Michael worked magic. When she'd left her hair had been a sculpture of curls that ringed her face. The sides were swept up and held by two silver combs and the back spilled over her shoulders.

Michael had insisted that as long as she was in the chair she let his wife, Karen, do her makeup and give her a manicure. Never felt beautiful when she left.

At her car she discovered she'd left one of the packages she intended to mail at home. It wasn't far. She decided to drop by her house and pick it up before going shopping for her dress.

Averal's jeep was gone, and a sad tug pulled at her heart. She knew he had to work, but it would have been nice to find him there when she returned. She pulled into the garage and went in through the kitchen. There was a note propped up against the coffeepot.

> *The coffee was good. Last night was incredible.*
> *Averal*

His signature was a flourish. A warm glow covered her when she had thoughts of last night. For a moment she let her thoughts run headlong. Her body began to feel cocooned in a heated glow.

Pushing her thoughts back to task, she rushed into the library—a room filled with books and computers and game machines—and picked up the package. *What could it hurt?* she asked herself. The most they could do is reject the game. Then she'd have proof her work wasn't marketable, and all argument about them would cease.

She had to admit she was a little bit excited. Suppose someone liked it? She pushed that thought out of her mind. She'd go to the post office and send them off before the analytical side of her mind talked her out of mailing it.

She was nearly out the door before she remembered the bedroom. Averal was still in the bed when she left. She had to clean the room.

Never was surprised to find the bed made, and more surprised to find a dozen, long-stemmed roses in a vase on the night stand next to the radio. She pulled the card free of the small envelope. It read,

> *You've added color to my life.*
> *Averal*

She read it again. He didn't know what he'd added to her life. She'd go to Jessie's. Jessie would have the exact dress for her. Her only condition was it had to be red.

Never was dressed and waiting when Averal arrived. The wide shoulders of the dress stood up like a queen's. She'd felt like royalty when she slipped the dress over her head and pulled the zipper. Jewels glittered from her neckline to her waistline, and then the fabric fell in a smooth line to her knees. The only addition needed was a pair of dangling ruby earrings that would brush her bare shoulders.

She turned full circle when he came in, modeling the outfit she'd spent hours finding.

"You look great in red," he said. "I knew you would."

He looked great, too. Never was used to him taking her breath away, but tonight his clothes, a black suit with a white shirt, didn't bowl her over nearly as much as the look in his eyes, the passion and love she saw when she looked at him.

"Don't you think I'll be a little overdressed for Riddles Place?" she asked when her heart would let her talk.

"Extremely overdressed," he agreed. "We're not going there." Looking at her, he didn't want to go out. He wanted to take her upstairs to that large bed they'd occupied last night. She was having her usual effect on his body. He wanted to take her in his arms and devour her mouth, push his fingers into her hair and peel that dress off and taste her body, square by delicious square.

"Where are we going?" Never asked when she'd been installed in a sleek black Jaguar and Averal was backing it down the driveway.

"Philadelphia." He angled the car toward Route 295, and thirty minutes later he handed the keys to a uniformed valet and helped her into Bookbinders.

Never noted the regal red and rich purple of the decor. The place was set up for royalty, and tonight she felt royal. They were shown to a quiet table in the corner and her feet placed on a cushion.

"Pinch me," she asked.

"Why?"

"This is a dream, and I'm going to wake up and find my prince has turned into a frog."

Averal laughed and gave a slight twist to the skin on her arm. "It's no dream." He couldn't stand it if this wasn't really happening to him. Over the candlelight Never's eyes sparkled with the same faceted brilliance of the jewels in her dress. He loved her. This was the woman he'd been waiting for. One he could easily spend his life with. The one he wanted to keep with him and share everything. Even his secret about Gabe. Thank God it was no dream.

The wine steward came, bringing the champagne he'd arranged for earlier. The black-coated sommelier poured the sparkling wine and allowed Averal to taste it. At his nod, he filled Never's glass. With the flourish of a knight courting his lady the tuxedo-clad waiter handed her an oversized menu—Averal thought he could serve any castle and any queen. Tonight he had his queen, and he wanted everything to be perfect for her.

He watched her over the top of his own menu. Only her eyes showed. She had gorgeous eyes, dark brown with shades of eyeshadow that blended from a soft red to light brown. Her hair bounced each time she moved her head, and for the life of him he could barely control the urge to plunge his hands in it.

She looked up, her eyes smiled, and she went back to studying the menu. The waiter returned as if on cue. As soon as they lowered the menus he was there to take their order.

"You know I know very little about you," Averal began after the waiter left with her order of crab imperial and his of lobster thermidor.

"Well." She set her chin on the heel of her hand. "I'm married. This is my sixth or seventh husband. I can't remember which. I have three children whom I feed bread and water and hide in the attic. My religion is devil worshipping, and under a full moon I grow fangs and hair on my chest."

Averal laughed. She could be so delightful when she wanted to be. It was sheer pleasure just to be in her company.

"Don't laugh." She acted affronted, sitting back in her chair and assuming her queenly attitude. "Let's see," she said with the precise control and order she was known for, "you know where I work, what I do, where I live and . . ." She stopped, then continued. "I think you know a lot about me."

"What was the *and?*" he prompted.

Never hesitated. She'd wanted to add that he knew what she was like in bed, but was too embarrassed to say it. Averal did make her lose her inhibitions, but that was too racy for her.

"Is that a question you're not going to answer?"

"Not today," she decided.

"But someday, maybe?"

"Maybe." She gave him an impish grin.

"What's your favorite color?" He changed the subject appearing to accept her decision.

She looked down at her dress and said, "Red."

He was sure she'd say black and white. "You remind me of a Christmas tree. All dressed in red with decorations all over you."

"I don't know if I like being compared to a tree, decorated or not."

"It was meant as a compliment." He bowed his head like one of the waiters.

"Thank you. Compliment accepted."

Averal took a sip of his drink. "You don't know how to accept a gift, do you?"

"Of course I do."

"Suppose I gave you a gift?"

He could see her stiffen. "Perfume and scarves are acceptable."

"Not dressing a woman from head to toe?"

She shook her head. "Very bad form."

"What would you do if I sent you a dress like that?"

"Return it."

"It's bad manners to return a gift. Especially one that fits in all the right places, makes you look like a queen, enhances your beauty, and shouldn't be worn by any other woman in the world."

Never glowed at his words.

"I'll bet no man has ever given you a gift."

"Don't be silly," she returned. "I've had plenty of gifts."

"Name one," he challenged.

"I got a set of wineglasses last Christmas from Sam Harris."

"Was that a grab bag gift?"

Never had to nod.

"Grab bags don't count."

"My nephews—"

He was already shaking his head. "Nephews are out."

"Martin gave me diamond earrings, and the jewels I had in my hair the night at the gallery."

He stiffened. "I thought you said gifts were perfume and scarves."

"I sent them back," she explained. "But they were gifts. Now, can we have a pleasant evening and not fight? I don't feel like fighting. I'm dressed like a crown princess." She tossed her head, repeating his words. "I'm out with an attractive man." She bowed to him. "And I believe the food's good here."

At that point the waiter returned with their salads. He lifted the napkin from her serving plate and with a snap opened it and placed it on her lap. Then he set the plates of greens in front of them with the flair of a ballet dancer.

"Which queen?" she asked, seemingly out of the blue.

Averal's brows went up. "Which queen do I remind you of?"

He cocked his head. "Queen Desirée," he offered with a smile.

"You're making that up. There is no Queen Desirée."

"Of course there is . . . or was. She was the wife of a French general. They emigrated to Sweden, and she became queen."

Never set her fork down and dazzled him with her smile. "You got that out of a Marlon Brando movie."

"There may have been a movie, but the story is true."

Never cut her eyes at him, retrieving her fork. "What did she look like . . . and don't tell me Jean Simmons."

"No. More like Wilhelmenia Fernandez."

"The opera singer? Star of *Diva?*"

Averal nodded.

Never knew of Wilhelmenia Fernandez. She was a beautiful woman, and had performed for some of the world's royalty. He couldn't possibly compare her to this sovereign of the operatic stage.

"You two have the same wine-dark complexion and expressive eyes. And with your hair styled like that you'd pass for her sister."

"I didn't know you were into opera, or is it women?"

"I happen to be acquainted with Wilhelmenia."

Never raised her glass and drank. "I am not surprised," she leaned forward and replaced the delicate fluted crystal on the table. "You seem to know someone everywhere." She remembered all the jobs he'd found for other people. She hadn't meant that as a reprimand. "I apologize. I didn't mean that the way it sounded. Where did you two meet?"

"In Paris. At the Opera House. She showed up at one of Anne's showings. She admires art and wanted to meet Anne. I introduced them. Whenever she's in the area I go to see her perform."

"I did notice her name in today's paper."

"I knew you'd be a quick study. I have tickets, four of them. Riddles and Vivette are taking two. I hoped you'd go with me."

"That's next Saturday, isn't it?"

He nodded confirmation.

"And the following week is Thanksgiving?"

He nodded again.

"Why do I have the feeling you're mounting a campaign?"

"Because I am, sweetheart."

That was the second time he'd called her sweetheart, and Never was thrown off kilter. The waiter arrived to take their empty plates away, and she had to wait for him to perform his ceremony before replying.

"What kind of campaign are you planning?"

"I intend to be part of all your waking hours, and if I'm lucky the sleeping ones, too."

He saluted her with his refilled glass. Heat stole up her neckline. She knew that if she were a fair-skinned person he'd be able to see the blush that ran wildly to her ears.

TEN

"Where are you going?" Averal grabbed her around the waist and pulled her naked body back against his. With one hand under her chin he turned her around to face him and covered her mouth with his. Never went slack in his arms and gave herself up to the longing that overtook her the moment his warm hands made contact with her body.

His mouth drugged her. "Let me go," she whispered. He responded by gathering her closer and raking his hands through the sleep-ravished curls that framed her face as he took her mouth in a soul-wrenching kiss. She needed him now! Just as she had needed him last night when they returned from the restaurant. . . .

Inside the door he'd taken her in his arms and they'd made a trail of clothes leading to her bedroom. Her dress rested on the stairs, discarded in a red heap by the grandfather clock that tolled one A.M. His hands slid up and down the silk pieces of underwear and connected with her skin, as smooth and soft as the transparent material.

By the time they had reached the bed the passion that gripped them was too intense to wait. Their lovemaking had been frenzied and fast. At the end Never was exhausted and sated. She felt as if she'd been on a long ride and finally reached the finish line.

Sleep came quickly for them. She woke cradled in his arms like a loving child. Trying to steal away, she roused him, and he wanted to continue where last night had ended. But this time he was pacing himself at great leisure. Open palms stroked her nipples, and she gasped as her pliant body acquiesced on a groan. She felt more than saw Averal smile.

"I love the way you do that," he said, open emotion unconcealed in his voice.

Never reached up and pulled his mouth back to hers. She turned her body into him as she ran her fingers over his smooth skin. Skin that reminded her of sunshine and spring. He smelled like soap and Obsession, and he had a taste all his own. Never's hands went over his shoulders and into his hair as he pulled her buttocks into contact with his libidinous pelvis. Anticipation and ecstasy made her cry out.

Averal quickly protected them and pulled her over him. She took control, impaling herself on his maleness and throwing her head back at the sensations that rocketed through her. Averal's hands came up and took her full breasts in them. They curved and swelled into his palms as if they'd been made for that purpose. Her nipples darkened even more as the timeless pulse of love began. Never wanted to give. She wanted her body to be the vessel that gave pleasure to him, more pleasure than any other woman had ever given. She wanted to be an indelible memory in his mind—one that brought a smile to his lips when he was without her, one whose body he couldn't wait to drink from.

She heard sounds, primitive sounds, animals noises that made her dance faster and harder. A drumbeat throbbed through her, setting a pace that drove her faster and faster. She kept up with it, dragging air into her lungs and fighting to maintain the spellbinding stronghold of mutual gratification that gripped them.

In the blinding light of consummation she collapsed against him. Her breath was as hard and ragged as his, and the blood beat in her ears with the pounding of ancient timpani that raced like a frenzied tribal seizure.

Averal reversed their positions and kissed her wet body. She was limp and weak. Her lids, at half-mast, told him how complete her surrender had been. He brushed the hair back from her face and tenderly kissed her lips.

"I don't think I'll be able to let you go." Averal's voice was hoarse with spent emotion. "What I did before you walked into my life, I don't know. Promise me you'll stay."

"I'll stay," she said on a breath. She didn't want to move. She was happy and content. The world couldn't bother her as long as she stayed here. Never snuggled against Averal, closing her eyes and positioning herself to draw on his strength. His arms held her caressingly. Lightly he massaged her, running his hand over her smooth skin.

She was drifting to sleep, her eyes heavy and languid. She blinked, pulling her head back to look at him.

"Oh my God!" She suddenly remembered. Never pushed him aside and dashed out of bed. "I'm going to be late," she threw over her shoulder, heading for the bathroom. She locked the door and turned on the shower.

There was no way she'd have time to put her hair up before she met BriAnne. Stuffing her mass of ringlets under a shower cap, she stepped under the water and quickly lathered herself with the lavender scented soap Donald had given her as a birthday present last July.

"Never." Averal knocked on the door. She knew if she hadn't locked it he would join her in the shower, and she wouldn't make her appointment with his mother. The water beat against her, and she couldn't make out what he was saying.

When she turned the taps off and wrapped herself in a towel, she heard him. "Unlock this door."

She pulled the door inward and passed him on her way to her dresser. He was wearing his slacks but his chest was bare. She snatched a bra, panties, and pantyhose from the drawers and went to the closet. Slipping the doors back on their sound-less hinges, she pulled a face at the absence of any color other than black and white.

"Why are you zooming around like a rocket out of control? Where are you going?"

She closed the closet and retraced her steps to the bathroom. "Princeton University," she answered, plugging in the cord of her electric curling iron. "I have an appointment there." Partially closing the door, she dropped the towel and ripped the shower cap from her head. Quickly she slipped into her underwear.

"Who's the appointment with?"

She opened the door its full measure. "Your mother," she returned, stopping briefly to take in his expression.

Averal went stark still. Only the muscles in his jaw worked feverishly. "You do know how to surprise a guy. I didn't know you'd been in touch with Anne since the night of the gallery opening." He was staring at the painting on the bedroom wall.

Never followed the direction of his gaze. "I met her in New York, last week. She's going to paint my portrait." At this, Never passed him again, going to the dresser. She lifted the nearly empty bottle of Passion and pushed her hair back to spray the perfume behind her ears. Walking in only her underwear and bare feet, she left the bedroom, Averal at her heels.

"Anne doesn't do portraits." He went to stand under the painting of the beach scene.

"Correction." She tossed her head, knowing he wanted to ask her about *The Edge*. Her hair bounced like a ball in a field of low gravity. *"Didn't* do portraits. Mine will be her first." She went into another bedroom and threw open the closet door. After rummaging for a few seconds she found what she was looking for—a purple suede skirt and jacket ensemble. She completed the outfit with a lavender blouse.

Averal watched her slip the blouse on and step into the skirt. He wanted to rip the clothes off her and take her again on the guest bed behind her. Its spread was so wrinkle-free that he was sure a quarter would bounce off it.

"Why didn't you tell me you owned the painting?"

"At the time I didn't think you needed to know." She gave him a direct stare.

"You seem to have become very chummy with Anne," he sneered.

"Why do you call your mother Anne?" She started for the master bedroom.

"It's her name. Before she became BriAnne Ball, she was just plain Anne Ballentine. What would you suggest I call her?" he asked following her.

"Mother would be nice." She stopped, turning to confront him. "Mom, Mama, and Mother Dear are all good terms for the woman who gave birth to you."

"We don't have that kind of relationship." He shrugged.

Never wanted to reply, but left him standing there and went through to her bedroom. She stepped on something. It was a cuff link. She picked it up and laid it on the night stand, then went into the bathroom. She draped the towel she'd left on the floor over the gold-tone rack. After testing the curling iron, she tried to repair her hair from Averal's finger combing. If there was one thing she knew about him, it was that he liked having his hands in her hair.

She checked the clock. There was no way she'd make it to the university by nine. It was three minutes to nine now, and she still had to make her bed. Never fixed the last of her curls and pulled the cord from the wall. The appliance had an automatic shutoff button, but she had a habit of unplugging and storing appliances.

Rushing back into the bedroom, she pulled the blue satin sheets from the bed and deposited them in the hallway chute that led to a hamper in the washroom. Taking fresh ones from the hall closet, she went back into the room. Averal, who hadn't returned to the bedroom, came up the steps and followed her.

"You have to have order, don't you?"

Never looked up as she dropped the clean sheets on a chair and threw the fitted sheet open to the air above the bed.

"You're going to be late for an appointment, yet you're taking time to make the bed." Averal had his shirt on, and was buttoning it up.

"This isn't about the bed. It's about me meeting your mother." She did like order, and she hated sleeping in an unmade bed. Of course, she wouldn't admit that to him. He'd begun to read her too well in the past few weeks.

"When did you two get together on this?"

"At Evan Dirkson's gallery. I ran into her and she asked me."

"You agreed."

"Averal." Never stopped her task and faced him. "If she weren't your mother, just a famous artist known the world over, and she asked you to sit for her, what would you say?"

"Is that your only reason?"

Why did he look so angry? "What does that mean?" She finished the bed and moved to lift a gold earring and push it through her pierced ear.

"You wouldn't have an ulterior motive, would you?"

Never was lost. She frowned at him, her hands dropping to her sides. "What are you talking about?"

"My mother didn't perhaps give you any family secrets, did she?" He sneered.

"All she did was ask me to model for her. And that's all I agreed to." She stared at him. Her gaze was steady and uncompromising.

"I apologize," Averal said at length. "I'll find my shoes and be gone." He turned on his heel and went to the door.

"Averal."

He stopped, but kept his back to her. She walked up behind him. She wanted to touch him, but he'd erected a wall between them.

"I don't want you to leave angry." Her voice was soft and low and sexy.

His head dropped and a moment passed before he faced her. "How can anybody stay angry with you?" he groaned, hauling her into his arms and covering her mouth with his. Never's mouth tangled with his in a kiss as demolishing as their lovemaking had been. Her hands climbed his biceps and briefly fondled his ears before clamping along the side of his head and deepening the kiss.

"I love you," Averal said when he finally came up for air. "I don't think I can live without you."

BriAnne stood in the arched entrance to Princeton University. Never's car screeched to a halt on the deserted main boulevard across from Palmer Square. She was fifteen minutes late. The century-old structure stood massive and majestic in its modern grandeur.

"Your hair," she greeted.

"I didn't have time to do it," she explained, not telling Bri-Anne it was her son who had kept her from being on time or getting her hair done. When she thought of what she'd done instead of her hair, she had no regrets.

"It looks wonderful," BriAnne complemented.

For several hours the tireless woman posed her and photographed her before the student union, under the gabled arch at the head of Witherspoon Street, by the fountain near the Woodrow Wilson School of Public Policy. Never lost count of the number of times BriAnne changed film.

"Are you tired, Never?" she finally asked as the noon hour rang out from the seminary school cathedral not far from the university.

"I can go on if you want to." She was tired. Modeling was fun at first, but smiling so much was like interviewing all day. After a couple of hours her face muscles wanted to fall, and she had to force them to stay up. Also, she was tired of everyone passing by stopping to stare as if she were a zoo animal. The young men smiled appreciatively, some even flirted. The women looked envious, or shocked that she was there. Others whispered to each other, making her paranoid about what they were saying.

"I think this will be enough. I'll go to my lab and develop this." She indicated the camera bag hanging on her shoulder.

"Tomorrow we can look at the pictures and begin deciding what we want to paint."

"What about my hair? I thought you were intent on the Nefertiti style."

"I was, but that was before I saw you this way. All those ringlets are a challenge." Never could see the excitement in her eyes. "I still want to try the style."

"I can do it for tomorrow," Never volunteered, feeling guilty that she'd forgotten about the appointment and been late.

"I like this look, too. It's more contemporary. What do you think?"

"I take it this is a collaboration." There was a smile in Never's voice.

"Definitely. Remember, this is new ground for both of us." BriAnne delighted her with a beautiful smile. She had straight, even teeth, and as always, was impeccably dressed—in green corduroy slacks and a white turtleneck sweater. Instead of a coat she wore a sleeveless deerskin jacket that left her arms free to focus the camera. "Never, would you like to go to the studio and see the development?"

The question seemed to spark an idea in BriAnne, and Never was intrigued. In minutes they were inside Never's car. BriAnne's studio was an upstairs apartment on Spring Street. The building sat even with the row of other buildings on the street, but it was higher than those around it. The inside structure had been converted to windows, and light poured in from every angle.

"Tea?" BriAnne offered.

"Please," she answered, hugging herself. The November wind had pierced her, but several times she'd discarded her coat so BriAnne could get a full-length shot.

There was a small kitchen area. Placed close to it was a square rug with a sofa and two chair combination. Never took a seat in one of the wing-back chairs while BriAnne put the kettle on.

"It'll be ready in no time," she said, coming back to set a tray of pastries on the low table between them. "I'm afraid my years abroad have made me develop a love for the English and their tea time, although I prefer croissants to biscuits."

Never smiled. Averal came back to her, and his anger when she told him her appointment was with his mother. What kind of family secret could he have, and why did he think BriAnne would have told *her* about it?

"Have you been here long?" Never asked, admiring the studio.

"Since permanently returning to the United States. That was about two years ago. For the most part I've been cloistered here, or up in the mountains painting."

"The show was a huge success," Never told her. "For your next one, are you going to have more portraits?"

"I'm not sure. I told my agent about the idea, and he was ecstatic over it."

Never looked pleased.

"He's ecstatic over everything," BriAnne explained. "I think he's been with me too long. But I have hopes for your portrait. If it's a success I'll do others, or at least add people to the landscapes."

The teakettle began to sing and BriAnne left to brew the English Breakfast mixture. She brought a tray back with more sandwiches than the two of them could eat.

"You must be hungry." BriAnne set the heavy silver tray down and went back for the tea. Then she settled herself in front of the low table and poured the tea.

Never chose a tuna sandwich and liberally added a pasta salad and potato chips to the small plate BriAnne had included.

When they had finished eating and were through with their second cups of tea, BriAnne said, "Grab that," indicating the petit fours. She led Never into a darkroom. Setting her tea tray down, she switched on a light. "Place it there." She indicated a cleared space next to the pot of tea. "We don't need absolute darkness except to transfer the film. You'll be able to see."

BriAnne left to get the camera bag and closed the door on

her return. Never poured two cups of tea and added sugar and cream.

She watched attentively as BriAnne set up the developer chemicals and water baths for the process. When everything was ready she told Never to take a seat.

"It will be absolutely dark when I turn this light off. You're apt to become disoriented, and when you can't see it's difficult to keep your balance."

Never knew that. It had been something she discovered during her pledging days at Howard University. Putting pledges in absolute darkness and letting them flounder was something the sorority sisters had found funny. Only now did she find a practical use for the exercise. Never sat down.

The lights were doused and the room plunged into darkness. Not even a sliver of light filtered into the room. Never heard the film cartridges being opened and slipped into something she couldn't identify.

"It won't be much longer," BriAnne said at length. "It just seems long because you're sitting in total darkness."

"I'm fine," Never commented. "Have you always painted this way?"

"What way is that?"

"With photographs."

"Heavens, no." Never heard the tinkle of disembodied laughter. "When I first started I used to sit on the stone steps of our house and paint the sea. Then I'd go on walks and paint whatever I saw. It's so much easier to transform the real canvas than to use photos, but they do capture a moment."

"Then you will want me to sit."

"Or stand," she answered with a laugh. Finally, a red light threw the room into surreal images. Never let out a sigh and stretched. She hadn't realized how stiffly she was holding herself.

BriAnne placed several canisters in a rack and switched on a machine which shook them gently. "The solution is being evenly distributed over the film. It reacts with the nitrate, and an image forms on the celluloid. The secret is to not let it stay in too long." She tapped a timer mounted on the vibrating machine.

Never sipped her tea and BriAnne lifted her cup, testing the liquid for heat before she took a long drink. The bell sounded, and BriAnne went back to work. "I didn't know it would take so short a time."

"Oh, the development happens quickly. It's making prints that takes the time, especially if you want special effects." She emptied the canisters and dropped the wet film into a bath. She pulled each roll out manually and washed it through, with hands encased in rubber gloves. When all the rolls were washed she hung them up to dry on a clothesline strung from wall to wall behind her.

Never was fascinated by the process. "We'll let them dry and then make some prints. "You'll be able to see yourself come to still life in a pan of water."

BriAnne took her back into the studio and gave her a tour of the room she used for painting. It was light and airy with sky-blue walls. Canvases lined the base like soldiers. Never recognized some of the Jersey shore scenes, the lighthouse at Cape May Point, a Victorian house along an empty beach, sand dunes in front of a snow fence. Without people, they looked lonely.

A bluish backdrop was suspended from the ceiling like a shade. A solitary chair stood in front of it. Other than the paintings there was nothing personal about the room except a single photograph on the wall. Never went over to it. Averal's young face smiled at her, his arm casually around the shoulder of a smaller version of himself.

"Those are my sons." BriAnne came up behind her. Never heard the pride in her voice.

"Averal seems so much like an only child." She studied the photo. Averal had the smile of a fortuitous child.

"Does that mean spoiled and self-centered?"

Never thought of the man who'd left her house this morning. He wasn't spoiled and self-centered. "I didn't mean it that way."

BriAnne dismissed Never's protest with a shake of her head. "He is spoiled, *and* self-centered. Gabe, my other son, died shortly after that picture was taken."

"Oh, I'm so sorry," Never consoled her. Averal was closed-mouth when it came to his family. Could his brother have anything to do with his comment this morning about a family secret?

"What was he like as a child?"

"Averal?"

Never nodded.

"I suppose he was like most boys—energetic, inquisitive, prone to getting into trouble." BriAnne smiled as if she were remembering some antic of his during a more innocent time. "After we moved to Paris he changed. I suppose it was the divorce. The children really are the silent casualties. Until Averal met Riddles he was unmanageable." She rolled her eyes to the ceiling. "Afterward he became a lot like he is now—silent, polite, intelligent, with a tendency to back away from relationships."

She stared directly at Never when she said that.

"I blame myself for that. Neither I nor his father gave him a good role model. His father moved away and remarried, and I—" She stopped. "Well, I didn't."

"Do you think Averal wants a family?"

"I think he's starving for one. He just doesn't know it." BriAnne sat down. "Riddles and I had many talks when he was growing up. We still do. Averal doesn't know, of course. He thinks Riddles is only his friend, but he's mine, too. Neither one of us would have survived if he hadn't been there for us."

Never knew what she meant. She'd met Riddles, and understood his silent method of support and reinforcement.

"I think the film is dry now. Why don't we go make some prints?"

When Never finally left the studio, darkness had fallen by

several hours. She found herself completely engrossed in a new world. BriAnne had taken several of the shots and superimposed one on the other to give an optical effect of being in more than one place at a time. She airbrushed a couple to exclude details she didn't want. In several she'd planned to add motion to the frame, and she enhanced the center image to sharp clarity, making it the focal point of the blur of purple suede.

The two women had made a decision. They both preferred the contemporary look. BriAnne suggested they search for a perfect dress for the portrait. Although the painting would be mainly a head shot, part of her upper body would be included.

Never already had the dress. She thought of it the way she'd seen it this morning, lying in the pile she'd left it in when Averal had slipped his arm under her knees and lifted her off the floor.

When she got home she pulled out the dress she'd hung reverently on a padded hanger and looked at it. The room reminded her of Averal. She didn't think she would ever be able to enter it again without remembering him standing there. His cologne lingered in the air. She closed her eyes, remembering the way he'd held her. Then the doorbell rang. Rushing down the stairs, she was sure Averal had returned. Flinging the door open she found Martin standing there.

A pang of guilt caught her. She hadn't thought of Martin since Averal had come into her life.

He whistled softly. "A study in purple." He closed the door and followed her through to the living room. "And I like the hair." He circled her, appreciation evident on his face.

"What are you doing here?" It was rare that he dropped by without an invitation.

"I got a call from a noted artist in the area. She asked me to lend some of my jewelry to a certain woman for whom I have a serious affection." He lifted the jewelry case in his hand.

"Martin, you're not walking around with precious stones on your person, are you?" she asked, incredulously. Whenever he'd sent her jewelry, a security guard had delivered it. And there was a safe installed behind BriAnne's painting in her bedroom, to ensure its safety. "You could get robbed, and your insurance company wouldn't pay on your negligence."

"I took precautions," he smiled. "I made sure no trench coats were following me," he teased.

"Be serious, Martin." Never frowned, then went to the alarm box concealed in her downstairs closet and engaged the alarm. They could move around the house, but all the windows and doors were now protected and the outside lighting was set for any unexpected movement.

When she came back, Martin was spreading small black velvet rugs on her highly polished coffee table. Diamonds twinkled at her like chips of ice. She smothered a strangled gasp at the sight of a long, antique necklace with matching earrings. Martin continued to unroll the small rugs, revealing some of nature's wonders.

The pieces were wonderful, and she spent a leisurely hour trying them on and looking at herself in the mirror. She felt good trying on jewelry that could only be viewed in museums.

"You look good in everything," he told her.

"But they're all wrong, Martin."

"How can diamonds be wrong?" Martin gave her his best salesmen's voice.

"It's not the diamonds. What I need is something simple, understated." She was thinking of the red velvet dress with jewels already woven into the fabric. Additional similar jewelry would be too much. She needed something to enhance the stones in the dress, but not overpower them. "Maybe I should show you what I'm planning to wear."

"I understand," Martin said when she'd run up the stairs and returned with the dress. "Can I take this with me? I'm sure I have just the thing to go with it."

Never went to get a dress bag to protect the garment.

"Now, how about something to eat?" Martin invited. "I have a taste for Mexican food."

Never's hand went to her stomach. She was hungry. The tea

and cakes she'd had at lunchtime had long since worn off. "I'll get my coat," she said by way of consent.

Martin helped her slip her arms into a short, western fringed jacket she pulled from the hall closet. "We have to return this jewelry first," she told him. "You shouldn't have brought it out without an armed guard."

"Sweetheart, this is Princeton, not New York," he teased.

"You can put that on the police report," she countered. "When someone else has that black case." Never pointed to it.

Martin sat on the sofa and rolled the little rugs into scrolls before replacing them in the specially made box.

She suddenly remembered she still had the Nefertiti comb and some other pieces. "Let me get the ones from my safe. You can take them all back at once."

Martin nodded, and Never ran up the stairs. She swung the painting aside and quickly dialed the combination. Three boxes of jewels were there. She picked them out and pushed the safe closed, spinning the combination. As she stepped back to close the painting her foot hit something sideways, and she lost her balance. Jewelry spilled everywhere.

"Damn!" Never cursed. Sparkling stones winked at her like stars spread in the nighttime sky. She stooped to retrieve them, picking everything up and replacing it in the boxes.

"We'll have to take inventory, Martin," she said, reaching the bottom of the stairs. "I dropped these on the bedroom floor."

Martin reached for the boxes. "I know what you have, and you can keep anything missing."

"Martin," she said, a warning clear in her voice.

"All right." He knew the tone.

"Check them." Never handed him the three cases and sat on the edge of the low table.

Martin opened the velvet-covered boxes and rearranged the bracelets, earrings, and necklaces. He studied the pieces for a long time, so long that Never thought something was missing.

"Is anything wrong?" she asked.

"That depends," he hedged.

"Depends on what?"

"Your point of view, I suppose."

"What's missing?" she asked, leaning forward to look at the jewels lying comfortably on the bed of blue velvet.

"Nothing," he said.

Never looked at him. His expression had changed. He was serious. She thought she saw a kind of hurt in his eyes she had not seen before.

"Then what's wrong, Martin?"

"Nothing is missing, Nefertiti. In fact, there's more here than I can account for." Martin opened his hand. In it was a single, gold cufflink with a crest on it.

Never stared at the gold emblem as if Martin held fire in the palm of his hand.

"There are few men these days who still wear shirts that require cufflinks," Martin spoke quietly. "There are even fewer of them with the initials A. B. Last Christmas BriAnne bought these for Averal. He likes cufflinks."

Never dropped her eyes.

"I know you've refused my proposals several times, but I thought in the end you'd finally marry me."

"I'm sorry, Martin," she said. "But we don't decide who we fall in love with. It just . . . happens." Never spread her hands. "I didn't want you find out this way. I wanted to tell you."

Martin took her hands. "Don't try to explain," he told her. "I love you. I always will."

"Martin," she began slowly. "You don't love me. I don't make your heart beat fast when you see me. I'm not the first person you think of when you open your eyes. It's not me on your mind when you close them at night. You're not breathless or weak-kneed in my company."

"And Averal is all those things to you?"

She nodded.

Martin leaned forward and pressed his hand against her cheek. "I thought I could be, in time."

Never took his hand and held it.

"I'm still hungry," he said. "How about it?"

Never laughed.

They left the house and got into Martin's Mercedes. He reversed down the driveway and pulled away. At the stop sign he rolled to a complete stop.

The light from the streetlamp and Averal's headlights illuminated the interior of the black two-seater, giving Averal a full view of Never's smiling face. The couple in the car failed to see him, or the angry rage that took over his handsome features when he realized she was out with another man.

ELEVEN

Never pursed her lips, trying to contain the wide smile that split her face when the man on the other side of the net saw his ball crash into the string barrier and bounce in his court. Averal wished he were in Mark Brown's place. He'd been watching them play for nearly an hour. Her body was toned and agile, and she was as quick on her feet as she was in the mental gymnastics she'd exercised with him.

Still, he wanted to spar with her. She was dressed totally in white, from the tennis shoes that protected her feet from the polished wooden surface to the circle of white ribbon holding back her curls.

He'd stayed away a week, even going out of town on a business trip someone else could have easily taken, to keep away from her. He couldn't stay away any longer. She was a fever in his blood, and it was useless to try to fight against her. He told her he loved her when he had no intention of doing so. Love meant one thing to a woman. To him it meant something else. He wasn't into the white lace and orange blossoms. He'd been married once, and that was plenty for him.

Yet all he'd done when apart from her was dream of her, compare every woman he saw to her, wonder what she was doing and if she was thinking of him.

The business he had to conduct went slowly. He blamed everyone else for holding things up, when he was the one who stalled the proceedings. He couldn't concentrate on anything except Never Kincaid.

He was jealous. That was the bottom line. When he'd seen her smiling and laughing and going out with another man after he'd just made a declaration of his love to her, he'd wanted to grab Martin and beat him to a pulp.

He didn't want to see Never Kincaid again.

Yet his own mind was his undoing. He couldn't stay away. She plagued him like an addiction. He needed her every day, every minute. He was watching her now, in a short dress that left her long, slender legs exposed to his survey, rushing for tennis balls and positioning herself in perfect form to return the hardest serves her opponent could send.

It was her turn to serve. The toss was high and sure. She waited for it to reach the proper height. Then, in one fluid movement, she rotated her shoulder and met the ball squarely with the center of her racquet. Aesthetically, she was beautiful. His eyes were like slaves as they followed her actions. She moved like liquid, twisting and turning in a poetic dance that placed her in complete agreement with the swiftly moving ball.

He enjoyed tennis, enjoyed playing and watching it. Seeing the long-legged creature on the floor perform her own athletic ballet gave him much more pleasure than any professional match he'd ever witnessed.

"Game and set." Averal could see Never mouth the words which confirmed she'd won today's contest. Her partner was Mark Brown, a man Averal had met while he conducted interviews in the Tax Department. Mark had survived the departmental reorganization, and joined the tax group at the headquarters location.

Averal watched them talking casually. He'd be jealous if he hadn't known the blonde, muscular he-man—who could easily qualify as one of the American Gladiators—had a new fianceé he adored. The man and woman on the court below him gathered their racquet covers and balls and headed for the stairway. Averal kept his position in front of the glass enclosure, following their progress until they disappeared through the shaded curtain and two other players took possession of the court.

Never was first through the door. Laughing, she tossed a comment over her shoulder, and the two of them separated as she headed for the women's locker room on the opposite side of the building. Averal stood directly in her path.

Never stumbled when she realized Averal stood only a few feet from her. His lion eyes met hers in silence. She couldn't tell what he was thinking. She hadn't seen him in a week, not since he told her he loved her, then apparently disappeared from the face of the earth.

Damn! she cursed silently. Why did he have to look like sugar to a diabetic? His suit was flawless as it stretched over his broad shoulders. She could tell the custom fit from the lines that nipped in at his waist and made him look like a male model. The dark-blue had a faint red line running through it. A line, which would be missed at a distance, was picked up in the slanted stripe of his tie. He exuded charm and confidence, while she looked like something dragged from a wet pond, her hair limp and her face sweaty.

"I hope you don't mind. I enjoyed watching the game," Averal said by way of greeting.

Never was already hot, but she felt her temperature rise. She had won today, beating Mark who appeared to be at the top of his game yet struggling to overcome her shots. The match had lifted her spirits. She'd poured her concentration into her strokes. She'd missed Averal. They'd fought before he went away, and she didn't understand his leaving without a word. Never had been determined not to let it bother her. She'd succeeded on the tennis court, but her work at the office this past week was poor and unproductive. She was more ready to begin her day this morning than she had been in the past five. She hadn't counted on seeing Averal before breakfast.

Never stopped when her gaze locked with his. "I guess it's an understatement to say I'm surprised to see you."

"I had some business out of town."

"So your secretary told me." She moved to brush past him.

He caught her arm. Never stopped, feeling the warmth of his hand and the small sensations that tightened around her heart. He said her name. His voice was a seductive whisper, his mouth close enough to her ear for her to feel his breath.

She wanted to lean into him, turn her head and feel his mouth on hers, but she jerked her arm free before she did anything like that. "I was under the impression we had a date last Saturday night. At least you could have called."

"I'm sorry." He looked about the room. Never wondered if she was causing a scene, but people weren't noticing them. "I wanted to call."

"So what stopped you? Did you go to some remote village where they don't have telephones? And your cellular unit got lost in a swamp?" She was angry. She wanted to see him every waking moment, yet he'd walked away from her without a word. She'd spent sleepless nights trying to remember what she had done to drive him away.

"Can we talk about it over breakfast? I promise I'll explain everything. All I ask is that you listen."

Curiosity and anger fought for survival within her. She wanted to be near him. She was interested in his explanation. Maybe she should be objective enough to listen.

She'd planned to be dressed and poised the next time she saw him. Instead of being confrontational, she'd wanted to be controlled. But look at her—her face flushed, her body glistening with sweat, and her hair falling about her face like slick oil.

Averal thought she was the most beautiful woman he'd ever seen. Her eyes were bright circles, and her skin had a healthy glow that radiated sex appeal. He wanted to reach into her hair and release the band holding it in place. It was slightly wet, reminding him of the first time he'd kissed her, when her collar was wet and the hair at her nape damp. The thought excited him.

"I won't be long," she said, her throat feeling like sandpaper. "If you want to wait in the dining room, I have a reservation."

"I canceled it," he said.

She started to pass him, but turned at his words. "You what!" She was about to explode. Never counted to ten. "Why?" she asked, her voice low and menacing.

"I made a reservation someplace else." He paused. "I think we need someplace quieter to talk. Take your time. We'll go as soon as you're ready."

If Never hadn't been so controlled, so able to handle anything, she'd have been shouting at him. Without a word she turned and disappeared through the door marked Women.

Thirty minutes later she was showered and dressed. Granted she could have taken a few more minutes with her hair, but for the moment this would have to do. Averal stood the moment she came into the waiting area. She had the feeling he'd been pacing the room like the caged lion his eyes reminded her of. She stopped, shifting her gym bag and clearing her mind of the memory that lion's eyes conjured. Averal met her, hoisted the bag from her shoulder. Placing his free hand on the small of her back, he guided her through the room and out to the parking lot and his jeep.

He handed her into the passenger seat as if she were made of fine crystal and would break at the slightest touch. Stowing her bag in the back, he went around the hood and climbed behind the wheel. Never didn't ask where they were going. Most of her anger had been washed away under the strong penetration of the shower. She sat without speaking. Averal was equally quiet as he maneuvered the vehicle into Princeton Borough. As they passed The Medical Center and the YMCA, Averal spoke.

"How long have you and Mark been playing tennis?"

"Two years. We used to play mixed doubles together. When the group broke up we started playing singles once a week, but it expanded into a daily game."

"You're really good at it."

"Thank you." Never was elated. She faced the window to hide a playful smile. His approval made her feel as if she'd just climbed Mount Everest.

Looking up, she noticed they were passing through a tree-lined street. The trees were bare and black against the morning sky.

"Where are we going?" she asked, not remembering any restaurants in that area.

"No place," Averal said. "We're here." He pulled the jeep into a long driveway. Several yards in front of them a wrought iron gate was electrically pulled across the roadway, allowing them access. The paved road wound its way past rhododendron bushes up a hill that ended in a circular driveway. A massive structure of red brick with four white columns stood before her.

She didn't need to ask if this was his house. "Chez Averal?" she commented.

"I couldn't fool you if I tried." He was being playful.

Never almost succumbed to it. Instead, she looked at her watch. "I have a meeting this morning, and we left my car at the tennis court."

Averal slid from his seat and came around to the other side. "I promise," he said, opening the door, "you'll be at your meeting with time to spare." He took her wrist and helped her down, holding onto her too long.

Never pulled herself free and adjusted her coat collar against the cold. She wasn't chilled at all, but she needed something to do to keep her hands from giving away her feelings.

Averal led her toward a set of double doors. Huge oval windows had been set into the black background. Passing through the portal, she found herself in a gargantuan foyer. A crystal chandelier lighted an entryway that opened into a large room with a matching set of curving staircases that wound up to the second floor.

"Breakfast is ready," Averal said. Again his hand found the small of her back as he led her through to the dining room. It was the kind of place where the President might have a meeting with thirty or forty of his most intimate friends. French doors leading to a patio and garden stood at one end of the room. The floor was dominated by a highly polished mahogany table.

High-backed chairs standing at attention outlined the perimeter. Intricate carvings spoke to her from the chair backs and table legs. Never tried to remember where she'd seen a table like it before. One end had been laid with place settings for two. Roses adorned the center between the two arrangements. Immediately, she was moved by the trouble Averal had gone to for breakfast with her, to apologize.

The door opened and a woman and three men came in to set silver chafing dishes in their frames.

"Would you like me to serve, Mr. Ballentine?" the woman, who must be Averal's housekeeper, asked.

"We'll serve ourselves, Alice."

The parade left. She was alone again. Averal started to move. Her hand, taking his arm, stopped his progress. "You planned all this?"

His smile was infectious. "It gets better. Come on." Averal slipped her hand in the fold of his arm and took her to a long sideboard. As he removed the lids she recognized the insignia of the best caterer in Princeton etched into them. Aromatic scents of bacon and eggs filled the room. Hotcakes and warm syrup joined the scents wafting through the air, causing her stomach to rumble. She was famished. He replaced the covers and joined her near the china plates and silver laid out in a widening triangle.

"I don't know where to start," she said, her first real smile curving her rose-red mouth.

"How about here?" Before Never knew his intentions, Averal slipped his arm about her waist and turned her body into his. His mouth was warm and moist as it found hers. The kiss was soft and controlled. Initially, Never held back. Averal didn't try to force her. If she pushed back, he'd let her go. But she didn't push him. Her arms, finding a life of their own, rose and wound around his neck. His hands on her waist fitted her into him, and his head dipped lower, deepening the kiss. Control in both of them evaporated like water droplets on a hot pan. His hands pushed deeply into her hair, releasing it from the confining style she'd fashioned.

It was still damp, as Averal had hoped it would be, thick and heavy. He let it flow over his fingers as he gripped her head and welded her mouth to his.

As he pushed his tongue past her teeth, Never arched closer to him. She couldn't get close enough. Her body ground into his, and the impression of his erection against her was unmistakable. The explosion around them engulfed her like a fiery mushroom cloud that fused her body indelibly to his. She wanted to raise her legs, wrap them around him, but her straight skirt confined her.

Averal broke free first, his breath hard and ragged. Never wasn't sure what had happened. She was clinging to him, knowing there was no support in her limbs. Her breath came in gasping drags as she tried to draw enough oxygen into her lungs to sustain life. She lay against him listlessly for several moments. Finally she began to breathe normally.

"How do you expect me to eat now?" she tried to joke, but the question came out strangled.

Averal raised his head. One pair of desire-laden eyes stared into another. "God!" he moaned, thrusting her away from him. He hadn't intended to do that, but when he looked at her the light had struck her in just the right place. Damp tendrils of hair slipped from the neat twist. He knew she'd rushed to dress, not taking the usual amount of time to dry her hair. The thought excited him and the sun caught the glistening strands and haloed her head. He couldn't have controlled his response if he tried, and he didn't want to try. He'd been suppressing his feelings, trying to exorcize her from his thoughts. Yet every morning she was there, and every night she disturbed his sleep.

No, Averal thought. His conscious mind might not have wanted to push her too quickly, but his subconscious had a stronger will.

Never braced herself against the sideboard. The chafing

dishes behind her were cold compared to the heat emanating from her body.

"I didn't intend to do that," Averal admitted.

"It's all right. At least it's behind us now."

Damn you! Averal wanted to shout. In seconds she'd ripped his resolve to shreds. Hers *had* slipped, too. Of that he was positive. Yet in seconds her control was squarely in place. He turned away, not able to look at her if his body were going to return to a presentable state.

"What do you mean, 'behind us'?" he asked when he faced her again.

"Behind as in gone, kaput, done with." Venom laced her words. She was upset that he could so easily get her to fall into his arms.

"It's nice you can be so clinical about it."

She made light of what had just happened, not sure why she was doing it. "It was just a kiss, Averal. Let's not get carried away."

"Why not? I think I'd like to be carried away." He took a step toward her, and was rewarded by her one step retreat. The corners of his mouth lifted. So she wasn't as indifferent as she pretended. He'd made his point, and he knew better than to press it. If he got any closer to her he knew he wouldn't be able to keep himself from taking her in his arms again. "Maybe we'd better have breakfast," he said.

Never let her sigh out on a long, even breath. She turned, attacking a plate as if it were a lifeline. When she sat down moments later, she had no idea why so much food covered the bone china dish. There was no way she could eat all that.

She lifted her juice glass and sipped the sweet orange liquid. Averal quietly walked behind her and took the chair at the head of the table. The moment was awkward, and she didn't know how to fill it. Idle conversation wasn't part of her make-up. So she resorted to the purpose of the meal.

"You had something you wanted to explain to me."

"Eat first." It was nearly an order. He bowed his head and

filled his fork with eggs. Never watched him shove them into his mouth.

"Averal." She pushed a strand of hair back from her face. She must look awful, with her hair wild and falling freely over her shoulders. There was nothing she could do about it until she got through this meal. "I'm sorry. I didn't mean to say that."

His sigh was a long disturbance of air that seemed to take his anger with it. "I'm sorry, too. You have a right to be angry."

Never felt better. She still wouldn't be able to eat all the food on her plate, but she'd try. They ate in silence, but it wasn't a hostile one. She knew something inside Averal made him push her back. She wanted him to trust her, tell her what it was. He had to do it. If their love was to survive, if it was to grow, he had to trust her.

Finally Averal put his fork down. Never's followed it, only a third of the food on her plate eaten. She picked up her glass and drained it.

"Coffee?" Averal asked.

She nodded.

He lifted a white Braun coffeepot and poured the black liquid into her cup, then his.

"Where did you go last week?"

She was still direct.

"Buffalo. It snowed." He stood up and took her cup and his and walked away from the table. She followed him into a library with book-lined walls, leather furniture, a desk that should have been in a museum, and a spiral staircase that led to another level.

He set the cups down on a table in front of a tufted maroon sofa. Taking her hand, he pulled her down next to him. Never leaned forward, lifting her cup and saucer.

She had restored her black and white color scheme. Her suit was as staunch and impregnable as a fortress—a black pleated skirt and blouse topped by a winter white blazer. Around her neck was a black and white polka-dotted scarf that she'd tied into several knots and wore like a necklace.

"After you went to see Anne I called several times." He'd

called her all day long, upset she hadn't returned home. He hadn't wanted to call Anne and ask if she were still there. "I went to see Riddles and Vivette, and when I left there I drove by your house before I went home."

Never knew what was coming. She had seen clearly the car that turned into her street as she and Martin left. It wasn't a car, but a jeep.

"You saw me leaving with Martin."

"I did, but that has little to do with it. I admit I was jealous." She smiled. Averal took her free hand.

"You scare me." He said it. He'd thought voicing the words would change something; but it hadn't. He was still afraid of her.

"How?" She didn't make light of his comment. She put the coffee down, turning to fully face him, her expression serious.

"I was married once. It didn't work."

"What happened?"

He got up and walked to the middle of the room. "We wanted different things. We grew apart." How could he tell her the break up was his fault? That his wife wanted children? He couldn't explain that he carried a gene that meant having children could cause them a lifetime of hardship, put a strain on their relationship so strong it would break under the strain, just as his parents' marriage had.

"Averal, I understand how a bad relationship can make you cautious about another one." Never moved closer to him. "Averal Ballentine, I'm in love with you. Don't you know that?"

He took her in his arms and held her tenderly. "No, Nefertiti Kincaid. Before this moment you haven't admitted it." He kissed her, his fingers spreading through her tousled hair. He didn't want to get involved with anyone. With Never it was already too late. He'd been involved with her from the first moment he saw her, and now he knew he needed her in his life. He didn't know how long. And he wanted to be honest with her.

"Never, I told you I was in love with you."

She moved her head from his shoulder and looked up at him.

"Except for my ex-wife, I haven't had any relationships that lasted for very long." A lump formed in his throat, and his head felt as if a fist gripped it. He swallowed hard. "Martin Caldwell. He's in love with you. You might be better off going with him. I can't offer you what he can." He could offer her a family, the usual life, the American dream. Averal didn't have the right.

"I'm not in love with him."

Averal stared at her. He was confused. His mind told him one thing while his heart drew its own conclusions. He wanted her more than he'd ever wanted a woman. His heart pounded just at the thought of her. When she was near him he wanted to rip her clothes off and make mad love to her.

She touched him and he drew her against him, reveling in the ability to have her nearby, smell her hair, her perfume, and that scent that defined the uniqueness of Never Kincaid. He was a fool, he told himself, wasting a week without seeing her, without making love to her. It was what he wanted to do this minute. Strip her of that expensive suit and feast his eyes on her brown body in the sunlight of his bedroom before joining it with his own.

"I had a brother, Never." He didn't know why he started to tell her the story. It seemed the right thing to do. He kept her in his arms, afraid he might stop if she could see his face.

"Gabe," she purred, rubbing her cheek against him.

"You know?" He frowned, but her face was averted and she didn't see it.

"There's a photo in your mother's studio."

"He died when I was eight. After that my parents argued a lot. I don't remember anything they said. I heard my name a lot so I assume it was because . . ." He choked.

Never slowly moved her head back. "Averal, you can't believe they were arguing over you."

"I asked Anne once. She refused to answer me."

"It wasn't you." She forced the words to sink into him.

"I could hear them from my bed. I used to cry myself to

sleep, praying for them to stop. And finally they did. I woke one morning to find my father gone. He'd left in the night like a thief. He didn't even say good-bye."

Never laid his head against her breast. "It's all right, Averal. I've met your mother. She wouldn't shut you out, blame you for living and your brother dying."

He pushed away from her like a bullet leaving a gun. "You can't possibly understand!" he shouted. "You grew up with people who loved you and wanted you around. When your sister died, you took your nephews in and gave them a home, and love. It's burned in you. How can you possibly know what it's like to have no one?"

"You had Riddles. You told me."

"It's not the same. They blamed me." He drove his point home by punching himself in the chest.

"I don't believe that." Never vowed to keep her voice level. Averal's was rising, and she had to remain calm. He needed her to be stable. He paced back and forth in front of the coffee table. She remained in place.

"Then why, in thirty years, have I seen my father only seven times?"

"I don't know that. He could have a perfectly good reason."

"Like what?"

"Fear." Never shrugged.

"Of me! I was only a child."

"A child who can look at you without words and make all your insecurities surface."

Somehow he knew she spoke from experience. She'd taken her nephews in. Had she been afraid of them, of their opinion of her? She had such a good heart. Anyone should be able to tell that. Yet maybe she'd just hidden her fear well.

"He wasn't afraid of me. He couldn't stand the sight of me."

"How do you know that?"

"He wouldn't look me in the eye. Whenever I was around there was tension, and arguments."

"So you denounced your family, and walled yourself up behind a façade that no one would ever be able to break."

He stared at her. Never saw a stranger looking out of his eyes. "They denounced *me*."

"You had a choice."

"What are you talking about? I was eight-years-old."

"You're not eight now. And you're not a child, although you are acting like one."

"What do you want me to do?" He spread his hands.

"Why don't you make an effort to heal the wound between you and your parents?"

He stopped dead. The glare he gave her should have made her shiver, but she stood her ground, accepting the invisible censure.

"Why don't you ask your mother what happened years ago? You could find your father and ask him."

"You're talking nonsense."

"Only to a man who refuses to listen."

Never went to him. She wound her arms around his middle and pressed her cheek against his heart.

"She might be ready to talk now. Those years could have been hard for your parents, too."

Averal set his chin on top of her head. It smelled clean and had the scent of fresh air in it. He squeezed her tightly against him. He loved her. And she made one thing clear to him—he wanted to know. That's what had plagued him all these years, his need to understand.

He had to talk to Anne, but would she tell him and if she did, could he stand to hear it?

TWELVE

The Jeep Cherokee ate the miles as they sped along Route 95 South toward Averal's sister's house in Arlington, Virginia. Never hadn't been to the capital city in a long time. She loved Washington, D.C., and looked forward to seeing Howard University again.

"We always stop here!" Never cried as she jumped down from the seat of the jeep. They had pulled into the parking lot of The Maryland House. It was the last rest area before they reached Baltimore, and from there the District of Columbia was only forty minutes away.

Never ran up the stairs, her hair swinging behind her, as she went to the ladies' room. Averal watched her from the best vantage point to view her round derriére. When she disappeared through the door, he went to get them something to drink. He was looking at the map by the front door when she joined him. Her lipstick had been refreshed, and her hair brushed. He had the urge to muss it up.

She wrapped her arm around his waist and looked at the red dot with the notation You Are Here. She ran her finger along the line pointing south.

"This is where we have to go." Her fingers stopped under Arlington.

"Another hour and a half," he said, as they made their way back to the jeep arm in arm. "If we're lucky." This was Thanksgiving weekend, and everyone seemed to be heading south.

"May I drive?" she asked.

Without a word or a bit of hesitation, he tossed her the keys. Reflex action had Never's hands up for the catch.

"Good," he complemented. "We'll have to get you a spot with the Nets."

"Knicks."

"Nets."

"Knicks." She unlocked the door, and climbed into the driver's seat with a bounce. Averal took her former position and locked himself in with the seatbelt. Never adjusted the seat for her shorter leg length and the two mirrors. Then they were back on the road.

"Tell me something about your sister."

"Half sister," he corrected. "She's clairvoyant."

"Really!" Never took her eyes from the road for a second to throw Averal a glance.

"No. I'm the only one she seems to read with crystal clarity."

"Ah, that must get under your skin." The way he'd said it Never knew it irked him. She didn't have to look at him to tell it was the truth.

"She says we're soulmates." His voice was dry.

"What do you think?"

"I'm not sure. Sometimes I can feel close to her, but I can't do any of the tricks she can."

"Like what?"

"She knows my moods better than I do."

"That's not hard." Never smiled at him and he squeezed her arm.

"Sometimes she can finish my sentences before I do. Then there are times she knows what I'm thinking and what I want before I ask for it."

"Oh," Never said. "I guess you'd better keep your mind on a purely platonic plane." She smirked.

"You're playing with fire, darling."

Never's ears warmed at the endearment.

"She had twins recently. I think they're six months old."

"Averal, you're an uncle."

"Half uncle."

"Why do you say that?"

"She's from my father's second marriage."

"Are there any . . . half brothers?"

"Three."

"And you don't consider them your family?"

"I consider myself W-F," he spelled out. "Without Family."

"No one is without family."

"I wasn't part of any of the things families do. It's only occasionally I come to these—"

"Family gatherings," she finished for him.

"Your sister obviously wants to include you in the celebration."

"And I wanted to see you. I'd have gone to the moon if I could spend the time with you."

Never swerved the jeep, then slipped into the passing lane to try to cover the thrill that ran through her.

"Will your father be there?"

"No."

He'd spoken quickly, and the monosyllable hung between them.

"How about your other brothers?"

"Caroline didn't say. Only two of them live in this area. The other one lives in New York."

"New York City?"

"Manhattan."

Never had to concentrate to keep her mouth from dropping open. Averal had family close to him and he didn't make any effort to see them, whereas her own family couldn't wait to get together. If it hadn't been for the holiday cruise her grandparents were going on and her nephews' ski trip, she'd be spending the day with her seven great-aunts, four great-uncles, and over thirty cousins who would be together on Thanksgiving.

"What are their names?" Never asked, shaking herself free

of missing her family celebration. She was with Averal, and she was happy.

"James, Calvin, and Edward."

Averal was wearing a green and white ski sweater with olive green wool slacks. His leather jacket was on the backseat with her coat. Nothing about him had the custom-made cut of his suits, except his mind.

"Which one lives in Manhattan?"

"Edward, the youngest. He graduated from law school last May, and he's studying for the bar."

"How old is Caroline?"

"Twenty-six. Calvin is twenty-seven, and James is twenty-five." His voice was a monotone.

"Do James and Calvin live in Virginia, or Washington?"

"James lives and teaches high school in Baltimore, and Calvin has a house in Rock Creek Park, but he lives at The Howard University Hospital."

"He's a doctor?"

Averal nodded.

Never stopped asking questions and let the miles roll past them. The traffic came to a halt just outside of Baltimore. It took them nearly an hour to get through the Harbor Tunnel. The sign flashing above the roadway said there was a longer backup at the Ft. McHenry Tunnel.

When they hit the Beltway the traffic crawled. For twenty minutes Never maneuvered her way to the Georgia Avenue exit. Driving across the city was preferable to trying to follow the traffic heading for Wilson Bridge and northern Virginia.

"I used to live here," she explained when she turned the car toward Silver Spring, Maryland.

"You went to Howard, didn't you?"

"Say that with admiration in your voice," she teased.

After she passed Colesville Road the flow seemed to pick up. The traffic jam here was on the other side of the divider, with people trying to leave the city.

He picked up on her humor. "Actually, I heard Howard girls were snobby."

"Vicious lie," she countered. "Started, no doubt, by some weak-kneed co-ed from Morgan State." She knew that was Averal's alma mater, the arch rival of Howard University.

"Watch how you say that. When you speak of Morgan State, you must bow your head and whisper a prayer."

Never laughed. She was nearing the turnoff for Alaska Avenue that would give her a straight run down Sixteen Street and make it easier to get to Key Bridge. Suddenly she wanted to go by her old school.

"Would you like to see Howard?" she asked.

"Not as much as you would," Averal returned with a smile. He could see she wanted to visit.

Never changed lanes and threaded her way through the holiday traffic until she reached Park Avenue. Making a left, she went over to Fourth Street and turned right.

"This is Drew Hall. It's a Freshman Dorm," Never said in her best tour guide voice. She went on to describe the Athletic Center with its football field, the Student Center with its restaurant called The Punch Out, and the School of Home Economics. They stopped briefly at the gates before Never went on to park behind the Old Freedman's Hospital building. They walked through Death Valley, and she explained why it was called that.

"In here," she said, turning around with her arms embracing the area, "is the School of Pharmacy, the Biology building, Chemistry Department, and Physics building and across there." She pointed between the Physics and Chemistry buildings. Many students have had intellectual deaths trying to negotiate the hardest science courses centered in these buildings below the hill, where the main campus lies. That's why they call it 'Death Valley', but if you don't want people to know you're from Morgan State, just call it 'The Valley.' "

Averal agreed, and took her hand. "What's up there?" He pointed to Founders Library.

"Let's go up." They ran for the stairs and raced up like two college students late for class. The main campus opened out like a carpet in front of her. Never felt at home here. She'd spent four glorious years with many friends, and she longed to meet them again.

Back in the jeep, she drove farther down Fourth Street and showed him the dormitory she used to live in. Then, doubling back, she went past the Schools of Medicine and Dentistry.

"Averal, do you have sickle cell trait?"

He felt as if a brick had been thrown in his gut. "Where did that come from?" He'd been wanting to ask her that question for weeks, but somehow he couldn't work it into the conversation. He'd been too afraid to ask. He wanted Never around. The way he felt, he wanted her for a very long time. Finding out she had sickle cell trait would change things. He knew that. It would change him, and there was nothing he could do about it. His genes dictated it.

Never stopped the four-wheel drive vehicle and stared out the window. A comparatively new building stood in front of them.

"This was a new research building when I was a student here. Now it's the Center for Sickle Cell Research."

He had to clear his throat. "What . . . what kind of research do they do here?"

"Everything. I worked here for Dr. Strom Washington. I fed statistics into a computer on cases of sickle cell that occurred anywhere in the world. The results were all sent here. Even if all you've had is a test, your results are somewhere in their computer system. I took the test. I don't have it."

He fought to get the words out—"My brother died of sickle cell anemia."

"Half brother," Never corrected.

"Brother," he said.

"Half brother," she countered.

"Brother."

Never turned from the window as realization dawned on her.

She looked steadily at Averal. "Averal, do you have the sickle cell trait?"

He nodded.

"Gabe died of the anemia?"

"When he was four."

She didn't say anything. Why hadn't anyone told him? How could she be the bearer of news that should have come from his parents?

"What's wrong?" Averal asked.

"Nothing." She attempted a smile. "I think we should get on to your sister's house." She reached for the ignition key. Averal covered her hand.

"What's wrong?" he asked again.

"It's not my place, Averal. You need to talk to someone in your family."

"I'm W-F, remember?"

Not in this, you're not, Never thought, but she didn't say anything.

"Tell me," he demanded.

"Please, Averal. Talk to BriAnne. Call her."

"I want to know now."

Never swallowed. "Generally, an offspring will be born with sickle cell anemia only if both parents carry the sickle cell trait." She paused, not wanting to go on, but Averal insisted. "In the case where both the male and female have the trait, the children born to them will have the disease."

"All children? Are you saying all children?"

"At least one in every four will have the disease. The others may or may not, but statistics show all children will have the disease."

"Does that mean I will get the disease?"

She shook her head. The air in the jeep's cabin was stifling.

"You're too old to develop it. It would have been detected at birth, or at least within a few months of birth."

"Then what does it mean?"

"Averal, please ask BriAnne," she begged.

He grabbed her arms and dragged her as far as her seatbelt allowed. Realizing he'd pulled her harder than he intended to, he loosened his grip. "I have to know," he said, lifting her chin to look into her eyes. There was pain there. He was causing it, but he had to know. "What does it mean, Never?"

"I may be wrong. There are cases where all the children don't get the disease."

"Don't pad it, Never. You've always been straight with me."

He was right. She wasn't one to skirt around details. But in this matter, she thought it would be better coming from Bri-Anne. Averal stared at her.

"I need to know," he said.

"BriAnne told me she had three miscarriages before you were born. That means you were the fourth child, and that Gabe could only have been a half-brother. In order for a child to have sickle cell disease, both parents must have either the disease or the trait. All offspring will have the disease. If you only have the trait, you and Gabe can't have the same mother and father." The last sentence was only a whisper.

"I have the trait, so if Gabe had the disease and I don't, it had to come from my mother."

His hands dropped from Never.

"Averal, don't jump to conclusions. Your case may be different."

"How rare is the incidence of one child not having the disease, if both parents have the trait?"

"I don't remember."

"Is it low, or high?"

"High," she stammered. "It's in the billion category."

"No wonder there were so many arguments with my name in them. My father must have found out I was his son, but Gabe wasn't." It wasn't his fault they fought. It had to do with his mother having an affair. Then why had he rejected *him?* It didn't make sense. Why didn't he fight for custody of him, or at least see him?

He couldn't blame Anne for keeping him away from his fa-

ther. Not one malicious word had ever passed her lips with
regard to his father. If his father had wanted to see him, Anne
would not have been an obstruction.

Never penetrated his thoughts. "Averal, don't jump to conclusions. It doesn't have to be that way."

"What do you mean?"

"You need to talk to them, Averal. It's why you don't know
the whole truth. You're speculating, drawing conclusions when
you don't have all the facts. It's not like you, Averal."

"You're right." He spoke more to himself than to Never. "I
could be the one. It would explain why he wouldn't look at me.
I'm not his son at all."

"Averal, stop it!" Never shouted. "Don't think about this until
you're able to get some real answers."

Averal stared at her.

"I'm sorry," Never said.

For a moment he'd forgotten she was there. He reached over
and disengaged her seatbelt, then cradled her in his arms. "It's
not your fault, but you were right about one thing. On this
question, I have to talk to Anne." He held her there for a long
moment. "We'd better get going. I told Caroline we'd be there
before the D. C. rush began."

Never glided across the seat and started the engine. Pointing
the jeep in the direction of downtown, she went as far as M
Street before turning toward Georgetown. She knew the traffic
there would be awful, but it was part of the excitement of Washington, and she thought Averal needed time to assimilate some
of the questions that must be running through his head before
he met his clairvoyant sister.

"Caroline, I'd like you to meet Nefertiti Kincaid." Averal introduced them outside her porticoed residence in the fashion-
able, Northern Virginia suburb. "Never, Caroline Taylor."

"It's nice to meet you." Never extended her hand.

She flashed a glance at her brother. "Welcome," she said as

they shook hands. "Averal has been very closemouthed about you." The comment was warm, and Never felt comfortable immediately. "Come in. You must be freezing."

"I'll get the luggage," Averal volunteered as she walked through the lighted doorway with Caroline.

He went to the back of the jeep and lifted the hatch. *Gabe wasn't my whole brother.* He stared into the dark cabin, unmoving.

Inside, Caroline took Never's coat and hung it in a closet. "Let me get you something warm to drink." Never instinctively liked the brown-haired woman with pecan-colored skin. Her hair was short and curly and reminded Never of black mink, as did her omniscient eyes.

She left, to return minutes later laden with a silver tray with both coffee and tea. The scent of raspberries wafted through the air.

"Averal isn't in yet?" Caroline commented.

Never didn't answer. She thought he might need a few minutes alone.

"Coffee, raspberry blend, or tea, apple spice?" Never opted for the coffee. Caroline poured a cup when she'd made her selection and handed it to her. She took it, adding cream and sugar.

"I tried getting him to tell me about you," Caroline started without preamble. "He wouldn't say a word. Have you two known each other long?"

Never was prepared for the third degree, but somehow she didn't think she was going to get it.

"We met in October at BriAnne's opening." Had it only been a month ago? Never felt as if she'd known Averal most of her life. He filled so much of the need in her.

"I wanted to come to that, but with the twins I don't have time to breathe."

"Averal said you'd just had babies."

"They're taking a nap now." She looked as if she were glad.

"Don't worry—before you leave, you'll have had your fill of them." She smiled, softening the words.

Caroline changed the subject deftly. "He doesn't come often, but he hasn't brought anyone with him before. You must be very special."

She emphasized *special*. Averal was special to her. She was in love with him. And he was in love with her. She sipped her coffee, not committing to anything.

"What do you do?"

Work, a safe subject. "I work for a chemical company. I direct one of their information services areas."

"Ah, then you and Matt will have plenty to talk about. Matt's my husband. He's in computer design. I sent him to the store to pick up some cheese. You'd think after I'd spent several hours going up and down the aisles there would be nothing I overlooked, but I had my mind on work and I forgot the cheese."

"Averal didn't tell me what you do." Never cradled the saucer in her hands.

"Before I had the twins I was a fashion designer. Now I do freelance design and consulting work." She took a sip of her coffee.

Never wondered if she'd designed the outfit she was wearing. It was a pantsuit with a long tunic top. The sleeves were long puffs of green silk with a line of buttons from elbow to wrist. The waist was nipped in, and the skirt opened over her hips in a circle of swaying pleats. Straight leg pants jutted from the bottom of the skirt and fell over matching green heels.

"I wonder what's holding Averal up?" Caroline looked toward the door.

"I'll go see." Never had only her turtleneck sweater and jeans on. She went outside. It was several degrees warmer than in New Jersey, but not warm enough to go without a coat.

"What are you doing?" she asked quietly when she found him leaning against the side of the jeep, one leg bent so his foot rested on the metal side.

"Contemplating the universe." He took her hands and pulled

her against him, wrapping his short coat around them. "Do you know how many stars are up there?"

Never looked up. "None we can see. It's still too light. We won't be able to see the stars for another few hours."

"There must be billions." He spoke as if he hadn't heard her. "About the same number as would make Gabe and me truly brothers."

"Averal, Gabe *was* your brother. Nothing has changed in the past hour to alter that. He's still the brother you remember."

"No he isn't. He's in the same category with—"

"They're your brothers and sister, too." She cut him off when he was about to lump his father's second family into a category. "No matter how you deny it, they're family." She shivered in the seeping cold. "You don't get to choose who you're related to, but you make the best of it. Granted, it's better when you love them unconditionally, but you love them because they're family."

"Averal, are you two going to stay out there?" Caroline was standing in the doorway, hugging herself for warmth.

"We have to go in, or she'll be out here," Never replied.

"Just a moment, Caroline," Averal called.

"Promise me you won't dwell on what you learned this afternoon, and that you'll try to enjoy the holiday?"

Averal heard the pleading note in her voice. Her body had blended into his like soft wax oozing down a candle. He could have stood here for the next hour just holding her close. But he looked into her eyes, eyes that wanted him to open up and let the hurt out. Eyes that were so sure the world was a good place to live.

"I promise," he said with a smile. He'd invited her here, and he wanted her to have a good time. He'd try his best to be part of the family. And to tell the truth, with Never next to him he thought he could do it.

THIRTEEN

The house filled quickly, and the noise level rose to a cheerful hum. Averal's three brothers showed up together, pulling into the driveway successively and giving the house a decidedly festive air. Matthew Taylor, a six-foot, bespectacled giant with broad shoulders and the look of an ex-football player, opened several bottles of Asti Spumante. Caroline brought canapes from the kitchen, letting Never know she'd expected them all along. Averal looked the loner in the group. While everyone joined in the harmony of being together, Averal remained aloof. He stood away from the conversation with as much purpose as the third person on a date.

When Caroline requested a fire, Averal volunteered. Never sat back and looked at the scene in the room. Edward and James were each holding one of Caroline's twins. The brothers looked enough alike to be twins themselves, each with dark skin that reminded her of a deep tan and clear eyes that told the world how they felt. Caroline favored the third brother, Calvin. He had an unsmiling countenance that said he could be serious, but underneath was the man his patients would see when they were in pain and needed compassion. In each of them she could find a resemblance to Averal.

The brothers talking and eating, along with the wine Matt poured into crystal wine glasses added to the party atmosphere.

"I think she wants her mommy." Edward stood ready to give the small bundle back.

"May I hold her?" Never asked quietly. Edward looked at her as if he were ready to give the crying child to anyone. He gently placed the baby in Never's arms. The child quieted as if she'd recognized her mother's heartbeat. Caroline had told her the twins were Laurence and Lindsay. She held Lindsay, tucking her finger in the child's tight fist.

"I guess she likes you better than she likes me," Edward teased.

Never had forgotten what it was like to hold a baby. Her nephews were grown men of nineteen and twenty. She'd only held them a short time before her sister and her engineer husband had taken off for Argentina to build a water treatment facility.

Averal joined her on the sofa. The fire blazed in the hearth, adding warmth to the room. Never turned her perusal to the man at her side. "Would you like to hold her?"

"No," he said too quickly, his hands coming up as if warding off something terrible.

"Don't be afraid," she said. "She won't break."

Never shifted the child and laid her in his arms. "She can support her head, but hold it, anyway."

He looked awkward and felt the same, but after a moment the toothless grin Lindsay gave him could have disarmed even the most hardened criminal.

Averal stared at the tiny creature in his arms. Her eyes were a bright black and her hair was a soft mass of curls. She squirmed and reached for his face. He had to smile at her. What was happening to him? How could such a small thing tie his heart in knots? She was so helpless. Everything had to be done for her. He wanted to cradle her closer to him and keep her warm and safe. With his free hand he touched her hair.

Averal thought of Never when he stroked it. It was silky like hers, only moist. He didn't realize the room had gone stark still, and that everyone was watching him. He felt hot and uncomfortable, with everyone waiting for him to do or say something. Lindsay reached for him again. Her miniature hand waved without control. It found his giant one and clasped his finger. What could he do? This was a foreign experience for him, but he couldn't say he didn't like it. He couldn't push the baby away. She was too beautiful, and her little hands caught in his sweater and held as if they'd caught his heart and pulled it out.

"What are you all gawking at? Can't a man hold a baby?" he asked the awestruck room.

Lindsay made happy gurgling noises, and laughter broke the tension.

"You're doing fine," Never whispered. "Just don't stand off from them. Let whatever happens, happen. Be a part of them," she instructed. "They want you to be."

Averal gave her a look that said I-love-you. And he did. He'd never felt so happy as he did right now, holding a baby and having Never close to his side, he wanted to scream to the world. But he sat quietly giving his attention to the soft bundle who had settled in his arms and into his heart with no effort at all.

"Averal, how are things going in Princeton?" Edward came over to ask. Never took his free hand and squeezed it.

"Things are working out." Averal returned a reassuring squeeze, and smiled at his brother.

"Good. I have a favor to ask." He threw a look at Never.

"I'll just go and see if I can help Caroline." Never stood and reached for Lindsay. Averal kept her, telling Never she was fine where she was.

Never glanced over her shoulder before going through the kitchen door. Edward was deep in conversation, and Averal was listening intently.

"Can I help with anything?" Caroline was reaching for a bowl on the top shelf.

"Can you reach that?" She stepped back on her heels and moved away. Never was several inches taller and reached the cut glass bowl with ease.

"How's Averal doing?" she asked.

Never took a seat in front of the butcher block island. "When

I left him, he and Edward were head-to-head in conversation, and Averal was holding onto Lindsay as if she were his own."

"I like you, Never," Caroline said. "We think the same way about my brother, and I can see you're in love with him."

Never didn't speak for a moment. She looked directly at Caroline, who busied herself by pulling things out of the refrigerator as if she hadn't said anything that was nervewracking. She *was* in love with Averal. She'd known she was falling, but she didn't realize how much until they were sitting in his jeep outside the Center for Sickle Cell Research. He was so hurt, and she'd wanted to take his pain, share it, and make it easier for him to bear.

"Is it that apparent?" Never asked. Her ears began to burn. "Or are you reading me? Averal told me you were clairvoyant."

"Women in love are easy to read." Caroline glanced up from her task. She dropped several apples on the counter. "And I'm not clairvoyant."

"What about Averal?"

She shrugged. "I do seem to know what he's feeling sometimes. Not always."

Never knew that wasn't how Averal saw it. "What about now?" Never asked. She deliberately didn't look at Averal's sister.

Caroline was making a fruit salad, and Never picked up a knife and began peeling apples.

"He's happier, a little calmer than when I last saw him. He likes having you near him." She paused. "Earlier, when you arrived, there was a sadness in him. Did something happen before you got here?"

Never knew what she meant. Averal had learned about Gabe, and the news was unsettling. It had to affect him enough for anyone close to see it.

"Something he needs to work out by himself." Never was sorry she couldn't help him work it out. She could be near whenever he wanted to talk. He'd carried this wound around for thirty years. It was time to heal it.

"He's different this time," Caroline went on.

"What do you mean?"

"I didn't think he was coming at all. The last time I saw him was at my wedding, three years ago. Then out of the blue he calls and says he's bringing someone."

"Were you surprised?"

Caroline stopped from her task of slicing bananas, using the knife as a pointer. "It was the first time I hadn't been able to read him in years. He asked if it was all right with me and Matt." She went back to the bananas. "And as soon as I said yes, he hung up. I couldn't get any information out of him, not even your name. He just said you'd be someone I'd approve of." She looked up at her. "He was right," she confirmed.

Before Never could say she liked her, too, James waltzed into the kitchen. "What are you two doing? Except for Lindsay, who's asleep on her uncle's lap, there's a stag party going on, and I, for one, need female companionship." Both women smiled at him.

"Then, Brother dear—"

James held his hands up. "Oh no." He faced Never. "Here comes the why-aren't-you-married speech from the only married member of the clan."

"What about the woman you introduced me to the last time I was there to visit? She was pretty interested in you, if I know my Cupid's arrows."

The smile on his face didn't waver. "She's no longer a part of my life. I'm back to being footloose and fancy free."

Caroline glanced up and Never saw the all-knowing set of her face. "And hating every minute of it." The statement was delivered in a calm, quiet voice that rendered them all speechless.

"Not now, Caroline," James cautioned. Never could tell she was about to do a character reading, and James was trying to avoid it.

"Maybe I'd better leave," she began, wiping her hands and preparing to leave brother and sister alone.

"Don't leave, Never." He looked Caroline straight in the eye. "You're right, Caroline." He turned to Never. "Caroline is always right. I do hate it. I miss Leslie more than I thought was possible, but there are some things that can't be repaired."

"Does she know you love her?" Caroline asked.

James nodded. "I told her. I asked her to marry me months ago. I can only surmise the answer is no."

Caroline left the salad and rushed to her brother. Tears formed in her eyes and spilled over her cheeks.

"Why didn't you tell me?"

"It didn't work out. I didn't want anyone to know and . . ." he broke off. "Well, it didn't work out."

"James—"

"Come on, Caroline," James interrupted. "Is this a party or a funeral? Let's join the others. And I'm starving. When do we eat."

"Now," Caroline said.

He took his sister's arm and held out his other one for Never to take. Then he led the women back toward the living room. They turned at the dining room, and Never placed the fruit salad on the table while Caroline set the dishes and silver next to it. The living room was alive with laughter and merriment.

"I'll get the rest of the food," Caroline said. "Why don't you call them to eat?"

Never returned to the living room. She sought out Averal. He was sitting in the same place she'd left him, but had shifted the baby to his shoulder, where she rested on a napkin. Obviously he'd known he should do something to protect his shoulder, but hadn't known quite what to use. The child's head and Averal's hair color were almost the same. Never observed this silently. She hadn't expected to see him holding a child. He looked entirely comfortable, holding the baby and continuing his conversation with his brother, Edward. Calvin had also joined them. They laughed at something Edward said, and then Averal remembered he had a child on his shoulder. Checking her, he found she was still asleep.

Wedging her way into the sea of legs, Caroline lifted the sleeping child from Averal, while Matt took the other one. Before they left for the nursery she interrupted the conversation to let them know it was time for dinner.

As everyone began to move, Never had the feeling that today was the first time these three had ever talked to each other as a family. Averal wasn't standing back and refusing to allow the family atmosphere to touch him. He was right in the middle of the action, and he looked as if he enjoyed it.

She remembered him at her grandparents' reception. At first he'd stood back, away from the group. She knew he needed to be accepted by them before he could join in completely, free his inhibitions, and become part of the group.

The floor of the living room in Caroline's house was like that now. Averal was joining in, not looking for any hidden meaning in what his brothers said or did. He was part of the family even if he didn't acknowledge it to himself.

The visit was going a lot better than he had hoped. Averal was glad Never was with him. Although he'd spent precious little time with her she was like an anchor, keeping him grounded. She came from this kind of background. It was foreign to him, but not at all dislikeable. After the news today about Gabe, he wasn't sure he'd be able to stand all the people around him, but as Never had pointed out he was having a good time. Of course the conversations with his half brothers had kept his mind active and unable to fully think about Gabe. He'd put it off for a while, and he'd talk to Anne when he got back to New Jersey.

Never was missing now. After dinner they'd returned to the living room and resumed the series of conversations, lies, memories, and stories that each one told about the other. Averal felt jealous of his half brothers, but not depressed that he hadn't been a part of some of the antics. He had memories of his past, too, not of brothers and sisters but of the friends he'd made in school and of Riddles. His life had taken him in a different direction than that of the people in this room, and he was glad he had a chance to get to know them.

He got up, holding the glass of bottled water he'd been drinking, and went to find out where she was.

Never didn't want to spoil the family camaraderie by intruding. She took a seat in the deserted library and listened to the happy noise. She heard Matt rejoin the group, but not Caroline. Averal's sister had disappeared a while ago, and seemed to be missing for a long time. Never assumed she was with the twins.

Leaning her head back against the soft leather of the oversized chair, she listened to the voices. Edward's was young and serious. James's was reserved with a happy lift to it. Calvin's was authoritative, but comforting. Averal's was easily discernible, deeper than his brothers. She heard him laughing and smiled in the knowledge that he was enjoying the reunion. The noise dissipated into a hum and then a lull, which had her head drooping.

She didn't know how long she slept, but she woke when someone lifted her and carried her upstairs. His aftershave told her it was Averal. Wrapping her arms about his neck, she rested her head against his shoulder as baby Lindsay had done.

"You must be tired," he said as he laid her on a soft bed in the room Caroline had assigned her. Switching on the lamp, he smiled at her. She smiled back, her hand on his arm.

"You're having a good time." It was a statement.

He nodded.

"Good. Go back and stay with your brothers—all night, if you have to."

"You'll be all right?"

"I'll be fine."

He brushed her mouth with his, and his fingers lingered on her arm until they reached the end, reluctant to forego contact.

"Good night, sweetheart," Never said as she turned her head into the pillow and closed her eyes.

"Are you planning to sleep in your clothes?"

She cuddled the pillow closer. "I'll change in a minute."

The babel downstairs was muffled when Averal closed the door. She fell asleep, content that he would be all right, that this afternoon's revelation hadn't spoiled his attitude and left him aloof and unwilling to participate. Instead, he was having a good time. It was going to be a wonderful Thanksgiving.

When she woke the house was quiet. No light filtered under the door. The digital clock on the bedside table read two A.M. She still had her clothes on. Averal must have pulled a blanket over her. She pushed it away as she sat up. Her head was groggy, and for a moment she considered lying back down and forgetting the nightgown.

Dragging herself to her feet, she found her suitcase and searched through it for her nightgown. Going into the bathroom she began her nighttime ritual of cleaning her teeth and brushing her hair.

By the time she finished and pulled back the covers of the rumpled bed she'd slept on, she heard the wail of one of the twins. She was already up, so she decided she'd go and see what was wrong. At six months, they should be sleeping through the night.

Never stretched her arms into the peach-colored, silk robe that matched her gown, and opened the door. She heard the cry again, and turned in the direction of the sound. Caroline came out of her room.

"I'll see what's wrong," Never told her. "Go back to bed."

Caroline looked tired. "There are bottles in the refrigerator if they're hungry."

"Don't worry. I've done this before."

Granted it had been a long time, Never thought as she saw Caroline go back through the doorway. Her nephews had been toddlers when they went to Argentina, and pre-adolescents when they returned to the United States. Never had loved sitting with them while her sister and brother-in-law had a night to themselves. She knew she remembered how to change a diaper or test a bottle for the right temperature.

In the nursery a pinkish nightlight provided enough light to see the two cribs, one pink, one blue, and the outline of Averal lifting Laurence into his arms.

"Is he all right?" she whispered.

Averal turned around, surprised. "Did he wake you?"

"No, I was just getting into bed."

Averal cradled the child in the crook of one arm. He squirmed and screamed, fighting mad.

"Maybe he's wet," Never suggested.

He felt for his diaper. "Do you know how to change a diaper?" he whispered, as if their voices would wake the house but Laurence's wouldn't. Lindsay slept silently with her thumb stuck in her mouth, oblivious to the noise her brother made.

Never took him and unsnapped the sleeper Caroline had put him in hours ago. Averal found diapers under the changing table, and together they dried the infant. When she finished she lifted the happy child and handed him back to his uncle.

"Somehow, I don't think he's sleepy anymore," Averal said, cradling the child. He pushed his finger into the baby's hand and the child grabbed it. Averal's attention was captured by the small bundle in his arms.

"I'll take him downstairs until he's ready. You go back to bed."

Together they left the nursery. Never knew that if he laid the child down he'd immediately return to his normal pattern of sleep. Averal wanted to hold him, but didn't want to admit it. Never let him play the game.

"In case he gets hungry," she whispered. "Caroline says there are bottles in the refrigerator. You have to warm the milk. He can't drink it cold."

He glanced at her. She could see the question in his eyes even in the darkened hallway.

"If he starts crying, come get me."

She went to her room but, like Laurence, she was wide awake.

She lay there thinking of Averal. Half an hour later she tiptoed down the stairs. As she turned on the landing she saw them. Averal was sitting on the sofa, his head back against the fabric, Laurence tucked in his protective embrace. A fire still burned in the fireplace. All the lights had been turned off. The room looked rosy. She smiled at the scene. Right now she needed a camera. This had been a breakthrough trip for him. He'd discovered he did have a family who was interested in him, loved him, and wanted to be friends with him.

She'd heard Edward asking his assistance for some of his friends who were having problems setting up their business. Calvin had told him about the hospital, and Averal had returned with how his own business was doing. James related the problems of inner-city youths in Baltimore, and Caroline hovered over them all like a mother hen. The warmth in the room hadn't been created by the gas furnace or the fireplace.

Never sat down on the step and watched them as if they were one of BriAnne's paintings. She didn't know how long she'd been there when Caroline crept down and joined her. She tucked her feet under her full-length gown and wrapped her arms around her knees.

"He's growing," she said in a hushed whisper, her gaze on her brother.

Never nodded. "I'm proud of him, and I think he's happier than he's been since his parents divorced."

Realizing what she'd said, she quickly whipped her head around. "I'm sorry, Caroline. I didn't mean—"

"I understand what you meant," she cut in. "My father hurt Averal by not spending time with him. I don't think it was intentional. I think Averal reminded him too much of Anne."

"He does have a remarkable resemblance to her."

"My father and mother married three months after he divorced Averal's mother. Anne immediately left for Paris, putting the Atlantic Ocean between Averal and his father. My father is not a poor man, though. If he wanted to see his son he could have."

"He doesn't know what a wonderful time he missed by shutting Averal out."

"I think it was Anne he was trying to shut out." Her voice was a soft whisper.

Never shifted to face Caroline.

"A little over a year after he married my mother, my brother, Calvin, was born, quickly followed by me and James and Edward. My father didn't say or do anything to make me believe he didn't love my mother. Until her death four years ago, he was a devoted husband." She paused and looked at Never. "But I know he's always loved Anne."

Caroline turned back to look at her brother and her child on the sofa. She looked at him as if she were reading his mind.

"There were times," she continued, "when I'd see him with a far away look in his eyes. He didn't know I was around, and I suppose all his defenses were down. I knew he was thinking of her."

"Are you sure you can't read minds?"

"Yes, I'm sure."

"Averal was only partially joking when he told me that. He meant you can usually tell what he's thinking or how he's feeling, much as twins can sometimes do."

"But Averal and I are only connected by one parent, and we're far from twins."

"Yet you can feel what he feels?"

"Sometimes, especially when his emotions are stretched."

"Like when he's in love, or when he's fighting with a huge problem."

"That's right. And tonight I saw him begin a healing process. Tonight, for the first time, he wanted to be part of the family. I think we have you to thank for that."

Never's eyes misted, and she blinked several times to push tears away.

"All we need to do now is get father and son to forgive each other. And I think they both need to let Gabe go."

"We talked about Gabe today. Averal didn't know he wasn't his full brother. The news came as a terrible surprise."

Caroline gasped. "I didn't know that, either." A light seemed to turn on in Caroline's eyes. "It makes sense," she said. "My father won't talk about Gabe. His name wasn't spoken in our house. I think it brought the war that raged within him over Anne to the surface. She was the true love of his life. He couldn't conceive of her having an affair with another man. And her producing a child by such a liaison crippled him emotionally. He struck out, first at Anne then at Averal, because he reminded him of the love that wouldn't die even when he was married to another woman."

Never turned her head to look at the man she loved. He lay in the same position, still protecting Laurence from harm.

"Will your father be here for dinner tomorrow?"

"That's today," Caroline corrected as the grandfather clock in the hall counted out the hour. "I invited him. Neither he nor Averal are aware of the other coming. Both would have refused to come. I'm not sure even you could have persuaded Averal, had he known."

"Let's hope what began yesterday will flow seamlessly into today," Never commented. "Now we'd better get them both to bed."

When the two women stood up, a new understanding had passed between them. Never didn't know which of them moved first, or if they moved together, but they hugged each other. A joining had taken place, and the occasion was marked by two gown-clad women, both loving the same man, but loving him differently—both caring for him and wanting him to rid himself of the sore that had left him alone and away from people who loved him.

Never lifted the paternal arm that enclosed Laurence, and Caroline slipped her hands under his tiny frame. She lifted him free and headed for the stairs with his head against her breast. She glanced back in time to see Never drop to her knees in front of her brother.

Never studied him. Was this the same man she'd climbed into a jeep with nearly a day ago? She stroked his chin. It was scratchy. He needed a shave. She found the contact strangely erotic.

"Averal," she said, keeping her voice quiet.

He stirred, but didn't open his eyes.

"Averal." This time he did open them. For a moment they were unfocused. Then they cleared, and reality hit him. He reached for Laurence.

"Caroline took him back to the nursery," she supplied.

He rubbed his eyes. "I didn't mean to fall asleep."

"It's been a long day," she replied.

He took her hands. "What are you doing here?"

"Just checking on you," she answered honestly. "A lot has happened today." She didn't elaborate, and Averal didn't acknowledge anything, but she could tell by the way his hands tightened on hers that he understood.

He pulled her forward, slipping one hand over the peach silk gown sliding like water over clear crystal. The other one buried itself in her hair. He angled his mouth toward her, and she saw the hunger in his eyes.

Instantly, she knew that same hunger reflected from her own eyes. "Averal, I love you."

He crushed her mouth to his, sealing his brand on her. Both hands slipped around the silk and pulled her closer to him. He massaged the velvety softness of her shoulders. Gathering her closer, he deepened the kiss. His tongue pushed past hers, and he filled her mouth with him. He wanted to fill her body the same way. He could feel her hand on his back. He knew the slenderness of her fingers, the softness of her palm. Thrills passed through him, making his body harden and strain against his clothes until he thought he would die if he couldn't feel her under him, feel himself inside her, feel her body convulse and accept the pleasure he could both give and take.

Pushing her back, he slipped off the sofa. In the small space between the couch and the coffee table he stared into passion-

drenched eyes. He wanted her, needed her, and he could take
her here, now. But reason lurked somewhere nearby. This was
the wrong time and the wrong place. He couldn't take her here
or in either of their bedrooms. He couldn't trust himself if he
made love here. She took possession of him whenever they
joined, and he had no control over the rapture she evoked in
him.

He lifted his mouth and looked at her. Her eyes shone with
passion, her hair, gently mussed from his fingers, framed her
face in a soft mosaic, and the ethereal light of the room colored
her skin in gold tones.

He gathered her to him, settling for a body-draining kiss instead of the blessed release he craved but knew he couldn't
sample. She wrapped her arms around him, her legs tangling
with his as she shifted herself as if to mount him. He wished
they weren't there. Her wanted her alone, instead of in a house
with relatives he didn't know what to make of. He wished they'd
stayed in New Jersey and that they were lying on the floor of
his living room or the comforter-mattress of her bed. He wished
they were any place where he could make love to her. He wanted
her slowly, all night, wanted her screaming his name in climax
and kissing his skin in mutual arousal.

He groaned loudly as he pushed her away. Averal stood, pulling her to her feet. She wore no shoes, and stood a head shorter
than him.

"Don't think I don't want you," he told her moments later
outside her bedroom door "Denying myself the sweetness of
feeling your naked skin next to mine right now is tantamount
to scaling the capitol building without ropes or support."

Never began to say something, but Averal stopped her with
one short kiss before pushing her through the door and pulling
it securely closed.

In his own room, he stripped his robe off and sat on the bed.
His body was hot and fully aroused. Never could make him
hard without saying anything. Her kisses made him dizzy. He
thought of holding her. She was as soft as the baby had been.

Suddenly he wanted his own baby. He wanted Never to carry his child. He wanted to watch her grow heavy with his child, feel her engorged belly and know that they'd made a child from the love they shared. And he wanted to be there to love it. Nothing could keep him from giving his son or daughter everything he hadn't had.

Tonight he had found out for the first time what it was to have a family around. He credited Never with making him see it. His half brothers were people he liked. He wouldn't say he loved them yet, but maybe in time he could have the same kind of relationship with his family that Never had with hers.

Averal lay back on the bed and extinguished the light. He closed his eyes with a smile. *Never,* he thought. *Pregnant.*

Then he remembered Gabe.

FOURTEEN

Thanksgiving Day dawned clear and sunny with an expected high of fifty-five degrees. The twins were up and in full voice at six o'clock. Never rushed in to grab one of them, but found that Caroline and Matt had beat her to it.

"They're hungry," Matt explained. "Go back to sleep. We're used to it."

Never returned to her room, but didn't go back to sleep. She showered and dressed, pulling her hair up in a style she was sure Averal would pull down as soon as he saw it. For the moment, she thought she'd help Caroline with the meal or the children. And she looked forward to him releasing the style. Her face warmed as she thought about Averal's hands in her hair.

"Can I help with something?" she asked, coming into the kitchen. Matt was holding Lindsay, spooning food into her mouth. Caroline was doing the same with Laurence. Both seemed to want to eat faster than their parents could get the food to them.

"I haven't heard anyone else yet, but you could put on some coffee," Caroline said. "It's in that cabinet above the stove."

Never found the package and filled the well of the coffeemaker with cold water. She took a seat watching the performance of parents. Within minutes the kitchen had taken on the homey smell of the brewing liquid. It was a smell Never liked. She closed her eyes, savoring the moment.

"Would you like me to make you a cup?" Never asked as the final gurgling sound indicated the mixture was ready.

"I'd love one," Matt answered. "But it's time I got this little lady into the bath."

"Me, too," Caroline echoed.

"How do you take it?" Never asked. "I'll bring you a tray."

"Black," said Matt. "Mine with cream," Caroline added. They headed for the door.

Never poured two cups and found cream in the refrigerator. Setting the two cups on a tray she found at the end of the counter, she headed for the stairs.

She heard the splashing of water and entered the nursery bathroom just as two small fists hit the water. Up the liquid jumped, catching Caroline in the eye. Matt was protected by his glasses. All four people seemed to be having a good time. Never didn't want to interrupt. She set the tray on the sink counter and left.

Back in the kitchen she poured her own cup and replaced the pot on the warming pad. Before she raised her cup she was whirled around and kissed. Averal caught her from behind and pulled her into his arms, his strong arms hugging her close.

"Good morning," he said. "I thought you'd be asleep for hours."

She didn't tell him she'd gotten very little sleep after their little interlude in the living room.

"Would you like some coffee?" she asked.

"Mmmm," he said, inhaling the aroma the black liquid made. "It smells wonderful in here."

Never lifted another cup from the cabinet and filled it. She handed it to Averal. He accepted the cup, but immediately put it on the counter behind her. Quickly he threaded his fingers into her hair, relieving it of the pins that held it in place.

"I knew you were going to do that."

"Then why didn't you leave it free?" he frowned.

Never returned his frown with a grin. "Maybe I like having you undo it."

He took the comment as an invitation. Without haste he stepped forward and took her in his arms. He kissed her. No matter how many times he held her in his arms, each was a new experience. She lit his blood with a fire that raged out of control with instantaneous fervor. She was better than coffee as a stimulant, and he was stimulated. He felt himself swell and bulge into her soft skin.

"Oh, God!" he groaned as he pushed himself away from her. "Why didn't I suggest we spend Thanksgiving at my house?"

Before Never could answer, James came through the door. "Sorry, I didn't mean to interrupt anything."

"It's all right, James." Averal greeted him with a frustrated sigh. He didn't release Never but held her loosely against him.

"I'm usually up early," James explained. "I was always an early riser."

Never wondered if the rest of the family followed the same pattern. "Why don't I start breakfast?" She pushed herself free.

"Can I help?" James asked.

Averal took his coffee mug, leaned against the counter, and drank the hot liquid. Edward and Calvin followed suit, and the camaraderie of last night spilled onto the morning. Never found bacon and eggs in the refrigerator. Under the counter she found an electric grill and set it up. Laying the bacon in parallel strips, she popped it into the microwave and whipped up some pancake batter. The grill was hot enough when she dropped a finger of cold water on it.

Pouring the batter, she instructed James to set the table and asked Averal to make another pot of coffee. She pushed the button to start the microwave. As Matt and Caroline joined the group at the kitchen table, Never was setting a platter of pancakes in the middle.

"Gee, I don't know when I've had a breakfast like this," Calvin muttered, stuffing a fork full of hotcakes in his mouth. "Never, will you marry me?" he asked.

Averal's heart thudded against his chest. His eyes flashed at his brother until he saw the humor mirrored in his eyes.

"She can't marry you. I want her to marry me," James chimed in. "Or at least can I hire you to make breakfast every morning?"

"Sorry, guys." She smiled. "I'm spoken for." Under the table she took Averal's hand. It was all he could do not to upset the entire arrangement.

When only the dregs were left and everyone was on their third cup of coffee, the doorbell rang. Matt looked at his wife. "Are you expecting company?"

She didn't answer him. "James, would you get that?"

Never watched Caroline busy herself clearing plates. Suddenly last night's conversation with James and his sister came back to her. And she remembered Caroline missing for a long time. Needing only a little deductive reasoning, she knew James was going to find his Leslie at the door.

Matt got up and started to follow his brother-in-law. "Matt, I need you," Caroline stopped him. "And the rest of you," she ordered, a soapy spatula in her hand, "don't even think of opening that door."

"Who's out there?" Matt thumbed toward the door.

"Leslie." All eyes turned to Never, but her gaze was directed at Caroline.

"How do you know?" Calvin asked.

"Women's intuition." A smile passed between her and Caroline that only they understood.

"Averal, don't tell me she's one, too," Edward piped up. "One soothsayer in the family is enough. With two, I won't even be able to think dirty thoughts."

Averal answered by slipping his arm lazily along the back of Never's chair.

"I'm not a soothsayer," Caroline defended.

"And neither am I," Never told Edward in the soft, quiet voice Averal loved. "I overheard her name last night. It could only be Leslie arriving this morning."

James burst into the kitchen several minutes later. A large

smile split his face. "Everybody, this is Leslie, Leslie Stone—soon to be Leslie Ballentine."

A stunned silence hit the room. No one moved or uttered a word for several seconds. Then everyone erupted into a collective cacophony of congratulations. Caroline was the first to hug the newcomer.

Leslie was a short, brown-skinned woman with expressive eyes and a dazzling smile. Her hair, no longer than an inch, crowned her head in a relaxed, even style that looked easy to keep but probably required just as much care as Never's did. She held onto James with an I-only-have-eyes-for-you look. Never glanced at Averal, and wondered if their own expressions were as obvious as this couple's.

"Welcome to the family," Caroline called over the chaos. "You'll find out who we all are before the day ends."

Calvin and Edward hugged her and added congratulatory comments. Averal was the last. He took her hand and affixed his congratulations to the others.

"Go on, Averal. You're one of the family," James said.

James didn't realize how much this comment meant to him. His throat closed off, and all he could do was hug Leslie. He felt awkward welcoming someone to a family in which he was the newest member.

"We just finished breakfast. Would you like something?" Caroline offered.

Leslie took the seat James had sat in. "I'm too happy to eat."

"Coffee, then." Caroline poured her a cup and set it in front of her.

It seemed they were going to spend the day in the kitchen. Averal got up suddenly. Never looked at him. He smiled and touched her cheek before leaving. She wondered where he was going, and if everything was all right.

She didn't want him crawling back into his shell or thinking about Gabe again, but if he was, it was a problem he'd have to work through. She poured herself another cup of coffee. She tried to listen while everyone bombarded the newly engaged couple with questions, but her mind was on Averal. He needed a little space. She knew that, and didn't want to burst in on him too soon.

"Sorry, guys," Caroline stood up and announced, "I have to put you out of my kitchen. If you want dinner today, I must get started." With false groans the entourage left her alone. All except Never.

"Do you want some help?" she offered.

"You did breakfast. And Averal didn't bring you here to cook. So enjoy." She smiled that knowing grin that told Never she knew something. Never didn't pursue it. She wanted to talk to Averal, probably as much as Leslie wanted to talk to James.

"All right," Never agreed with a smile. "Call me if you want anything."

"I will. Now go see what Averal's up to."

Never almost ran from the kitchen. She found Averal in the living room. All the brothers were there, but Averal looked alone again. Never joined him at the door which led onto a porch.

"How many stars do you think are out there?" she asked, near his ear.

His arm circled her waist, pulling her body into contact with him.

"Billions and billions," she said, looking at the clear morning sky and the complete absence of any nighttime visions. "But that clump right there." She pointed to a place in the western sky. It was filled with streaks of white clouds. "That's where the Ballentine clan comes from. Can you see it?" she teased.

"Just barely." He shaded his eyes as if he were truly looking for stars.

"Don't worry, it will become clearer to you in time."

"Want to go for a ride?"

"Need a little air?" she questioned.

"Yeah."

Minutes later Averal was crossing Key Bridge and heading toward Georgetown. Even on Thanksgiving Day the District of Columbia was teeming with people. Averal inched the jeep through the traffic until he reached Wisconsin Avenue. Making a left, he headed through the heart of the area.

Street vendors lined the walks, hawking their wares to the crowds on the sidewalks and showing them to passengers in the slow moving cars.

"I thought the place would be deserted," Averal opened, having been quiet since they left the house.

"Not Georgetown. Look, even the shops are open here." Georgetown, named for George Washington, was the home of Georgetown University and site of the filming of *The Exorcist*. The less than one square mile area was a famous tourist area, known for its small boutiques and cobblestone streets.

The jeep's suspension didn't register the bumpy ride as they moved up the main boulevard. Since walking would be faster than driving, Averal searched for the rare parking space. He found one on O Street. Never got out, and hand in hand they made their way back to the busy town center. She had to stick close to him to avoid being separated by the crowd of moving flesh. Instead of being draining as it would have been in New York City, here it was invigorating. Never's hair flared in the wind.

Averal browsed in bookstores and let the street vendors go through their entire repertoire before refusing to purchase anything.

They headed back toward M Street, a major road today, but Never wondered at the small buildings that flanked it. What must this section of the city have looked like when Congress was in its first year? Across from them a carriage house style restaurant had a black and white horsedrawn brogan pulled into its off-the-street entrance. She didn't know if the restaurant had sat there for nearly a century or if it were only made to look that way, but its presence was enough to make her wonder about the city and its beginning. The wide crossing at Wisconsin and M Streets had directional signals that held the crowd back for a long moment. On the other side of the street they started downhill, silent, holding hands, in tune with each other. There were less people on that side. Averal and Never swung hands like the happy lovers they were, and went toward the river.

The Potomac passed right along Georgetown, separating it from the businesses that had grown up on the Virginia side. Averal stopped under the K-Street off ramp. The hum of traffic above them reminded her of a distant crowd, talking low, waiting for something to begin, like the hush over a Thanksgiving Day parade crowd just before Santa Claus arrives. It was soothing, and after a moment faded into oblivion.

Averal leaned against one of the posts. There they enjoyed a quiet moment. Never found a niche in his side and molded herself to him. She rested her head on his chest and listened to the steady beat of his heart. Without words they let their problems float away on the waters of the river. The sound of rubber tires on the cement roadway above them created a lull that washed out the noise and honking of horns atop the rise behind them.

"What happened at breakfast?" she asked gently, not wanting to disturb the untroubled moment but feeling he'd wanted to leave the house for a reason.

"Nothing," Averal said, no emotion betrayed in his voice.

"Why did you leave the room?"

"I needed some air."

"Averal." She turned her face to look at him. "This is Never. You can talk to me."

He shifted, his back leaning against the bridge support. She linked her fingers in his and stared at him. Averal released one of her hands and laid it against her face. With no effort he cupped her neck and repositioned her head to his chest. He held her there, his chin on her hair.

"I don't have much experience at this family stuff," he began. "James threw me with his comment."

Never remembered James saying Averal was part of the family. She'd seen the expression on his face when James had said it. He'd looked stunned. The day before had been new for him. He needed time to get used to acceptance. His heart was beating faster now. She could tell he needed time to learn to trust the feelings of his family, to know they would always be there. Even during disagreements and times when one person did or said something the other disapproved of, it didn't mean they would turn their backs and walk away. It didn't mean that years would separate them. It meant love would grow.

"Suddenly, there wasn't enough air in the room," he said. "I felt as if I were going to explode. I had to get out of there."

Never's arms went around his waist and she hugged him closer.

"I don't deserve them, Never. I haven't done anything to deserve their love."

"That's the thing about love, Averal." She stepped back and shook him slightly. "You don't have to do anything for it. It can't be bought or bartered. It's given fully, unconditionally, and without reservation, by the giver. You can't refuse it, for that will not stop it. And taking it is nothing to have angst over. Just accept. It'll make everyone feel good . . . including you."

"You like them, don't you?" he asked, pressing a kiss in her hair.

A note of hope entered his voice. She didn't know if he wanted her to hear it. "I like them a lot. What about you?"

"I don't know what I'm feeling." He caressed her back. "For everybody except you."

Never pulled back to look at him. He groaned again. "I don't think I can ever bring you here again."

Her brows went up and hurt flooded her eyes.

"I want you, too much," he explained. "Not being able to make love to you is a physical pain." His voice was deep, and Never saw his Adam's Apple bob up and down. She felt him grow warm against her, and the same fire that ignited his blood heated hers to a boiling point. She knew what he meant. Her eyes clouded, and she pressed herself closer to him. His arousal was evident to her.

"I can't believe I screamed and shouted at you," she said. They were so compatible in every way. How could she have fought him when he came into her office? Turned her back on him in the bookstore?

"Let's walk," he said, taking her hand and pushing her away. "I need the space." Never needed it, too. Her thoughts had begun to run to hotel rooms and a few hours alone with nothing between them, not even air.

They went back into the busiest part of the square mile and folded into the crowd. Never led him into a bookstore, where she found one his books on the shelf. It wasn't the latest one, and she already had a copy of it. She had all his books, but decided to buy this one, anyway.

"Would you like an autograph?" he teased. She remembered her previous attitude to having a book autographed by him.

"Yes, I would." She opened her purse and extracted a ballpoint pen. "Make it out to Stephen. That's S-T-E-P-H-E-N." She laughed at his pained expression. "I already have a copy. This one is for my nephew."

Never paid for the book and Averal penned his signature to the cover page.

"Stephen agrees with your methods." They stepped onto the sidewalk and slowly worked their way up the street.

"He goes to MIT?" he asked.

"I couldn't get him to go to Howard." She stalled his why-didn't-he-go-to-Howard-look. "MIT has a better computer science program."

"That's what he told you," he teased. "The real reason was those snobby women. He's even heard about them."

"Averal Ballentine—" She turned, beating at him with his own book. "If you say that once more, I'll drown you in that river."

"I give, I give," he conceded, warding off her attack. "After all," he said pulling her back against his hip. "you're not nearly as snobby as you were that first day I saw you."

Never would have pulled away, but he tightened his grip on her waist, keeping her close to him. They walked on. Street vendors stopped them every few feet. Averal would listen intently, then walk away. A few feet before turning toward the parked jeep, Averal stopped. The hawker went through his wares, showing Averal scarves. He used adolescent psychology to entice Averal. Several silks he placed against Never, to show him how the colors enhanced her rich skin.

Never held her laughter in, but was surprised when Averal pulled several bills from his pocket and purchased one.

"Scarves and perfume are acceptable gifts." He repeated words she'd said and placed the scarf in her hand.

Never took it, and rewarded him with a dazzling smile and a peck on the cheek. "Scarves and perfume are acceptable," she said.

FIFTEEN

Never's dress was Christmas green and Averal's gift scarf had several red and green stripes running through the geometric pattern. Her neckline was high, and the scarf added to the dress. She tied it around her neck, then moved the knot to her shoulder, where she used a circle pin of pearls to anchor it in place. Pearl drop earrings were her only other adornment. She twirled around before the full-length mirror, watching as the full skirt swished about her ankles.

As she descended the stairs she found Averal's eyes meeting hers. He didn't say anything, and she knew words were unnecessary. She stopped for a second and looked at him as he admired her. Her breath did its familiar disappearing act at finding him dressed in evening clothes. The only other times had been in the gallery that first night and at her grandparents' reception. He'd taken her breath away then, too, but she'd hidden her attraction. Now she had no reason to hide anything from him. His black tuxedo was contrasted by a white shirt and black bow tie. It wasn't the clothes. It was the man wearing them that made her knees weak.

The others hadn't come down yet. They were alone. She relished having him to herself for a few moments before giving him back to his newfound family.

On the bottom step he took her hands. "Where is everyone?"

"In the other room. They won't stay there for long."

"A little too much family?"

He shook his head. "It's been good. But, until they find us, let me look at you and tell you how beautiful you are." He opened his arms lifting her hands up as his gaze skittered over her dress, from her neck to her toes. "I can't wait to get you home."

Never smiled. "Gee, I wonder what smells so good." Never lifted her nose to analyze the savory aromas coming from the kitchen and deliberately ignored Averal's comment.

"You do," he told her. She had put Passion behind her ears. "I love that perfume." He kissed her quickly on the neck and stepped back.

Averal threaded her arm through his and drew her into the small den, away from the hub of activity in the living room. The roar and crackle in the hearth reminded her of last night and finding Averal asleep in the chair holding one of the twins. She sat down.

"Would you like a drink?"

Never shook her head. He was all the intoxicant she needed. "Sit next to me." She patted the seat beside her and he dropped into place. His arm snaked across the back of the chair. He looked at her, eying her hair. "Don't you dare," she told him, feeling his hand come up and knowing his penchant for digging his fingers in her hair and pulling it down.

"So here you two are." Caroline's voice interrupted Averal. "We've been waiting for you. Everyone is watching the game."

Averal looked at Never. "Do you like football?"

"I had the television on upstairs before I came down."

He smiled, "So did I."

They got up and followed Caroline to a game room. There a wide screen television sported a game in progress. Several smaller sets were playing other games. Thanksgiving Day must be second only to New Year's Day as a football fan's worst nightmare. It was a production just to try to resolve which one to watch. Every station had some kind of game on. There were too many to possibly see at one time, even with the arrangement that Matt had worked out.

"Averal!" a roar went up as they entered the room.

"Hi, pretty lady." Edward bowed in mock gallantry. "May I get you a drink?"

"A white wine would be nice," she told him.

"Averal, this creature says he favors Dallas over the Redskins." Calvin spoke in shocked surprise. "Can you trust a man who'd root for guys who wear grey?"

"I wouldn't," Averal answered, joining his brothers. "At least, not if I lived in this town."

Never found it confusing to have so many sets on at one time. She concentrated on the one with the large screen. Edward returned with her wine, and she took a seat near the edge of the room.

Caroline ran in and out, checking on the dinner. Matt played with the twins as they climbed over him on the floor. Leslie was tucked securely in James's arms and Calvin sat quietly on the end of the sofa next to Averal.

"Averal told me you're studying for the bar," Never said, turning to Edward.

"Yes." His young face brightened. "I thought law school was grueling, but studying for the bar is murder."

"What do you plan to do when you finish?"

"I work for the prosecutor's office in New York. I'll probably stay there to gain some experience. What I want to do in the future is wills and estates."

"Some of those take years to resolve. Do you have the staying power for that kind of work?" Never knew she'd be bored working on the same thing for years at a time.

"My mother used to say I could roll a pea around the world and not notice when I got home."

Never laughed. "Well I guess that's perseverance."

"You work for a company that's just recently merged." It was a statement. She assumed Averal had told him about working with the newly formed Cedar-Worthington. "I have several friends who went to work right out of undergraduate school and their companies merged. Several of them lost their jobs. I guess you're one of the lucky ones." His smile was genuine.

Never hadn't wanted to be reminded of Cedar-Worthington. She only nodded, and tried for a smile as genuine as he had. Averal hadn't told him of his involvement with her future. She wasn't sure of the future, and hadn't thought of it in the last few days. Edward brought it back to her. She was going to have to face it soon.

"I'm glad I went into law," Edward continued. "I'd hate to lose a job after only a few months."

It was worse after years. "I understand," she said. "We'll always need good lawyers."

"There's a glut of them, too," he frowned. His face cleared quickly. "But I'm going to be a better one."

Never looked at the face of ambition, idealism, and invulnerability. She remembered when she'd felt as Edward did now— before life and reality merged into one. When had the idealism gone away? When had her ambition been tethered? And invulnerability? Where had she hidden it?

Edward called her back to the present. "Your glass is empty. Would you like another?"

She looked at the empty glass. "No, thank you." At that moment Caroline called her and motioned for her to come over. Never left Edward and went through the door.

"It's nearly time to eat. The rolls are browning, and my father's car just pulled into the driveway."

"You want me to warn Averal?" Never's heart dropped. She'd forgotten in the wake of the good time everyone was enjoying that his father was due to arrive.

"I don't want him to make a scene when he sees him."

"I don't think Averal will do that. What about your father?"

"They're both stubborn when it comes to the other. If you'll take care of Averal, I'll tell Daddy."

Never put her hand to her temples. This was a headache she didn't want thrust on her.

"All right, Caroline. I'll tell him, but I can't guarantee he won't refuse to sit at the same table with him."

"He seems happy for the moment, but I don't know what to make of him at these times."

She looked distressed. Never felt her own blood pressure rising. She'd hate it if someone did this to her. And she had to tell Averal. She was the only likely choice. His brothers were ill-equipped to do it, and Caroline had to talk to their father.

"Thanks, Never." Caroline took her silence for acceptance. "I knew you'd be a treasure."

"I don't feel like a treasure," she muttered. She felt like the Wicked Witch of the West about to steal the ruby slippers.

The two women returned to the game room. Never didn't know how much time they had before Averal's father rang the doorbell or someone else noticed a strange car. Luckily, they couldn't see the driveway from there.

"Dinner is served," Caroline announced. "We will be eating in the main dining room, *without the television.*" Her voice defied anyone to argue with her.

Men and women grumbled as they filed out of the room. Leslie passed her carrying Laurence, a smile on her face. Never stood near the door, her gaze reaching out to Averal. He returned it without moving. When everyone else had gone she closed the door.

"You look as if you have a secret," he teased.

"I do." Never heard the muffled roar go up from the crowd gathering in the other room. Someone had obviously seen the inevitable. "I don't think you're going to like it."

"What is it?"

She went to him, raising her arms and putting them around his neck. Without preamble she went up on her toes in her three-inch heels and pressed her mouth to his. Averal's body was stiff, but he relaxed in seconds. His arms encircled her, caressed her back, and drew her closer to him. She could feel every part of him, feel the heat that generated in him, feel his heart beating fast against her own. Her breasts pressed into his strong chest as his arms banded across her back.

She loved him. If she'd been in any doubt, it was now gone. Never wouldn't be able to explain in words the way he made her feel, but the stirring inside her told her all she needed to know. She felt as if generations of Kincaids were behind her, cheering her on for finding the love of her life. She'd waited decades to find him, longer than most of her friends who were married now, some with children. She didn't regret one minute of the wait. Averal was who she wanted, and she told him with her mouth, her tongue, her hips, her body.

When she pulled away and lay limply against him, she regretted the words she would have to say. For the last twenty-four hours they'd been together constantly and loved every minute of it. She didn't want it spoiled, but she had no choice.

"Who's out there?" Averal whispered through her hair.

Never's head snapped up and she stared at him. "You already know, don't you?"

"I won't go," he exclaimed, he dropped his arms and walked away from her. He was at the door. Never felt cold and alone. The shared moment was gone.

"Why not? Who are you that you can't sit at the same table with your father?"

"We don't even know if he is my father."

"We don't know that he's not." She went to him, walking around to stand in front, forcing him to look at her.

"Even if he is, he's a stranger."

"And that's the way you want to keep it!" she shouted at him. "You don't want to understand. You've been living with this hate so long that you don't know anything else."

"I wasn't the one who refused to see him."

"You're the one who's doing it now. I've haven't met your father, but I'd lay book he's exactly like you—stubborn, self-righteous and bullheaded."

The lethal gaze Averal leveled at her should have burned holes in her brain. She steeled herself for his assault. Anger spurred her on. "By now he knows you're here. You haven't heard a door slam or tires squealing down the driveway. He must be willing to see you. It's time for the two of you to break down the barriers you've erected. Are you going to deny him that? Is it you, now, who won't see him?"

She paused to catch her breath. Her heart was thumping in her chest, but she wouldn't give up.

Averal stared at her. Myriad emotions distorted his features. His fist came up and slammed into the door next to her head. Never felt her hair stir, and fear ran from the center of her breasts to her toes. She didn't move.

"How long have you known he was coming?"

"Caroline told me last night. I didn't know before that."

"Why didn't you tell me?"

"I forgot." She spread her hands in a gesture of truth. "We were having such fun in Georgetown. It completely slipped my mind." Never took Averal's hand. She rubbed her fingers over the knuckles he'd hit the door with. "I don't fully understand, Averal. My family is different. We rally together whenever we can. Family division is foreign to me, but the two of you are here together. Isn't this what you've wanted your whole life? For him to come to you and talk? Do you seriously want to go through this door knowing you have a chance to fulfill a lifetime wish and not take it?"

There were few instances in Averal's life when he didn't know what to do. This was one of them. He'd painted his father as a monster years ago. What could he do now? His newfound family waited for them to open the door and step through. He didn't want to lose the friendships he'd just sealed, but having to confront the man who'd sired him but had only seen him seven times in the past thirty years left him at a loss as to what to do.

"Never, I don't know what to say to him."

She melted as surely as warm butter at the resolution in his voice. Her arms circled him, and he took refuge in her strength.

"Just say hello." Her voice was strained, as if she were holding back tears. "See what happens after that."

"Suppose we argue?"

"It takes two people to argue. Refuse to be one of them."
She pushed herself back and stared up into his eyes. "You didn't
think you had a family yesterday. And look at what happened."

"But with my father I'll need a miracle."

Never smiled. "Remember those stars we looked at this
morning?" He nodded. "One of them is your miracle."

"You believe I can do this?"

"I believe you can do anything you want to do." She kissed
him on the cheek. "I'll tell him you want to see him."

She waited for Averal to agree. He hugged her tight, cutting
off her breath and drawing on all the strength she had. She gave
it freely. When he released her she slipped out.

Averal had nearly asked her to stay, but he didn't. This was
his father, and *his* battle. He'd been fighting it for as long as
he could remember. He had scars, sores that hadn't healed, although he'd told Never it was in the past and he was over it. At
thirty-four he was still carrying the baggage of that twelve-year-
old boy.

He resolved to get rid of it today.

Averal took a deep breath. If he could have sucked all the air
in the room into his lungs, he would have. He didn't know what
he was going to say. He'd had a lifetime to prepare for this
meeting, and now that it was about to happen he could think
of nothing. How would he begin? He'd written six books on the
management of people. He'd been involved in countless interviews, had trained people in conflict resolution, dealing with
hostile employees, getting work done through cooperative efforts, yet all his knowledge deserted him now in the face of a
meeting with the man whose gene pool matched his own.

The door across the room was an ocean of distance between
them. Averal's legs were as heavy as iron. He couldn't move,
even though he wanted to. Then it swung inward. He stared at
the space, unaware of what to expect. Averal Ballentine, Sr., his

father, stepped across the threshold and closed the door. Averal stared at him. He couldn't count the years since they'd last seen each other. If he'd seen him on the street, would he know him? Would he recognize anything about him if Caroline hadn't provided the standing ground?

He was as tall as Averal. His hair had not thinned from the mass that Averal remembered covering his head, although it was shorter, conforming with the current style.

Averal remembered him as a younger man, without the grey hair. He was good-looking, the college professor type, with greying temples and an intelligent look in his eyes. He didn't look at all nervous about this meeting. Averal hoped he was holding onto his own outward appearance. Inside, he was shaking. He didn't understand why. For years he'd told himself this did not matter, that he was over the time when his father's attitude could reduce him to the twelve-year-old he had once been.

He was wrong.

"Hello, Averal."

Averal stared at him as if he hadn't heard anything. He was wondering if any part of his father were visible in himself. Then he looked at his father's eyes. They had the same eyes, although his father's were older, the creases about them more deeply set than his own. Other than that, Averal looked like Anne. Hadn't he seen his eyes when they were divorcing? Hadn't he known he was his child?

"What do I call you?" Averal asked.

Because Averal was already looking at his father's eyes, he noticed the change in them. He'd hurt him. He hadn't expected that, and it made him feel small. Never had pointed out that his father hadn't been the only one keeping them separated. He'd played a part in it, too.

"Why don't we defer that for a while?" he said.

SIXTEEN

Never merged into the traffic on the Beltway and quickly brought the jeep up to cruising speed. The traffic was light since many people would stay over another day before beginning the trip back to their homes. She glanced at Averal for the hundredth time since he'd emerged from the game room the night before and they went into Thanksgiving dinner.

He and his father had come out of the room after forty agonizing minutes of people outside waiting, pacing, and listening. They could hear nothing—no angry words, no laughter,

"All right," she began. "You've been smiling and trying to keep us all from knowing that you're riding on a cloud. I want to know everything. Tell me what happened."

"First we were hostile to each other. I didn't know what to say, and neither did he. Then we blamed Caroline." He laughed.

"You blamed Caroline?" she glanced at him.

"Not exactly. Neither of us expected to see the other this weekend. It was Caroline's engineering." He paused and sobered. "Then we started to talk. He told me how I reminded him so much of my mother that he couldn't look at me without thinking of her. His behavior appeared as hatred to me. The truth was, he was hurting, too."

Never noticed it was the first time he'd referred to Anne as his mother, and called her that. She also remembered her talk on the stairs with Caroline, and her belief that her father had been seriously hurt by Averal's mother.

"We talked about Gabe and his death. You were right." He paused and looked at her. Never smiled. "Gabe wasn't his son. He told me about an affair my mother had. He knew about it, but didn't realize Gabe was the result until he developed sickle cell anemia."

"The love he felt for your mother and your brother was so intense that when he found out he wasn't normal. He had too many emotions to overcome in too short a time. The result was divorce."

She understood that love. She wouldn't have thought she was capable of it a few months ago. Since she'd met Averal her life had changed, and now she couldn't imagine it without him.

"He's still in love with her," Averal said quietly. "All these years, and he's still in love my mother." Averal lowered his eyes while Never retraced their route up Interstate 95. "He thought remarrying would solve his problem, exorcise his love for her. He said it eased it for a while, but it was always there lurking, waiting."

Averal went on with story after story of how he and his father had talked about his childhood. His visits, though infrequent, had been lonely voyages that neither of them enjoyed. It was a relief on both their parts when they were over, and both of them admitted they hadn't missed the time they were together. After that admission others came forward, until all the demands were gone.

Never listened while Averal went on and on. The two hundred miles were eaten up in understanding and forgiveness. Eventually they lapsed into silence. Averal spread his arm along the back of the seat and played with her curls.

Pulling into her driveway she cut the engine and leaned into his hand. It was comforting, and she pushed the button on her seatbelt and slid across the seat.

"Glad to be home?" he asked.

She nodded.

"I am, too. I had a wonderful time."

"Me, too," Never said, and turned her head. She kissed Averal on the cheek.

"Let's go in."

Averal opened the door and they both slid out on the passenger side. Never lifted the key ring to open the back door where their luggage was stored. Averal covered her hand.

"The luggage can wait," he said. "I want you. I've been hard since we passed The Maryland House."

He waited only until she'd closed the door before pressing her up against it and covering her mouth with his. He abandoned any thoughts he might have had, and his mouth ravished hers. His tongue brushed past her teeth and mated with hers. He wanted to mate with her, wanted to know all the things that he'd learned this weekend with her. He wanted to possess her, spend time with her, spend . . . He stopped. His mouth lifted. Was he thinking happily ever after?

Her mouth was swollen, her eyes half-closed and full of passion. Her arms lay around his neck, and her body was hot against his. He wanted to say something, tell her his feelings, but he couldn't do anything more than take her mouth again and let her know every ounce of love he felt was in his actions.

He kissed her again, devouring her, wanting to make the two of them one unit. He squeezed her tightly to him. How could someone so soft be so strong? How could arms like hers pull him so securely against her? He didn't have time to think about it any longer. His hands were reaching for the hem of her sweater and he pulled it over her head, separating his mouth from hers only long enough to remove the fabric.

She breathed hard against him, her body molten and pliable. Averal pulled her away from the door, bending her over backward as he squeezed her closer to him. He wanted her. He wanted her to cry out for him, her body so much a part of his that no clear division between them was visible.

He pulled his shirt off. Never's hands caressed his chest, causing his entire being to tighten into a harder mass. Her mouth replaced her hands as she kissed his skin. For sure, the two of them would spontaneously combust. Never continued to kiss his chest, inch by inch. Her fingers teased his flat nipples into response. Then she replaced her hands with her mouth. He groaned at the sensations rocketing through him.

Her hands went to the snap on his jeans. The sound was an explosion in his head. With it went any control he had left. In seconds he was undressing her, feeling the heat on her skin, the smoothness of her arms, the flatness or her stomach, and knowing he wanted her forever. He lowered her to the floor and covered her with his own body. For a second he looked into her dreamy eyes, feeling her hands as they ran the length of him. In one easy movement he spread her legs and thrust himself inside her. She convulsed as her body took his in and held him. He was moved by her, more than by any woman in his past, and he knew there would be no other after her. This was where his life had brought him. His love for her was as she'd told him love was meant to be—total, without reservation. His body moved inside hers. Life began here, and he wanted her to know that life with her was a given. Nothing would come between them. Forever. This was what he wanted, and what he wanted to give to her.

He felt it with her, felt the level of trust, the wanting, knowing, feeling the knowledge that after today they would be together. She had his heart. He'd given it to her freely, without reservation, and he trusted her to hold it securely.

His body mated with hers, loved her, found all the places that were in tune with hers. He remembered that first day when he wanted to play the sounds of her feet on his sax. Now he wanted to play her body, play it every day, the way he was playing it now, with the fiery frenzy that made him crazy. He opened his body to her. She'd already learned the tunes that made him dance. And tonight he was doing the dance of a lifetime. He loved her more than he knew he was capable of loving anyone. A groan escaped his throat, and he knew he couldn't hold himself back.

Never's fingers laced with Averal's. She squeezed hard. Her

long body was wracked under his. She wasn't sure what was happening to her. They'd made love before. Yet this was different. She heard his groans, heard her own sounds, and knew this time any bars between them had disintegrated. She loved him, and her body was telling him that, just as his communicated to her.

"Averal," she breathed. "I'm burning up."

"Baby, I'm dying here."

Yet neither of them felt the need to stop. Never wrapped her arms around him and kissed his shoulders. She had ceased trying to stop the feelings that ran unchecked inside her. Averal had taken their lovemaking to a level she'd thought was only available in fantasies. They had crossed the fantasy threshold, only to find reality much more satisfying. When Never felt herself rushing toward the area of sensation that Averal created, she knew she couldn't stop the runaway train they were on. She didn't want it to stop. She wanted it to go on forever. She wanted this sensation, this pure love, to continue until she died, and she wanted to be with Averal when it happened.

Then she felt herself screaming. She called Averal's name loudly as they found that place, the lover's leap which they took together, life spilling from body to body.

Never pulled a sheet of monogrammed stationery in front of her. She'd been home nearly a week. It was well past time to send Caroline a thank-you note. Since she'd returned she couldn't forget what a wonderful time she'd had with Averal's family, or the nights they'd spent in each other's arms. Even the tense moments that passed before the meal in Caroline's dining room were worth seeing father and son emerge from the game room less than friends, but no longer enemies.

Never addressed the envelope in a strong, flowing style. She couldn't explain to Caroline in a thank-you note what had happened to her during the few days she'd spent at her house, but then Caroline couldn't explain what had happened in her family. Finally the link between all of them was sealing.

Never smiled as she placed the card in the pink envelope. If she hadn't already been in love with Averal, that weekend would have sealed her fate. Since they returned Never had rarely been without him. They ate dinner together every evening, and on weekends, after she sat for BriAnne, they went to a play or joined the crowds in the shopping malls. They held hands and talked about everything. Afterward, they'd make love. She couldn't remember being so happy. Waking up in Averal's arms, coming to life like a cat stretching, was something Never hadn't thought was in her stars, yet here she was—in love and loving it.

She stamped the envelope and dropped it into her briefcase. Checking the clock, she snapped the leather case closed and went out to get into her car.

Work was different these days. With Averal no longer a fixture in the office, morale had gone back to being low man on the totem pole. Never's had moved up a notch, and she floated about the office, frequently humming or singing softly.

"What have you got to be so happy about?" Barbara asked as she plopped into the chair in front of Never's desk. It was rare these days that Barbara did anything except make wedding plans.

"Isn't this better than being down in the dumps?"

"Yes," Barbara agreed quickly. "I'll bet it has something to do with that handsome man you couldn't keep your eyes off."

"What are you talking about?" She and Averal hadn't discussed keeping their love a secret but Never hadn't made any announcements.

"I'm talking about Averal Ballentine. I expected him to drop by this office today."

"Why is that?"

"Never, I've seen the way he looks at you, and the way those sexy eyes of yours drop to half mast every time he's in the vicinity. If you don't know you have the hots for him, you're the only one who doesn't.'"

Never was stunned. "Barbara!"

"I didn't start any rumors. You two did, by avoiding looking at each other, fighting whenever you came into contact with each other, and all the while you couldn't keep your hands off each other. Now tell me it isn't true?"

Never hesitated, thinking about confiding in her secretary. Then she decided if she didn't tell someone she'd burst. "I can't. It is true. I love him."

Barbara started up from her chair. Never came forward across the desk, cutting Barbara's exuberant howl. "You can't run around here telling everybody. I don't want to be the subject of any more rumors."

"This won't be a rumor. This will be confirmation," Barbara returned.

"I just don't want anything said." Never was too new at being in love. She and Averal were still learning about each other, and while she wanted to stand on her desk and shout how she felt, she was too leery of the tenuous thread to chance it. If they parted, she didn't want to be the subject of silent pity.

"All right," Barbara consented. "That's probably why he didn't come by."

It wasn't. Never frowned. She hadn't even known he was going to be in the building.

"Sharon did say he left King Boris's office in a foul temper."

Sharon was Boris King's secretary. And, as in any office, the secretaries were the ones who owned the grapevine. The remark had upset her. What had happened? She'd ask Averal that night over dinner.

"They're probably sending him over to Accounts Payable." Barbara was babbling, but Never was no longer listening to her. "Rumor has it they're next on the chopping block. We haven't heard anything here since he left. Any word?"

Never shook her head. She knew her secretary was trying to get information to take back to the anxious people on the floor.

Never had been so wrapped up in herself that she'd forgotten the insecurity of the people she worked with. She didn't have any information, and couldn't give it even if she did. She and Averal had discussed everything from solar flares to why people use circles over their 'i's' instead of dots, but they had missed Cedar-Worthington as a topic of conversation. She hadn't done it consciously, and wondered if he had. Suddenly, she realized the position she was in now.

Averal didn't come to dinner that night or the next, or the one after that. On the fourth night his jeep was parked in her driveway when she pulled in after work. Averal stepped down from his seat as she got out of hers.

All her doubts and fears that he wanted to end their association fled when she looked at him, and moments later she ran into his arms. He caught her and kissed her, kissed her hard and passionately, as if he'd been in the desert and she was his first drink of water.

"Where have you been? I was so worried."

He took the bags of groceries she set in his arms and followed her through the garage door.

"I had something to work out."

Never assumed he was still trying to resolve the years of dispute with his father. He'd been talkative on the drive home, but now that he was back on familiar ground had all the old insecurities returned? Had he talked to BriAnne? She had not mentioned it when Never went for her weekly sitting.

"I thought you'd decided I was no longer what you wanted, and you wanted to stop seeing me," she joked. Her voice was light as she dropped the bags on the kitchen counter.

"Don't ever say that again."

Never turned at the vehemence in his tone. "Averal."

He came to her, slipped his arms about her waist, and pulled her against him. "Don't ever doubt how I feel about you. You're the only sane thing that's happened to me. And I'll die before I let you go."

He squeezed her closer. Never knew something was worrying

him, but she didn't know what, and somehow now wasn't the time to ask. She let her arms slide up his and held him. They stood in the kitchen among bags of unpacked food and drank of each others' closeness. Averal's fingers were tangled in her hair, and his mouth moved seductively over the scented skin of her exposed neck. Never was easily aroused. After three days of missing his attention, she craved him.

His mouth covered hers as his arm bent down and the back of her knees folded against his arm. Her feet left the floor. Averal knew exactly how to get to the bedroom. He carried her there without relinquishing her mouth or giving her time to protest. No protest would have come.

Laying her on the satin coverlet, he began a slow, seductive and erotic ceremony of taking the clothes from her body. His fingers slid over her smooth skin, making it hot and pliable as liquid gold. As each sensuous inch of flesh was exposed he pressed lips equally hot and equally aroused against her.

He loved her. She was what made him whole. His tongue circled her extended nipple, and she gasped as pleasure flowed through her. Averal could have cried at the enjoyment that sound gave him. He wanted her. He wanted to dig deep into her and fill her body with himself. He wanted her to know she was his, and wouldn't belong to any other man for the rest of her life. He wanted to tell her everything that had ever happened to him, and know everything that had ever happened to her.

He wanted to fill her body with his child and hold her swollen belly in his hands. He groaned at the pain-pleasure the thought gave him, and bit slightly harder against her nipple. Never groaned and he loosened his grip.

"I won't hurt you," he murmured. Her skirt had come free, and he tediously released one leg of the panty hose she wore and then the other, all the while exploring her form.

When she was fully exposed, Averal stood back and looked at her. She accepted his perusal without modesty or comment. Rising on her knees, she pushed the coat from his shoulders and began her own seductive adventure, into the regions of his body. She loosened his tie and used it as a lasso to pull him to her. Her mouth fused with his in the heat that sprung up around them. She arched her aroused body against him, moving provocatively, and hearing him groan egged her on. She wanted to rip the clothes from his body. Three days was like a lifetime. She was starved for him, yet she forced herself to have patience.

Her unsteady fingers pushed the first button through its hole. She slipped her fingers inside the shirt and rubbed his skin. She had to close her eyes at the pleasure that ran through her just being able to touch him. The second button came loose. Never replaced her fingers with her tongue. His heart thudded against her, and she felt the shudder that passed through them.

Button number three was followed by four and five, and she had enough room to slip her hands inside the confining fabric. His breasts were flat, but hard work and hard play had developed his chest in muscular sections. Never's hands felt on fire as her open palms brushed his nipples into hard pebbles.

Averal pressed her closer to him. "Never, I won't be able to hold back much longer." His statement was an agonizing groan that had her dizzy with power. She unbuckled his belt, and the zipper of his pants gave way. Seconds later he was free of them. He'd taken over. Pushed her back on the satin cover and spread her legs. "I need you, Never. I need you *now.*"

He joined with her. Never's gasp at the initial penetration was due to the point of elated bliss that promised and gave so much. The ancient art of lovemaking was shared between them. Averal had thought he knew how to make love, but with Never he found he'd only had sex before—with *her* he made love.

He wanted only to give her what she needed. He wasn't out to take from her, only accept what she had to give him, and she held nothing back. He could tell from the ragged breathing and the body that writhed beneath him like a fighting lioness—a soft, wonderful lioness who controlled herself in any situation but could be a clawing cat when aroused as he aroused her.

He smiled, plunging deeper into her. Never's legs locked him to her. Her body took the punishing demands of his, consolidating his need for her with hers for him. He was on a high ride, one no aphrodisiac could produce, one that only Never Kincaid could extract from him. All his strength concentrated in one pool of need, and he heard himself cry out at the explosive release that rocked them both.

Their fall back to earth from the climax only lovers know was slow and uncontrolled. Their breaths mingled as Averal rained wet kisses over her face and neck. "I love you," he repeated over and over.

Never's words weren't lost on him, either. They vowed their love for each other and, wrapped in a tangle of arms and legs, clung as if one could not breathe without the other.

Never woke with Averal lying across her. It was dark, and she could only see him in the half-light that filtered through the curtains.

She stretched and he stretched, joining her. They came awake together, just as they had fallen asleep.

"I'm hungry," Never said.

"Again!" Averal's brows went up.

"For food, you dope." She made a swat at him, but he stopped it, imprisoning her hand in his and capturing her mouth. Lightning snaked through her at how quickly she could be made hungry for him.

"It's your night to cook," he told her.

"Cook?" she said. "Maybe leftovers." She pulled on a robe and headed for the kitchen.

Averal got up slower, grabbed a towel from the bath, and wrapped it around his middle. He found her in the kitchen, a container of Haagen Daz dripping from her hand. He went up behind her and put his arms about her waist.

"I believe I can live without ice cream, but I'm not so sure about you." He pulled her against him, her head leaning on his chest, and his hands cupped her breasts.

"Averal," she breathed with uncontrolled passion. "Don't do that."

"Why not? I thought you liked it."

"If you want to be drenched in ice cream, keep it up."

His hands massaged gently, bringing her body to life. When she could stand it no longer she turned in his arms and smeared his chest with gobs of the cold cream she held in her hands.

He jumped at the initial surprise, then pushed her face into it. Never began to eat the sweet strawberry goo from his bare chest. Her tongue savored him. Quickly his heart rate accelerated. When her hand released the towel covering him he lowered her to the floor and made love to her until she cried again and again.

Never finally got something to eat about ten o'clock. In the meantime Averal had carried her to the shower, where she washed him clean of the sticky residue she'd applied to his chest. He'd taken her again under the cascading water, and finished on the satin spread which showed their wet indentations.

"Never," he began, carrying her cup of coffee to the living room. "I have some—"

The ringing of the phone interrupted them. Never went over to answer it. After a second she handed it to Averal. "It's Vivette. She's calling for Riddles,' she said.

"This'd better be good," he said into the mouthpiece, then listened quietly. Never watched him tense. "I'll be right there," he said, and hung up.

"What's wrong?" Her heart thudded.

"I don't know. I have to go to Riddles Place."

"Is he all right?"

"He's fine." Averal took the stairs two at a time. Never found him dressing several seconds later.

"Is there anything I can do? Should I go with you?" She watched him moving quickly, much as she had done the first morning she met BriAnne and he'd made her late.

"No." He was fully dressed, his tie hung like a flat arrow around his neck.

"Averal, what's happened? What did Vivette say?"

"My father is at Riddles Place." He pulled his socks over his feet and stepped into his shoes.

"What's he doing there?"

"I don't know, but Vivette says it's urgent. I should come."

"Are you sure you want to go alone?"

Averal nodded, standing up. At the door he reached for her and she came to him. He hugged her to his side and kissed her longingly.

They walked down the stairs, arms wrapped about each others' waists. At the bottom of the stairs he stopped and turned to her. "I need to talk to you later." After a swift kiss that drugged her, he went into the dark.

SEVENTEEN

"Averal!" Surprise registered on Anne Ballentine's face as she opened her studio door and stared at her son. "What are you doing here?"

"Mother," he said, at a loss for what he would tell her. Until he saw her small frame he hadn't known he'd feel this protective of the woman he thought he only tolerated. Now he knew he loved her, and had loved her all his life. He'd always thought of her as a strong woman, able to withstand whatever life threw in her path. Now he didn't know.

After Thanksgiving he'd talked with her. For the first time since Gabe had died she told him how she felt about losing his father and about the brief affair she'd had with Gabe's father. She poured out the love she felt for Averal, and how devastated her life had been when his father remarried so quickly.

Averal felt as if his life were a huge puzzle with some of the pieces upside down. And over the weekend following Thanksgiving, some of those pieces had been revealed.

"May I come in?" he asked.

"Yes . . . yes," she said, standing back to allow him access. Averal walked into the room. He'd been at the studio only a few times. "I was just cleaning up." She looked at her hands, held out in front of her. Paint coated her fingernails. "I'll be right back." She left for several minutes. Averal heard water running in the bathroom.

He dropped his coat on the chair near the studio door and

walked to the area his mother used as a sitting room. It had a rose-colored sofa on top of a white area rug. Chrome and glass tables flanked the ends of the L-shaped sectional, and a square coffee table stood in front. Two matching chairs completed the grouping. On the low table were several art magazines, the anniversary clock that had twice crossed the Atlantic with them, and two picture frames. His heart missed a beat on seeing the photos. He had not seen them in years.

His seven-year-old face smiled from one glass frame. His brother Gabe, four years younger, looked clear-eyed and unchanging from the other. Averal lifted the heavy carved glass with his brother's likeness in it. Memory transported him back to Lake Como, a year before Gabe died. The two of them had been fishing with their dad that summer. It was the last happy memory he had of his childhood, as part of a family.

Anne came back breaking the fragile thread Averal had on the past. "You surprised me, Averal. I don't think you've ever been here unless I asked you to come."

He looked toward his mother, the frame still in his hand. "It's been a long time since I've seen these," he told her.

Anne took the frame from him. "I know. I found them the night of the opening. For some reason I had to see your faces again." She looked at her surviving son. What Averal saw had been lost for years. His heart stopped, then beat faster. Suddenly he was a small boy again. A child who needed to know he was loved. It was all there. In his mother's eyes was the love and compassion he'd craved all the years in France. All the years since Gabe's death. The look that said *I love you.* He didn't know who moved first, but he was hugging his mother and she was holding him. Years fell away. He was her child, and she was soothing his hurts and pushing the dark away when he was scared.

He realized she was crying. "Mom, don't cry."

"You haven't called me that in a long time," she said through hiccups.

Averal's eyes were moist, too. It had been so natural, calling her Mom. In the years they had lived in France and since re-turning to the United States, he'd called her Anne. It was formal and distant, as he'd felt she was. He used the name to make her remember she wasn't BriAnne Ball, but Anne Ballentine, his mother. Tonight she was close. Tonight, without words they had found each other again. But tonight he had something to tell her, something that might hurt her. He didn't want to have to do it. Not tonight. Not after they had just become a family. But he couldn't put it off.

"Mom, sit down."

Anne Ballentine pulled a tissue from a box on the table and wiped her eyes. Then, curling her short legs under her, she sat on the sofa.

"Can I make you a cup of tea?"

"No," she said, patting the sofa next to her. "Let's just sit here and talk."

Averal sat next to her. "I do want to talk to you, Mom."

"I know something must have happened. You didn't just de-cide to visit."

"No," he shook his head. Their recent talk had brought them closer, but an uneasy alliance existed until tonight.

Vivette's call had told him his father was at Riddles Place. Averal didn't fathom why he'd come when he left Never's house, and he'd broken speed limits to reach the bar. He knew it had to be important.

Riddles was behind the bar drying glasses when he came in. He caught Averal's eye immediately and motioned toward the end of the room. A solitary figure occupied the booth at the end of the bar. Averal Ballentine, Sr. looked every one of his sixty-two years. He caught Averal in a bear hug. It was the last thing he had expected. When they parted at Thanksgiving they'd agreed not to be enemies, but there was no agreement they were friends, and although Averal had released the pent-up anger of his father-son relationship his father wasn't privy to that reve-lation.

Averal felt strange with this man holding him. He was his

father, and he wanted to return the hug. Before he could decide what to do, his father released him and sat down again. Averal Ballentine, Sr. had already emptied a glass. It sat on the table. Riddles brought Averal a drink and removed Averal's father's glass. Averal noticed he did not replace it with a fresh drink.

"How did you know where to find me?" he asked, hiding the emotion he felt for the man across from him.

"Anne told me about Riddles years ago."

She had not mentioned it to him. He wondered when that was. Maybe the one and only time he came to see him in Paris. Riddles was giving him saxophone lessons. But as far as he knew, his mother and father didn't see each other then. Averal's father had brought his second wife with him, and he met them at the hotel. This wouldn't explain how he knew about the restaurant in Princeton. The only other source had to be Caroline.

"I had a good time at Caroline's," Averal said. "After we talked, I felt a lot better. And I talked to Anne. I know we'll be able to mend some of our differences in time."

"Time." Averal, Sr. grunted. "I'm here, Averal, because I'm running out of time."

Averal felt numb. Air whooshed out of him like a deflating balloon. He didn't understand why. This man had been nothing to him. "What are you saying?"

"I want to see Anne before I die."

"You're . . . dying." Averal couldn't get the word past the lump in his throat.

The older man nodded. "I have a rare heart disease. It has a long, unpronounceable name, but what it means is the walls of my heart are deteriorating."

"When did you find this out?"

"The Friday after Thanksgiving. I've had a lot of tests recently. This was the result."

"Have you had another opinion?"

His father was nodding before Averal finished. "I've been to groups of specialists. They've all come up with the same diagnosis."

"What are you going to tell Anne?" An unfamiliar concern gripped him. Protection of Anne's feelings wasn't one of his emotions. She could take whatever life threw at her. But suddenly Averal knew she harbored a love for his father. And he wasn't sure how this news would affect her.

"I don't know. I just want to see her again."

Averal remembered Caroline's game room. He'd told him he was still in love with his mother. Averal had related none of this to Anne. He didn't know how she'd feel. In the past thirty years he'd thought he knew these people. But it had turned out he didn't really know any of them. It had taken Never to open his eyes.

"Are you going to tell her about the heart disease?"

"I don't know."

"She'll wonder why you're showing up after so many years of silence."

"I hoped you'd brace her. Let her know I'm here. If she refuses to see me, I'll go away without a word."

Averal took his drink and threw the contents into the back of his throat. The hot liquid was like fire as it hit him. Warmth spread over his tight chest and into his stomach.

"When do you want to see her?"

"Tonight, before I lose my nerve."

He was surprised, but he hid it. "Maybe I should call."

"Don't." A brown hand reached over to stop him from rising. "Can we just go by? I'll stay in the car until you let her know."

They'd left the bar. Averal acknowledged Riddles, and his father had shaken his hand as if they were the best of friends. Averal suddenly felt as if his life had been under glass. Everybody around him knew what was going on, and he stood in the middle with blinders on. . . .

His mother called him to the present. "Averal, you said there was a reason you came by tonight?"

Averal lifted the picture frame with Gabe in it. "I've wanted so much for things to be as they were before Gabe died. But so much had happened to us, and it was so long ago. You're the success you wanted to be."

She dropped her eyes. "I'm a success. But it isn't what I thought success would be." Her voice was devoid of emotion.

Averal was silent.

"When I took you to France I thought it would be good for both of us. We'd get away from your father's new family, the old house, and memories of Gabe. I didn't know it was hurting you until it was too late."

"I wasn't hurt," Averal said.

Anne took his hand. "I hurt you. Riddles told me."

"Riddles?"

She nodded. "It was why I let you spend time with him. You needed someone like him. I couldn't be a father to you. Riddles promised me he'd look out for you, guide you the right way. I trusted him, and he didn't let me down."

"He used to defend you to me." Averal could see why now. When he complained about his mother, Riddles would tell him she was only looking out for him, that she was busy trying to support him, and that everything she did was out of love. Why he'd rejected that explanation, he didn't know now.

"Averal, I'm sorry your father and I failed you."

His father. Averal remembered his purpose for coming. "I've seen him, Mom," Averal said.

He looked carefully at Anne Ballentine's face. Her chin dropped a fraction before she pulled it up again. "How is he?" she asked with the grace of a woman born to duty.

"He's here."

Anne looked at him as if he'd dropped a bomb.

"He wants to see you."

"Me! Why?" For the first time in his memory, Averal thought his mother was flustered.

"We talked a long time tonight." He squeezed the hand his mother was holding. "He's not well." Averal spoke softly.

Anne's head snapped up, and she took a deep breath. "Where is he?"

"Downstairs."

Anne was suddenly on her feet. "You left him in the car? Averal, go and get him."

"He wanted me to tell you—"

"Go and get him. He can tell me." The old Anne was back—the pint-size woman who could take anything.

Averal stood and hugged his mother. "I love you, Mom," he whispered, pressing his lips against her hair.

Her arms tightened around his waist. "I love you, too, Averal. I always have."

When he released her, there were tears in her eyes. "I'll get him now."

Averal went out and moments later came back with his father. Anne's back was to them.

"Anne." His father's voice was hoarse with emotion.

Averal watched as his mother stiffened. Slowly she turned around, her hand going to her throat as if she were going to choke.

Averal didn't know what to expect but he didn't think he'd discover his mother was still in love with his father. When he saw their eyes lock on each other, he knew. What passed between them had the same lightning bolt effect that made him reach for Never. Between them was the space of the room, but there was a love so tangible he could almost touch it.

Both of his parents took a step toward the other. Then they were in each others' arms. His mother was crying, and his father was smoothing her tears away. He felt like an intruder. Why hadn't he seen it before? Why didn't he realize his parents had always loved him, and loved each other? He knew they would be all right. He didn't have to fear telling his mother. His father would do that. He'd leave them to remember and rediscover each other. There would be time for the three of them to talk later.

The last puzzle piece was turned over, and the picture was

clearly visible. It was a giant heart. A heart encompassing love and understanding, with bonds strong enough to withstand time and tragedy. Inside was his family, bonded together and loving each other. He wasn't without family. They had always been there, protecting him from a perceived hurt. And he'd pushed them out, not allowing them to get close enough to his real feelings to know how much they loved him, or to know how much he needed them.

Averal retrieved his coat from the chair and slipped his arms into it. As he turned to leave he saw the scarf on the chair in the studio. If the moon hadn't been so bright or the studio had less windows, he would have missed it. It was the one he'd given Never. He went through the studio and picked it up. He could smell her perfume.

The portrait. He remembered his mother was working on a portrait of Never. And she had paint on her hands when he came in. He saw the canvas on the easel. It faced the east windows. He was drawn to it. He had to see it. Stepping in front of it, Averal stopped. Moonlight struck the canvas and Never stared at him, lifelike and beautiful.

Her face filled the canvas. His mother had captured her essence. On a flimsy piece of fabric, large expressive eyes looked full of love. Averal knew that look. It was how she looked at him, how her eyes had looked when he left only an hour ago.

Only the top of her red velvet dress showed. Splashed over her shoulder was the scarf he'd given her. She wore it like a tartan cloth.

Averal left the portrait. As he turned away, the scarf slipped like water from his fingers. He let himself out without being aware of the two reunited lovers in the other room.

EIGHTEEN

Fired! Never was stunned. It had finally happened. The decision had come this morning. She'd been summoned to King Boris's office the moment she arrived.

"The decision," he told her, "is that your department is essential to the organization."

Elated, Never smiled at him. His expression was austere. She knew there was more.

"However," Boris continued, "under the new organization it will be put under the direction of Jason Bartholomew."

Never didn't move. The bottom had dropped out from under her. Her department would stay. She would have to go. She remained calm and listened as Boris went through telling her what a valued employee she was. They would recommend her without reservation for another position, but there were none available at Cedar-Worthington at the moment.

When she just stared at the short fat man, he went red with discomfort. Never knew what she was doing, but she kept it up. When he began going through the severance package, she was no longer listening. She saw the Ballentine and Associates stationery lying on the desktop, and her only thought was *Averal knew.* He knew, and he didn't tell her. He'd made love to her, and all the while he could have told her. Yet he hadn't.

Never was calm by the time she passed through the gauntlet of curious stares on the way to her office. She closed the door and stood against it. Her body was numb. She didn't know how she felt. Was she relieved it had finally happened? Did she have a plan for the future? Now she had no choice but to accept the New York offer.

Maybe it wouldn't be so bad getting on the train each morning and commuting into the city. Hundreds of people did it. She could too.

A soft tap came on the door. Never stepped away from it and Barbara turned the knob and came in.

"What happened?" she asked.

"Would you please ask everyone to meet in the training room in ten minutes?" Never replied.

"Sure." Barbara hesitated, then backed out of the partially opened door and closed it behind her.

She couldn't get it out of her mind that he knew. All the way to the crowd waiting in the room at the end of the hall she thought of Averal, and how he'd made such beautiful love to her last night. All the time he'd known she was going to be fired today, and he withheld it from her. How could he? If he loved her, how could he?

The room was silent when she walked in. She felt nervous around people she'd known for years. They watched as if she were about to drop the guillotine on them. Never tossed her head and smiled. She broke the ice. "Don't worry, the news isn't that bad."

She didn't stand on the presentation stage, but opted to lean against one of the tables in the front of the room.

"Mr. King didn't ask me to speak to you, but I wanted to. Cedar-Worthington-" The name felt strange to her tongue. "Cedar-Worthington has finished their review of our department. The decision is that this department is essential to the corporation, and will be left intact." An audible sigh of relief came from the gathered crowd. A second later conversations and smiles began to filter through the group. A smattering of hands clapped, and then it broke into full scale applause.

"There's one more thing." Never put her hands up to regain their attention. "The reporting structure has been altered." She forced herself not to choke on the words. "The department will no longer report to me. Jason Bartholomew will have responsibility for Corporate Systems, along with the other groups which already report to him."

"Where are you going, Never?" Barbara stood at the end of the room. Her question echoed the thoughts of those present.

"I will be leaving to pursue other interests." She attempted to smile. The phrase *pursue other interests* was a catchall when there was a difference of opinion between the new management and the old. "I would like to say that I've enjoyed working with all of you, and I'm glad the merger will allow you to keep your jobs. Thank you."

She didn't wait for anyone to leave. She went through the door and back to her office. The rest of the morning a steady stream of people came in to say they were sorry she would no longer be there. Never kept her head up until Aletta came in with tears in her eyes.

"Don't do that, Aletta," she cautioned. "I've managed to get through this without breaking down. You wouldn't want to ruin my reputation as a hard-nosed director, would you?" Aletta burst into laughter, which did nothing to stem the tears flowing from her eyes. Never handed her a tissue.

"I thought we'd all go," she said.

"I'm glad we didn't. Mergers aren't personal," she told her friend. "It's business sense. A new organization needed to be formed when Cedar Chemicals and Worthington Pharmaceutical merged. Some of us have to go. I won't take it personally."

"They don't know what they're doing, firing you." Aletta sniffed.

"Thank you, Aletta." She hugged her. When Aletta left, Never began packing her personal belongings in a cardboard box.

By lunchtime she'd said good-bye to everyone and talked to personnel. She picked the box up and looked around for anything she'd left. It amazed her that ten years of her life fit into a box she could hold in her arms. A few plaques, two service awards, her monogrammed pen and pencil set, a few photos, and three plants. Not much to show for the hours she'd spent there.

She kissed Barbara on the way out. "I'll see you at the wedding," Barbara told her. Never walked toward the exit. She felt strange. A phone rang behind her.

"Never," Barbara called when she reached the door. "It's for you."

She turned back. "Transfer it to Jason Bartholomew."

She smiled as she stored the box in her car. What a great exit line. But the humor wore off when she pulled into her driveway. It was quiet when she went inside the house, too quiet, and when she woke tomorrow morning she'd have no place to go.

Never wasn't used to being home in the afternoon. When Averal had left last night she'd curled up on the sofa, waiting for him to return. She woke at three o'clock in the morning, cold and wondering why he'd hadn't called.

The bedroom was a mess. She stepped out of her heels and pushed her feet into flat shoes. Taking off her business suit, she donned a faded sweatsuit.

Keeping busy was good for her, she thought. If she kept her hands and mind busy, she wouldn't dwell on being fired. She ripped sheets off the bed as if the movement had enough force to send her back in time twenty-four hours. But it didn't. These sheets had to be sent to the cleaners. She folded them neatly and got fresh ones from the hall closet. Remaking the bed made her feel better.

But the moment she finished, the memories came back. She had been fired this morning, and Averal knew about it. Why didn't he tell her? She put the sheets on the pile to take to the laundry, and picked up some furniture polish. An hour later there was no dust to be found on any surface in the small house on Library Place.

The dishwasher was running and the kitchen was clean enough to eat off the floor. All the food had been unpacked and put away. The empty bags were stored on a basement shelf.

It was two o'clock, and she was finished. Damn! she cursed.

She was out of things to do. Maybe she could work on a program. The newest one had been completed and mailed weeks ago, though. She wasn't even working on one at the moment.

Going to the door, she checked the mailbox. The flag was down, meaning the mailman had already been there. Opting to disregard the cold, she jogged to the country style mailbox and retrieved her mail.

Back inside, she closed the door. The wind had picked up, and she was cold all the way through. There wasn't much in the mail, a few bills, a few flyers for local stores and a business envelope from the video company where she'd sent the games.

Her breath stopped. It was a letter, not a package. Rejections came in packages, when they returned the games. She'd included enough postage for their return. But she had a letter. She closed her eyes, hoping. Maybe they did like the games. Maybe they wanted to buy them. Maybe she would find another career on the same day she'd lost one.

She was afraid to open it. She stared at it for a long time before she picked up the letter opener and slit the top. The white piece of paper with the blue and white logo almost fell out. Opening it as if she needed to hold it for future fingerprinting, she pulled the flaps back.

Seconds later tears were running down her cheeks. The letter expressed their regrets, but at this time her games did not meet their specifications. Never didn't read any further. She balled the letter into a small wad and threw it toward the garbage can. It missed, finding a place between the refrigerator and the door leading into the dining room.

Myra's voice came over the intercom. "You have a Barbara Dixon from Cedar-Worthington holding."

"Thank you, Myra." Averal grabbed the phone. He hadn't been able to find Never for a week. He'd heard about her being fired and rushed to her house, only to find it empty. Her car wasn't in the garage, and when he called, her answering machine had said she wasn't available.

"Barbara, this is Averal." He was anxious.

"Hi," she greeted. He could hear her smile through the line. "I was wondering if you could tell me where Never has gone? I've been calling her, but I get no answer."

"I don't know where she is. I was hoping, when Myra said you were on the phone, that you'd be able to answer that question." Averal's spirits plummeted, and he fell back against the leather chair. "I've been trying to call her for a week, but all I get is her answering machine." Averal knew the message by heart. He'd dialed Never's number until that message had him wanting to climb through the phone line and yank the machine from the wall. "I've been trying to reach her, too."

"When she left here she seemed fine." Concern laced Barbara's voice. "You think she's all right?"

"I think she's fine," Averal lied. "She probably just needed some time alone."

"It's not like her." Barbara hesitated.

"I'm sure she'll be back soon." Averal wasn't sure of anything except he wanted to wring Never's beautiful neck, just as soon as he knew she was safe and unharmed.

"I'm calling because they're remodeling her old office for the new director." Barbara stopped to clear her throat. "I found her extra set of keys, and I didn't know what to do with them."

Averal sat straight up. "I know this is going to sound strange, Barbara." He spoke very slowly, as if he needed to make sure she understood English. "Can I come by and pick them up?"

"You're worried about her, too."

"Extremely." Averal controlled his breathing, not wanting her to know how much Never's disappearance affected him. He *was* worried. He was nearly out of his mind thinking horrible things that could have happened to her. He'd called everyone he could think of who might know where she was. Even his mother hadn't seen her. She told him she'd finished the portrait, and Never wasn't due for another sitting.

No one answered the phone at her grandparents' house the one time he'd called. He'd been reluctant to do that, not wanting to worry them, but after four days he'd needed to know if she was there.

Barbara spoke again. "Averal, why don't I meet you at Never's house in fifteen minutes?" Averal looked at the clock on his desk. It was quarter to one.

"Fifteen minutes would be fine." He was already getting up.

Barbara and Averal pulled into the driveway at nearly the same moment. Barbara had the keys in her hand.

"There's an alarm system," Averal told her. "I have the code." It was Never's nephew's birthdays.

Barbara opened the door and Averal pushed the codes into the electronic alarm system. They went through the house. Nothing looked out of place. All traces of Averal ever having been there had been removed. Her house was as neat and clean as one of her starched blouses.

"There's nothing here," Barbara said as they both ended the search in the kitchen. "Never could have disappeared from the face of the earth, but she'd clean her house first."

Averal stared at Never's former secretary. His eye caught the wad of paper lying near the dining room door behind her.

"Yes," Averal agreed. "And she'd make sure every bit of paper was properly disposed of." He picked the paper up and straightened it out.

"What is it?" Barbara asked, and when he didn't answer she tore the letter from his fingers.

"Oh my God," she said on a breath. "By the date on this letter, it must have come the day she was fired."

Averal had already calculated that. To be fired and rejected on the same day. And to know that he could have softened the blow, and he didn't.

He had been going to tell her. He knew Boris King's decision. He'd wanted to let her know. But his father had called.

The news of his health and the renewed love between his parents had made him forget about Never's problem. By the time he remembered it was much too late to call. And in the morning he'd overslept. Each action was small, but the combination of them made for one grand fiasco. Unfortunately, Never was the person to feel the effect. She was alone. Somewhere out there she was alone and miserable.

He had to find her.

"Barbara, you know Stephen and Donald's birthdays."

"I'm a good secretary." She pouted.

"I'm counting on it. What about their addresses and phone numbers at school? Do you know them?"

"Yes," Barbara said, as if it would be outrageous for her not to know.

"She wouldn't disappear without letting them know where to find her."

"You're right. Every business trip she went on she left them specific itineraries, even connecting airline flights."

"Oh, Barbara, I could kiss you."

Averal felt his spirits lift. They would know where she was, and how to get in touch with her.

But he was surprised later that evening when he finally reached Stephen. "She didn't have any particular destination in mind when she called," the young man said.

"She was just going to get in the car and drive?"

"She's done that before, and when someplace looked interesting she'd stay there and she'd call. The last time it was the mountains. She went skiing."

"Where did she go skiing?" People were incessant creatures of habit. They liked familiar things. Never might return to the same ski area.

"It was a lodge in the Pocono Mountains. I don't remember the name. I just took the phone number at the time."

"You don't still have it?" Averal knew he was hoping against hope, but he needed to do something.

"I don't," Stephen confirmed. "I wouldn't worry about her. She'll be all right. She's a very resilient person."

Averal knew that. It didn't keep him from worrying. He

wanted to know where she was. He didn't want her going through this alone. It wasn't necessary. She had him to lean on.

"I've got to talk to her," Averal kept his voice from sounding too rough. He wanted to grab Stephen and make him talk. But he knew shouting would get him nowhere. "She was fired."

"She told me."

"I've tried her grandmother's, and got no answer."

"I'll give her a message if I talk to her."

How could he tell this young man he was in love with his aunt? How could he tell him she wouldn't talk to him because he had known she would be fired and he didn't tell her, even as he shared her bed and the floor of her kitchen? That he'd had so many opportunities to let her know and he'd kept the knowledge to himself?

And now what kind of message could he give her? What could he say through a medium?

"Averal?" Stephen called from the other end of the line. "Do you want to leave her a message?"

"Yes," he conceded. "Tell her I love her."

He hung up without waiting for a reply. His desk was a mess. His life was a mess. With both hands he raked his hair and leaned back in the chair. It was quiet, as it had been the night she came to his office with three different kinds of chicken. She'd been willing to eat crow for him.

Now it was his turn. And he'd gladly do it, if he knew where she'd gone. Why hadn't she called?

And why hadn't he returned to her the night his father called him?

The moment Never arrived at her grandparents' house she thought of Averal. Despite the cold and rain, her grandparents swung the door open as she got out of the car. Both of them were down the porch stairs and hugging her, welcoming her into their loving home as if she were a prodigal daughter returning after years of absence. This was the kind of homecoming Averal longed for. She knew Averal would not get this kind of welcome from his parents or his half-family. Caroline might try, but Averal would back off, the same way he backed away from her.

"I'm so glad to see you," her grandfather said. "Your Grand's been fretting ever since you called."

"I have not." Never's grandmother threw a protesting look at her husband as she hugged her granddaughter.

"I'm fine," Never said.

"It's just unusual," her grandmother continued, "that you'd come in the middle of the week."

Never didn't answer that. She pushed the button on the key chain in her hand. The trunk of the car popped open, and she turned toward the rear of the car.

"You're getting wet," she said. "Go inside. I'll get my suitcase."

The house was a huge Victorian structure. Cape May had many of these built as refuges from the summer heat of New York during the early 1900's. Never's parents had bought this house the year she was born. When her father and mother died, her grandparents took over the house and brought her and her sister here during the summers. The house had a center foyer with a wide staircase that stood across the back wall. Along the side a small elevator had been installed when her grandparents could no longer climb up and down.

When Never walked inside the house was as cozy as she remembered it being during the many summers they had spent here. Never left her suitcase by the wide staircase. A fire burned, cheery and inviting, in the living room hearth. A live Christmas tree filled the air with pine scent. Never breathed it in. Everything was perfect. This was exactly what she needed to get her mind off her problems—to come home.

Removing her coat, she hung it in the closet and walked through the arched doorway. She stopped in front of the grate and faced the room.

"I was fired today," she said.

Neither parent said a word. They stared at her, at a loss as to what to do.

Her grandfather recovered first. "You'll get another job. In the meantime you can stay here as long as you like."

"Thank you," Never said.

"What happened, Never?" Her grandmother looked stunned. She had worked most of her life as a nurse in hospitals along the shore or near the Princeton corridor. Since there was always a shortage of nurses, unemployment for her had been a choice.

"The company merged several months ago. Mergers create duplicate departments. Mine was evaluated, and it was determined that we didn't need two department heads. I was let go."

"I'm sorry. I know how much you liked that job."

"I will find another," she said cheerfully. She didn't want her grandparents to know how bad she really felt. And she didn't mention a word about Averal, although he hadn't been more than a nanosecond away from her mind since she got the news two days ago.

Staying in her house had only reminded her more and more of Averal. The phone would ring and she'd hear his voice but wouldn't answer it. Then she couldn't stay there a moment longer. She'd packed, called her grandparents, and started for the shore.

"We can bake cookies and make Christmas decorations for the tree." She glanced at the fully decorated tree. It needed nothing added to it. Holly was strung along the mantelpiece, and white lights twinkled in the cloudy afternoon light.

Her grandmother came to her and took her hand. "Don't feel you have to put on a show for us," she said. "You take as much time as you need. When you're ready you'll find a job. In the meantime, your room is still at the top of the stairs."

Never hugged her grandmother. She should have realized her attempt at cheerfulness would be lost on the person who had raised her from childhood. Her grandmother saw through her, but understood. Never knew she could count on them. She'd always counted on them.

Carrying her suitcase, Never went up to her room. The sleigh bed she'd slept in since childhood stood in place like an old friend. She'd spent many nights here looking at the stars and listening to the incessant ocean only a few steps from the back door. Her sister, Samantha, used to creep into her room after their grandparents were asleep, and they would talk for hours and hours. Never missed her sister, and the nights of planning for their futures. Neither of them knew what was in store for them. She still felt a sense of security within these walls.

Three days later, Never pulled her sheepskin jacket closer around her. Wind from the ocean cut through her body, but she refused to go in yet. She liked the beach, liked walking here. Today she only stood and stared. The waves crashed against the winter shoreline. She loved this sound. It reminded her of strength, freedom, unharnessed energy, and a mystery that no one could find or divulge. Averal had those qualities, too. She knew now that was what had attracted her to him. He was like the ocean—unpredictable and intense—yet he could be calming and adaptable. There he was again, she thought, at the front of her mind. Everything reminded her of him—the ice cream her grandfather had made a special trip to purchase, the sunlight streaming through her bedroom windows in the morning as it had shone across his body mornings after they made love, the sound of a deep voice in the stores and shops, even the polished wooden surfaces of the dining room furniture that mirrored the same dark color of his passion-filled eyes.

She should have just given up. She was in love with him, and nothing could change that. Now even her place of solace—the ocean—had been invaded by his veiled presence.

Never sat down. The temperature of the sand penetrated her jeans. She ignored the discomfort and watched the horizon. Gulls flew overhead, their persistent cries blending with the salty air and ocean's voice. She hoped the sounds around her would block out the chant in her head, but they seemed to conspire against her, calling Averal's name with surprising harmony.

She'd told her department it wasn't personal, that the merger was business, yet she felt Averal should have warned her. And he'd said nothing. She'd known it was coming. She'd been around long enough to know how the corporate world worked. She'd also seen what happened in the departments. The Cedar people prevailed regardless of logic, regardless of education, experience, or general know-how.

Well, she told herself, it was time to stop feeling sorry for herself and make some decisions. Never hugged her knees and placed her chin on top of them. She'd accept the job in New York City.

She stood up, dusting sand from her bottom. She might as well go in and call. One decision would lead to many more. The wind blew sand in her face as she crossed the beach, re-tracing her steps back to the house. Her grandfather met her before she reached the back stairs. He handed her a cordless phone.

"It's Stephen," he told her.

She smiled, taking the instrument. "Hi," she said cheerfully. "How was the ski trip?"

"Just wonderful. I really enjoyed myself."

"And Donald?"

"He didn't break anything, if that's what you're worried about."

"I wasn't worried," she lied. She knew she wasn't fooling him. She couldn't help being worried. The feelings, the need to worry, came with the role. "You're not calling to tell me there's another trip over the Christmas holidays, are you?"

"No, I'm not calling for that. I called to tell you I spoke to Averal."

Never's heart leapt. Her hand came up to calm herself. "What did he say?" Her voice was only a whisper.

"He wanted to know where you were."

Never remembered her grandparents going for a short walk and the phone ringing. She hadn't answered it. The answering machine wasn't on, and somehow she knew it was Averal. She'd watched the machine go through eight, nine, ten rings before it stopped. Whoever it was would call back, she told herself. No one except Stephen and Donald knew she was here. There was no need for her to answer.

"I didn't tell him," Stephen was saying. "I do think you should call him."

Stephen was very mature for his twenty years. He was also right. She should call Averal, if for nothing else to let him know she was all right. He hadn't really needed to tell her anything. No one else had known prior to being terminated. Why should she be any different? Just because she was in love with the guy was no reason he should compromise his professionalism.

"I'll call him," she told him.

"There's something else. It happened on the ski trip."

"What?" She braced herself for bad news.

"One of the chaperones has a toy company. He got some of the games you'd sent us, and he wants to see you about buying them."

"Stephen, you know I only do those games for you guys." They'd covered this area before. Her nephew's persistence was a quality to be admired, but right now she was in no mood to talk about games.

"Hear me out," he insisted. "After we got back he called to remind me of my promise to meet you. I made an appointment for you, and I want you to keep it."

"An appointment with who?"

"Whom."

"Stephen—"

"You remember Brad Hilton," he interrupted. "You met his mother at Parent's Day."

"I remember her."

"Her husband owns the toy factory in Lawrenceville, and he wants you to come by for an interview. You haven't accepted that job in New York, have you?"

"Not yet. I was about to call them."

"I think you should go to this appointment first."

"Why? I know nothing about toys."

"Aunt Gee." She heard the incredulity in his voice. "You know a lot about electronics, games, programming, and management. That's why he wants to see you."

Never decided her nephew had given her qualities she didn't have. This man probably had nothing for her. It would be a waste of both their time.

"The appointment is for tomorrow afternoon at three," Stephen continued. "Don't be late."

He gave her the address. Never wrote it on a piece of paper. She could decide later if she really were interested in a small company in Lawrenceville. She'd always worked for large companies, places with many opportunities for advancement. She didn't want to work for a mom-and-pop operation where decisions were made by the family. She wanted to be part of the decision making process, and for that she needed a multi-national corporation like the one in New York.

"Don't forget—three o'clock."

"I won't forget. I'll go for the interview." It meant she had to leave tonight or drive a couple of hours tomorrow.

Maybe this was what she needed. It was time to go back. She'd walked the beach and eaten her grandmother's meals, even had her laundry done by her grandmother. She knew how easy it could get to sit around and let herself be pampered, but that wasn't what she wanted. She'd been here long enough, and she needed to start making plans for working in New York. She'd attend the interview, then call the New York people.

"I'll talk to you soon," she said, preparing to hang up.

"All right. Oh, there's one more thing."

"What's that? I already promised to go."

"It's something Averal told me to tell you."

Never's mouth went dry. "What is it?"

"He says he loves you."

Stephen hung up. Never held the phone to her ear, trying to hear him say it again. *He loves you.* Were the gulls chanting that now? She loved him, too. Things would be all right. She knew that. She'd go home tomorrow. She'd find him and . . . she didn't know what she'd do. He might not want to talk to her, but Stephen had told her he loved her.

She'd hold that thought. Everything else was unimportant.

NINETEEN

Music blared from the stereo. Never turned the knob to make the sound even louder as she danced about the room. It was good to be home. She felt like dancing. How could she possibly have known the good fortune waiting for her at the interview Stephen had insisted she go to?

Snow had nearly blinded her for the last eighty miles before she reached the Township of Lawrence. Never had set out at noon, kissing her grandmother—who insisted she should stay a few more days—good-bye. Never promised to return soon.

The roads were clear and the temperature in the thirties when she got behind the wheel. The closer she got to home the heavier the snow became. Instead of the two hours it normally took to cover the hundred and ten miles, she'd pulled into the driveway of the toy factory forty-five minutes late. She'd hoped to have time to go home before the interview, but as it stood she had to go as she was, dressed in a blue suit and flat red shoes.

Never kicked her shoes off and danced about the room. She was practically bursting with happiness. She wanted to celebrate. She wanted to tell someone. *Stephen,* she thought. He was the reason it happened. She called him. His answering machine spoke to her. Donald was also out when she dialed his number.

Averal came to mind. She wanted to call him. The urge was so strong her fingers were punching in the numbers before she could stop them. There was no answer at his house, and none at his office.

She dropped back in the chair, feeling alone. There wasn't anyone who would appreciate her victory. She did need to let her grandparents know she was home. At their house, she got another machine, and left only the message that she had arrived safely.

Impulsively she pulled on her boots and a thick coat. She'd go to Riddles Place. Maybe Averal was there. She'd promised Stephen she'd call him. And she had done that. But now the need to see him, touch him, was too great for a small snowstorm to keep her grounded.

Her hair was loose, and she pushed a red felt hat with a turned up brim on her head. She pulled the lapels of her coat closer as the wind blew snow in her face. Driving was too dangerous, so she trudged forward in the deepening snow. It took a long time to walk the seven blocks, and she was a white ghost when she rushed through the door of the bar.

There weren't many people inside. The weather frightens New Jerseyans, who clear milk and bread off the shelves of grocery stores and hibernate until the white powder is nothing more than dirty piles of melting water.

Riddles was the first to recognize her. Averal, following the line of his gaze, was off his stool in a second and coming toward her.

"Where the hell have you been!" he shouted when he got close enough to her. He took her arms and shook her. She could see the indecision in his eyes. He didn't know what to do to her. He wanted to kiss her—she could see the depth of emotion in his eyes—and he wanted to throttle her for disappearing and not calling. Quickly he turned and pulled her behind him, through the bar and out a door at the end of the room. Never didn't resist. She followed him until he slammed a private door closed. They were in a small entryway with only a stairway in front of them.

Averal pulled her around and pushed her against the door.

Then he crushed her to him. His arms went around her, but he didn't choke the breath out her. He held her tenderly. Never felt him kiss her hair and her neck. Her arms hugged him. She felt sorry she'd made him worry.

"I've been going out of my mind worrying about you," he whispered so softly it was almost a prayer. "Where were you?"

"I went to my grandparents'," she answered quietly.

"I called them. There was no answer."

It was Averal, she thought, when I heard the phone and refused to answer it. "I needed some time alone."

"Are you all right?"

She nodded.

"I'm sorry," he said. "It wasn't my recommendation. I suggested they keep you, and get rid of Bartholomew. I was floored when I found out what had happened."

Never put her fingers over his mouth when he started to speak again. He kissed them.

"It doesn't matter." She slid her hand around his neck and aligned her body with his. "So much has changed."

"I've been out of my mind," he groaned. "If it hadn't been for Riddles I don't know what I would have done." His mouth sought hers. She moved into him. "Don't ever do that to me again," he spoke against her lips. "I'll die without you."

Snow coated Never from head to foot. Averal felt none of it. He took her mouth like a convict deprived of sexual contact for generations. His body drove into hers with an arousing force that made her scream for him to make love to her.

Averal stepped back and looked at her. Quickly he took her hand and yanked the door open. They retraced their steps through the bar at a fast run. Averal stopped only long enough to shrug into his coat and say good-bye to Riddles.

The four-wheel drive vehicle covered the distance to Never's house in record time. Never went into the bathroom to shake the snow from her hair. Averal found her there. He slipped his arms around her. He nipped at her ear. "I would say I was going to take my time, but in the last week all I've had is dreams of you slipping away from me."

He twirled her around to face him. They didn't speak. He kissed her and fire ignited. Never could almost hear the snow-flakes hissing as they went directly from water to steam. How they got to the bedroom, she didn't remember. How they got undressed, she didn't remember. She remembered him cupping her neck and pulling her to him. His head slanted, and his mouth found hers. Passion easily overtook them. Averal's hands slid up from her hips on a slow journey to her breasts. Her nipples tightened into hard pebbles. Sensation spiraled inside her like a hot arrow heading straight for her core. She could feel her body become wet and ready for him.

"I missed you," she moaned, lifting her leg to wrap it around his.

"Baby, if I'd known where to find you nothing could have kept me from coming."

His mouth tugged at her lower lip, then kissed the skin under her lip and along her jawline to her eyes. Never's head fell back when he went for her neck and the sensitive skin of her ear. She gasped at the pleasure that went through her. How could she have denied herself this? Averal's hands caressed the heated skin of her back. He lowered them to her buttocks, sliding them over her like velvet gloves. Rapturous wonder rioted within her. The scream that wanted to escape her throat died in Averal's mouth as he kissed her again.

He laid her on the bed, his body, long and hard, next to her softer one. Never panted. He bowed his head and took her nipple in his mouth. Her eyes closed with the ecstasy he created. She'd be delirious soon, and she didn't care. Her fingers held his head, inviting his mouth to continue the exquisite torture he was al-ready proving against her breast. Moving from one to the other, Never's mouth went drier. She heard her own moans and knew she wanted him inside her.

"Averal," she groaned, almost out of breath. "Now!"

But he wasn't finished torturing her. She could feel him

against her, hard and hot. Her legs separated and she moved under him, her hand seeking him. She found his erection and circled it. He jerked at the contact, then settled into the gentle fingering she performed. She could hear his ragged breathing and knew she tormented him, too. Her hands moved slowly, not like the pounding of her heart. Blood rushed in her veins as she guided him to the one spot on her body made only for him.

Averal thrust himself inside her. He filled her with all of himself. Completely they joined and held. Her inner muscles clenched and released once, twice, silently communicating to him her need. He moved, taking himself out until only the tip of his erection remained connected to her, then thrust inside her again. Never learned the rhythm and danced to it.

The room was filled with grunts, moans, the sounds of love. She heard her own high-pitched voice mingled with the dark notes of his. Averal drove her higher and higher, taking her harder than he'd done before. She writhed under him, giving as much as she took, driving hard and fast, wanted nothing more than to stay there, to be with him, to tell him how much she loved him. To let him know he'd made her his for all time. They were joined together in more than body—her soul had bonded, entwined, merged with his. Together they climaxed on a resounding shudder.

"Averal," she murmured when his winded body began to return to a sense of normalcy. His heart no longer thudded against her, but beat a steady rhythm. "I had an interview this afternoon."

"I know," he crooned.

"Not you." She swatted him. "His name was Roger Hilton."

Averal lifted his head and stared into her eyes. "President of Janssen Toys?"

"One and the same." She smiled in the darkness. "He wants to buy my games."

Averal reached across her to the switch near the edge of the night stand. Light flooded the room, and he pulled her next to him.

"Roger Hilton doesn't conduct interviews to buy games." He said each word succinctly as if he were speaking to a child.

"I didn't know that. He asked to buy my games." Never was smiling widely.

Averal stared at her. Happiness shone in her eyes. The woman looking out at him was beautiful from the inside, like the portrait his mother had painted. Her beauty shone through. "Never, you can't know what that means. Those games gross millions."

"I know that." She paused. "That's not all."

He raised his eyebrows for her to continue.

"He offered me a job. Vice-President of New Development."

Averal pulled himself up in the bed, resting his back against the headboard. "Tell me how this happened."

"Stephen, my nephew, is always after me to send my games out, to try to sell them."

Averal nodded.

"I did send some, and they were rejected."

"I know. Barbara and I were trying to find you. We found the rejection letter."

"It doesn't matter." Never smiled. It seemed as if that rejection letter had come a lifetime ago, not just a few days. So much had happened. "Anyway, for Thanksgiving my nephews went on a ski trip put together by Roger Hilton's son. The lodge where the students stayed was owned by Roger Hilton. When he saw them playing night after night he tried one of the games, and insisted that my nephew call me. During the interview he offered to buy the games, and any more I might have, and he offered me the VP position."

Never had been speechless when she'd heard his words. Suddenly all her problems were solved. She didn't have to go to New York City. She could work near her home and stay in the corporate arena. She had a manufacturer who liked her games, and wanted to market them. And, more important, he was one of the biggest toy manufacturers in the country.

"I held my control as long as I could. Then I jumped for joy and came to find you."

"Oh, dear," he said his shoulders falling. "This is terrible."

"What do you mean, terrible?" She sat up to look at him.

"This is really bad. You're going to have to back out of this deal."

"Averal Ballentine, what are you talking about?" She pulled him over to look at him. He was laughing. For a moment Never had thought something was seriously wrong. Now she knew he was joking with her.

"I'm talking about marriage—you, me, us. If I ask you to marry me, you'll think I only want your money."

Never stared at him. She'd thought she was as happy as she could get in one day. "Are you asking me to marry you?" she murmured, hardly able to get the words out.

"I was thinking about it."

Silence stretched between them.

"Ask," she said.

"Will you marry me?"

"Yes!" she shouted. "Oh God, yes." She rained kisses all over him—each one punctuated with a *yes*.

The snow from two weeks ago had melted after only two days on the ground, but on Christmas Eve the white stuff came down again. Averal's place was already full of guests, and more were still arriving. Never looked out from one of the lighted windows of the mansion-size home. She didn't know where they were going to put everyone who promised to come for the holiday. She was looking forward to seeing them all and catching up on what'd been happening, especially since she had doubly good news to tell.

Averal, Sr., and BriAnne Ballentine arrived looking as much in love as they must have on their wedding day.

"Hello, darling," BriAnne said to Averal as she lifted her cheek for his kiss. Averal bent and kissed her. "I've brought you a gift."

His father was holding a large rectangle covered with bright paper and tied with a large, red ribbon. Averal knew without opening it what was inside. The size was right. She would have added a frame, and BriAnne knew he wanted the painting more than anything she'd ever done.

"Mom, thank you." Averal's smile was wide and loving.

"Don't thank her yet," his father said. "It could be cufflinks in a big box."

They both laughed.

"Can I open it now?"

"Of course." His mother beamed. Averal pulled the wrapping aside just as he'd done during his childhood Christmases. Never came up behind him as the final piece of wrapping dropped to the floor. "It's her," Averal said. "I'll always love her." He looked at both his parents.

"And I'll always love you."

Averal turned and pulled her to him.

"It's a wonderful portrait," she told BriAnne. "I can't believe you made me look so good."

"She didn't," Averal replied. "She just captured what we can all see." He bent and kissed the tip of her nose.

"We'll go in and join the others." His father gave BriAnne a slight nudge, and they went in to greet the other guests.

Never's grandparents arrived with several of her aunts and cousins. And Calvin, James, and Edward came en masse, with Leslie, of course, in tow. Then Riddles and Vivette moved into the decreasing space. A steady stream of people joined the holiday hub for most of the next hour. Never and Averal divided themselves between the kitchen and greeting guests.

Caroline and Matt pulled into the circular driveway. Never spotted them from one of the large windows. She left to pull the giant door inward and help them with the twins.

"Glad you could make it," Averal greeted, on her heels. He shook hands with Matt. Then he took Laurence, and Never took Lindsay, straight into the warmth of the living room, where they were immediately swarmed over by family. Everyone wanted to see the two youngest arrivals. Matt and Caroline followed.

"You two are the last to arrive," Averal told Matt as he led his sister and her husband into the room covered with wall-to-wall people. "These are all Never's relatives, and I won't even try to introduce you." Laughter rang out.

He couldn't remember half the names of the people who reduced his spacious living room to postage stamp size. Never's grandparents sat near the piano, and in the distance Stephen and Donald were helping themselves to the shrimp canapés. Leslie and James had made their own private conversation group on the fireplace hearth, and his parents were talking and smiling with Never's cousin—Francis, he believed. The scores of other people were aunts, uncles, and cousins—first, second, third, he wasn't sure which.

Caroline and Matt joined in, and soon everyone was toasting and singing Christmas carols. Never's grandmother played the piano to the discordant voices.

Averal watched the room for a private moment. He wouldn't have believed this would happen this Christmas. He'd hadn't had a family since Gabe died, and he didn't think he would ever have one again. But the woman with the long, dark hair, happily smiling and singing across the room, was responsible for the change. He liked the new Averal Ballentine. Gabe would always have a special place in his heart, but he was glad he could see clearly now, see that love lasted through both time and hardship. His parents showed him that.

Never showed him how great the world can be. When her own was falling apart, she'd had the advantage of a loving family who would be there to support her and help her through any crisis that came her way. And she'd been there with him during his crisis period. This would be the best Christmas he'd spent in a long time, but it wouldn't be the last. He could see a future of holidays, weekends, and weekdays, a lifetime of wonderful experiences awaiting them because they had each other.

Never stood by the fireplace. Averal worked his way through the crowd and tapped her on the shoulder as she sang out heartily to "Jingle Bells."

"Excuse me," he whispered in her ear. "But we'd better check on the food in the kitchen."

Never let him take her hand, and followed him through the obstacle course of people until they reached the hall. She knew he'd hired caterers for this gathering, and they'd checked on them only a few minutes before Matt and Caroline arrived.

"Which way is the kitchen?" she teased, knowing there was some other place he wanted to take her.

"This way." Averal led her around the side of the library and into a small room that had a circular stairway. He pushed her up the steps first, and she came through into his bedroom.

"I didn't know this was here," she said when she stepped into the brown and maroon room.

"It was here when I moved in," he assured her. "But I do have an ulterior motive in taking you away."

"I would never have guessed." She went up on her toes and planted a kiss on his mouth. His arms wrapped her as if she were his personal Christmas present.

He stepped back a moment later. "I want you to open your present." He walked to the dresser and opened a drawer. Out of it he pulled a box. It was too large to be a ring box, and too small for a dress.

"You don't want me to wait until tomorrow?" She took the square container with gaily wrapped colors of purple and gold.

He shook his head, a sly grin twisting his mouth.

"Scarves and perfume are acceptable?" she teased, remembering their walk in Georgetown at Thanksgiving.

"Scarves and perfume are acceptable," he repeated.

Never sat down and tore away the ribbon and bright colored paper. Inside was a silver box, and in it was the largest bottle of Passion she'd ever seen.

"I was nearly out of it," she said.

"I know." He took the bottle from her and held it up to the light. Never's eyes widened, and her mouth opened when she saw the ring lying at the bottom of the jar.

"Oh my God! Averal." The stone in the ring was easily three

carats. "Am I going to have to wait until I use all this to get the ring out?"

"Not on your life." Averal opened the bottle and upended it over her.

"Averal!" She grabbed for it and righted the perfume, before she and the room were reeking. "I love you." She smiled.

"I love you, too. More than anything in the world. And I want to marry you, have children with you, and I'll always make you happy."

"I am happy, honey. Happier than I thought possible."

He kissed her, deeply, passionately, until she didn't remember there was a crowd of people only a flight of stairs away.

Dear Reader

Creating characters is one of the most enjoyable parts of writing. As I worked on *Opposites Attract,* Averal Ballentine emerged as one of the most charming and vulnerable men who's ever walked into my consciousness and demanded to be in a book. Losing his brother and virtually his entire family made him strong on the outside, but on the inside he had the same wants and needs of any child. It took Never to help him see that people without a blood relation could be a family. In Averal's case, he already had a family. All he needed to do was accept them. I hope you enjoyed sharing in their story.

I receive many letters from the women and men who read my books. Keep them coming. I appreciate your comments.

If you'd like to hear more about *Opposites Attract,* other books I've written, and upcoming releases, send a business size, self-addressed, stamped envelope to me at the following address:

Shirley Hailstock
P.O. Box 513
Plainsboro, NJ 08536

Visit my web site: http://www.geocities.com/Paris/Bistro/6812

Sincerely yours,

Shirley Hailstock

Shirley Hailstock

ABOUT THE AUTHOR

Shirley Hailstock, a short-story writer and award winning novelist, has been writing for more than ten years. Holding a bachelors degree in Chemistry from Howard University and an MBA in Chemical Marketing from Fairleigh Dickinson University, she works for a pharmaceutical company as a systems manager. She is a past President of the New Jersey Romance Writers, a member of Women Writers of Color and a Regional Director on the National Board of Romance Writers of America. She lives in New Jersey with her family.

COMING IN APRIL . . .

A TIME TO LOVE   (1-58314-008-5, $4.99/$6.50)
by Lynn Emery
To discover his roots, Chandler Macklin takes a job in Louisiana. He's interested in Neva Ross's insight on the history of Louisiana . . . and her charm. Neva's hesitant. Her past relationships failed—why would this one be any different? When his ex-wife wants to reconcile, Chandler's torn between giving his son a stable family and a true love with Neva.

ISLAND ROMANCE   (1-58314-009-3, $4.99/$6.50)
by Sonia Icilyn
Cara McIntyre, co-founder of a London advertising agency, is in Jamaica for her agency's first major international account. With business resolve, she meets with coffee plantation owner Cole Richmond. But she loses her poise in his presence, and Cole's set on proving he's the one for her . . . even when someone from his past threatens their chance at love.

LOST TO LOVE   (1-58314-010-7, $4.99/$6.50)
by Bridget Anderson
To start over after a painful divorce, family counselor Deirdre Stanley-Levine returns with her daughter to her hometown in Georgia. But after an article by journalist Robert Carmichael is featured in his newspaper, Deirdre becomes the target of a madman. Now, while falling in love, Robert must help save the woman who roused his burning passion.

SWEET HONESTY   (1-58314-011-5, $4.99/$6.50)
by Kayla Perrin
Samona Gray falls for the handsome writer who moved in next door. He's the first man in a very long time she feels she can trust. Then she learns that Derrick Lawson is really a Chicago cop on a special assignment: to get close to her and learn the whereabouts of a fortune in missing jewelry. Her faith in men is tested once more, and ultimately, her faith in love.

LOOK FOR THESE ARABESQUE ROMANCES

AFTER ALL, by Lynn Emery   (0-7860-0325-1, $4.99/$6.50)
News reporter Michelle Toussaint only focused on her dream of becoming an anchorwoman. Then contractor Anthony Hilliard returned. For five years, Michelle had reminsced about the passions they shared. But happiness turned to heartbreak when Anthony's cruel betrayal led to her father's financial ruin. He returned for one reason only: to win Michelle back.

THE ART OF LOVE, by Crystal Wilson-Harris   (0-7860-0418-5, $4.99/$6.50)
Dakota Bennington's heritage is apparent from her African clothing to her sculptures. To her, attorney Pierce Ellis is just another uptight professional stuck in the American mainstream. Pierce worked hard and is proud of his success. An art purchase by his firm has made Dakota a major part of his life. And love bridges their different worlds.

CHANGE OF HEART   (0-7860-0103-8, $4.99/$6.50)
by Adrienne Ellis Reeves
Not one to take risks or stray far from her South Carolina hometown, Emily Brooks, a recently widowed mother, felt it was time for a change. On a business venture she meets author David Walker who is conducting research for his new book. But when he finds undying passion, he wants Emily for keeps. Wary of her newfound passion, all Emily has to do is follow her heart.

ECSTACY, by Gwynne Forster   (0-7860-0416-9, $4.99/$6.50)
Schoolteacher Jeannetta Rollins had a tumor that was about to cost her her eyesight. Her persistence led her to follow Mason Fenwick, the only surgeon talented enough to perform the surgery, on a trip around the world. After getting to know her, Mason wants her whole . . . body and soul. Now he must put behind a tragedy in his career and trust himself and his heart.

KEEPING SECRETS, by Carmen Green   (0-7860-0494-0, $4.99/$6.50)
Jade Houston worked alone. But a dear deceased friend left clues to a two-year-old mystery and Jade had to accept working alongside Marine Captain Nick Crawford. As they enter a relationship that runs deeper than business, each must learn how to trust each other in all aspects.

MOST OF ALL, by Louré Bussey   (0-7860-0456-8, $4.99/$6.50)
After another heartbreak, New York secretary Elandra Lloyd is off to the Bahamas to visit her sister. Her sister is nowhere to be found. Instead she runs into Nassau's richest, self-made millionaire Bradley Davenport. She is lucky to have made the acquaintance with this sexy islander as she searches for her sister and her trust in the opposite sex.

Available wherever paperbacks are sold, or order direct from the Publisher. Send cover price plus 50¢ per copy for mailing and handling to Kensington Publishing Corp., Consumer Orders, or call (toll free) 888-345-BOOK, to place your order using Mastercard or Visa. Residents of New York and Tennessee must include sales tax. DO NOT SEND CASH.

ROMANCES THAT SIZZLE
FROM ARABESQUE

AFTER DARK, by Bette Ford   (0-7860-0442-8, $4.99/$6.50)
Taylor Hendricks' brother is the top NBA draft choice. She wants to protect him from the lure of fame and wealth, but meets basketball superstar Donald Williams in an exclusive Detroit restaurant. Donald is determined to prove that she is wrong about him. In this game all is at stake . . . including Taylor's heart.

BEGUILED, by Eboni Snoe   (0-7860-0046-5, $4.99/$6.50)
When Raquel Mason agrees to impersonate a missing heiress for just one night and plans go awry, a daring abduction makes her the captive of seductive Nate Bowman. Together on a journey across exotic Caribbean seas to the perilous wilds of Central America, desire looms in their hearts. But when the masquerade is over, will their love end?

CONSPIRACY, by Margie Walker   (0-7860-0385-5, $4.99/$6.50)
Pauline Sinclair and Marcellus Cavanaugh had the love of a lifetime. Until Pauline had to leave everything behind. Now she's back and their love is as strong as ever. But when the President of Marcellus's company turns up dead and Pauline is the prime suspect, they must risk all to their love.

FIRE AND ICE, by Carla Fredd   (0-7860-0190-9, $4.99/$6.50)
Years of being in the spotlight and a recent scandal regarding her ex-fianceé and a supermodel, the daughter of a Georgia politician, Holly Aimes has turned cold. But when work takes her to the home of late-night talk show host Michael Williams, his relentless determination melts her cool.

HIDDEN AGENDA, by Rochelle Alers   (0-7860-0384-7, $4.99/$6.50)
To regain her son from a vengeful father, Eve Blackwell places her trust in dangerous and irresistible Matt Sterling to rescue her abducted son. He accepts this last job before he turns a new leaf and becomes an honest rancher. As they journey from Virginia to Mexico they must enter a charade of marriage. But temptation is too strong for this to remain a sham.

INTIMATE BETRAYAL, by Donna Hill   (0-7860-0396-0, $4.99/$6.50)
Investigative reporter, Reese Delaware, and millionaire computer wizard, Maxwell Knight are both running from their pasts. When Reese is assigned to profile Maxwell, they enter a steamy love affair. But when Reese begins to piece her memory, she stumbles upon secrets that link her and Maxwell, and threaten to destroy their newfound love.

Available wherever paperbacks are sold, or order direct from the Publisher. Send cover price plus 50¢ per copy for mailing and handling to Kensington Publishing Corp., Consumer Orders, or call (toll free) 888-345-BOOK, to place your order using Mastercard or Visa. Residents of New York and Tennessee must include sales tax. DO NOT SEND CASH.